DEATHWATCH
'39

Also by Jack Gerson

DEATH'S HEAD BERLIN
DEATH SQUAD LONDON

DEATHWATCH '39

Jack Gerson

St. Martin's Press
New York

Library of Congress Cataloging-in-Publication Data

Gerson, Jack.
   Deathwatch '39 / Jack Gerson.
     p.   cm.
   "A Thomas Dunne book."
   ISBN 0-312-05412-2
   I. Title.
PR6057.E72D44   1991
823'.914—dc20   90-49300
                                                  CIP

First published in Great Britain by W. H. Allen & Co.

First U.S. Edition: January 1991
10 9 8 7 6 5 4 3 2 1

For my daughter, Natasha

DEATHWATCH
'39

PROLOGUE

On a warm London evening early in August 1939, a tall, attractive woman walked from Curzon Street into Shepherd Market towards what she considered to be her beat. Also, although she was not aware of it, to her death.

The name she had assumed for the last of her twenty-eight years was Antoinette Valois, and she claimed to be a Parisienne. In fact, her name was Josie Leibnitz and she had been born and raised in comparative poverty in the port of Le Havre. She had come to London illegally in 1936, under the aegis of two Maltese brothers who described themselves as company directors. In the case of the Maltese brothers this was a euphemism for pimping. A speedy and arranged marriage had given Josie Leibnitz British nationality and frustrated a threat of deportation when she had been arrested some months before on a charge of common prostitution. As it was a first offence she had escaped with a fine.

Although Josie lived in an apartment in a tenement block in Bermondsey, her Maltese associates had provided a lavishly furnished room in Curzon Street where she conducted her professional activities. The ensuing police investigation revealed that she had left this room at seven-thirty that evening, was seen by an acquaintance in the same profession returning at eight o'clock with a tall middle-aged man. By eight-thirty she was seen walking back to Shepherd Market. The same acquaintance believed she had been on her beat beside a corner public house in the Market sometime after

7

nine. She was not seen alive again by any other witnesses who came forward.

At ten minutes past midnight, Police Constable Ernest Walker, checking that premises in the Market were lockfast, shone his torch into a doorway some yards from the public house. He saw what he thought was a bundle of coloured rags lying against the door of an antique shop.

A closer examination revealed the blood-spattered body of Josie Leibnitz aka Antoinette Valois.

The forensic report delivered to the CID officer in charge of the ensuing investigation, Detective Chief Inspector Charles Ainsley, revealed that the woman had died by the entry of a knife into her stomach just below the navel. With great force, the knife had then been drawn upwards laying open the torso to the throat. The wounds struck a chord in Ainsley's memory and, consulting old records, he realised that they resembled the wounds inflicted on the victims of Jack the Ripper some fifty years before. There were differences of course. None of Leibnitz's organs had been removed. And those murders had been committed in the depths of the East End of London. The victims had been prostitutes of a lower class. This crime had been committed in a fashionable part of the West End and, although the victim had been in the same profession, she was one of a group of what the French would have called *poules de luxe*.

Random killings of this nature presented considerable problems to the police. The motive is almost certainly sexual aberration; and generally there is no connection between perpetrator and victim other than the simple pick-up and the killing itself. Also the killer himself, while possibly a Londoner, might equally well be one of the enormous influx of tourists who had come into the metropolis that hot summer.

Press coverage of the crime was not extensive. A much bigger crime threatened the nation. Having swallowed Austria and Czechoslovakia, Adolf Hitler had turned his attention towards the Free City of Danzig and behind it the Polish nation. The British press and public, having been lulled a year before by the Munich agreement into a grateful acceptance of the possibility of peace, were now coming to realise their hopes had been ill-founded. Despite the angular figure of Neville Chamberlain brandishing a scrap of paper and announcing 'Peace in our time', it had become obvious that the old man with the umbrella had been deluded by the Charlie Chaplin figure with the little moustache. The murder of Josie Leibnitz, having appeared in two columns at the foot of page two of the *Daily Express*, soon became a paragraph on page five, and eventually disappeared from the paper altogether.

Chief Inspector Ainsley braced himself. The murder of Josie Leibnitz appeared to his practised eye to be what might well be the beginning of a series of killings.

It seemed he was wrong. By September the country, and indeed the police, had other matters with which to concern themselves. And there was no repetition of the crime. While no murder case is ever completely closed, in time the Leibnitz case was filed as open but inactive. And Ainsley believed that the killer was caught up in the holocaust of war that followed, perhaps even killed in it.

But Ainsley was not wrong. It was simply that the location of the subsequent crimes was several thousand miles away in another country.

Thomas Jefferson was the first American president to have his inauguration in Washington DC, in 1801. In time the Jefferson memorial was erected to celebrate this fact. At that time Washington was a sprawling village and the Capitol building was unfinished and described by the locals as 'two wings without a body'. In 1939 Franklin Delano Roosevelt, thirty-second President of the United States, was nearing the end of his second term. And while war had broken out in Europe, the avowed intention of the United States was to keep out of foreign wars and entanglements. If Roosevelt himself had other ideas, he could not state them publically. At the same time he was determined to render to the Allies as much assistance as he could in their war against Germany. There was no doubt where his sympathies lay. Nonetheless there were strong factions throughout the USA who were only too willing to lend support and sympathy towards Hitler and the expanding Reich.

There were also many who had little knowledge or appreciation of the Nazi peril. Indeed they lived in their own small world. One such person was Mary Lou Hancock; though she would have denied indignantly any resemblance between herself and Josie Leibnitz they did have some interesting points in common.

Mary Lou had been born Marie Pulaski in Pittsburgh some twenty-five years before. After winning a local beauty contest – Miss American Steel of 1934 – she had gravitated to Washington on the arm of a lobbyist for steel interests who, having a wife and three children in New York, had installed Mary Lou in an apartment by the Potomac. His heart attack while *in flagrante delicto* had terminated their relationship and made it necessary for Mary Lou to find another method of paying for her apartment and commensurate expensive tastes.

In time she made the acquaintance of Mrs Sadie Vavasseur who operated an escort agency to provide female companions and a degree of comfort for lonely businessmen and out-of-town politicians. Mary Lou soon became one of her favourites in so far as the girl established a wealthy and distinguished clientele without forming any permanent and exclusive liaison. She now paid her own rent and her attractions ensured regular clients who returned again and again. Until, that was, 30 September 1939. On the morning of that day the caretaker of the apartment block observed, while vacuuming the corridor of Miss Hancock's floor, that the door of her apartment was open. Calling out to her, he received no reply.

10

Cautiously he entered the apartment. He came out rather more quickly, face white, and rushed to the nearest telephone to call the police.

Officers of the Police Department of the District of Columbia found the body of Mary Lou Hancock lying naked on her bed. The bed was soaked in blood and Mary Lou had been stabbed below the navel and an upward movement of the knife had ripped her torso open to her throat.

London

ONE

He lay, stretched out on the single bed, dressed in crumpled flannels and open-necked shirt. It was just after eleven-fifteen. From some three floors below the window the Sunday sounds of Museum Street came faintly to his ear, competing with the voice from the radio. The radio was small, its frontage of polished wood broken only by a tiny illuminated window showing the various gradings that could be adjusted to different channels and wavelengths; the whole resembling a foot-high Gothic cathedral. From its speaker came a voice, a mournful, querulous, slightly nasal drone.

'. . . and so consequently, this country is at war with Germany.'

So, thought Ernst Lohmann, it's done. After all these years, this Sunday, 3 September 1939, the angular old man has belatedly and grudgingly taken the necessary action.

The voice went on, reiterating all the efforts the speaker had taken to avoid this outcome. As if showing how hard he had been treated, how wronged he was. No word of those who had warned him, pleaded with him one, two years before. No mention of Czechoslovakia. What was it he had said? '*A quarrel in a faraway country . . . between people of whom we know nothing . . .*' Something like that.

Lohmann could see the speaker in his mind's eye. And not just from newsreels and newspaper photographs. They had met briefly some three years before. The tall angular Victorian figure, hard edged, cold of aspect, mouth turned

15

down at the corners, forever a mourner at unseen funerals.

He switched off the radio. He'd heard all he wanted to hear. The fact and not the excuses. The key words still echoing in his head: '*consequently this country is at war with Germany*.'

Thinking now of Germany, of those places that endured in memory. The linden trees in bloom in the spring in Berlin, summer on the grass in the Tiergarten, the waters of the Wannsee rippling in the breeze. And the Gothic majesty of the buildings, Frederick the Great's palace at Sans Souci near Potsdam, only one of the legacies of the Hohenzollerns. Where he had entertained Voltaire, whose books had now been burned by the Nazis. Lohmann's Berlin. Not the city draped with black swastikas on scarlet banners; and the picture of the Führer gazing into the middle distance in a simulation of mystic rapture. Not the country of Brownshirts and black uniforms and desecrated synagogues. No longer his Germany; the old Germany was six years dead and in a mass grave along with so many of his friends.

Yet in Lohmann there was still a stirring of conscience. Should he have stayed in Germany five years ago? If he had acted differently perhaps he could have stayed on to fight, in his own small way, against the criminals that had taken over his country. Inspector Ernst Lohmann, Criminal Police, Berlin, he had been. His official title. Still that had been nothing more than a minor official position, one cog in the vast machinery, latterly thrust onto the larger canvas at the behest of Rheinhardt Heydrich and Hitler himself. At the end Lohmann had had little choice but to escape; to join the thousands of refugees who had gone into exile in the West, first in France and then in England.

He reassured himself it was not just to save his own skin. There'd been Anna, his daughter. Anna, who was becoming tainted by Nazi ideology. And was now safe in America, learning all that he would wish her to learn, away from the spreading evil in Central Europe.

He sat up, on the edge of the bed now, staring at the

sunlight slanting through the window. A good day and a bad day. But the evil of the day, the commencement of war, was a necessary evil. And there was still the question, could the Allies prevail a second time? And at what cost to themselves? And to Germany.

He lit a cigarette, inhaling deeply. Inducing in him a lessening of tension. The boundaries had been defined, the lines drawn. It was something to be grateful for. He must not dwell on future nightmares. He glanced at his wristwatch. Eleven twenty-six now. He would have to be off soon, expected at Bush House at the end of the Strand at midday. There he had one of his small jobs, translating radio reports coming out of Germany. With the promise that in a proposed service to be beamed to Germany he would be used as a commentator. But then that had been a week ago. With the declaration of war, circumstances might well have changed.

Particularly his own circumstances. There was irony there. He, who had opposed the Nazis, would inevitably be classed as an enemy alien. Had he opposed them enough when he was still with the Berlin police? That was a question he had often asked himself. Certainly in his last case he had. And since then in the business of Beth Kovel. Also, in Germany he could imagine how an enemy alien would be treated. The fortunate might well be returned to the country of their birth. God help him if the British followed that example. It would be tantamount to ordering his execution, he'd be dead within twenty-four hours – no legal formality, no trial; a bullet in the back of the neck, or maybe the rope. And an unmarked grave. Heydrich would see to all of it.

Outside, the air raid sirens went off.

Lohmann had heard the sinister wail, rising-falling-rising-falling, before in practice runs to familiarise the civilian population with the sound. But this would be no practice run. The Germans had received Britain's ultimatum to withdraw from Poland the previous evening; if no reply was sent by eleven o'clock, they would know Britain considered itself at

17

war with Germany. Easily time for the Luftwaffe to plan and execute the first air raid of the war. And they'd had experience – Madrid, Barcelona, Guernica. Lohmann had spoken to a Spanish refugee who had been in Guernica, a small town of around ten thousand people obliterated by aerial bombardment. Now it could be London's turn. Seven million people under threat of Armageddon.

He rose from the bed and went to the window. Police whistles were blowing. Pedestrians were scurrying towards shelters in and beside the Museum. He knew he should join them, seek cover somewhere close by, yet a leaden fatalism embraced him. His death would be of little consequence, that was the first thought. Only Anna in America would mourn. He would like to see her at least once again. She would be eighteen, far removed from the tenets of Nazi philosophy which Germany had started to teach her. And possibly Reiner, his old sergeant now also in America, too would mourn. But there would be few others. A part of Lohmann looked with envy at the prospect of death; at joining his wife Magda, ten years gone. Here, in London, he wouldn't mind dying so much. But not in Germany, he would hate to give them the satisfaction of executing him.

Another wail broke into his consciousness. The siren again, this time the steady note of the all-clear. So much for his meditations on mortality. It had either been another practice or a false alarm. He stubbed out his cigarette and tied his necktie. Time to get down to Bush House and the job. He had never been late. Police training died hard.

Somewhere below he heard the telephone ring. Norman, the caretaker would scurry from his basement apartment to answer it. Norman had little life other than a preoccupation with his tenants' affairs. Lohmann had straightened his tie and was donning his jacket when he heard him calling.

'Mister Lohmann! Telephone for you.'

Lohmann went out, locking the door behind him. He'd grown accustomed to the tiny, cell-like room. It had become

18

his bolthole, a sanctuary from the alien city whenever he felt the need for solitude.

The public phone was on the ground floor, on the wall under the staircase. He lifted the receiver.

A pause. 'Well, that's the thing. I . . . I'm afraid we're not going to need you, for the time being . . .' Ollinshaw stopped, obviously waiting for a reply. He got none. This time Lohmann paused. 'Eh, hello! You still there? Hello. Lohmann?'

With a sigh, Lohmann replied. 'I am still here.'

'Of course I'm arranging for two weeks' money for you. The Corporation always looks after its own, eh? And . . . and as soon as . . . as everything is cleared up, I'm sure . . . yes, I'm sure we'll have you back. I'll arrange for a cheque to be put in the post. Might take a week or two, you know how accounts are.' A deep breath. 'You do understand, old man?'

'I understand,' Lohmann said in hollow tones. 'Thank you.'

Ollinshaw was still talking, explaining, apologising when Lohmann replaced the receiver. There was, after all, nothing more to say. He understood. He was an enemy alien. He could obviously not be permitted to work on in broadcasting. Who knows what threat to national security he might present?

Nauseous, he felt a need for fresh air. Anyway, there was no point in going back to his room, to brood on the injustices of life. For four years he had been in this country, mostly in London. And for all those years he had expressed his disgust with the government of his homeland. He had even argued with Englishmen, some of whom had insisted Hitler was harmless, Hitler was the best thing that had happened to Germany, the fellow had the right idea about the Jews. It was surprising how many anti-Semites he had met who were members of the political party that had once been led by Benjamin Disraeli. He had seen the British Fascists march in the East End . . . been present at the Battle of Cable Street . . . seen the slogans on East End synagogues, the Star of David

19

scrawled on shop windows . . . were they indications of a coming *Kristallnacht* in London? How many of the people who had expressed such ideas would now be spouting patriotic slogans, loudly asserting how they were once again going to defeat the Boche? Would they count him one of the hated enemy?

Lohmann walked along Museum Street heading for the West End. Above him the barrage balloons gleamed in the sun, floating with elephantine grace. Pedestrians gazed up at the sky, searching for something above and beyond the balloons, not so much fearful as determined not to be surprised by anything that might happen. Over their shoulders were slung the square cardboard boxes containing their gas masks. It was only when he reached Tottenham Court Road that he realised he had forgotten his own, and momentarily hesitated, wondering whether to go back for it. He decided the day was too pleasant to waste time. And he was thirsty. Most of the pubs had either not opened or did not intend to open. He headed towards Cambridge Circus and Soho. He would go to the Gog and Magog. It would be open. It would be open on Judgement Day, God permitting. Only God, and certainly not Hitler, could close the Gog and Magog.

Situated on a side street off Old Compton Street, it was a drinking club in the top floor of a tenement building. It was patronised by artists, poets and refugees. And minor BBC production executives. Lohmann was greeted by the elevator attendant in his shirt sleeves beside the control box on the wall at the side of the elevator.

' 'Morning, sir. Bit of bad news, eh?' the man said, wiping his brow with a greasy hand.

'Yes. I have heard the Prime Minister on the wireless.'

'Oh, that. Well, we was expectin' that. No, this is serious. The bloody lift's broken down. Club's open all right, sir. But you'll have to walk up four flights of stairs.'

Lohmann nodded. 'I will climb your stairs.'

As he walked up the first step he heard the attendant

20

mutter, 'Don't 'ave much bleedin' choice, do you?'

Five minutes later, gasping for breath, the ex-police inspector reached the fourth floor landing and the entrance to the Gog and Magog. Despite the declaration of war the club was as busy as it had been in the last few weeks. Which was to say it was not as busy as it used to be. But then, over the last two months, many people had moved from London seeking boltholes in the country, in the North, even as far as Scotland. The clubroom was simple. A long room with a bar, tables, chairs, window seats and a few alcoves. There was no restriction against women guests, but they were usually few in number, and this Sunday Lohmann could see none. The drinkers and talkers seemed to be split into two groups. The younger men were joking and laughing in clusters, talking noisily: a few of them were in uniform. The older men were quieter, there was no laughter, indeed some had a grim air. Memories, too many memories, of the last time, of mud and clamour, stagnation and death.

Lohmann could see it behind their eyes. He could see it because it was there behind his own. Then he had been on the opposite side, but it had been the same mud, too often the same trenches, newly vacated, and later to be handed back. The smell of earth and cordite, chlorine and human sweat in his nostrils. And the smell of death too. Like the odour in a butcher's shop, of open bleeding flesh; and worse, the putrid smell of gangrene; that had always been there. For two years he had lived with it as he had fought in Flanders and been wounded twice. The first time it had not been serious, a graze across his shoulder, an hour in a dressing station. The second time he'd been shot in the thigh and spent three fortunate weeks out of the line. The scar was still there.

He made his way across the room towards a familiar face at the rear, catching fragments of conversation as he moved. '. . . she wouldn't believe it was serious . . . wouldn't listen. Until she saw for herself. Greenfly . . . all over the bushes . . .'

'. . . the old boy was very annoyed, ranted at the producer.

21

My church service, he insisted. On the wireless eleven till eleven-thirty this morning. *Why didn't it go out?* What he wanted to know . . .'

'. . . waiting. Just waiting. In vacuum. On the edge. Positively on the circumference. Going on for days . . .'

'. . . Halifax, it'll be. Chamberlain'll go and it'll be Halifax . . .'

'. . . won't have Churchill at any cost . . . bloody right they won't. Lloyd George maybe, but not the other . . .'

'. . . never get through the Maginot Line. Never get into France. All we have to do is sit there and wait until the Jerries starve . . .'

Lohmann reached his objective, the end table at the window, and two familiar faces. Joe Kahn looked up.

'Thought you were working, Lohmann?'

'So did I. But the BBC called off.'

Kahn sighed. A deep Semitic sigh. Containing sadness and resignation. 'So, for you it starts.'

'For myself too. Any minute,' said Kahn's companion, a man called Leibermann. A Jew and once a prosperous furrier in Vienna, he and his wife had escaped from the Nazi invasion by hours. 'A drink, Inspector Lohmann?'

Leibermann insisted on calling him Inspector. To the furrier, professional titles were a matter of right and not to be dismissed because of the vagaries of governments or pogroms.

'Thank you, a lager, Herr Leibermann.' Lohmann replied, grateful of being relieved of the effort of pushing his way to the bar. He had still not recovered from climbing the staircase.

'And the same for you, Joseph?'

Kahn nodded and Leibermann went off to the bar.

'I suppose I'm lucky,' Kahn said.

'If it *is* luck not to be an enemy alien,' Lohmann replied. 'You may be less lucky. Called to the army.'

'If I'm not, the anti-Semites will enjoy themselves. *These Yids, always get out of fighting.* Heard it all before. The last

22

time. The few times I was on leave.'

Lohmann nodded. He knew Joe Kahn had served in Allenby's army in Palestine, fighting the Turks. 'I avoided the mud,' Kahn often said. 'Got sand and sunburn instead. When I got home my cousin called me Kahn of Arabia.' Kahn of Arabia had been wounded at the second battle of Gaza, buried by a Turkish shell and invalided out of the army.

'Still, this time it was inevitable,' Kahn went on. 'Have to stop Hitler once and for all.'

'It will not be easy.'

'You think so? Some of them here say it'll be over by Christmas.'

'In every war, they say it will be over by Christmas. Better not to specify which Christmas. The paper still going?'

Joe Kahn was a journalist, running a small left-wing paper in the East End. He was also a member of the Communist Party of Great Britain. Lohmann had met him in the Gog and Magog four years earlier just after arriving in England. Later, Kahn had been instrumental in involving him in the Beth Kovel murder, also in the East End. Even that was three years past.

'I closed it down,' Kahn said. 'Two weeks ago. And I'm resigning from the Party.'

Lohmann looked at him, inwardly surprised but showing nothing.

'I had to go,' Joe went on. 'The minute Molotov signed that pact with that bastard Ribbentrop, I knew what would happen. Oh, Harry Pollitt's got the right idea. To hell with the Molotov-Ribbentrop pact. The Nazi, he's the enemy. But he'll be out of the leadership and in the cold, the minute the word comes through from Moscow.'

'What will you do?' Lohmann asked.

'Join the Labour Party I expect. Why not? Lot of good Socialists there. Nye Bevan and Cripps have the right idea.'

'I meant, for your living, Joe. Now that you've closed the paper.'

23

Kahn sat back in his window seat and smiled for the first time. 'Got a job already. The *Daily Mirror* took me on. Sub-editing. Well, they reckon a lot of their youngsters will go into the forces. Being in my forties, it'll take time to get around to me. Oh, I'll go if I'm called. But I always think I did my bit last time.'

They were around the same age, Lohmann thought. And both of them abhorred the Nazi regime. Yet because Kahn's family had arrived in London a matter of fifty years before Lohmann, Joe Kahn could fight the enemy but Ernst Lohmann would be considered one of them.

Kahn seemed to read his mind. 'They won't intern you, Ernst. Surely not after the Kovel business . . .?'

'Will that count? I doubt it.'

'You had . . . friends. Influential ones.'

Leibermann returned, carrying a tray with three full pint glasses on it.

'Here we are!' the furrier said. 'While we can enjoy, enjoy! Tomorrow we are interned, eh?'

For a while, they drank in silence, each man lost in his own thoughts. As if they were waiting. For God knows what. Later Lohmann bought another round and the lager seemed to cheer them.

'At least we know where we are now,' Joe Kahn said.

'Mister Chamberlain will not shilly and shally any more,' Leibermann added.

A young man, in his late twenties, passed the table, hesitated and looked down at Kahn. 'Hear you left the Party.' A very BBC voice. A touch of arrogance in the handsome face. The typical upper-class Englishman.

Joe Kahn shrugged, a very Jewish shrug. 'In anticipation.'

'Too soon, Joe, too soon. That treaty . . . only tactics. Stalin knows what he's doing.'

'You have specialised knowledge of Stalin's mind?'

The young man smiled. 'Why not? You're too hasty, my dear man.'

'That's me. Fast Joey from Whitechapel.'

The young man matched his shrug and moved away.

'Want to watch that one,' Kahn said. 'Still waters running very deep.'

'Seems pleasant,' said Leibermann. 'Who is he?'

'I wonder if he knows, himself. His father was pally with the Arabs. He was in Spain, reporting the civil war. From Franco's side. They say Franco gave him a medal. Philby's his name. Kim Philby. Seems to get mixed up between his arse and his elbow.'

'So many do,' said Lohmann. 'I think it is time I went. Too much lager, too little air.'

He rose wearily. 'I hope I may see you soon, Joe.'

They shook hands. 'If you are picked up, Ernst, try and get word to me.' Kahn said. I'll do what I can. Not that it'll be very much.'

'Thank you. Take care, Herr Leibermann.

Deciding he was hungry, he strolled down to Leicester Square and ate a small meal in the Lyons Corner House, telling himself he had to be careful with money. He was unemployed now and could survive only a few weeks on his small savings. Perhaps, he told himself, arrest and internment would solve that problem.

He walked back to Museum Street, staring at the changes that had come over London in the last week or so. Sandbags against so many buildings, windows taped with strips of adhesive paper to prevent fragmentation in the event of bomb blasts: at least there were signs of readiness on the streets.

Back in his apartment he read the *Sunday Express*. It carried news of embattled Poland fighting with cavalry against German tanks. On the radio at six o'clock it was announced that Churchill was back in government, at the Admiralty. It was a small consolation. Lohmann had met Churchill during the Kovel business and had some admiration for the old man who had opposed Hitler from early on.

25

At least there was someone in the government who knew the enemy.

He picked up *The Sorrows of Young Werther* in a battered volume he'd brought out of Germany. To find a kind of reassurance, he told himself, that there had been, perhaps still was, a civilised and enlightened Germany. As if to feel he had something in common with Goethe who also had translated foreign works into German. To tell himself translation was an honourable and worthwhile profession.

Lohmann went to bed at ten o'clock. He'd got into the habit of going to bed early. And, without work, he'd be doing so from now on.

Three weeks later, at six in the morning, there was a knock on his door. Two plainclothes policemen and a uniformed constable stood outside his door with Norman, the caretaker, hovering nervously behind.

He was under arrest as an enemy alien.

He was relieved, without work he had been coming close to the end of his resources.

TWO

They searched his room, quickly but, to Lohmann's practised eye, efficiently. The only item they could find that they viewed with suspicion was his copy of Goethe in German. The younger of the two plainclothes men thumbed through the volume and then glared at him.

'Looks like subversive literature to me.'

'I am sorry to disappoint you, sir,' Lohmann replied, 'But

it is merely a German classic. I don't think you will find much subversion there.'

'Ah, but you would say that,' the officer replied, brusquely. 'Anyway, it's coming with us. As are you . . . bloody Nazi . . .'

'Be quiet, Wilson,' said the older of the two. 'I'm sorry, sir, but we'll take it along just in case.'

'I am a refugee from National Socialist Germany,' said Lohmann. 'So why am I being arrested?' He knew what the answer would be, but he wanted to hear them say it.

'According to our information, you may be a Nazi sympathiser. Possibly even an agent of their government.'

'A number of people in high places would know it is not so.'

'Aye, sure. You would say that, wouldn't you?' said the young detective constable, who appeared to have a limited vocabulary.

'We have a warrant,' the older officer said.

'May I take a change of clothing?'

He was permitted, under their supervision, to pack a small suitcase. Throughout this and the search, Norman had hovered on the landing, literally wringing his hands.

'You'll look after my things, Norman?' Lohmann said as he was ushered out of the room.

'I'll do that, Mister Lohmann. I'm sure there's been a mistake. You'll be back soon.'

'Perhaps.'

A police car was waiting at the kerb. Lohmann was hustled into the rear with the older of the two men. 'May I ask where I am being taken?' he asked.

'Brixton, sir,' replied the senior man. 'For the time being. And I've no doubt, if what you say about being a refugee is true, they'll let you go, in time.'

Lohmann was handed over to the prison officers at Brixton and left in an ante-room for some time. Finally the chief warder, or so he appeared from his uniform, appeared with a tall, thin, grey man in a sports jacket and flannels.

'I'm the governor of this prison,' said the tall thin man.

'Your name is Lohmann? Ernst Lohmann, formerly a police officer working for the German government?'

'I was appointed by the previous German government,' Lohmann replied.

'But you served under the present regime?'

'For a time. Hoping that regime would not last. In that, I was mistaken. I left Germany in 1934. Had I not done so, I would have been arrested by the Gestapo.'

The governor coughed. He looked embarrassed. 'Yes, well, that of course is for others to judge. Meanwhile you are to be detained here. Shortly we hope to transfer you to another establishment, but while you are here you will be restricted to your cell. You will be permitted to wear your own clothes. Any complaints to be made through the usual channels. Good day.'

The governor went to the door and hesitated, turning again. 'Unfortunately we are fairly crowded. You will have to share a cell with one other internee.'

A nervous nod and he was gone, leaving Lohmann in the custody of the warder.

'Have to take your personal possessions. You can keep cigarettes and matches. And small change. With that you can purchase more cigarettes if you wish. Otherwise you are to be confined to your cell. And it is requested that you have no contact with the regular prisoners.' The warder recited this as if by rote. He had been reciting it all morning.

The cell Lohmann was escorted to was small and cold, with that unpleasant odour peculiar to prison cells; a mixture of human sweat, excreta and carbolic. It had two bunks and in one was a pale youth of Austrian-Jewish extraction.

'Name of Meyerstein,' the young man introduced himself. 'Formerly of Vienna. I play the violin and I don't know why I'm here.'

'I imagine we can all say that.'

'But sir, I am a Jew. A musician. My parents sent me out of Austria when Hitler marched in. I haven't heard from them since.' His voice trembled. 'I am fortunate to be given sanctuary here last year and now I'm put in prison as a suspected Nazi sympathiser. It is insane.'

'You will not be the only one, Herr Meyerstein. I think a great many mistakes are being made. And I think, in time, the British will rectify them.'

The pale young man rested his head on what passed for a pillow and sighed. 'I suppose you're right. But how long will that time be? I had, just a week ago, obtained a position with the London Symphony Orchestra. Now I will lose the job.'

'I think we can only blame Hitler. Now, I was disturbed in my sleep. Would you mind if I lie down and catch up on that lost sleep?'

For the next four weeks Lohmann and Meyerstein ate and slept and talked together. They talked of everything and nothing. They avoided talking of their situation. Of that there was little to say. They were waiting, they acknowledged, but for what they had no idea. On the third day Lohmann's volume of Goethe was returned without explanation. Library facilities were granted to them although Meyerstein had difficulty in reading English. Lohmann started to tutor him. At the end of four weeks, they were informed by the warder that, in a few days, they could expect to be moved to somewhere out of London. A camp at a race course in Surrey was mentioned. They began looking forward to this. Anything must be better than the cell in Brixton.

The next day, however, the Governor appeared outside the cell.

'Ernst Lohmann?'

'I am Lohmann.'

Without further words, the cell was opened.

'You will take everything with you.'

Lohmann complied, pocketing a toothbrush and the few cigarettes he had left. As an afterthought he handed the cigarettes to Meyerstein.

29

Meyerstein gave a pale smile. 'Thank you, Herr Lohmann. Good luck to you.'

He was escorted to the ante-room in which he had waited on his arrival four weeks before. Here, his personal possessions were returned and again he was left with one warder waiting. Ten minutes later a door opened and two men in plain clothes came in. Policemen again, thought Lohmann. He could always recognise policemen, whatever garb they wore.

'Good evening, Herr Lohmann.' This from the smaller of the two men, but, from his manner, the superior in rank. 'You remember us?'

Only then did Lohmann look up at the faces.

Before he could speak, the man confirmed their identity. 'Chief Superintendent Thornhill. And you'll remember Charlie Newton. He's an inspector now.'

He recognised them. Remembered them. Newton had saved his life three years ago, during the Kovel business. And Thornhill too had been deeply involved on a personal level. The Superintendent had been engaged to Beth Kovel before she had been killed. It seemed to Lohmann that his past was rising up in front of him.

'I'm to be released?' Lohmann asked.

'Not our decision, old man. We're simply Special Branch coppers. Do what we're told. But you have to come along with us.'

It was a cold November morning. A mist had drifted up from the river and settled on the streets. Lohmann thought, it was still autumn when I arrived. Now winter has come. An unmarked police car was waiting for them. Inspector Newton drove and Thornhill sat in the back with Lohmann.

'All of three years since we met,' said Thornhill. 'What have you been up to?'

'I have worked for the BBC. And I have been arrested as an enemy alien. How is the war going?'

'Quietly. Except at sea. Lot of your U-boats sinking our ships at sea.'

A scowl came over Lohmann's face. 'Not my U-boats, Thornhill. Hitler's.'

'Of course. I was forgetting . . .'

But had he really forgotten, Lohmann asked himself? Or was the Scotland Yard man merely baiting him? God knows, Thornhill of all people should know he was anti-Nazi.

'But what is happening on land?' he asked quickly, deciding he must not show his chagrin. 'Those damn trenches been dug again in France?'

Newton, behind the wheel, laughed. 'Gawd, I remember them. I was at the Somme. Got trench foot at the Somme, so I did. And a shell fragment in my back. Bloody hellish, the Somme. Thank God, none of that, this time round.'

'Oh, they're much more comfortable this time,' Thornhill said. 'The French are sitting in the Maginot Line making faces at the Germans, and the Germans are sitting in the Siegfried Line, making faces at the French. They're beginning to call it the phoney war.'

'Some air marshal wanted to bomb Jerry's munitions factories in Essen and the Black Forest,' Newton continued the theme. 'Kingsley Wood, our Air Minister, said, "Good God man, you can't do that. Don't you know it's private property." Nutcases, the lot of them, if you ask me. Thank God Winston's back anyway. Only one with guts.'

'He is a good man.'

Lohmann peered out of the car. They were heading north, towards the river. 'Where are we going?'

'See when you get there.'

Some minutes later they were crossing Westminster Bridge. Big Ben was barely discernible in the mist and the barrage balloons above the city were invisible. Newton swung the car into Whitehall and drove towards Trafalgar Square. But, before reaching the Square, he pulled into the kerb.

'This all right, Superintendent?'

31

Thornhill opened the door and stepped out. He motioned Lohmann to follow and turned to Newton. 'You can go back to the Yard now, Newton.'

The Inspector looked glum. 'Same old story. Anything interesting happens, I get sent back to the office.'

Thornhill gave a small tight smile. 'Never mind. You'll get in on it all when you make superintendent.'

The smile disappeared as he turned to Lohmann. 'Right, this way.'

They walked passed sandbagged buildings and came to a door manned by a begaitered naval rating wearing battle webbing and with a rifle on his shoulder. Inside, a naval officer sat at a desk, another rating, bearing side arms, behind him.

'Identification?' the naval officer demanded of Thornhill.

The superintendent showed his warrant card, which was scrupulously examined. Then the eyes behind the desk focused on Lohmann. 'What about him?'

Thornhill produced a letter. The officer scrutinised it with an increasingly deepening frown, 'Ernst Lohmann! That's a German name.'

'Yes. Herr Lohmann is a German national.' A smile hovered on the police superintendent's lips.

'You can't bring an enemy alien into the Admiralty!'

'Oh, I think I can,' Thornhill replied. 'I would refer you to the signature on that paper.'

The officer's eyes turned reluctantly from Lohmann and settled on the signature.

'Oh, yes. I see. Sorry.' He pressed a button on his desk. 'Can't be too careful, you know.' From somewhere behind him a young woman in the uniform of a WREN rating appeared. 'Take these two gentlemen to Room 26. They're expected.'

They followed the WREN into the depths of the building, Thornhill now smiling broadly.

They went down to the multiple basements below ground

level. And finally were shown into an ante-room. Behind a desk sat another WREN, this time a junior officer.

'Two gentlemen to see him, ma'am.'

The WREN officer rose. 'Come in. He's running late as usual, but I'll tell him you're here.'

She disappeared through a door at the rear of the room. They waited some minutes until eventually she reappeared.

'You can go in now.'

Thornhill led the way. It was a large room, functional, without decoration, the dun-coloured walls covered with maps. Behind a desk a figure familiar even to Lohmann was sitting, head down, spectacles perched on the end of his nose, studying a document.

Without looking up the figure spoke. 'Pray sit down.'

They sat on two uncomfortable chairs facing the desk.

'It appears,' the figure went on, 'That we may be facing a German pocket battleship loose in our South Atlantic shipping lanes.'

The face finally looked up and Lohmann found himself staring at the First Lord of the Admiralty, Winston Spencer Churchill.

'Your fellow countrymen build excellent ships, Herr Lohmann. It is a pity they build them for such fearsome warlike endeavours. However, have no doubt, we shall send the *Graf Spee* to the bottom.'

Lohmann nodded, uncertain of what was expected of him. Surely he had not been brought from prison to discuss naval warfare.

At once Churchill clarified the issue. 'However, you were not summoned here to talk of the *Graf Spee*.' He looked at Lohmann. 'You know that we had some difficulty finding you?'

'I did not know that, sir. Surely there was no difficulty since your government placed me in Brixton prison as an enemy alien?'

Churchill snorted. 'Unfortunately too many people in this

administration deem it necessary not to inform the left hand what the right hand is doing. It took Superintendent Thornhill some days to ascertain your whereabouts. However now you are here. It is three years since we have met.'

'Yes. Three years.'

'And you have been interned for some four weeks?'

'Something like that.'

Churchill produced a cigar, clipped the end of it expertly with a small implement and then, as an afterthought said, 'Would you care for a Havana?'

'Thank you, no.'

'We shall have some tea, shortly. Meanwhile, Herr Lohmann, I must ask you a question.'

'Sir?'

'I have no doubt that you still oppose the government of your country and Herr Hitler?' Churchill managed to inject into the name of the Reichschancellor of Germany a combination of scorn and contempt. 'That is so?'

'It is so.'

'Good. But now I have to ask you whether you would be prepared to engage in the war against Germany? Opposition to Hitler is one thing but to take up arms against one's own country is another matter. I wish to assure you that if you were disinclined to do so, for obvious reasons, I would understand. Indeed, I would respect such a position.'

Lohmann hesitated. Not that he had doubts about what his answer would be. But he was curious as to why he should be brought before a British cabinet minister to answer such a question.

'As you have said, Mister Churchill, I abhor the present regime in my country. I have already clashed with that regime. I would be only too pleased to see the Nazis swept away. And I realise now it will take a war to achieve that end. I have no doubt the war will be necessary to restore Germany to sanity and I would have no hesitation in taking an active part in that process.'

Churchill nodded, pleased at his answer, pleased also perhaps, that the man, albeit a German, could express himself in a manner as verbose as his own.

'Good, good. That is why you have been brought here. I have a job for you, Lohmann. I believe it will be not without danger. You may well be working on your own and have no claim to aid from us if you are in trouble.'

He's going to ask me to go back to Germany as a spy, Lohmann told himself. Well, he determined, he would be prepared to do so.

Churchill went on. 'I wish you to go to the United States of America. On a mission classified as top secret. And also on a matter of multiple murder!'

THREE

Churchill sat back in his chair and, rubbing his eyes, glanced at a clock on his desk. The famous polka dot bow tie was slightly askew. With a surprisingly swift motion, he pressed a button on the desk.

'Time is of the essence,' he said. 'I have to be in the House in half an hour. If I do not cover everything, Superintendent Thornhill and the gentlemen who are presently joining us will answer any further questions you may have, Herr Lohmann.'

He cleared his throat, then drew on his cigar. Waiting. Finally the door through which they had entered opened again and two men entered. One was a tall, middle-aged man in a rather crushed tweed suit. The other was a naval officer, of senior rank, in uniform.

Churchill did the introductions quickly and off-handedly. 'Rear Admiral Gaunt is Director of Naval Intelligence. Professor Lindemann is one of my advisers, and was at one time a fellow countryman of yours, Lohmann.'

There was no hand-shaking. Nods were exchanged. The new arrivals gazed with some curiosity at Lohmann; the Admiral possibly with a degree of suspicion. Lohmann returned their gaze without expression. Lindemann took up a position leaning on a bookcase on Churchill's right. The Admiral positioned himself against the wall at the side of the door as if mounting guard duty. During these moments there was a silence finally broken by Churchill. When he spoke it was out of a haze of cigar smoke.

'First, understand that this mission is top secret, apart from the people in this room, the Prime Minister has some knowledge as has my Permanent Secretary. When I have finished, you too will know, Lohmann.'

Lohmann frowned. 'No one on the American side?'

Churchill scowled. 'Very perceptive. Naturally certain individuals in the United States will know. I have personally informed President Roosevelt of the broad outlines of the affair. Knowing the President, I have no doubt Harry Hopkins will have been informed. And certain aspects are known to J. Edgar Hoover, of their Federal Bureau of Investigation. Only certain aspects. You will learn why as I explain.'

Lohmann said nothing now, but waited. Conscious, it seemed, that Churchill was enjoying drawing his explanation out. But at this point, Churchill turned to Thornhill.

'The first part should be yours, Superintendent. Please proceed.'

Thornhill said: 'Early in August the body of a prostitute was found stabbed to death in a doorway in Shepherd Market. You may have read something of the case.'

'I saw a newspaper report,' Lohmann replied. 'It had certain points of interest. Unfortunately the story disappeared very quickly from the papers. Doubtless the pressure of international events . . .'

'Exactly,' Thornhill paused and threw Lohmann a thoughtful look. 'Why did you find it interesting, Inspector Lohmann?'

It was the first time Thornhill had used his old rank. Lohmann wondered why the acknowledgement, as he replied. 'Such crimes can of course be motivated killings. A prostitute has a dispute with her . . . *Zuhälter* . . . her . . . ?'

'Pimp,' Lindemann interjected, his accent thicker than Lohmann's.

'Yes, her pimp. Or another girl. Perhaps even a customer. And she is stabbed . . .'

'This girl wasn't just stabbed. She was eviscerated,' said Thornhill with some reluctance and a glance of seeming embarrassment in the direction of the Admiral. Why the Admiral? Lohmann thought.

He said: 'Ah, yes, I wondered about that. There was a hint in the newspaper. It interested me. As a retired police officer. You have perhaps had other similar murders since?'

'None in this country. So far.'

Churchill leaned forward. 'Why do you ask this, Herr Lohmann?'

'Because this might be the beginning of . . . *Fortsetzungsroman mord. . .*'

'Serial murder,' Lindemann provided the translation.

'What is . . . serial murder?' The Admiral spoke for the first time.

Thornhill told him. 'Multiple killings. Usually without motive . . . Like Jack the Ripper. Or, in Germany, Peter Kurten – which Inspector Lohmann worked on.'

It was Lohmann's turn to interrupt. 'I would not say without motive. The motive is not . . . normal. It is often sexual aberration. The murderer is a psychopath . . . with some grievance, imaginary or otherwise. Or he is a sadist . . . and the killings are random. Or as in the Ripper murders,

37

against prostitutes in general.'

The First Lord of the Admirality twisted uncomfortably in his chair and frowned. 'I find these . . . eh . . . psychologists' theories questionable, to say the least.'

'The killing of the woman is not questionable, sir. It is hard fact,' said Thornhill with a sharp tone that did not please Churchill. The frown grew deeper.

Thornhill turned back to Lohmann. 'The officer in charge, Inspector Ainsley, was prepared for a further murder. And of course, as you will know, Lohmann, it is difficult to catch such a murderer. Ainsley was relieved when no further killings of a similar type took place. However he followed through his investigation to the best of his ability. With no result. And with the outbreak of war, the police were under considerable pressure. The case has not been closed, but it is dormant.'

'That is all?' Lohmann said.

'Not quite. On September 30th in Washington DC, a woman the Americans describe as a call girl was found dead in her apartment. The body was mutilated in the same manner as the woman in Shepherd Market.'

'Exactly so?'

'Exactly so.'

'If it is not coincidence, this might suggest someone whose occupation is that of a traveller. Perhaps a merchant seaman, an airline pilot . . .?'

'Good thought,' said Rear Admiral Gaunt. A man clutching straws, it later became clear.

Lohmann looked at Thornhill, a puzzled look. 'But how did you become aware of this crime in the American capital? Have you such a strong liasion with the American police forces?'

'Normally no. Of course we co-operate in the matter of extradition of known criminals. But there are considerably more murders in the United States than here. We have no record of them . . . why should we? Unless British nationals are involved.'

'Ah, yes. British nationals.' Lohmann ran his hand across his chin, a meditative action. 'Please proceed.'

Thornhill looked at Churchill. The First Lord cleared his throat. 'The narrative now falls to me, and at first it will appear there is no connection. However, I have to go back to the beginning of September when the Prime Minister asked me to take over this office. Among the many matters and papers on my desk for action and information was one which seemed to be of considerable import.'

Another pause. His timing for the maximum dramatic effect was impeccable.

He went on. 'This paper was . . . is . . . highly confidential.' A glance at Lindemann, who nodded enthusiastically. 'It necessitated confidential contact between certain individuals and the President of the United States. The Prime Minister – who was highly dubious of the whole affair – left it to me to deal with. I, on the other hand, entertained no doubts of the importance of the matter. I therefore found it necessary to use a naval officer to arrange the various details that would lead to the meeting with Roosevelt. I chose an officer with admirable qualifications . . . some specialised knowledge was involved. The officer, a captain, was sent to the United States as assistant naval attaché to our Embassy in Washington. He is there now, engaged upon his task.'

Again the frown. Churchill crushed the cigar out on an ashtray on the desk.

'We have reason to believe that attempts will be made in America to frustrate his mission, even discredit him. Possibly by the pro-Nazi element.'

'Then such elements are aware of his mission?' Lohmann asked.

'It is possible. The individuals who must be put in contact with Roosevelt are . . . Europeans. One, like yourself, is a refugee from Nazi Germany. They approached us, as belligerents, for assistance. Professor Lindemann assures me of their *bona fides*. Yet it is possible the Gestapo and German intelligence are watching these men and know they are in America. It is also possible that they may know our new assistant naval attaché has certain specialist skills which would link him with these men. Attempts could be made to discredit our man. His life may even be in danger. As may the lives of others. Your task in America would be to protect and watch over our man, forewarn him of any such dangers.'

Lohmann searched in his pockets for a cigarette and then remembered he had given them to his fellow internee.

'Have you a cigarette?' he asked Thornhill who at once produced a packet and threw it to him.

'Keep them,' Thornhill said.

Under the glowering eye of Churchill, Lohmann lit a cigarette. 'Why me?' he asked, inhaling. 'Excuse me, Mister Churchill, but you surely have your own operatives in Washington. Your own trained agents.' He glanced at the Admiral, who looked down at his shoes.

Churchill, on his part, looked towards Thornhill as if seeking help. None was forthcoming; Thornhill was staring at a picture of Nelson's flagship *Victory* on the wall behind Churchill.

Gruffly the old man endeavoured to reply. 'You speak German. You *are* German, you will be able, if necessary to . . . to contact, perhaps even infiltrate pro-Nazi groups. You would appear to be unconnected with us or our embassy . . . Damn it, man, we want you!'

Churchill's face was flushed. Something, Lohmann decided was embarrassing the First Lord. As if he was reluctant to continue. As if he wanted now for Thornhill to take over.

'And there is another reason,' he added.

Lohmann said, 'Apart from the question as to why I am selected for this mission, what connection has this with the two murders you have spoken of?'

'That is the other reason,' Churchill said and nodded towards the policeman. 'Thornhill!'

It was an order. Thornhill took his eyes from *Victory*.

40

'The naval officer chosen for this mission was Captain Robert Edgar Pardoe. After Pardoe had been sent to America, Inspector Ainsley came to me with his name in connection with the murder of the Valois woman in Shepherd Market. This was ten days ago.'

Lohmann looked puzzled. 'Ten days ago. How did he come across the captain's name and why so long after the actual murder?'

It was Thornhill's turn to flush. 'Ainsley had been trying to find Valois' pimp, a Maltese by the name of Cazalis. The man went to ground and was only apprehended ten days ago in Manchester. In his possession was Antoinette Valois' appointment book which Cazalis had appropriated from her apartment in Curzon Street before the police got there. His name was also in the book. But it appears Captain Pardoe was a . . . a regular client of the lady's.'

'Pah!' Churchill's expression was one of disgust. 'A naval officer . . .' He glared at Admiral Gaunt.

'Pardoe is unmarried,' Gaunt said evenly. 'He was stationed for two years at Singapore, flag officer rank, and only had recently returned to this country. While I am not condoning his . . . relationship, surely in the circumstances it is understandable?'

'In an ordinary seaman possibly. But Pardoe is an officer. He should not be patronising a woman of the streets!' Churchill produced another cigar and clipped the end from it viciously.

'He should not be murdering her, either,' Professor Lindemann muttered with what he obviously imagined was a mildly humorous remark.

'There is no proof that Pardoe killed this woman,' Gaunt insisted stridently, defending the honour of the Royal Navy.

Lohmann had to agree.

'Loneliness can cause a man to seek sympathetic company. It is understandable if he has been away from the country for some time. And knowing he may be away again, he may prefer to form no more permanent liaisons. Especially in wartime.'

41

Remembering Berlin and his own friendship after the death of his wife. A girl in a house, no obligations, someone with sympathy. It was all a time ago but still there in memory. Lohmann had no regrets about the girl, only to the English would such a relationship appear improper. A nation of hypocrites, it had been said. He turned back to Thornhill.

'Being one of many clients would not mean he had killed the woman. Unless you have other evidence?'

Thornhill's eyes narrowed. 'He had an appointment with her the night she died.'

'Certainly he should be investigated. But it is not conclusive evidence of anything other than an active sex drive.'

Thornhill pressed on. 'The reason the Washington police contacted us was because in the apartment of the girl murdered in their city – name of Mary Lou Hancock – they found, in her address book, the name and address of a member of the staff of the British Embassy.'

'Captain Pardoe?'

'Captain Pardoe.'

Churchill leaned forward across the desk now. 'It was Thornhill who pointed out to me that you have had a great deal of experience in the apprehension of perpetrators of multiple murders.'

'So have many of your own police officers.'

'None of them are German.'

'The crime took place in America. Not in Germany.'

Churchill sighed. 'My dear Lohmann, German Americans ... those in sympathy with Hitler ... are our adversaries in America. You can mix with such people in a way none of our people can. I urge you, pray accept this mission. We will provide all resources. However, if you fall into trouble with the United States government, we will not be able to acknowledge you in public. Roosevelt will know of you, but, as President, he will not be able to acknowledge you. Now, sir, what do you say?'

Lohmann stood, stretching his legs. He walked to the side

of the bookcase against which Lindemann was leaning. On the wall was a map of the South Pacific ocean.

'At this moment I can say nothing.'

Churchill made a face. 'You will of course be paid. A fairly substantial salary. Intelligence officer level. Civil service grade . . .'

'Money is not relevant, sir. I would presume to be adequately paid.'

'Then what?'

Lohmann spun around on his heel and faced the Minister.

'You've told me most of the circumstances of this matter. But you haven't told me what you want of me. What am I to be doing? Trying to prove your Captain Pardoe is a murderer? And, if he is, am I to arrest him? Or am I there to protect Captain Pardoe from possible enemy plots to subvert his mission . . . whatever that may be?' The old man broke the silence that followed Lohmann's question.

'Your prime task is to see that Pardoe carries out his mission without interference from the enemy. Also while he is carrying out his mission, you will see that he does not engage in any other activities, such as killing young women.'

Rear Admiral Gaunt took a step forward. 'I must protest, First Lord! We do not know that Captain Pardoe is responsible. '

Without taking his eyes from Lohmann, Churchill went on, 'That is of course, *if* Captain Pardoe makes a habit of killing young women. But the mission comes first.'

Lohmann said, 'Why can you not send another officer?'

'Because Pardoe is particularly qualified for this mission. Anything else, Herr Lohmann?'

'If Pardoe is a killer and I permit him to complete his mission –.'

'You will *ensure* he completes it!' Churchill growled.

'Very well. But presumably the American police will also be pursuing the killer. If they should –.'

'You will do everything to prevent the American police

43

apprehending Pardoe.' A glance again at Gaunt. 'If Pardoe is guilty.'

Lohmann nodded. 'I see. I ensure he completes his mission. I keep the Nazis from interfering. I keep a watch on Pardoe, should he show the inclination to kill anyone. A kind of *Tod ansehen* . . . a deathwatch. And when the mission is over . . . what?'

'If he is not guilty, then he will return to duty here in England.'

'And if he is guilty? Do I hand him over to the American police?'

'No!' Churchill jerked the word out. 'I do not wish this matter to be used as anti-British propaganda.'

'If the Americans believed he was guilty, they would arrest him,' Thorhnill said bleakly. 'Of course, you could avoid that by claiming diplomatic immunity.'

Lindemann nodded his agreement. 'Pardoe is a member of your Embassy. It could be done.'

Again Churchill barked, 'No! There will be no immunity. Hardly good for our image, demanding they let a cold blooded killer free. Hardly good for our image that we have such a man representing this country. No, there will be no arrest and no plea for immunity.'

He looked down at his desk pensively, plump fingertips brushing imaginary dust from the polished surface.

'If,' he went on in a quieter tone, 'if Captain Pardoe is guilty of these crimes, he will face the ultimate penalty. But there will be no trial.'

Again Gaunt felt the need to protest. 'Without a fair trial, you propose to execute a naval officer?'

Churchill sighed, eyes still on his desk. 'War, Admiral. The necessities of war. Would you rather have one of your officers exposed as a murderous pervert? No! If Lohmann here tells me Pardoe is guilty, that will be enough. You understand, Lohmann?'

44

'I understand what you are saying, sir. But I am not an executioner.'

'You have killed men in the course of your duties as a police officer? So the record compiled by Thornhill tells me.'

'I have. But in self-defence. Or for the protection of the public. Under those circumstances only.'

Yet another pause. this time, a brief one. Then Churchill nodded. 'So be it. We have people who will do what is necessary if the man is guilty.'

For the second time during the meeting he looked at the clock. 'I am expected in the House. You will have to excuse me. One thing more. I have said, if you believe Pardoe guilty, you will inform us and we will take the necessary measures. But more than that. Whether Pardoe is guilty or not, if he appears to be guilty in the eyes of the American authorities, you will so inform me, Lohmann. Even if innocent, appearance of guilt is just as bad from a propaganda point of view. So if Pardoe seems to them to be guilty, we are forced to treat him as if he is guilty And he will still be . . . eliminated.'

FOUR

Churchill rose wearily from his desk. 'I wish you good fortune, Herr Lohmann.' He then surveyed the others. 'It is understood, gentlemen, that this meeting never took place.'

He went from the room, a rotund figure, with an air of the previous century. The aroma of Havana cigars enfolded him. Lohmann realised why the old man could be so greatly admired and so vehemently hated. The benevolence was genuine but the ruthlessness, the cold determination, was appreciable too.

Lindemann, leaning against the bookcase, coughed and straightened up. No surprise to him, the old man. He was adviser, friend, acolyte. Lohmann had heard of him. A clever man but replete with his own prejudices.

'You'll excuse me, gentlemen,' Lindemann said. 'Mister Churchill may have need of me at the House.' He went out, a large man scurrying like a small one. Leaving Lohmann with Thornhill and the Rear Admiral. Gaunt turned and addressed Lohmann.

'You realise, Lohmann, that on your accepting this mission the First Lord will have erased this matter from his mind. It is his way of coping with so many matters. He will only bring up the subject again briefly to hear that there has been a successful conclusion.'

'I hope he will hear what he wants to hear. But now I have some further questions.'

'Of course, of course. Perhaps we might adjourn to my office?'

Again Lohmann found himself being led through the maze of corridors in the depths of the building. Finally he found himself sitting, side by side with Thornhill, in front of another desk in a smaller office.

'Now, Mr Lohmann . . .?'

'There are a number of things I have to . . . eh . . . *enklären* . . .'

'Clarify,' translated Thornhill. 'Go ahead.'

'This mission Captain Pardoe is carrying out in America. It is so important that pro-Nazi elements are trying to jeopardize it . . .'

'Almost certainly, and backed by the Abwehr,' Gaunt said. 'My opposite number, Admiral Canaris, is an old hand.'

'Yet, you have given me no details of this mission,' Lohmann said.

Thornhill cleared his throat loudly, with a knowing look at

Gaunt. 'The mission is designated "need to know". Mister Churchill has decided that you do not come under that classification. If, when you are working beside Pardoe, he finds it necessary to inform you, he has permisison to do so. But only if he believes it necessary.'

Lohmann frowned, 'So I am to have one hand tied behind my back?'

'Your task is basically to ensure Pardoe is free to operate,' Gaunt insisted. 'And investigate the two murders. The details of Pardoe's task are not relevant.'

'Your opinion, Admiral. And Captain Pardoe – what is he to believe I am there for?'

Thornhill replied. 'Security officer. Sent to protect him that's all.'

'Protect him?' Lohmann mused. 'From Nazi sympathisers, the American police, and possibly his own penchant for murder?

'You expect a great deal. Here I shall need at least an assistant. In Germany I was used to working with a police department behind me.'

'Our naval attaché at the Embassy, Captain Greenock, is in effect Pardoe's superior. He has instructions to lend you every assistance. Without, of course, embarrassing Lord Lothian, the Ambassador, or openly involving the Embassy.'

'Not enough!' Lohmann insisted. 'I'm talking of someone with experience who can work closely with me, take my place watching Pardoe if I have to disengage myself to conduct investigations into the German-American Bundists. You will understand, I cannot be in two places at once. My former sergeant, Paul Reiner, is in America. Cincinnati I believe. I wish to recruit him as my assistant.'

'I don't think . . .' Thornhill started to say.

'I am not asking your permission! I am telling you, Superintendent. You will arrange payment at the same scale as myself for whatever time he spends on the case. If you cannot agree to this, then you will have to inform Mister

Churchill that he should get someone else for the job.'

Gaunt said quickly, 'It can be arranged for payment to be made through the Embassy for this . . . Mister?'

'Reiner, Paul Reiner.'

'He will be your own responsibility, Lohmann. He has no security clearance.'

'Have I?'

'We have investigated you.' Thornhill said.

'I should be disappointed if you hadn't.'

Thornhill shrugged. 'I don't like it. Bringing an unknown into this. But if Admiral Gaunt feels as he does, and you insist, Lohmann, then I've no further objection. One other thing, though.'

'And that is . . .?'

'You have a daughter in New York.'

'Yes.'

'You will not be able to visit her until this whole business is finished. We must insist on that. Visiting your daughter could give away your true identity.'

'Agreed,' said Lohmann. Glumly. But knowing it was for the best. Apart from calling attention to himself, he could endanger Anna. And that he would not do.

'Anything else?' said Gaunt.

'Details. Passports, transportation. My identity. And I would like to see the file you presumably have on Captain Pardoe.'

Thornhill stood up. 'At my office at Scotland Yard, we'll sort everything out.'

Gaunt rose and stretched a large hand across his desk. 'Good luck, Lohmann. I sincerely hope you can prove Bob Pardoe is innocent of these murders. For the Navy's sake. I personally find it difficult to believe he could be anything else but innocent. I know him and he doesn't look like some kind of sexual sadist.'

'They never do, Admiral Gaunt. If they did it would make the task of the police so much easier.'

48

Twenty minutes later Lohmann was in Thornhill's office, a tiny room, high up in the building at New Scotland Yard. Ensconced at the Superintendent's desk, the two men discussed the details of Lohmann's mission.

'You will have a British passport,' the Special Branch officer informed him. 'Under the name of Ernest Lomond.'

'Hardly very imaginative,' Lohmann said.

'Churchill's idea. He has incidentally suggested that when this business is over, if you wish to retain the passort, you may do so. In other words, you will officially be a British citizen.'

'I thought it took five years.'

'Without influence, yes. But now you have influence. If you wish citizenship, it's yours.'

'Please thank Mister Churchill. If he does not consider it necessary to . . . eliminate me in the interests of the United Kingdom, I may take up the offer.'

Thornhill expressed surprise. 'Wait a minute, Lohmann, you don't think . . .?'

'I think the possible elimination of Captain Pardoe, if he is innocent but might appear to be guilty, is a subject of concern.'

'Won't be your affair. If he is innocent, you prove it and the question will not arise. If he's guilty . . .'

'That is another matter. But I will need more than one passport.'

Again Thornhill looked surprised.

Lohmann went on, 'I will need a German passport. If I find it necessary to infiltrate the German-American Bund, I will need authentic credentials.'

'Yes, I see.'

Thornhill pressed a button on his desk. A moment later the door opened and Inspector Charlie Newton came in.

'We want one authentic German passport, Newton. Lohmann's photo on it. Have to do that later. Made out in the name of . . .?' He looked across the desk at Lohmann.

'Something fairly common. Muller, I think. Bruno Muller.

Take them time to check up on all the Mullers in Germany.'

'Anything else?' Thornhill asked.

'Photographs, suitably aged, of Bruno Muller's wife and children. Two children, I think. All of them blonde, in line with the Führer's ideals. Some letters from Frau Muller . . . how she is, how the children are, and so on. And business letters. Authorisation as representative of Siemens, the electrical firm, something like that. Muller in America to sell German products. Everything in a used wallet made in Germany.'

'Special Branch can do that, Newton?' Thornhill looked at the inspector.

'Naval Intelligence will provide the wallet from a captured submariner,' Newton replied. 'The rest we can do.' He grinned at Lohmann. 'We've got some bloody good forgers working for us these days. Anything else?'

'Labels on my clothes to be German. Also a Mauser automatic, easy to conceal some place in my suitcase to get through American customs.'

'You give us the suitcase, we'll do the job. And ammo, I suppose?'

'And ammunition, Mister Newton. Thank you.'

'We'll call at your flat in a short while,' Thornhill said. 'Collect your case and clothes.'

'Good. And I want copies of your files on the murder of the woman in Shepherd Market. And the file on Captain Pardoe.'

'You'll have them.'

'Only one thing more.'

'And that is . . .?'

'How do you get me to America?'

Forty-eight hours later, Thornhill and Lohmann were on the night train to Scotland, a sleeping compartment to themselves. The compartments were drab, dusty and ill-lit. The carriages were over-filled with soldiers, sailors and airmen. During the journey, Lohmann sat up on his bunk bed in the compartment, and in the blue light of the partially blacked-out train read with difficulty the file on Captain Robert Pardoe.

Robert Edgar Pardoe, born 1899. Unmarried. Only son of Henry Pardoe, JP (deceased, 1936) and Alice Greer Pardoe (deceased 1938). Henry Pardoe owned a reasonably successful yacht-building business in Lowestoft which he sold in 1930 on his retirement. Robert Pardoe was educated at a private school and entered Dartmouth Naval Academy at the age of 14. In 1916 passed out seventh in his class and was gazetted to *HMS Gladiator* as a midshipman. Mentioned in dispatches at the Battle of Jutland. In 1918 promoted to sub-lieutenant. Seconded to university course, Oxford, reading Physics. 1st class honours degree, physics and dynamics. Advanced torpedo course, Portsmouth, 1923, promoted to lieutenant. 1924, officer commanding minesweeper *HMS. Coleander*; 1928, Lieutenant-Commander, followed by staff course; 1930, Commander. Promoted Captain, 1933. CO destroyer *HMS Lotus*. 1935, staff officer, S. Pacific flotilla, stationed Singapore. 1938 posted to Admiralty experimental unit. 1939, assistant naval attaché, Washington, special assignment, ref. Rear Admiral Gaunt.

That was it. A reasonably distinguished career officer, with a degree in physics and dynamics. To do with torpedoes? Unmarried? Why not? Many career officers were married, many were not. Pardoe had made his way up the promotion ladder pretty well between the wars. Probably because of his technical qualifications. With the war, he could go all the way to the top.

Except for the fact that his name appeared regularly in the diary of a whore who was murdered in a doorway in Shepherd Market.

One more question. If he had regular access to Antoinette

51

Valois' apartment just around the corner in Curzon Street, why kill her in a doorway in a public thoroughfare?

He returned to the police report. Nothing new there. Detailed description of the wounds on the body. Thornhill had been right, she had been eviscerated. With a sharp knife not found. Every appearance of a motiveless sex crime. According to her diary, Pardoe had visited her on an average once every two weeks. No indication that it was other than straight sex. He did pass the entire night with her. So? Nothing unusual in that, could be argued it was more normal than a quick thirty minutes. An additional question was noted in the report: Could the girl have tried to blackmail him? Learning of his career prospects, deciding there might be money obtainable from him, if she threatened him with exposure. A possibility. But why mutilate her body? Unless he wanted to make it seem like a sex crime. And, if he was involved in the killing in America, then this lessened the blackmail motive.

In the dim light of the compartment, Lohmann's eyes began to ache. Opposite him, stretched out on the sleeper bunk, Thornhill was fast asleep, breathing easily. After a time, Lohmann replaced the reports in his suitcase and stretched out, convinced he would never be able to sleep. He was wrong. Twenty minutes later he slept.

It was twelve hours before they pulled into Glasgow Central on an ice-cold, rain-soaked morning.

'I could have been back in London,' Thornhill complained, as they stepped onto the platform. 'Working from behind my desk on a nice little espionage case. Instead of shivering in this God-forsaken rear end of the universe.'

'You are having a hard war, Superintendent?' said Lohmann sardonically. 'The poor fighting men on the battlefields will feel sorry for you.'

Thornhill flushed. 'All right, all right, point taken.'

Lohmann let it drop. Instead he asked. 'Where do we go now?'

'A car is laid on to Prestwick.'

During the car journey, Thornhill explained that just before the war a small civil aerodrome had been opened there, and the RAF had now taken it over.

'It's comparatively fog free,' Thornhill went on, 'and at the limit of German bomber range. You'll fly from there. Refuel in Greenland or Iceland or some cold spot like that and end up in Canada. From Canada you'll drive into the United States. But I'm glad to say I stop at Prestwick. Although I envy you the American end of the trip,'

Another icy blast was blowing across the airfield, straight off the Firth of Clyde. The sky was grey and heavy with cloud above a wild sea. The car deposited them in the teeth of the wind, outside an unprepossessing Nissen hut. Inside, a pot-bellied stove provided some trace of heat. Lohmann sat on his suitcase in front of it and waited, Thornhill pacing impatiently behind him. An RAF sergeant brought them two mugs of tea.

'We'd appreciate some breakfast,' remarked Thornhill. 'Mister Lomond has a long flight in front of him and I have to travel back to London.'

'See what I can do, sir.'

The sergeant did rather well. Ten minutes later they were driven to a hotel at the edge of the airfield which was now the officer's mess. They were provided with a thin strip of bacon, one fried egg and three plump sausages. A Flight Lieutenant appeared and apologised profusely for the delay and for the breakfast.

'Bloody food rationing. Sorry about the bacon. Give you plenty more bangers, though.'

'Thank you, this'll be no more than adequate,' Thornhill replied dryly.

'Never mind,' the Flight Lieutenant said cheerfully. 'Other side of the drink, you'll both get anything you want. No war over there, eh?'

All this was addressed to Thornhill who gazed bleakly

at the young officer.

'Unfortunately only Mister Lomond is flying. I am returning to London.'

'Oh, well, never mind, sir. They say it'll all be over by Christmas.'

Lohmann thought, the ever present cry he'd heard even in the Gog and Magog of hope in any war; that all would be well at Christmas. Knowing Hitler, Lohmann had his doubts.

After breakfast they settled in front of a wood fire in the mess bar, neither felt like drinking. It was too early and anyway the grease from the 'bangers' had had a not entirely pleasing effect on their stomachs.

Two hours later, a senior officer appeared and introduced himself. 'Group Captain Munroe. I think we can take Mister Lomond to his plane now.'

Lohmann, his stomach still feeling queasy, shook hands with Thornhill.

'Have a good flight,' said the Superintendent.' And luck with the . . . eh . . . the job.'

Lohmann wasn't thinking of the job. He was thinking of the coming flight. He had flown occasionally in Germany but only on short flights. Now, with a sickish stomach, feeling cold and utterly miserable, he was about to undertake the longest flight of his life, and that mostly across a November ocean – not a warming prospect.

Reluctantly he followed Group Captain Munroe across a wind-swept tarmac towards the shadowy outline of a large, quivering machine, propellers already spinning; to the flight and to his immediate destiny.

Washington

FIVE

Julie Neuberg was twenty-five, blonde, and nurtured by an expensive upbringing and latterly a practical education. All of which meant she had few ideas, but was technically efficient. She worked in the offices of Senator Sam Neuberg in the Capitol Building. Senator Neuberg was the Senior Senator for one of the smaller Mid-Western states. A tall, grey-haired man with a long aquiline nose below a high forehead, and a skin tone that resembled burnished leather, he presented the ideal figure of a statesman. In fact, he was a shrewd local politician, adept at wheeler-dealing in the party machine of his state. He'd been elected on the Democratic ticket but was known as one of the more conservative democrats. Beneath the outer shell was a small-minded man, elected for his looks and a command of empty rhetoric. A supporter of the two Neutrality Acts, his favourite campaign speech emphasised his avowed belief that '*not one boy of an American mother was gonna ever be sent again to die on a European battlefield.*' He had also been heard to express his belief that '*Jest maybe that guy Hitler had the right idea about the Jews. And Mister Roosevelt seemed to have too many Yiddish pals around him in Washington.*' The Senator also never forgot to stress that his ancestors came over just behind the *Mayflower*, before the Roosevelts, and were of good Dutch stock.

Julie was Sam's niece, daughter of his brother Joe Neuberg, a younger and less adroit replica. Joe was sometime dead.

Sam had undertaken to look after his unfortunate brother's

family, arranged for Joe's wife to buy a modest but comfortable home in the state capital, ensured that Joe Neuberg Junior obtained a cadetship at West Point, and at her own request gave his niece a secretarial position in his office at the Capitol and introduced her into Washington society where, he hoped, she would make some kind of useful, possibly influential, marriage and remove herself to the care of other hands. To the Senator's surprise, Julie had proved to be an excellent worker and after a year he had promoted her to be his assistant secretary. (He did not consider it wise to make her his secretary as there were certain personal matters to which he did not wish family attention to be drawn; including his relationships with more than one Washington hostess.)

Julie had taken a small apartment in Georgetown, a bright suburb of the city that always looked as if it had been newly painted. She had made a number of impeccable Washington social connections (in other societies they would have been considered quite dubious) and become popular among Washington's younger set. It was rumoured that for a time she had been escorted by one of the younger of Roosevelt's sons. To the Senator's relief and certainly the President's, nothing had come of this. Neuberg and F.D.R. were never on the best of terms.

Julie had then shown a penchant for being escorted by young army and navy officers, up-and-coming career men, the clean-cut variety that looked like the hero characters in comic strips. Again Neuberg approved providing they had money.

She did not confine her social activities to the armed forces and was, on occasion, and to the approval of her uncle, seen on the arm of the younger sons of wealthy industrialists. She had even been escorted several times by the young, if rather oddball millionaire, Howard Robard Hughes, but after a time Hughes had disappeared back to California and his movie studio. After Hughes, there had been a brief fling with one of William Randolph Hearst's sons but this too had petered out.

Nothing had come of any of these liaisons and the Senator had begun to despair of getting his niece off his hands. Still, he told himself, Washington had a floating population of celebrities and there would always be some new and promising prospect on the horizon.

Julie, on her part, had been enjoying herself. She had met royalty, been flattered by the very rich, and, most important of all, she had discovered sex. (Until coming to Washington, three years before, she had been a virgin.) She took to it like an Olympic diver in training, diving in with enthusiastic abandon almost daily. No thought of marriage, not yet; there were too many attractive men around her. And, of course, word of her enthusiasm got around. For a time, until she deserted the navy, always her first love, she became known as the 'Fleet Bicycle'. Not that she ever knew this. Not that she would have minded. She was an honest girl, according to her lights.

That was, until a week in late October. It was then she met the man she determined she would marry. Now, in November, she finished work every evening on the dot and rushed home to the apartment in Georgetown to await the man she loved. She liked the phrase. *The man I love*. Like the song. The man she had made up her mind she would spend the rest of her life with. It didn't matter they'd only known each other . . . what . . . three weeks?

They would marry at Christmas. He'd said that himself. Oh, yes, he'd told her he was as much in love with her as she was with him. He had some matters to attend to but, by Christmas, they would be settled. He promised it. Promised her while in bed in her apartment in Georgetown. In bed on top of her, inside her. Before the onset of that mutual wildness in their lovemaking which left her soaked in perspiration, every nerve of her body trembling, her large breasts bruised by his open mouth, nipples still hard and erect. And then her mind, her voice, her body, pleading that he would start again. She'd given up taking precautions now, given up asking him to take precautions. She had no need to care, anyway. If she did become pregnant, it wouldn't matter. They could marry even earlier.

After three weeks, she was convinced she was pregnant. No. she hadn't seen a doctor and her period was only a few days late. But it was something she knew in herself, in the depths of her mind and body. She was carrying his baby.

Tonight, she was waiting for him. No desire to go out on the town. Rather be alone in the apartment. She would have dinner ready for him and then everything would follow. She had cooked steaks. He couldn't get enough of big thick T-bone steaks; he'd been deprived of them too long. The wine was in front of the fire, its deep red hue emphasised by the flames behind it. She was dressed in casual elegance; a silk sheath that dived deeply to the cleavage between her breasts. And opened easily down the front so that it slipped off like a négligé. Underneath, nothing. Two minutes to eight. She looked around the room. Nothing out of place.

The doorbell rang. Eight o'clock on the dot. He was the most punctual man she knew. Never late, not even by a minute. He had told her that was the only way to make things work. Be on time. She hesitated briefly. He'd warned her about opening the door without asking who was there. After all, he'd said, a girl had been murdered a few weeks ago. She'd read of the killing herself in the *Washington Post*.

She opened the door carefully, peering around it.

No-one!

Then he stepped into her vision.

'For God's sake! I told you, never open the door without asking who's there!'

He stepped forward and she was in his arms, Chanel 5 driving away the cold, foggy aroma of the city. They kissed with all the passion of a love-affair at its early flowering. Her tongue found his lips and prised them open. He responded with a brief enthusiasm.

'Let me come in!' he said, gasping for breath and smiling at the same time.

She shut the door behind him and turned. They were facing each other. Like two adolescents at the beginning of a first affair. Looking each other up and down with approval, and laughing at their own fascination. Then she remembered her duty.

'One pink gin coming up. And dinner is just about ready.'

She poured and handed him a pink gin, took one herself – good enough for him, good enough for her.

'How do you do it?' he said. 'A Washington working girl by day, turned into a vision of glamour by night.'

'Magic, honey. And just for you.'

He stared out of the window at the lights of Georgetown.

'Don't you ever want me to take you out on the town?' he said.

'Why should I?'

'I might like to show you off,' he said, sipping pink gin.

'That's nice,' she replied. 'But we'd have to behave ourselves. And I don't want to behave. Not yet. Not until we're an old married couple. If we went out, I'd probably attack you and we'd be barred from *Le Lion D'Or* for life. Rather have you here, all to myself.'

Then the thought came to her. Was she being selfish?

'But if you really want to go out . . . ?' she said quickly.

He shook his head. 'No. No, I prefer it here. For all the same reasons as you. Anyway I hate other people watching us.'

She kissed him again. And ten minutes later, served dinner. He could think to himself, never before had he been served by a waitress so glamorous. After dinner, they relaxed side by side on the sofa, listening to Jack Benny on the radio, brandy glasses in hand.

Julie thought, how successful she'd been this evening, as every evening with him. He was relaxed, at ease, feeling good with the world, talking about his day, and they were laughing

61

together. So far, a perfect evening. And later, in bed, they made love, coming together with the customary passion of their weeks together, moving each to each, with the kind of perfection that pleased and stimulated all their respective desires. When it was over, they lay in each other's arms. She felt warm, protected, satiated for the time being.

She told him she thought she might be pregnant and, to her delight, he drew her closer to him. He too felt relaxed, at ease. More, he felt still a sense of anticipation . . . of waiting.

Some time later, as the evening wore on, he moved again onto her body, stroking her hair and her neck.

She closed her eyes, embracing the warm darkness. Happily. So happily. She could feel his body moving on hers, his flesh against her flesh. One hand caressed her face, lips, cheeks, forehead. So very gently. The other was on her body, smooth on the smoothness of her belly. A sudden chill came over her, drawing some of her warmth from her body. Still, she could tell herself she was coming to the end of her perfect evening.

And of his.

The next morning, Lohmann arrived in Washington. Three days earlier he had finally reached Montreal, unshaven, exhausted, and suffering from the after effects of hours of air sickness. He'd been met by a young man with a trace of a French accent and the aroma of a strong after-shave lotion, dressed smartly in a too-trim grey flannel suit.

'Pierre Murat.' A neat hand grasped Lohmann's. 'Inspector, RCMP Special Branch. I have been asked to meet you by Superintendent Thornhill. It is an honour to meet the Inspector Lohmann.'

This was what the Mounties, heroes even in Germany of his childhood reading, had become. They had stood, side by side with the German writer, Joe May's 'Old Shatterhand' character. Dismissing the thought, he said, 'For this journey, the name is Lomond.'

'Ah, oui. But I have followed your career until you left Germany.'

'Inspector Murat. I have flown in one aeroplane over the Atlantic. From Newfoundland, I flew in another. I don't like flying. But I have done it. And I am very tired. I would like to wash and sleep.'

'Follow me, Inspector . . . Mister Lomond. I have booked you a large pleasant room at the Bellevue. And a Cadillac.

'A Cadillac!'

'The smallest of the range. It is yours for as long as you are on this continent. You will be driving to Washington tomorrow?'

'If I'm still alive.'

In the large and pleasant room at the Hotel Bellevue, Lohmann surveyed the king-sized bed with approval. 'Thank you for meeting me, Inspector Murat,' he said. 'Now, if you will leave me the car keys, tell me where the car is, I will go to bed and sleep for as long as I can.'

'The car is in the basement carpark. Washington DC registration as on the key ring,' Murat replied. 'You report to the British Embassy on your arrival.'

'I know.'

'And I am instructed to give you this.' Murat handed him a long fat white envelope. 'Ten thousand dollars, US. Authorised by Naval Intelligence. And Mister Thornhill. Expenses. Thornhill informs me that the Admiralty may require an accounting when your mission is over.'

'I wasn't sure Thornhill would get around to that. Thought I'd have to draw money from the Embassy in Washington. I brought £100 of my own.'

'Keep it. This ten thousand had to be handed over to you here. The British Treasury has certain wartime restrictions. Now, if I can call you later, I would be delighted to take you to dinner, show you a glimpse of Montreal . . .'

'Thank you, but no. I intend to sleep until tomorrow morning. Then I will breakfast and be on my way.'

The next morning, he ate a large English breakfast, found the Cadillac and drove south, out of Montreal. After an hour he crossed the American border and drove down the side of Lake Champlain towards the Adirondack Mountains, capped with the first snows of winter.

His boyhood reading of westerns included Fenimore Cooper and other writers of early frontier stories. It was therefore with fascination that he read the modern road signs with the familiar names from his childhood. A sign to the west indicated St. Francis and later Ticonderoga, once Fort Ticonderoga. It was as if he knew these places and he had to resist the temptation to take detours.

He drove through Albany, capital of New York State, and was sorely tempted to go on towards New York. Anna, whom he had not seen for four years, would be at university in New York. Columbia, that was the university. Later when the job was done he would see her.

In Albany, assisted by a kindly woman Western Union operative with a sense of humour, he sent a telegram to Paul Reiner in Cincinatti.

"Lafayette, I am here. Meet me soonest British Embassy, Washington. The Chief."

After an overnight stop in the grey, unlovely industrial Allentown, Pennsylvania, he arrived in Washington at midday, cheered by the whiteness of the city, its broad avenues and breathtaking vistas. But this in contrast to one of the poorer suburbs he had driven through. There was a predominance of black faces in those streets. For the first time he was seeing something of the two societies that existed in 1939 America.

The British Embassy was an elegant building, a part of white America. Yet, once inside, he was reminded of one of the more exclusive clubs in London, wood panelling, polished silver, a hushed atmosphere, and a trace of expensive cigars. The receptionist was a tall brunette in her late twenties, dressed in skirt and sweater with a single string of small pearls around her throat, a suggestion of pink lipstick faint but perfectly shaped on her lips. An English rose tanned with that tan all Americans seemed to pick up. Could there be a tanned rose? She stirred a memory within Lohmann; of his only love-affair in England, with Rue Scott-ffoliot. There was the same elegance, the same cool beauty and intelligent brown eyes. In a low, cultivated voice she asked him for his passport.

'Ah, yes, Mister Lomond, you are expected. The Naval Attaché is waiting for you.' She beckoned to an elderly man in a peaked cap and dark suit. 'Will you show this gentleman to Captain Greenock's office?'

Lohmann followed the elderly man up a broad staircase and along a corridor. He was shown into a small outer office in which sat another young woman, a clone of the receptionist, only this time a blonde. And, being a blonde, she had a double string of pearls.

'Mister Lomond? Go right in.'

Captain William Greenock, of medium height, with a thickening waistline and a nose threatening to rival that of W. C. Fields, was standing at the window of his office. He was gazing towards the dome of the Capitol as if on the bridge of his ship contemplating a possible target. He was in a dark civilian suit, white shirt and conservative blue tie. As Lohmann entered, he turned quickly.

'Been waiting for you. Thank God you're here.' He crossed the room and shook hands quickly, obviously distressed.

'Something has happened?' Lohmann asked.

'Another of these ghastly murders. Identical to the previous one. Same . . . what do they call it . . . *modus operandi*. Yes, that's what the police said.'

'When?'

'Body discovered this morning. Apartment in Georgetown.'

'A prostitute?'

Greenock looked suitably appalled at the suggestion. 'God,

65

no. A secretary, this one. More importantly, the niece of a senator.'

Lohmann expressed no surprise. He was too used to the twists and turns of convoluted murder searches. 'Where is Captain Pardoe?'

'Left Washington. Didn't tell me why. Went south to Kentucky, I gather. Something to do with his mission.'

'Then, if he can prove he was out of the city, we can clear him of any suspicion of involvement in these killings.'

Greenock now shook his head regretfully. He tugged at the knot of his tie. ' 'Fraid not,' he said. 'Y'see, he told us he was leaving last night. Left his office at six o'clock. Said he'd be back in a day or two. But we know he stayed in Washington all evening. Went out of his apartment about seven-thirty, came back before midnight. Seen by the porter there. Could have easily gone to this girl's place in Georgetown.'

'He was seen there?'

'No, no, not as far as I've heard. But he could have gone . . . and . . . and presumably started off south early this morning. So we have to say he was in Washington last night. Could have done . . . whatever was done. Not that I believe he did it. Not . . . not for a minute . . .'

'But he could have,' Lohmann echoed the Captain's words.

SIX

They drove from 'Embassy Row' along Massachusetts Avenue to Georgetown, Captain Greenock behind the wheel of his large Ford.

'Used to be a tobacco port,' Greenock explained. 'Nice place to live, Georgetown. If you can afford it.'

Lohmann gazed out at the neat rows of houses, with their bow windows and their unity of small bricks and white wood; life-sized dolls' houses for the wealthy.

'Period stuff,' said Greenock. 'Nearest thing they have to history.'

He drew the Ford to a halt outside one of the three-storey terraced dwellings. Ahead of them police cars were parked at the kerb and, at the entrance to the building, a uniformed cop (Lohmann could think of no other word to describe the man in his loose-fitting uniform, peaked cap and belt with its holstered revolver) surrounded by a group of clamouring civilians.

'Journalists,' Greenock said. 'Ignore them and say nothing. We don't want to be identified by the press.' Greenock led the way, pushing through the crowd of newspaper people.

'Hey, who are you?' A large round face with a large round mouth loomed up in front of Lohmann.

Greenock half turned and replied, 'Police laboratory.'

The lie was accepted without any show of interest by all but one small woman reporter who, bird-like, popped up in front of Greenock.

'Hey, Mac, was she raped first?'

Ignoring her, Greenock reached the police officer at the doorway and produced a small card.

'Oh yeah, they're expecting you,' said the officer laconically.

'He's with me,' Greenock explained, grasping Lohmann by the arm. They were waved into the building despite an increasing clamour from the newspaper people.

'All this,' said Greenock, 'makes me wish I was back at sea. To hell with the U-boats. I'd settle for the smallest tramp steamer rather than this. Breathe fresh salt air again. Give my pension for that.'

They were climbing stairs now. 'And Captain Pardoe? Would he feel the same?' Lohmann asked.

'Pardoe's different. Quieter type. Got some kind of scientific degree. Other interests. But I daresay he'd agree with me.'

The apartment was on the first floor, another policeman standing at the door. Again Greenock was waved through after producing his identification. They walked into a large room, expensively furnished, and filled with a number of men in plain clothes, some of them merely standing around, others, on their knees, dusting the furniture for fingerprints.

A tall man, running to fat, in a creased suit and still wearing a soft hat, slouched over from the window; a large, wrinkled sack with legs.

'Hi, Cap'n Greenock.'

'Mister Thompson.'

'Looks as if your boy's been at it again.'

Greenock flushed. 'You have no proof of such an accusation, Thompson.'

'A friend of Mary Lou Hancock's. Mebbe a friend of this one too. And this one was no hooker, Greenock.'

'And I would remind you the man you may be accusing is a British Naval officer . . . and a member of the diplomatic corps.'

68

'Doesn't mean he can't be a bad person.' Thompson stared at Lohmann, heavy red-rimmed eyes looking him up and down suspiciously.

Greenock followed the look. 'This is Mister Lomond. From London. Lomond, this is Bernard Thompson, Chief of Detectives, Washington police.'

Thompson nodded curtly. No handshake. 'What's he doin' here? Some kind of Limey lawyer?'

'Mister Lomond is from the Admiralty. By permission of your Secretary of State. To keep an eye on this matter as far as it affects us.'

'That right? Well, just as long as he keeps out of my hair.'

'Chief Thompson!' The voice came from behind, sharp and authoritative. A youngish man, with a fresh out-door complexion, impeccably dressed in grey flannel, fair hair smooth and short. A complete contrast to the chief of detectives, a clean-cut figure, so clean-cut, Lohmann thought, as to be sharp at the edges. 'I got to remind you, Chief,' the man said. 'You're no longer in charge of these two killings. As far as we're concerned you're here as a courtesy.'

'Oh, yeah. A courtesy!' Thompson practically spat out the last word, his expression venomous.

The youngish man turned to Greenock, hand outstretched. 'Collins. Whitney Collins. Federal Bureau of Investigation.'

'Greenock. Senior Naval Attaché, British Embassy. And this is Lomond.'

Whitney Collins' grip was firm and assured. 'I have to tell you, gentlemen, in view of the possible diplomatic implications of this case, the FBI have taken charge of the investigation.'

This brought a snort from Thompson. Without a glance at the chief of detectives, Collins added, 'Working, of course with the Washington police force.'

'While you gab with the diplomatic corps, I'll get on with my investigation,' Thompson said morosely and moved away.

'You'll have to excuse Thompson,' Collins said. 'He's a

69

good detective, but when it comes to the niceties of tact and diplomacy, he's got rough edges.'

'I had noticed,' Greenock replied.

But now Collins turned to Lohmann. 'You'll have just arrived, Mister Lomond. Of course your people in London told us you were coming over. Kind of awkward situation for us all, I guess.'

'It is only awkward, Mister Collins, if Captain Pardoe turns out to have homicidal tendencies,' Mister Lohmann said quietly.

The flush was on Collins' face now. 'Sure, sure . . .'

'And so far, I gather, you have no firm evidence.'

'Pardoe was a client of Mary Lou Hancock's.'

'He denies that,' Greenock cut in.

'Okay. But his name was in her address book.'

'And the victim here?' Lohmann asked.

'A dead ringer for the Mary Lou Hancock killing. Identical wounds. A knife thrust in below the navel and drawn up to the throat. With considerable force. Scraped the ribcage.'

'Eviscerated,' Lohmann said.

'Yeah, you could say that. Entrails and everything out. Very nasty.'

'The murderer must have been covered in blood.'

'Sure. No sign of forced entry. He was invited in. Tracks of blood on the carpet leading to the bathroom. And blood in the shower. He was in bed with her. Or on the bed. Probably naked when he killed her. We're sure he took a shower afterwards.'

'Fingerprints?'

'Only the victim's. And some smudges. He was damn careful. Looks like he rubbed out any prints before he left.'

'There is nothing to connect Captain Pardoe with this crime?'

Whitney Collins looked down awkwardly at his feet. 'Well, it being the same *modus operandi* as the killing of Mary Lou Hancock . . . and his name being in her diary . . . that's the main link. Of course we haven't finished around here. Body was only discovered at nine o'clock this morning. By the cleaning woman.'

'But you have no real evidence against Pardoe?'

Collins straightened up and stared directly into Lohmann's face. 'We also know about the killing in London, Mister Lomond.'

Lohmann was taken off guard. Of course the killing of Antoinette Valois had been in the London papers. But not extensively reported. And no link with Robert Pardoe had appeared. How the devil did they know . . . ?

'We have our sources, 'Collins seemed to read his mind. 'I wouldn't know the details. But Pardoe was linked with that murder and the Hancock killing. If we can tie in a connection here, it's going to make us all think, isn't it?'

Lohmann could only nod briefly. Feeling uneasy. Why was he here? A deathwatch assignment, it had already been said. But everyone seemed to have made up their minds already that Pardoe was guilty. Except Greenock, who was looking rather shaken. Lohmann knew he had to meet Robert Pardoe and quickly.

'You want to view the scene of the crime, Mister Lomond?' The doc's still examining the corpse.'

'I would appreciate it,' Lohmann said, with a glance at Greenock.

'Of course you realise you have no jurisdiction here,' Collins added quietly. 'Because of the diplomatic situation, I'm instructed to give you the courtesies, but the investigation is entirely ours.'

'Of course,' Lohmann replied as they moved towards the bedroom. Thinking, this is a courtesy, viewing the mutilated body of a young woman? He could only hope there would be no more courtesies. Greenock, pale faced, had declined.

It was obviously the bedroom of a young woman with money. It was expensive, in pink and with chintz around the dressing table and throughout the room. It was a large powder puff of a room. Even the drapes and the bedsheets were pink although the latter were now soaked in a deeper, darker, more sinister colour. The nude body lay twisted across the bed, almost a question mark on the pink sheets. The head, in one corner, was turned back, sightless eyes staring at the ceiling, mouth open. The expression was one not of pain but of surprise. As if, in her last conscious moments, astonishment had taken the place of pain; amazement that the act of love should be so terminated. If indeed she had been engaged in the act of love. The wound itself was a gaping red chasm, an enormous welling-up of blood.

A small, elderly man, with a stiff collar above a tweed suit, a pince-nez on the end of his nose, a shapeless tweed hat on the back of his head, was straightening up from examining the body.

'Doc Sanders, Medical Examiner,' Collins said by way of introduction. 'Got anything for us?'

Doc Sanders was not without a grim sense of humour. 'She's dead,' he said blandly, eyes shining behind the pince-nez. Lohmann thought a sense of humour had to be necessary to stay sane in such a job.

Collins sighed. 'Anything else?'

'Won't have it all until I get her on the slab.' Sanders scratched his head. 'Tell you this though. She had sex before she was killed. Be able to confirm that at the PM but I'm pretty sure of it. Could almost say she died happy. Except nobody could be happy with that done to them.'

He scratched the back of his head, contemplating the corpse. 'Oh, and it was a pretty sharp knife. Thin blade. If it was a knife.'

'What do you mean, if it was a knife?' Collins said.

'Something with a thin, thin blade. Fine incision, but deep. Deep enough so the body just burst open. But from the initial incision, you can reckon it was a thin blade.'

'Like a surgical scalpel,' Lohmann said.

72

The pince-nez turned towards him. 'Yes. Exactly. Good. Very good.'

Lohmann thought of the reports he'd been given on the murder of Antoinette Valois: A thin blade, inserted below the navel.

'Like the Hancock girl. Something familiar in both killings,' said Sanders.

'What do you mean, familiar?' Collins asked.

'Not sure. Something I've read about.'

'Jack the Ripper?' Lohmann prompted.

The pince-nez was riveted on him. 'Yes. Yes, indeed. You got experience of this kind of business?'

'Some,' said Lohmann.

'It's true. Jack the Ripper. Although he removed some of the internal organs, didn't he?'

'Took them away with him. And decorated the bodies with the remaining entrails.'

'Christ!' said Collins.

'You're a knowledgeable man, sir,' observed Sanders. The pince-nez turned to Collins. 'Who is he?'

'Oh, I'm sorry. Mister Lomond. From England.'

The Medical Examiner nodded. 'I'll not shake hands. A little sanguinary, my hands. So you've had experience. I'm interested. Any particular cases?'

'Kürten. Denke. Haarmann. Not that they used knives. Denke was an axe murderer. Kürten strangled women, often after attempting intercourse. Haarmann was possibly the most unpleasant.'

'I've read about Haarmann,' Sanders could not conceal his fascination with the subject. 'Murder and cannibalism. Also he and Denke were homosexual, weren't they?'

'Only Jack the Ripper killed like this.'

'They never found him, did they,' Collins cut in on them. 'How long ago . . . ?'

'Over fifty years,' said Sanders, with a small smile. 'You'd be looking for rather an elderly gentleman, Collins. And the

73

unofficial version was that the Ripper died. Am I right, Lohmann?'

'You are, doctor.'

'Pity,' chimed in Bernard Thompson who had been standing at the bedroom door listening to them. 'But I do reckon we're looking for a much younger guy. Oh, sure, he'll be a foreigner. Bet your life on it. Americans don't kill like that – with the knife.'

'We've had our knife murderers,' Sanders said, with a brief glance at Thompson. 'But serial killers are usually insane, are they not, Lomond?'

'That would depend on the parameters of what is considered legal insanity,' Lohmann replied. 'But, yes, in my opinion that is so.'

Thompson snorted indignantly. 'Whoever did this ain't going to get off with an insanity plea. Not if I got anything to do with it!'

'You haven't,' said Whitney Collins roughly. He turned to Sanders. 'You'll let the Bureau have your report, doc?'

'Soon as I do the PM. Twenty-four hours.' He was suddenly querulous. 'Your boys finished in the bathroom? I want to wash my hands,'

'They'll let you know. Now, Mister Lomond, I have instructions to take you to meet the Director.'

'Captain Greenock and I will be pleased to –'

'Not Captain Greenock. He can wait for you at the Embassy. We'll drive you back there. Now, unless there's anything else you want to see here . . . ?'

The office of J. Edgar Hoover, Director of the Federal Bureau of Investigation, was large yet spartan. Despite wood panelling, and a few framed photographs on the walls, there was no decoration other than the flag of the United States behind the desk. The desk itself was neat and uncluttered. Two upright and rather uncomfortable chairs faced it.

The man behind the desk had broad shoulders and a round,

almost bulldog-like face, cheeks running to fat. The hair was cropped short and below a wide forehead were small, penetrating eyes. When Lohmann entered, ushered in by Whitney Collins, the man did not rise but looked up, eyes peering at Lohmann.

'Take a seat. You can stay, Collins. You'll have gathered, Mister Lomond, that Collins is case officer for this business.'

Lohmann sat, facing the man behind the desk. 'I have gathered that.'

Collins did not sit, but stood, almost at attention, near the door.

'And he'll have told you, you have no jurisidiction here?'

How often was he to be informed of this?

'Yes, yes. But I am accredited to the staff of the British Embassy.'

A plump, well manicured hand waved the air. 'I know that. Gives you diplomatic immunity, nothing else.'

Lohmann was suddenly weary of these preliminaries. Hoover had not asked him to come here to tell him he had no standing in the United States. The man was merely using the obvious as if to place himself on some elevated and authoritative level. He had no need to. His position as Director of the FBI already gave him all the authority he needed. And his reputation underlined that authority.

'I expect nothing else, sir.'

Hoover continued to glower at him. 'Yeah, you say so. But I have to tell you this. The President of these United States has authorised me to investigate all subversive activities being conducted in the country by communists, fascists and so on. I intend to do this. I intend to do it without interference from any foreign governments. That includes the British.' He took a deep breath and seemed to swell out like some large bird puffing up its feathers. 'That doesn't mean that we are slowing down on our battle with lawbreakers,' he went on. 'Particularly murderers.'

75

'I am glad to know that, even as a simple visitor to your country, sir.'

Now Hoover smiled but that smile was devoid of humour, merely a contortion of the facial muscles. 'Neatly said, sir. But we know about you, Lomond.'

He opened a drawer and took out a large folder which he slapped on the desk loudly. 'It's all here, Lomond, or should I say one-time Inspector Ernst Lohmann of the Berlin Police.'

They had done their homework, Lohmann told himself. And waited to see exactly how well.

'Left Berlin in 1934.' Hoover had opened the folder and was flicking through it. 'Reasons never fully explained?'

'I could explain them, sir.'

'But would I believe you *Herr* Lohmann? Later, in London as a refugee, you were involved with some opposition to Sir Oswald Mosley's Fascist Party . . .'

'I would have thought that would have met with your approval, Mister Hoover.'

Another page of the file was turned over. 'Not necessarily. There are people we classify as prematurely anti-fascist.'

'Can one be *prematurely* anti-fascist?'

'We think so. At that time in London, you had close connections with a journalist, one Joseph Kahn, a member of the Communist Party of Great Britain.'

'That is so. I also had connections with another perhaps premature anti-fascist. The name was Winston Spencer Churchill.'

Hoover did not like such contradictory indications and showed it. 'We know you are here at the behest of Mister Churchill. Or at least with his knowledge. That does not absolve you from such Communist connections as you undoubtedly have. Oh, I'm sure you'll deny being a Red. But that doesn't mean we believe you. And certainly we intend to keep an eye on you.'

'I am accredited to the British Embassy,' Lohmann repeated sharply. 'And I have British citizenship.' Did he?

Could he lay claim to that? He hoped like hell he could. Otherwise, a sudden thought, these people could ship him back to Germany.

'Reds have fooled the British before now,' Hoover insisted.

The two men stared at each other in silence for a moment. Lohmann broke the silence.

'What is the purpose of asking me here, sir? I know I have no jurisdiction. Everyone emphasises that. I am here on a mission for Mister Churchill, a mission not unfriendly to the government of the United States.'

'So you would say!' Uttered as a reptile would flash out its tongue to catch an insect.

'I do say!'

'You are here, Lohmann, to watch over Captain Robert Pardoe.'

'To aid him with his mission!' Lohmann snapped back.

'To keep him from killing any more prosititutes!'

'There is no direct evidence that Pardoe has killed anyone. Only some vague circumstantial –'

'We're not naive, Lohmann. Your British friends are worried. They sent Pardoe here on a mission and then afterwards discovered they might inadvertently have sent a maniac. So they sent you after him. Your job is to watch over him, keep him from . . . misbehaving. At least until his mission is done.'

Hoover stood up now. A barrel-chested figure, smaller than Lohmann would have imagined.

'The man's sick, Lohmann!' he said. 'A sick, depraved creature. A pervert from a sick continent, come among us. And I am the one to stop him.'

A touch of the prophet or the poet there, Lohmann thought. The man must have ideas above his station.

'Europe is not the only continent with a premium on perverted criminals, Mister Hoover. Your own organised crime factions . . .'

Hoover flushed, thumping his desk, angry now. 'We have

criminals, sure! But we have no organised crime in America.'

'Surely the Mafia influence is well known?'

'There is no Mafia! A few hoodlums get together and it's called a conspiracy! Lies. And we will get these hoodlums – as we got Dillinger and Floyd and Nelson and all the others.' He paused to draw breath. 'As, Herr Lohmann, we will get Captain Pardoe. Oh, your government may be able to get him out using diplomatic immunity. But we'll get him, understand that, and we won't hide our knowledge of his guilt.'

'If he's not guilty . . . ?'

Hoover had been crouched over his desk. He straightened up now, the smile returning.

'He's guilty. Of murdering that hooker. And, much more seriously, of murdering Senator Neuberg's niece. The senator is a personal friend. This ugly, unpleasant killing has to be solved by the Bureau. And will be!'

'And if you have no real evidence . . . ?'

'But we have now, Lohmann. We have the first piece of real evidence. Collins!'

The agent reached into his pocket and produced a small cellophane envelope.

'Tell him!' said Hoover.

'I found this in Miss Neuberg's apartment.' Collins passed the envelope across to Lohmann. 'At the side of the bed. Could have been loosened and fallen off, or could have been torn from his jacket.'

Lohmann looked at the cellophane envelope. Inside, he could clearly see the gleaming round shape of a brass button typical of the jacket of a British naval officer.

SEVEN

Whitney Collins escorted Lohmann to the main door of the Department of Justice building.

'We can lay on transport, Mister Lomond. Get you back to the British Embassy.'

'Thank you, no. It is my first day in Washington. I would like to walk a while.'

'Well, if you're sure. But you don't know the way.'

'I shall walk a while and then get a taxicab.'

Collins shrugged. 'Yeah, well, I reckon we'll be in touch.'

'I am sure.' Lohmann edged towards the door. Anxious to be out of the building; away from the heavy, accusing atmosphere of J. Edgar Hoover. He felt uneasy, as if there was something sinister about the Director of the FBI.

Collins seemed reluctant to see him go. 'Lomond . . . about the Director. Mr Hoover is a very great human being. As a man and as a detective. If he seems overly suspicious of your part, it's not . . . not personal. He has to be alert to every possibility.'

'I am glad it is not personal. But, you know, it felt personal.'

'Look, honestly, he'll be pleased to have you around. This case could be dynamite. I mean, your Captain Pardoe being with your embassy and all that. And tied in to these killings. Very tricky . . .'

'If he is guilty. Which we have yet to determine. Good day, Collins.'

He went from the building on to the street. And started to

79

walk along what what he learned later was Constitution Avenue. Ahead of him the dome of the Capitol building seemed to shine in the dying afternoon sun. Yet, despite the sun, an ice cold breeze was blowing up. The traffic was building up on the streets. It was nearing the end of another working day. Four hours, he mused, he had been in Washington and in that time he had visited the scene of a particularly brutal crime and met the most famous policeman in the country, maybe in the world. The number one G-man. He'd even been known as that in Germany. A pity the man was so unlikeable.

Lohmann put these thoughts behind him and concentrated on the man who was following him.

He'd been aware that he was being followed the moment he'd stepped out of the building. While he'd been talking to Whitney Collins, he'd noticed the man standing leaning on a pillar in the entrance hall, ostensibly reading a newspaper. When Lohmann walked out of the building, the newspaper was crammed into a raincoat pocket and the man moved after him.

And kept going after him.

One of Hoover's minions . . . agents, he called them, or operatives? That was more than likely. Hoover would want to note Lomond's every move. What better time to start than at once.

Alternatively the man could be of some other group. One of *die Schlägertyp*. Heavies, Reiner would have called them. Reiner was a movie addict, especially American movies. Boasted he'd seen the James Cagney movie *G-Men* eight times. Lohmann wondered if Reiner had reached Washington. A momentary thought; he would know soon enough. Meanwhile forget Reiner, concentrate on the Follower.

At first Lohmann deliberately walked quickly. Without looking around, he knew the Follower had matched his pace. So then he slowed down, looking around him, for all the world a first-time tourist in the city. An average Herr Muller, from Hamburg or Frankfurt, taking in the sights. As he slowed, he saw to his surprise, out of the corner of his eye, that the Follower had not also slowed. If anything he was moving faster towards his quarry.

Lohmann stopped, staring at a building on his left, still playing the tourist.

'Mister Lomond?' The voice was breathless and slightly too highly pitched.

Lohmann turned to face the Follower.

'Yes,' he said, staring at a young man, barely thirty. Hatless. Over the grey flannel suit, the man wore a clean, uncrumpled trench coat. If it was for effect, Lohmann thought, it should at least be crumpled. Like that actor who played gangsters in the movies. What was his name? Reiner would have known. Bogart, Humphrey Bogart. But this fellow was too young, too clean, too well-scrubbed. His face while tanned was tinged with pink. His teeth were very, very white. He talked nervously.

'I . . . I wanted to get away from the Justice Building before I made contact.' The accent was unfamiliar to Lohmann. Broad A's and the high pitch quality he had already noted. Despite this, well spoken. 'Name's Straight. James Henry Straight. The Third, to be exact.'

'So? James Henry Straight the Third, to be exact, what can I do for you?'

'Known as Jimmy, more often than not. I'd like a word. But I shouldn't be seen with you. If I am, it gets back to the Great Panjandrum.'

Lohmann looked puzzled.

'My name for the Director, Mister Hoover. Gets back to him, I'm the little boy in trouble.'

'You are a Federal Agent?'

James Henry Straight smiled awkwardly. 'Yeah. You could say that. I . . . I got a Justice Department number. I'm a lawyer. Harvard Law School.' He pronounced it *Ha'vahd*. 'Look, we can't talk here, still too near the Justice Building.

81

Meet me. Half an hour . . .'

'Where?'

'The Lincoln Memorial. Where else would a tourist go? It'll be quiet just now. You get a cab. See you there.' He walked away before Lohmann could reply. A slim, neat figure, medium height, fair hair rumpled by the breeze.

The street lights were on now. Night was coming. Lohmann thought, had he time to get back to the Embassy? Not yet. This young man, James Henry Straight, seemed considerably concerned. Insistent. All right, he would visit the Lincoln Memorial.

He flagged down a cab.

Fifteen minutes later he was climbing the steps into the building and towards the massive nineteen-foot high statue of the Great Emancipator. It rose in front of him, in dim light seemingly infused with life, enshrined in this classic design of a Greek temple and staring ahead into the distance, towards the Capitol. As if he had to keep his eyes on the present day rulers.

Lohmann swung around a full 360 degrees. On the walls of the chamber the words of the Gettysburg Address and the Second Inaugural were carved. He stood for a moment, impressed. And then aware that the great chamber was almost empty. A black couple with two small children had been staring in awe at the great figure. Now they turned and went out, footsteps echoing on the marble floor. A young woman came in, putting out a cigarette as she did so, as if entering a church. She read the Address and the Inaugural speech, contemplated the statue, looked nervously at Lohmann with a half suppressed smile, and then went out.

Lohmann waited.

No sign yet of James Henry Straight.

A couple of figures walked in shadow clockwise around the statue. Lohmann walked, counter-clockwise, around its massive bulk. Into shadow.

Too dark here, he thought. As if some of the lighting had

82

gone. He walked more quickly. James Henry Straight should have been here.

The blow came from his right. Something flashing through the very corner of his eye, a dark speeding shape. Instinctively he twisted aside, ducking his head. And was struck heavily on his shoulder. A stabbing pain shot down his arm.

The second blow came from his left. Another shadow figure kicked out at him towards the groin. In twisting he took the blow on the side of his leg. He felt his leg buckle and he went down on one knee.

In Berlin, as a young policeman, he'd been used to street fighting, standing between the Stahlheim and the Communists. The Stahlheim had been the precursor of the Nazis, dissident ex-officers from the exiled Kaiser's army, extreme right-wingers. It was the Stahlheim who had murdered Rosa Luxemburg and Karl Liebknecht, the Communist leaders. And later most of them were absorbed in the Nazi Party. And the street fighting continued. A young policeman trying to separate the warring factions had to learn the dirty tricks of the street. He was nearly ten years away from all that. Yet the instincts were still there.

He lashed out with the side of his hand and connected with the soft midriff of one his two assailants. He heard the gasp as he spun aside to avoid the boot that came from the right, felt the air as it missed his head. Then he was on his feet again, and kicking out with his own right foot; feeling it sink into one of the shadows. The man screamed. Lohmann felt a flash of reassurance. He had not forgotten the technique.

Then he felt the blow on the side of his body. The second assailant had connected with a vicious kick. Lohmann went sideways and down. The marble floor seemed to come up and meet him. Cold, hard marble. And the thought came with the blow . . . he'd been set up. By James Henry Straight the Third; whoever he was.

He knew then another blow would come, this time to his head. He rolled over on the floor, away from the attacker.

83

And heard the voice, echoing against the walls.

'Stop it! Stop it or I shoot!'

The high-pitched voice. Then the sound of running footsteps on marble. The sound dying into the distance.

He tried to get up, feet slithering. Pain stabbing below his left kidney. A hand reached out and helped him to his feet.

'You okay?' James Henry Straight staring at him.

'I . . . I thought you had . . . set me up. That's how you say it?'

'That's nice, that is. *Me*? Set you up? I thought I was on your side.'

'Then who were they?'

'I should know? Couple of heist men. Or else . . . ?'

Lohmann swayed, holding his side. Or else . . . ?'

'The bad guys?' Under the fair hair, the pale face creased into a smile. Lohmann thought, he has the face of a porcelain statue.

'Let's get out of here,' said the porcelain statue.

A ten minute cab drive later they were sitting in a booth in a small dimly lit bar, a barman standing over them.

'What you drinking?' Straight asked.

'A brandy, I think.' The pain in his side was beginning to ease.

'And a glass of milk. With a little rum in it. Barbados rum.' Straight smiled at Lohmann. 'Keeps the chill out and does you good at the same time.'

The barman brought the drinks and vanished.

'Those gentlemen behind Lincoln,' Lohmann said. 'They were waiting for me.'

'No mystery. They followed you. Hoover had you watched from the moment you arrived at the Embassy.'

'They were Hoover's men?'

Straight shook his head. 'I wouldn't think so. But if he knew you were coming – and he did, we all did – then others would know too.'

'How?'

'Your Embassy . . . leaks like a sieve. The German Embassy knows everything eventually. I think you encountered a couple of Krauts. Only a guess, but not a bad one. You came here to keep an eye on Bob Pardoe. And Captain Pardoe is of interest to everybody. The FBI, the US government, the Washington police, and the German Embassy. And me, of course.'

Lohmann took a gulp of brandy. His side throbbed. 'Who are you?' he asked.

'I told you. James Henry Straight the Third.'

'So? Who is James Henry Straight the Third?'

'My father is James Henry Straight the Second. Family got frightened by the numbers racket, I guess.'

Lohmann had believed himself fluent in English and with a good knowledge of English idioms, Until now.

Straight grinned. 'Okay. My old man is Senator James Henry Straight. He was the second of the line. J.H.S. the First made a fortune out of chewing gum. Me, guess I'm the prodigal grandson. Not too prodigal. Law degree, Harvard Law School.' Lank blond hair fell over his forehead. 'The old man is a pal of J. Edgar's. Hoover made me a kind of honorary agent.' Again the flashing grin. 'Well, I didn't quite measure up to the physical. So I sit behind a desk and give erudite legal opinions on behalf of the Bureau. I also go overseas for them. My old man's on the Foreign Relations Committee of the Senate. So when he goes abroad, I go abroad. And send Hoover reports. Since we're filthy rich, it costs the Bureau damn all.'

'You are a kind of amateur agent . . .'

'Yeah, something like that. But with official status. My old man loves it. People ask him what his son is doing, he can say I'm a G-Man.'

'So why are you so interested in me?'

'Because of Bob Pardoe.'

'You know him?'

'Good friend of mine. Met him a time ago in Singapore on a

little vacation. A small job for Hoover. We met up at some dreary official reception. Hit it off right away. He was fed up to the back teeth, they were sending him back to London and he didn't want to go. All the glamour of the East and he was going back to a dreary desk job. Know how he felt. We went out on the town first night. He showed me a sailor's eye view of Singapore. And that was sure something. Do you know there's one street in Singapore . . .'

Lohmann shut his mind to the effusive description of the Far Eastern city. He was thinking, what might Pardoe have in common with this rather effete young American?

Straight was chattering on. '. . . after that, I moved on and he went back to London. But he gave me his address in London and then later I found myself message boy for Hoover again. Wanted his own report on the situation before war broke out. Knew I was friendly with the Kennedy family, and old Joe Kennedy was Ambassador to the Court of St James's. I like that. Not Ambassador to the UK, but to the Court. I like it.'

'And you visited Captain Pardoe?'

'Sure I did. And more. Bob Pardoe introduced me to one of their Members of Parliament. Guy who'd been an American too. Got himself knighted and took British citizenship and ended up in Parliament. Channon. Sir Henry Channon. Everybody called him Chips Channon. Friend of friends. Like the Duke of Windsor. Knew everybody worth knowing. Gave me a lot of stuff I could report to Hoover. Like who was screwing who in London. Hoover likes that kind of thing. Also told me the British would never fight Hitler. Chamberlain hadn't the stomach. Boy was he wrong! But I was meeting . . .'

Would the man ever stop talking? Lohmann had to make him. 'Why do you want to speak to me?'

Straight looked surprised. 'I'm telling you. Bobby Pardoe is being set up. Of course he contacted me when he came here to Washington. Didn't tell me why he's here. Just some secret

86

job he was on. But then I saw the reports come into the Bureau. They think he murdered that hooker. And one in London. And the Neuberg broad last night. He knew it too.'

'Did he kill these women?'

'Like hell he did. I don't believe a nice guy like Bob Pardoe would do anything like that. You only got to know him.'

'A number of seemingly nice people have committed murders in the past.'

'That's why you're here, isn't it? To investigate.'

Lohmann didn't reply. He determined he was the one who asked the questions.

'Okay, okay. Not my business,' said Straight. 'But they're out to get Pardoe. And because you've been sent to investigate him or whatever, they're likely out to get you too. Like those two guys in the Lincoln Memorial.'

'If those people were out to get me, as you say, why didn't they kill me?'

'Maybe they were just trying to frighten you off. Maybe they would have killed you. And like, I just turned up in time.'

'And saved my life?'

'Well, if you want to put it that way. Gee, first time I ever saved anybody's life.'

'The Chinese believe, if you save somebody's life you are then responsible for them for the rest of your life.' Lohmann drained the last of the brandy from his glass.

'That right?' Straight laughed. 'You going to hold me to that, Mister Lomond?'

'Who were these people who attacked me?'

Another shrug from the American. 'The bad guys. If we're the good guys, they have to be the bad guys. But what bad guys, I don't know. Krauts maybe. That would be logical.'

'German agents.'

'German agents. They're around, you know. We got dossiers on them in the Bureau. Nazis, communists . . . Hoover's a great man for keeping dossiers.'

Lohmann rose to his feet. The brandy had warmed him. 'I shall have to meet your friend Captain Pardoe very soon. But he's in Kentucky.'

'Kentucky? That's what he'd tell the Embassy people. But he knows the place leaks. They say the Germans want to know anything, they just contact their little listening post in the British Embassy. Pardoe didn't go to Kentucky.'

'No?'

'Has to cover himself. Went to New Orleans.'

'Why should he go to New Orleans?' Lohmann affected a mild curiosity over a seemingly general indifference.

Straight gave a small twisted smile. 'Better ask him. When you catch up with him. When you do, look out for him. Keep him out of trouble. But then that's what you're here for. See you, Mister Lomond.'

EIGHT

Greenock said: 'New Orleans?'

'I have been so informed.'

Greenock hesitated. Looked around at his office, at the city beyond the window.

'Who told you this?'

'A man called Straight. James Henry Straight.'

'He's with the FBI.'

'He also told me that. He claims he is a friend of Captain Pardoe's.'

'True enough. Pardoe met him somewhere abroad some years ago. He looked up Straight when he came to

Washington. As Straight was an FBI operative, Pardoe thought he might be useful, regarding the mission.'

'And he *is* in New Orleans?'

'Yes. I was the only person in this Embassy to be told.' Greenock suddenly had become very formal. 'It is necessary that he do so. Should the Embassy wish to contact him. Matter of protocol.'

'Yet Straight knew. Straight maintains the Embassy has leaks. And, not only the FBI but German agents have access to everything that goes on here.'

Greenock's eyes flashed angrily. His cheeks reddened. Matching his nose, Lohmann thought inanely. 'That would imply a spy within the Embassy.'

'Yes.'

The momentary silence seemed to scream at them.

'I don't believe it,' said Greenock, but his tones lacked conviction. He drummed his fingers on the edge of the desk.

'I think you should, Captain Greenock. It would be the sort of thing the Abwehr would do. You have an intelligence officer in the building?'

'Yes, of course. Charlie Markham.'

Greenock went behind his desk and lifted the telephone. 'Would you be good enough to ask Mister Markham to come to my office. At once.' He replaced the receiver.

'He's pretty new here. Only recently sent out. And orders are he must have as little contact with Pardoe as possible. Markham as a security officer will become quickly known in Washington. The word gets around. We thought it best that Pardoe should have little contact with intelligence people in view of his own mission. But if there is a leak in this building, then it's certainly Markham's job to find it.'

'Why did you insist Pardoe has gone to Kentucky? Why Kentucky?' Lohmann asked.

'No mystery there. He happens to have a cousin living in Louisville. It was a good cover.'

'And why has he gone to New Orleans?'

'To do with . . . with his mission. That's all I know.'

Damn this blasted secret mission, Lohmann swore to himself. Ernst Lohmann, aka Lomond, trying to solve three murders with access to only a part of the possible evidence. A boxer with one arm tied behind his back.

Charlie Markham was in his thirties, dapper, thin and elongated. Over six feet in a grey suit and Guards tie. And an expression that made him look as if he was suffering, stiff upper lipped, from a bad smell beneath his nose.

Lohmann thought: he reeks of the English public school and Oxford, Chamberlain, Baldwin, dusty old country houses with even dustier squires. Markham as the younger son who might have gone into the ministry or the City. True-blue, politically sound, believed in England, Home and Beauty (didn't acknowledge anyone he thought might not have his beliefs). Instead went into MI6. To spy for England, specifically. Didn't acknowledge Scotland except for grouse moors. And Wales only as a supplier of coal.

'Ah, yes,' he said, after the introductions. 'Sent by naval intelligence to aid Captain Pardoe on his . . . unspecified mission.'

'But you would not know what my mission is?' Lohmann asked quietly.

'Hardly my affair, old man. May have heard a few whispers. But only within the building.'

'Exactly. Yet the FBI knows why I'm here, Mister Markham. And other people seem to know it too. I'm even attacked on my first day in Washington.'

It was the first he'd mentioned of the attack. He had to explain it further to both men.

'That proves it. There's been a definite security breach,' Greenock insisted.

Markham's tone to Greenock was respectful but with a slight condescension. 'Not necessarily from the Embassy. If Mister Hoover's lads know why Lomond is here, they could have let the fact be known in . . . other areas. Or Pardoe could have talked.'

'Pardoe would not have talked. And I always heard Hoover guarded his information jealously,' Greenock said.

'Unless it suits him,' Markham replied. 'We should talk to Captain Pardoe.'

'When he gets back,' Greenock said formally. 'Meanwhile you will handle the security side of the matter.'

'I shall of course institute an investigation into security within the Embassy at once. And, naturally, the Ambassador should be informed.'

'I'll see Lord Lothian myself,' Greenock said.

Markham nodded perfunctorily, and moved towards the door, exuding men's after-shave and the Brigade of Guards. At the door, he hesitated, and turned.

'Unless of course the FBI instigated the assault on Lomond.'

He went out.

'A thought,' said Lohmann.

'Rubbish,' said Greenock. 'And now I have to introduce you to the Ambassador. Oh, I've booked you a room at the Mayflower Hotel. Pardoe stays there. It's expensive, but I gather you have to be close to him. And I've allocated you an office here. It's tiny but we're cramped for space.'

'I'm sure it'll be satisfactory,' Lohmann said. 'I'm expecting an old colleague, by the way.'

'Man called Reiner. He's waiting in your office.' The naval attaché hesitated. 'He is a former German national, I understand. Although he took up American citizenship this year. You will vouch for him, Lomond?'

The meeting with the Ambassador was brief. Lord Lothian examined the papers supplied to Lohmann by the Admiralty. And then gazed bleakly at the latest acquisition to his embassy.

'I don't wish to seem unfriendly, Lomond, but you and Captain Pardoe are, I gather, on some highly confidential mission. That would be an intelligence matter and I have no wish to know about it. But I must emphasise that should you disturb Anglo-American relations, this Embassy will at once disown you. You understand this?'

'I understand, sir.'

'Good. Having said that, I wish you every success. Good day.'

Outside the Ambassador's office, Greenock said. 'He means it, y'know. You get into trouble with the FBI or the police, the Embassy will claim it has no knowledge of your activities.'

'So everybody tells me. And if Pardoe is arrested for murder . . .?'

'God knows! That, as the Americans would say, is a whole new ball game.'

'Would he get diplomatic immunity?'

'I can't answer that. You're here to see it doesn't happen.'

'Then I shall have to attach myself to him as soon as possible. I will have to go to New Orleans. Tomorrow. You have an address there?'

'The Fairmont Hotel. Near the university.'

'Good. Can I fly down?'

'I'll get you a ticket. That's the least and probably the most I can do.'

'Thank you, Captain Greenock.'

'Don't thank me. I think I may sleep easier when you and Pardoe are out of Washington. Come on. I'll show you to your office. And your colleague.'

'One last thing, Captain. A room in my hotel for this colleague of mine.'

Greenock sighed. 'You'll want to move into the White House next.' He led the way down into the depths of the Embassy.

It was indeed a small office. Lohmann had the instant impression it might have been a large cupboard. It was windowless but contained a desk, two chairs and an air conditioning unit high up on the wall. And Paul Reiner.

'Hello, chief,' Reiner said, smiling.

92

'I'll leave you,' Greenock said and did so, aware of the fact that there was barely room for two people in the office, far less three.

Left alone, the two men stared at each other for a moment. Then they embraced awkwardly, not something they had ever done before. But it had been five years since their last meeting. In a scruffy hotel in Paris. The embrace affirming their old friendship, they stepped back to survey each other.

Reiner was now in his late thirties, an inch shorter than Lohmann, dark hair now slightly greying at the temples. The boyish look Lohmann remembered from Berlin had gone. In those days, he had worn a flat cap from which his hair had untidily protruded. His clothes had always looked in dire need of a hot iron. Now, he was bareheaded, the hair cut neatly and shorter than it had been. He was dressed in a well cut grey serge suit, a white shirt and a rather garish tie. Over his arm was a heavy raglan coat. He looked like so many prosperous Americans Lohmann had seen in the streets. And this had been his untidy but efficient sergeant in Berlin five years before.

'Reiner,' Lohmann said awkwardly. *'Geht es Ihenen gut?'*

'Nun gut!' Reiner replied, equally awkward.

'Perhaps in English, I think,' Lohmann went on. 'We are in the British Embassy.'

'Of course. I am okay. Doing well. Chief security officer for a large company with ten department stores throughout the North-West.'

'Sounds prosperous.'

'It is, chief. Do you know, I have more people working under me than we had in the whole of Berlin Criminal Department in the old days.'

'Good. Very good. And your wife?'

'A typical American *Hausfrau*, these days. And I have two children now. Regular American boys. And you, sir?'

'As always. Now working for the British. Does that worry you, Reiner?'

Reiner shook his head. 'You're working against his lot. Hitler. That's enough.'

'I hoped you would say that.'

'So . . . what's the job we're on? I've taken three weeks holiday. I'm due it. I'm at your disposal.'

Lohmann squeezed himself behind the small desk and indicated Reiner take the other seat. 'But your family . . .?'

'Sir, if it hadn't been for you, we would still have been in Germany. I think we would have been in a *Konzentrationslager*. As it is I am now a Yank! And doing well at it. Helga also insisted I help you. If you wish it.'

'I do.'

'Then there is no discussion. I am yours for three weeks.'

Reiner grinned suddenly, and Lohmann saw the awkward young police officer he had brought in from the streets to the Criminal Department so many years before. Within a year that awkward young man had learned the game.

'Like the old days,' Reiner added. 'Of course I realise it won't be a murder hunt . . .'

'It *is* a murder hunt,' Lohmann said. And then proceeded to tell Reiner the whole story.

When he had finished, Reiner gave a low whistle. 'A serial killer! *Just* like the old days. Only we know the man. This Captain Pardoe. And the British picked him for a special mission. Very tricky.'

'If he is the killer,' Lohmann said.

'The coincidences pile up, chief.'

'I know. And, if he is the murderer, then I have to stop him. But most important of all, let him complete his mission.

'Which we know nothing about.'

'Not yet. Not until I meet Pardoe. And hopefully work myself into his confidence. Which is why I intend to leave for New Orleans tomorrow.'

'I come with you?'

'No. You stay in Washington. I want you to find out all you can about the two victims, Mary Lou Hancock and Julie

Neuberg. Any further links with Pardoe. Also James Henry Straight . . . the Third. Is he genuine? Anything about him of interest. But you must remember, you have no official standing.'

'Oh, but I have some official standing, chief.'

Lohmann looked puzzled.

Reiner grinned, produced a small leather folder, flipped it open to reveal a silver badge and an identification card.

'I told you I was head security officer for Solomon's department stores. As such I have aided the Cincinnati Police Department. And have been made an honorary captain. I know it has little standing in Cincinnati, still less here. But it looks impressive enough to be useful now and then.'

It was Lohmann's turn to smile. 'Use what you can. But you have nothing behind you. No department to call on. And something else. You may well have German agents watching your every move. Perhaps more than watching.'

Reiner was serious now. 'I will expect it.'

'That's the one area where Hoover and the FBI may help us. I gather they have made moves against German agents.'

'Wouldn't put too much trust in that, chief. He moved because he had to. But it is reckoned he's more interested in going after the communists than the fascists.'

Lohmann looked at Reiner curiously. 'How do you come to be so well informed?'

'I know the station officer of the FBI in Cincinnati. Friendly with the German-American Bund. Very active in Cincinnati, the Führer's friends are. Heard I was German, they invited me to join.'

'And you told them to go to hell!'

Reiner flushed. 'Not exactly. I remembered something you taught me years ago. Keep all options open. I hate the bastards but I got to thinking: mustn't turn them down flat. Never know when it might be useful to learn what they're up to.'

'Reiner, you would have been a senior inspector at least if

95

we'd stayed in Germany.'

'Oh, I know it,' said Reiner with a trace of his old impudence. 'Anyway, I didn't join but I didn't turn them down.'

'Good. Might be useful. Go on, tell me more.'

'The company I work for, Solomon's. Harry Solomon's Jewish. Obviously. Third generation American. The Bund, needless to say, don't like him. A few incidents. A few window smashings, graffiti, that kind of thing in some of our stores. We informed the FBI. They did bugger all. But they knew every left-winger in the building. Got a couple of card-carrying American communists sacked.'

'And what did Solomon say about this?'

'Not much. Very typical American, scared of the Reds. Bred into him.'

'And the Bund?'

'Doesn't fancy them either. But what can he do? I tighten up on security for him. Oh, it's not like Berlin in the old days. Not yet, thank God. One of the reasons I didn't turn the Bund down. Thought I might find out who was at it. Certainly Hoover's boys weren't very concerned.'

'Interesting,' said Lohmann. 'Useful to know. Anyway you know what I want from you?'

'The women, Hancock and Neuberg . . . all I can find out. And Mister Straight. Whoever he may be.'

'Fine.' Lohmann rose. 'There should be rooms for us at the Mayflower Hotel. We should go now . . .'

Lohmann drove the Cadillac. On the way. Reiner talked of his life in America, his job, his family, his enthusiasm for this new way of life.

'Of course, everything's not honey and roses. The poverty's as bad as Berlin in the old days. And, as I said, there's anti-Semitism and worse. The negroes have the worst of it.' Cleaning people, sweepers of the white man's debris, this they can be. But not much else. Of course old Solomon's a Republican . . . can't stand Roosevelt . . . times I think the

Yankee's not the brightest in the world.'

'And we Germans are?' Lohmann said sardonically. 'We allowed Hitler in. Allowed the worst pogroms for centuries. Can we criticise your Yankees?'

Reiner twisted awkwardly in the passenger seat. 'Okay, okay, I forget things. And one thing they're good at here . . .'

'What's that?'

'Crime is so beautifully organised. You can't help admiring it, chief. The Italians, the Mafia, they have it all their own way. They operate like big business, they own police, politicians, judges. If we were Criminal police here, what a time we'd have.'

'We may still have a time, Reiner.' Lohmann suddenly thought he should call his old assistant Paul now. There was no longer any rank between them. Paul Reiner was a good friend. Yet Lohmann couldn't get out of the old habit, calling him Reiner. Awkwardly, he voiced the thought.

Reiner grinned. 'Surprised you don't call me sergeant. Still, wouldn't feel the same if you call me anything but Reiner. Wouldn't feel right. It took you six months before you knew my first name was Paul.'

'Which reminds me, Reiner,' said Lohmann 'I am Lomond now. Lomond.'

'I'll remember.'

The reception area of the Mayflower had a rather dusty elegance. Brown panelling gave it the appearance of a private club. And, indeed, many of the regular patrons did nothing to disabuse the casual *habitué* of that fact. Among these regulars could be counted a number of senators, many members of the House of Representatives, and at least two Justices of the Supreme Court.

After they had registered, Reiner suggested they go into the bar while their luggage was taken up to their rooms. Lohmann was surprised. Reiner would occasionally take a drink but never with any great enthusiasm. Perhaps America had changed him. The bar was busy. Well-dressed grey

97

flannel escorting the latest Paris and New York fashions. The conversation was loud and uninhibited, much of it political. Reiner ordered a seltzer for himself and a lager for Lohmann and they withdrew into a corner of the room.

'You are desperate for *Mineralwasser*?' Lohmann asked.

'You're losing your touch, chief,' Reiner said quietly.

'Eh?'

'In the foyer. We were expected. A man in a blue suit hiding behind the *Washington Post*. Became very interested when he heard the name Lomond.'

'Is he in here?'

'Yes. Wandered in just behind us. He's at the far end of the bar. Behind the lady with the black dress and the large bosom.'

It seemed to Lohmann that most of the women had large bosoms but, after a moment he identified the black dress and, at the wearer's side, the man in the blue suit. The man was of medium height, body running to fat and face catching up fast. Black hair was thinning in front and a five o'clock shadow shrouded his face. For a brief second the man's eyes met Lohmann's and then swiftly turned away.

Reiner lifted his seltzer and took a sip. 'Not Department of Justice. A little too overweight for that. Hoover likes his agents slim and clean-cut. Like characters in the funny papers.'

The allusion was lost on Lohmann. No one at the FBI had seemed remotely funny to him.

'Another little job for you, Reiner. While I'm in New Orleans. See if you can find out who he is.'

Reiner nodded. 'Look at the hands.'

Again Lohmann studied the man, through the ebb and flow of the crowd across the room. After a moment he caught a glimpse of the man's hands. Fat fingers, like sausages, and each ringed with gold. Too many rings, too much gold.

'Cannot be sure,' Reiner said. 'Too many people in America with so little taste. But it is possible.'

98

'What is possible?' Lohmann felt testy. Reiner was enjoying his longer experience of America.

'He looks the type. The rings, the complexion. Italian-American. Mafiosi, maybe. Gangster.' A pause. 'Time we went to bed. I'll take your room, you take mine. We can eat in your room.'

Lohmann drained his glass, eyebrows raised at Reiner.

'A small precaution. I can stay alert all night. You have to get your sleep if you are flying to New Orleans. I'll see you at breakfast. Let you know if you would have been disturbed.'

They left the bar, moving past the be-ringed man in the blue suit who studiously ignored their passing. They were alone in the elevator. It was early for Washington, the night life of the city barely begun. The flow was from the rooms, not to them.

'Why,' asked Lohmann, 'should Mafia gangsters have any interest in our business?'

Reiner gave his habitual shrug. 'I don't know, Except one thing. They kill people. Not for political or ideological reasons. Just for money.'

Louisiana

NINE

He lay in the darkened room, staring at the ceiling, still trying to sleep. The daylight was beginning to filter through the shutters on the windows of the room, a feeble grey light becoming brighter as the sun rose. His body was damp with sweat, his eyes burning. Change of climate, he told himself, from Washington winter to the heat of the delta. Even in winter, this winter, it was still hot. And he'd spent a long day looking for a man who was no longer where he should have been. And there were other images to keep him from sleep. Visions at the edge of consciousness, pictures in his head, waking nightmares that came uncalled into his mind.

Somewhere in the distance, he heard the rattle of the St Charles streetcar starting off towards the Garden district.

Away from Singapore, he had believed he might get away from . . . from what? The nightmares? The picture of the girl in the crib, near Changi, broken body lying across what passed for a bed. The bright colour across the sheets. Scarlet under the throat; an extra mouth, ragged, contorted into a sickly grin. The eyes were turned back in the head, sightless yet seeming to stare at him.

Not . . . not to do with me . . . nothing to do with me . . . never seen her before . . . no, that wasn't true . . . the girl had been with them the night before . . . nothing to do with him . . . somebody else . . . her pimp . . . they say they all had knives . . . not to do with me . . . yet why was I there? Was I there? How else could one see so clearly the girl lying there . . . no, no, still not to do with him . . . someone else . . .

In London, it was better. He could forget the pictures at the edge of his mind. And now there was something worthwhile to do. The First Lord, sitting nursing his Havana cigar, explained something he didn't understand himself across a desk at the Admiralty.

'You appreciate the significance of all this, Captain Pardoe?'

'I do indeed, sir.'

'Only the Americans have the resources.'

'But will they understand? After all, they will almost certainly be neutral.'

'That is why you are being sent. I have been asked by the Prime Minister to look into this matter. You are one of the few naval officers who can understand what could happen. I'm told the possibilities are terrifying.'

'Indeed they would be, sir, if the thing is possible. But can I convince them?'

'Not them. One man. President Roosevelt. But you will not have to convince him alone. Your job will be to enable others to do so.'

'With respect, sir, why can you not convey this matter to the President yourself?'

The old man smiled. Sourly. 'A pertinent, impertinent question. It must not come from me. Otherwise this government could be accused by certain of the more isolationist politicians in America of trying to draw the Americans into the war. And it may be necessary that some of them know what is going on. Therefore this matter must come from knowledgeable people outside my own sphere. Which is why I can't send you alone and directly to the President. At least not as a serving naval officer. The others will have to do the convincing. And indeed it is from them our original information comes.'

'Yet the mission will be secret?'

'Top secret. It will only be official between us. These names . . .' A sheet of paper pushed across the desk; he'd heard of the names on it; three names . . . these are the people you will assist, when you make contact. Then the real job will be up to them.'

Baffling at first. Official but not officially so. In a neutral country. In Washington. On the spot. The old man at the Admiralty his only authorisation. Under direct orders from the new First Lord.

Yet still there had been one night in London.

That night. When Singapore had been forgotten. As if it had never happened. You could tell yourself it hadn't happened. A nightmare. But not me. Nothing to do with me.

Still the night in August had brought it all back. The images, the fear, the questions. Everything suddenly coming back. If he could only remember . . . not that he'd been drinking, not that much, he didn't think so. But it had all become vague. Starting in the Savoy Grill and then the bar. With friends. And then alone. Sometime finding himself in Shepherd Market. But nothing had happened, he told himself. He'd been there, and before that in Piccadilly and Half Moon Street and later in Park Lane.

There was only that uneasy feeling. He'd read about the girl the next morning. Nothing to do with him, he could tell himself that. Case dismissed, in his mind.

Yet, still, the uneasiness.

Like a forgotten nightmare. You knew you'd had the nightmare but you didn't remember what it was about. Not at all. Not even a detail.

To be forgotten. Linking something in Singapore with which you had a silent connection, with something in London with which you had no connection. All imagination. Had to be.

He went to America, the mission was everything . . . Until it happened again.

You're on your own that night. Drinking again. Too much. Okay, you're off duty. You're waiting. To go on with the mission. Nothing. Nothing to be done that night. So you have a drink too many. And wake up in your own bed. With blood on your sleeve. And the newspaper the next morning telling you a whore had died somewhere in the city. Can't have anything to do with you. No possible contact. That you could remember.

The telephone by the side of the bed rang.

Forget these insane ideas. Nothing to do with you. Only the mission is important. Answer the bloody phone.

He lifted the receiver.

'Mistah Pardoe!' The receptionist's voice with its deep southern accent. No Captain Pardoe on this trip. Mister had to be enough. 'A gen'leman to see you, sah. On his way up. Said not to be disturbin' you, but I thought it better to . . .'

'You were quite right. Thank you.'

He was up and on his feet now. Opening his suitcase. The revolver was there at the foot of the case. Loaded but with the safety catch on. He would be ready for the visitor. Whoever it might be. Only Greenock was supposed to know he was in New Orleans at the Fairmont.

He opened the shutters, letting sunlight flood into the room. He donned his dressing gown, still holding the service revolver.

Waiting.

The knock on the door came two minutes later. Pardoe slipped the revolver into the pocket of his dressing gown.

'Yes?'

'Captain Pardoe?'

'Who is that?'

'My name is Lomond.'

The man from London. The only person Greenock would have told.

He unlocked the bedroom door and opened it. The figure was in shadow.

'Good morning, Captain Pardoe.'

Stepping out of the shadow was a man of medium height, in an overcoat, soft hat in hand. With some trace of an accent Pardoe couldn't place.

'Come in,' Pardoe said. 'You didn't have to come to New

106

Orleans. I expect to be back in Washington in a day or so.'

'I was to join you as soon as possible. Orders.'

The two men faced each other. Appraising looks were exchanged. Pardoe thought, this is my bodyguard. Or is that the right word? Is he here to protect me, or to protect others from me?

'Yes, well, you've joined me. I suppose we'd better have breakfast. Or did you eat on the plane?'

'I would enjoy taking breakfast with you. Here?'

Pardoe shook his head. 'Downstairs. The breakfast room is quiet enough. And I have to go out shortly.'

'Good. I shall of course come with you.'

He's going to be everywhere with you now, this Lomond character. Have to accept it. The job is more important than any other considerations. It could be a good thing. The words of the old song, 'Someone to watch over me.' Like a child now. The man would even be there in your nightmares . . . if they recurred. Might even keep them at bay. For that, you should be grateful.

He dressed while Lomond sat at the window of the bedroom looking out onto University Place. A quiet man, for which Pardoe was grateful. But he had no doubt that in time the questions would come. He dressed for the climate and the trip he was to make. In slacks, open necked shirt and lightweight jacket.

It was nearly ten o'clock when they entered the restaurant. The large room was almost empty, for which Pardoe was grateful. At this time of the year the hotel was only half full, the residents being mostly business people and they would already be about their work. He ordered a full breakfast, English breakfast. Bacon and eggs, tea, toast. Like showing the flag. He had always believed, when abroad, forget the alien milieu; behave as you would at home.

He told Lomond, 'Going to be a long day. As well to have a good meal.'

Lomond shrugged. 'Just coffee and rolls for me, thank you.'

107

'Up to you. If everything goes well, we should fly back to Washington tomorrow. But I think you should book a room here tonight.'

'I will do so. As close to your room as possible, I think.'

'Is that so very necessary?'

'It would be best.'

Don't argue with him. Play it his way. He'll have his orders just as you have yours.

'Where do you go this morning?' the man asked, sipping his coffee.

'To find a man called Duplessis. Henri-Georges Duplessis.'

'This is the part of your . . . mission?'

'Yes.'

Lomond beckoned the waiter to refill his coffee cup. 'Am I allowed to ask who this Duplessis is?'

Now come the questions. You should tell the man everything and get it over. After all he is on the same side. But the orders were only to give information when necessary. Still, there were some things he could say.

'He was on the staff of the university here. I'd hoped to see him yesterday and fly back this morning. But I learned he is no longer a resident at the university. It seems he has retired and moved.'

'This Duplessis, he is French?'

'Creole. American citizen born in New Orleans of French origin.'

'Ah, yes. Creole. And you know to where he has moved?'

Such precise English! Wasn't his native language. But then when they notified you of Lomond's coming, something had been said about that. You wonder where they find such people. And whether or not you can trust them. Still, he'd been sent by Churchill. The old man must know what he was doing.

'I know where to find him. He has a small house on the bayou. So the university people informed me. On Bayou

108

LaFourche. With luck we should see him late this afternoon and be back this evening.'

'Very good.' Lomond drained his coffee cup and rose to his feet. 'Please, finish your breakfast. I will reserve a room for myself and make one telephone call. I have to confirm with Captain Greenock that I have made contact with you.'

He went out. Pardoe finished his breakfast and some minutes later found Lomond waiting for him beside the reception desk.

'They have given me a room. Would it inconvenience you if I took my case up and had a quick wash?'

'I have a cab ordered and a boat fixed up to take me into the bayou. Look, there's no real need for you to come. As I said, I should be back this evening.'

Lomond was insistent. 'My orders are to accompany you. I shall not be long.'

Pardoe waited. Impatiently.

Thinking. When he talked to Duplessis, would Lomond have to be present? If so, the aim of the mission might well become obvious. Which might be inadvisable. On the other hand, it might even help if Lomond knew . . .

Forty-five minutes later Lomond reappeared. He had divested himself of his coat and hat and was dressed in a smart grey flannel suit. And wearing light shoes. At least the shoes were more suited to the climate.

The cab drove south-west. It crossed an avenue called Humanity, which seemed to Pardoe a rather all-embracing name for an avenue. Behind them, lay the sprawling city of New Orleans, quaint, irregular and decadent.

They were driving now onto the delta of the great Mississippi river, a vast flat outcropping of land and water and marsh that protruded into the Gulf of Mexico. A flat terrain pockmarked and riddled with tributaries and lakes and reeds, flatland under the sky, as if designed by a map-maker gone mad. This was the home of the Cajun and the Acadian; French Canadian refugees despatched here in the

1750s because they were hostile to British rule.

For a time they drove along a great highway built by the late Governor Huey Long, the Louisiana Kingfisher, who managed to bring fascism to America in the guise of populism and was, mercifully perhaps, assassinated on the steps of the Governor's Mansion. Finally they turned off the highway, drove along a rutted track to a landing place on the water.

Here, they transferred to a flat-bottomed boat ordered by Pardoe. It was powered by an outboard engine and crewed by the imposing figure of a large Cajun, high-cheekboned, broad shouldered, morose and suspicious of manner. He informed them in a Cajun accent, a mixture of deep-south American and French intonation, that his name was Joe and he understood they wanted to visit *P'fesseur* Duplessis.

'He 'spectin' you?' Joe went on.

'I have to see him,' Pardoe replied. 'You know where he lives?'

'LaFourche way. House out on B'you. On his own. He on his own very much.'

'Then he may be glad of company,' the man called Lomond said.

The Cajun shrugged. Not his concern. He sat in the stern of the boat and steered it out into midstream, south-west on an infinity of sky and water and reeds and grasses and little else. The sky, blue when they had left New Orleans, was now a dull slate colour. Somewhere a solitary bird, species unknown, emitted a mournful cawing. Pardoe thought, with the landscape's bleakness, it might have been a pterodactyl. The water was a muddy brown colour, the mud a residue of half a continent swept towards the Gulf and, before reaching the sea, stranded among this maze of tributaries of the great river.

The boat moved on. Time passed. They had been on the water for nearly two hours. In almost total silence.

The landscape by the water was unchanging but for an occasional shack in the distance. Most of these were built on stilts above the water. Pardoe was reminded of the shacks on

110

the rivers around Singapore and the Malay Peninsula, except that there they were villages on the water, crowded together, busy. Here too he knew there were villages, even towns, on the bayou but they couldn't see any.

At last the boat swung towards the southern bank. From behind the reeds a battered wooden jetty came into view. Moored beside the jetty was a motor boat, a gleaming power craft, obviously new.

'Dat's the P'fesseur's boat,' the boatman said, easing his craft onto the other side of the jetty. Standing, the Cajun balanced himself on the bottom of the boat, moved to the bow and, lifting a rope, reached out for a wooden upright on the jetty, drew the boat in and with a quick flip of the wrist, twisted it around the upright.

'You go see him now. I wait.'

Pardoe jumped, with all the confidence of his naval background, onto the planks of the jetty to find them creak and almost give under his weight. Part of the edifice was obviously rotting. With greater care. Lomond climbed from the boat behind him. Pardoe looked around, a full 360 degree turn. He could see nothing but the river, the reeds and a flat horizon broken only by clumps of undergrowth. There was no sign of a human dwelling-place.

'Where . . . ?' he started to say but the boatman cut in on him.

'Jest follow the track. 'Bout half mile walk. Keep on the track. T'ings off track not always friendly. Snake, mebbe 'gator.' Said with a grin, as if he relished the thought. Which, Pardoe told himself, he obviously did.

Off the jetty was the track. A path worn through reed and marsh. Sometimes ahead, the marsh encroached on the path. In a moment the boat, the jetty and the river were out of sight. There was only the track and the undergrowth. And pools of water and patches of mud. The two men walked in single file. Only way to go.

'Your friend likes the wilderness, it seems,' said Lomond.

'He's hardly a friend. Met him once years ago when he was visiting Cambridge. He was being shown around the Cavendish by Rutherford.'

'The Cavendish?'

Lomond obviously had gaps in his education.

'Physics laboratory,' Pardoe replied. 'I was a student then.'

'Thought you were in the British Navy?'

The British Navy? He was right, Pardoe told himself. Lomond's origins were certainly not British. Had they been, the man would surely just have said the *Navy*.

'I also have a degree in physics. I suppose the Navy thought it might come in handy.' Which it had, now.

'This Duplessis, he is also connected with physics?'

Pardoe stepped carefully around a large patch of brown mud. 'He was professor of physics at New Orleans university. Until he decided to take an indefinite sabbatical. They told me that was only a few months ago.'

'An important post,' said Lomond ineptly skirting the mud patch and slithering on the edge, almost losing his balance. 'Why should he give it up?'

'A sabbatical, I said. Not necessarily for good. A lot of these old boys like to take time off. Be on their own. Gives them time to think. That's when theoretical physicists really do their work.'

They walked in silence for some minutes more. And then, as if it had risen unbidden from the bayou, ahead of them they saw the house. In fact it was more of a large clapboard shack, perched on the customary wooden piling to raise it above the dampness of the swamp. The shack was quite large, though all on one level. A wooden stairway led up to a porch, a balcony almost, which seemed to go all the way around the building. In the centre of this was an open wooden door and over the entrance was a second door, this one closed and made up of a lattice of wire netting.

Pardoe leading the way, they climbed the stairs to the porch. At the door, Pardoe called out.

'Professor Duplessis!'

The only reply was from a solitary bird, cawing as it winged its way high across the bayou.

'Professor! My name is Pardoe! I wrote to you.'

The lattice door creaked.

'Doesn't seem to be here,' said Lomond.

Pardoe took a tentative step towards the door, hesitated, and then pushing it open, went in.

It was a spacious room, and well furnished. Large bookcases covered two walls. On a third wall, above a wide fireplace, was a large stuffed fish of indeterminate species. At the side of the fireplace a bundle of fishing rods leant against the wall. A suite of battered leather furniture surrounded the fireplace, cracked and worn, stuffing protruding from the rear of the sofa.

On the armchair facing the door sat the figure of an elderly man. Dressed in a open necked shirt, once white, and a pair of denim slacks, he sat quite erect, eyes open, staring in front of him. He was quite dead.

His throat had been cut.

The top and front of the shirt were stained a dirty brown colour. Blood, many hours dried.

Pardoe bent over the body. 'It's Duplessis.'

'Dead for hours. Looks like since yesterday.'

Pardoe nodded. 'God! Poor old boy. Who the hell would . . .?'

'Don't you know?' said his companion coldly.

'How could I know this would happen? How the devil does the other side know?'

'Do they have to?' The cold voice went on. 'Or haven't you just turned your talents with a knife onto old men now, Pardoe?'

Pardoe straightened up and turned angrily. 'What the hell do you mean?'

Facing the man called Lomond. Facing the muzzle of a Mauser pistol. 'You . . . you think I did this?'

113

'Came out yesterday. Heard what you wanted from him. Or perhaps he wouldn't help you. So you made sure he wouldn't help anybody.'

'That's stupid. I needed him. I wanted him to come to Washington with me.'

'Ah, yes, your mission. You're an easy man to follow, Captain Pardoe. You leave a trail of dead women behind you. From Singapore to Washington. And now, this old man.'

Pardoe took a step forward.

'I wouldn't,' said Lomond. 'I'm good with pistols. Get you between the eyes with one shot. Regular male Annie Oakley, I am.'

The accent had gone, Pardoe suddenly thought. Almost mid-Western.

'I didn't do this.' Pardoe said.

'And the others?'

'I know nothing about the others.'

'But you know there were others. Women. I find that interesting. How would you know?'

'Look,' Pardoe insisted, 'I have a job to do. And your job is to help me carry it out.'

'Can you still do that without Duplessis?'

'Yes, I can. He would have helped but there is another way. After the job is over, we can turn to the problem of these murdered women.'

'So easy, Captain Pardoe. So easy. But just maybe I can carry out your job without you.'

That wasn't the plan. Wasn't the way it was supposed to be. Unless those in London had changed their minds, had another operation in mind. Or knew something else. About the dead women. About Changi . . .

'So what do you propose to do now, Lomond?'

'I think, make an end to it. Judicial execution. Nobody'll blame me. You could count yourself lucky, Pardoe. I'm going to shoot you. It'll be very quick.'

TEN

He had the feeling he was being followed. He'd had the feeling since he came into the country. He'd had it before in London and in Washington; and he'd been right in Washington. But now he began to wonder whether a kind of paranoia was setting in, as if everyone in the street was a potential enemy. The sidelong look from the stranger with whom he brushed shoulders assumed some sinister significance. The passer-by seemed to be staring at him with a penetrating look. No, it was too much. A nervous reaction. Or he'd been out of the game for too long. Perhaps should never have come back in.

He was waiting now, merely passing time. He'd wandered into the French Quarter, feeling more at home there than he had since he'd arrived in America. Paris again, but not quite Paris. Tropical but not quite tropical. At least some of the faces were friendly. The black ones. He could feel more at home with black faces, some smiling, others gently curious, than with the white faces coldly ignoring him as they moved by.

He finally went back to the hotel. And waited.

It was nearly seven o'clock in the evening when the face he had been waiting for came in. It was recognisable at once from the photograph. He rose from the corner of the foyer and went over at once.

'Captain Pardoe?'

The man swung around, a jerking nervous reaction. His

hair was awry, his face flushed.

'What do you want?'

'I'm Lomond. I've just arrived from Washington.'

Pardoe recoiled two steps backwards as if an electric shock had gone through him. His hands, shivering, clenched. His face paled, blood draining from it. He said nothing for a moment as if it was some considerable effort for him to speak. Lomond thought, he's ill, he has to be. Some kind of fever. Malaria perhaps, he'd known a few navy men who had recurrent bouts of that.

Then Pardoe managed to speak. 'You . . . you have identification?'

Lohmann produced his new British passport and his document of accreditation to His Britannic Majesty's Embassy in Washington.

Pardoe scanned them carefully, hands still trembling.

'Yes, yes, I see,' he said, almost gasping for breath. 'I should have known. I should have . . .' He thrust the documents back into Lohmann's hands. 'We have to talk. Come up to my room.'

'Something's happened, Captain?' Lohmann asked quietly.

He nodded. 'Come on.'

By the time they reached Pardoe's room, he had become calmer. 'Sit down, Lomond. Would you like a drink? I need one.'

Lohmann accepted a Scotch and Pardoe poured two large measures. Lohmann took his with water, Pardoe gulped his neat.

'Medicinal,' he explained. 'Or Dutch courage or something.'

'You will tell me what has happened?'

'Yes. You . . . you tried to kill me.'

'Please?' Lohmann looking utterly baffled.

'This morning. You turned up. Or rather this character came here. Introduced himself as Lomond from London. I

116

was expecting you. I . . . I accepted the man. Completely. Didn't even ask for identification. Bloody stupid of me.'

Lohmann was beginning to understand. 'No, not stupid. He would have had something to identify himself.' They were certainly quick off the mark, he thought. One step ahead. Efficient. Whoever they were. 'Please tell me what happened.'

Pardoe told him of the journey into the bayou, the discovery of Duplessis' body and finding himself facing the pistol.

At this point, Lohmann interrupted him. 'You wouldn't happen to know the type of weapon?'

'A Mauser. Is that important?'

'No. But it is accurate. I too use a Mauser. They are doing their homework rather well. Please, you were facing the Mauser and the man announced he was going to kill you. A disturbing experience, but you are here now. He decided not to kill you?'

'I decided he wasn't going to kill me, Mister Lomond. There were fishing rods and tackle leaning against the fireplace at my side. Large hooks for deep-sea fishing. While this character seemed to be enjoying his moment, I reached out and grabbing the tackle, threw it at him.'

The whisky and his story were having a soothing effect on Pardoe. He seemed more relaxed now, a man to whom confidence was returning. Lohmann had time to study him. Tanned face running to fat. Clear blue eyes, sandy coloured hair. In his forties, looking slightly older, the result of tropical weather and a shade too many pink gins in too many wardrooms. An earnest man, capable in his own field. But now out of his depth. Also a man suspected of the perverse murders of at least three young women. But Lohmann knew, to look for any sign of such perversion was futile. The psychopath would never reveal any outward signs of his proclivities. In a normal context, they appeared completely normal. He could remember Kürten, the Dusseldorf murderer, a seemingly quiet man, intelligent, attractive to

117

women, looking like a well dressed bank clerk. A mass murderer described at his trial as being 'the king of sexual perverts'. You could never tell.

'The tackle struck him in the face,' Pardoe went on. 'And one of the large hooks caught him around the eyes. He screamed and fired wildly. I grabbed his gun hand and took the Mauser from him. That part was easy, he was clawing at his face trying to get the hook out.'

'You were fortunate, Pardoe,' Lohmann said. 'Or the man was over confident and foolish. Challenging people who present a loaded weapon at you is usually extremely foolish and generally unsuccessful – despite the imaginings of popular novelists. I know. I have had some experience. So, next?'

'I left him there. I think the hook was in his eye. He was screaming.' This was said with little emotion. But certainly without relish. 'I knew the old man, Professor Duplessis, was dead so I ran back to the boat and told the boatman to bring me back here.'

'Of course,' Lohmann took a sip of whisky. 'And you had never been out at the Professor's house until today?'

'Look, I knew of his reputation as a physicist but I'd only met him once, years ago. I thought he was still at the University here. They told me he'd taken a sabbatical, gave me the address of his house on the bayou.' Pardoe hesitated and then at once his face flushed. 'Good God, you're not thinking like that bastard . . . that I actually killed him?'

'I simply wondered if this *doppelganger* of mine had any assistance in the vicinity.'

Pardoe looked puzzled. 'How could he? He didn't know where we were going.'

'He or someone else had to know you were coming to New Orleans to see this Professor Duplessis. They could have followed the same course as you. Enquired at the university and obtained his address. They would then be able to get out there last night and kill Duplessis.'

A silence. The sound came to them of the St Charles streetcar, followed by a foghorn sounding from the river.

'I hadn't thought of that.' Pardoe broke the silence. Looking genuinely distressed.

'Who knew you were coming to New Orleans to see the Professor?' Lohmann asked.

'Well . . . Churchill. And . . . and Captain Greenock. Not that Greenock knew why.'

'None of us do, as yet,' Lohmann observed with mock regret. 'No one else?'

'No one.'

'What about your friend, James Henry Straight? The Third.'

The haggard, drawn look returned to Pardoe's face. 'He . . . he's a friend. I may have said something to him. But he wouldn't know why I was going to see Duplessis.'

'But he still knew where you were going, who you were going to see. Straight works for the FBI. And therefore the FBI knew.'

'I suppose that's so. But the FBI . . . they're not the enemy.'

Lohmann finished his whisky. 'Captain Pardoe, the more I learn about the world today, the more I realise that one never knows who is on one side and who is on the other. The National Socialists make a point of infiltrating the most innocent-seeming of organisations. And, indeed into the minds of people one would never suspect. This Professor Duplessis, he was essential to your . . . project?'

'He was a friend of Roosevelt's. He would have been of great help. But he was not the only one. There are others.'

'Good! In New Orleans?'

'No, I'm finished here. I must get back to Washington.'

'Then pack. You were planning to fly back?'

Pardoe produced a small case from the wardrobe and laid it on the bed.

'Are you coming with me? I won't be long. Just washing kit, a suit and some extras. We can get a taxi to the airport.'

'Oh, yes, I'm coming with you. But I doubt if we'll be flying back.'

Pardoe's head jerked up. 'Why not? It's the quickest way.'

'And the most obvious. You didn't by any chance kill my *doppelganger* out at the Duplessis house?'

'I told you. I certainly injured him . . .'

Lohmann nodded. 'It's a pity you didn't kill him.'

Pardoe gave Lohmann a peculiar, strained look. 'I'm not a killer, Lomond!' he said quietly.

'That is something we will have to consider at another time.' Lohmann avoided Pardoe's instantly altered look, indignation mixed with fear. 'Since you incapacitated him, but not too severely, he will have had time to be in touch with his associates. I'm sure he will have associates. To go to New Orleans airport is to ask for trouble. They will be there. Waiting for us.'

'You can't be sure of that!'

'Also they will almost certainly be in this hotel, watching you. If they see you leave, I think the possibility of you meeting with a fatal accident is rather high.'

Pardoe finished his packing. He shut and locked his case. 'If they'd wanted to kill me, they'd have had the opportunity in Washington.'

Lohmann rose wearily. 'I think, in Washington they would have been content to . . . to discredit you. Or let you discredit yourself.'

'What the hell does that mean?'

'I think you know. Also, killing you in Washington could precipitate a serious diplomatic incident. But killing you here could be attributed to local criminals. Yes, they are now prepared to kill you. The incident on the bayou proves that. I am not prepared to have you killed, Captain. I therefore suggest we make our way out of New Orleans by another route and catch a plane elsewhere. Of course they may expect us to do that. So we shall have to move quickly.'

120

Pardoe took his case in his hand. 'I'll just go down and settle my bill.'

'I think you can forget that. We go out a back door without announcing it to the world. If you're worried about the hotel, send them a cheque from Washington. If we get back there.'

'You . . . you're serious. You really think we are in danger?'

'Everyone's in danger in this world today. With us it is slight more excessive. Let's go.'

They made their way along the corridor, ignored the elevator to the main foyer, found a stairway, and walked down. Pardoe seemed to accept that Lohmann was in charge now. Lohmann gave silent thanks to the naval officer's training: always obey a superior order. In this case he had acceded to obvious authority and experience.

'You've done this before, Lomond,' he said as they moved down the stairway.

Lohmann gave a small smile. 'Usually I have been the one being evaded.'

They reached the ground floor. To their right the corridor led to the main reception area, a sign indicated that to their left there was an emergency exit. They followed it. The corridor twisted and turned before they finally arrived at the rear entance to the hotel. There was no one in sight. Lohmann led the way through the door. They found themselves in a narrow alley between the hotel and the adjacent building. It was starting to rain and the street lights to their right at the end of the alley were reflected on damp cobbles. To their left, the alley ended in a high brick wall.

Lohmann scowled. 'Takes us to the front of the hotel. Pity. We'll have to move quickly.'

They came out onto University Place. Early evening traffic surged along the street, a moving carousel of light and sound.

'Where to now?' Pardoe asked.

'We hire a car.'

They crossed the road, Pardoe looking nervously behind him.

Lohmann said. 'Don't look behind, please. If someone is looking out for us, it is a giveaway. If they are following us, we will soon know. Look for a car hire firm. Or a garage.'

'How the devil do we know we're going in the right direction?'

'We don't. We just put distance between us and the hotel.'

Two blocks on, they turned up another street, moving north. They were now on Basin Street.

'Why this way?' Pardoe asked.

'Because if the man I think may be following us, is really doing so, he will come after us.'

'We're being followed?' Pardoe couldn't resist looking over his shoulder.

'It is possible. He was outside the hotel. A smallish man with a large wide-brimmed hat.'

'I didn't see anybody.'

'You were not meant to.' Lohmann thought of Reiner in Washington accusing him of being out of training. At least now he was getting back to form. 'It is a matter of knowing where to look and what to look for. We will get rid of him; one way or another.'

'How do we do that?'

'Move faster than him. Or face him and frighten him away. Might be interesting to face him and find out who sent him.'

In front of them, on their right, the buildings ended. A large gate loomed out of the darkness; beyond it, an even deeper darkness.

'Through the gate,' ordered Lohmann, moving faster.

Through the gate, they ran into the darkness. They followed a pebbled path, grass on either side, and beyond the grass were shapes rising six, seven feet in height. As if there was an uneven wall lining the path.

'Where are we?' Pardoe asked.

'I think we are in a cemetery.'

He'd heard about these cemeteries called cities of the dead. All of the tombs were above ground, because the city was built on marshland. Out of respect for their dead, the citizens of New Orleans had created impressive above-ground tombs which dwarfed the two running men. As their eyes became more accustomed to the darkness they could make out the ornate shapes of the tombs. The form of a winged angel arose on one side of them. Further on they came face to face with the door of a small pseudo-Greek mausoleum. And even further into the cemetery there was a large, impressive tomb with strange crosses marked on it and above the crosses the name, 'Marie Laveau'.

'We stop here and wait,' Lohmann said in a whisper, looking around.

There was no sign of Pardoe.

Lohmann swore under his breath. In the blackness Pardoe must have lost sight of him and veered off into the maze-like avenues of tombs and statues which surrounded him on all sides.

All right, the detective thought, I stand here and let the man who was tailing us, find me. Doesn't matter if I make a noise, all the better for him to find me.

He called out quite loudly, 'Pardoe! Where the hell are you?'

Nothing. That is, nothing but a sound like an owl hooting nearby. And feet on the gravel, just audible, treading slowly and carefully. Lohmann flattened himself against the tomb of Marie Laveau, and waited. The thought came to him; what the hell am I doing here, standing in a cemetery in the city of New Orleans in damp darkness? In some ways like the old days in Berlin. But then the terrain would be familiar to him. And he would have all the authority of a metropolitan police force behind him. Here, he had virtually no authority, no idea of what he was doing. Except that he was protecting a man who might well be a multiple murderer. He wasn't even sure why he was protecting the man; and from whom he was protecting Pardoe.

The owl hooted again. And the feet came off the gravel,

swishing through long grass nearby.

The street lights, quite distant now, still gave some illumination to the shadowy outline he could just discern coming closer. The shape of a wide hat on the head of a small figure with wide shoulders, moving nervously towards him. Lohmann felt in his pocket and produced the Mauser. The Mauser ready in his hand, he was sweating. Sweating in the thin rain that was falling on the tombs all around him. The man was close now, and breathing heavily. Lohmann could reach out and touch him.

He did so. Leaning forward, he threw his right arm around the man's neck, left hand pressing the pistol into his back. The wide-brimmed hat fell into the darkness. The man was a small, square shape in the darkness.

He screamed, a high pitched, keening sound.

'Be quiet!' Lohmann hissed in his ear. 'Or I'll shoot you. The revolver is pressed against your spine. I press the trigger and, if you live, you'll never walk again.'

'*Grâce a Dieu!*' the man said. 'I thought it might be her.'

The accent was French, or rather French-Creole. A thick accent.

'Might be who?' Lohmann demanded.

'Her! Behind you. *La Reine!*'

'*Quelle Reine?*'

'You know whose tomb you stand against, monsieur?'

'Tell me!'

'The queen. Marie Laveau. Her tomb. If she is still in it. If she is still dead. Which they say she isn't. You can just see the crosses on the stone. *Gris-gris.* Voodoo. The great Voodoo Queen of New Orleans. I thought she had come alive.'

Keeping the revolver pointed at the man, Lohmann released him from the neckhold and swivelled him around until they were facing each other.

'You have a cigarette?'

'*Oui.*'

'And a lighter?'

'*Oui.*'

'Light two cigarettes. One for each of us. And let me see what you look like.'

As the lighter flared, Lohmann found himself staring into large eyes, the whites like small saucers, gazing up at him from a dark-brown face. A negro, smallish in stature and far from impressive with slick black hair. The man wore a jacket widely padded at the shoulders and tapering down to just above his knees. A zoot suit, that was what they called it.

'Why are you following us?' Lohmann said.

'I am not following you. I am following the other man.'

'Why?'

'Because I have been paid to do so.'

'There must be a reason.'

'I do not know the reason.'

Lohmann took a deep breath. Exasperated. Either the man was very clever or very stupid.

'Let's start at the beginning,' he said.

'The lighter. It burns my fingers.'

'Then put it out. But if you move I'll shoot you.'

The flame went out.

'Your name?' Lohmann asked.

'Call me Billy Bones. That's what they call me. 'Cause I'm good with the bones – the dice. I can throw a seven whenever I want to.'

'Your real name?'

'Amboise. William Amboise. Got nothing to do with anything.'

'You were told to follow us. Who told you?'

'Man I know. Look, could we move away. That tomb . . . *c'est mauvais!*'

'We stay until you talk. Who told you to follow my friend?'

'Big man around here. Tell me, "Boy, you follow that Englishman if he come out of the hotel." I don't do it, they . . . they take me . . . maybe string me up.'

'Who's the man?'

125

'Call him Colescott. He a Yankee. Came down from Indiana. He a big man . . .' Billy Bones' voice trailed off nervously.

'A big man in what?'

'Them that wants you followed. You gotta know.'

'You tell me.'

'The Klan, mister. KKK.'

Lohmann knew. He'd read of the Klan.

'But you . . . you are a black man?'

'Sure I am. But if I don't do what they tell me. I'm a whupped black man. Maybe a hanged one.'

'This Colescott, you say he's from the North?'

'Came down special. Two, t'ree days ago. 'Bout you friend.'

They were interrupted. A strained voice from the darkness to Lohmann's left. 'That you, Lomond? I lost you . . .'

'So you have found me now. Stay near me. I have found our follower.'

Pardoe, breathing heavily, came up beside Lohmann. 'Thank God I found you. This is the man?'

'He tells me we have the Ku Klux Klan following us now.'

'But this fellow's a negro . . .'

'He's only doing what he's told. So he tells me.'

'*Cest vrai!*' said Billy Bones. 'I only follow because they make me . . .'

'And pay you?'

'*Peut-être.*'

The splinter of stone hit Lohmann on the cheek. And then the sound of the shot, muffled by a silencer but instantly recognisable to Lohmann.

'Down!' said Lonmann. He and Pardoe dropped quickly onto the damp grass. But Billy Bones seemed slower. He went down as if he was trying to stay on his feet but was being impelled slowly to the ground. Lohmann pulled him down by the legs.

'We're being shot at!' Pardoe said, enunciating the obvious

126

in a hoarse whisper! 'Thank God, they can't see us.'

'They were close enough. See if we can get behind the tombs.'

Pardoe lead the way, wriggling across the grass around the monument to the Voodoo Queen.

'Move,' Lohmann whispered to Billy Bones, hands still on the small man's folding legs. But then he realised the legs felt rubbery, lacking strength. The man collapsed on top of him.

Another sound, another shot, the dull *plop* of the silencer in the distance. Thank God, in the distance. Whoever was firing was far enough away. Had probably focused on the cigarette lighter before Bones had extinguished it. No splinters from the shot this time. The bullet had winged its way into the blackness.

Pulling the black man's legs behind him Lohmann crawled behind the sheltering facade of the tomb and found himself huddled beside Pardoe.

'You all right?' gasped the naval officer.

'I'm all right,' Lohmann replied. 'But our friend seems to have fainted.' He felt the little man, hands searching for the pockets of the zoot suit. And found the lighter.

'Keep your head down,' he whispered to Pardoe. 'I'm going to light this cigarette lighter. I want to see if he's all right.'

It burnt for two seconds before Lohmann switched it off. In the two seconds he saw all he needed to see.

Billy Bones was lying on his side. There was a small damp red patch on the back of his head. At the front, his forehead had turned into a large bloody hole. Billy Bones would no longer have to worry about being whupped or strung up by the Klan. The bullet had killed him instantly.

ELEVEN

Pardoe said, 'The police! We have to go to the police.'

'We have to get out of this cemetery alive,' Lohmann replied in a hoarse whisper.

'What about him?' In the darkness Pardoe raised a damp hand, barely perceptible to Lohmann, and indicated the body of Billy Bones.

'There is nothing we can do for him.'

A pause. From the tone of Pardoe's voice, Lohmann judged him genuinely shaken by the black man's death. Not that he could be blamed for that. For all his experience with sudden death on the pavements of Berlin in the old days, Lohmann could still feel nauseous at the sight of violent death, phlegm rising at the back of his throat. And pity, for the waste and futility of it, no matter to whom it came. He reached out and grasped the naval officer's shoulder.

'Come!'

They crawled away from the tomb of Marie Laveau and the body of Billy Bones who had feared it; at the end, with cause. They crawled around the tombs, pressed close to wet grass, under the stone-bound bodies of the New Orleans dead. They headed towards some distant street lights. Any moment Lohmann expected to hear another sound, another muffled shot. The assassins, whoever they were, had lost sight of their quarry.

Finally they reached a small doorway that led into Basin Street. The street seemed busier now, cars and taxis

128

beginning to pile up in a minor traffic jam. It was after eight o'clock and New Orleans had come alive with the evening crowd. From an open window, a radio blared the Jack Benny show. Further along the street, from a basement doorway, came the muted sound of a jazz trumpeter beginning to warm up.

'We should go to the police now,' said Pardoe.

'Although it goes against all my training,' said Lohmann, aware that he must sound rather pompous, 'I think we should avoid the police. We're in a strange city a long way from Washington and, while our Embassy credentials might help in the long run, I think we might be held up here for some days. Could you afford the time?'

'They wouldn't do that, surely?'

'If I was the investigating officer, I wouldn't let us out of the city. And, as long as we are here, we are targets for the people who shot your Professor Duplessis and that little man in the park.'

'But can we just go back to Washington . . .?'

'Would you be prepared to inform the New Orleans police of the details of your mission? They would want to know everything.'

'You've convinced me,' Pardoe said, running the back of his hand across his forehead. He looked down at his clothes. He was damp and mudstained, As was Lohmann. But Pardoe still clutched his suitcase. Lohmann had nothing.

'You've no luggage,' Pardoe said, a belated discovery.

'Left my case with the hotel reception. No loss. One pair of pyjamas and a toothbrush.'

He flagged down a garish yellow vehicle with long fins at the rear. They climbed in. 'We want to hire a car. You can take us to a hire company?'

An hour later they were driving north out of New Orleans, in a rented 1938 Chevrolet. Hired to one Bruno Muller; Lohmann had used the other passport. Might just confuse

129

someone looking for Lomond.

'Once we're well clear of the city, we'll find a hotel in some small town,' Lohmann said.

'I don't mind if we drive through the night,' Pardoe replied. 'The sooner we get somewhere we can catch a plane to Washington, the better.'

Lohmann pursed his lips. The man wasn't used to this kind of pursuit. He had no doubt they were being searched for, and might well be pursued. If they had to deal with that, they had to be alert and wide awake.

'We should get some sleep. We can cope with tomorrow so much better.'

'If you think so. But I have to get to Washington as quickly as possible. I may even have to go on to New York.'

'In the event, we must both go to New York. My orders are to stay with you.'

Pardoe shrugged and settled back in the passenger seat of the Chevrolet. He appeared to accept the situation. He stared at the darkness ahead and the strip of Huey Long's State Highway 10, illuminated by the twin headlights of the Chevrolet. After a ten-minute silence, he spoke again.

'You're not just a bodyguard, are you Lohmann?'

'Not just a bodyguard, Captain Pardoe.'

Another silence. Broken this time by Lohmann. 'Did you kill those women?'

The naval officer shifted uneasily in his seat. 'Women? What women?'

'In London, a prostitute called Antoinette Valois.'

'I know nothing about that.'

'She was found a day or so before you left for America.'

'No one ever contacted me.'

'Because your name was not found in her diary until two weeks after you'd left. It was considered unwise to disturb your mission. Her body was found in Shepherd Market; throat cut and eviscerated.'

'Christ!'

'You didn't know her?'

Pardoe took a moment to reply. 'I knew a girl who had an apartment near Shepherd Market. But I only knew her as Toni. I met her at the bar in Claridges. I suppose we . . . we picked each other up.'

'Toni. Antoinette. The same girl?'

'I don't know. Oh, for Christ's sake, it was only one night. I went back to her apartment for an hour or so. I never . . . harmed her . . . I never saw her again. And that was a good two months before I left for Washington.'

'And Mary Lou Hancock?'

'I *never* knew her. The police said my name was in her diary. And she used to hang around the bar of the Mayflower Hotel. So they told me. But I never knew her.'

'Yet in London, you picked up this Toni who may have been Antoinette Valois in a hotel bar. You could make a habit of picking up women in hotel bars.' Lohmann rubbed his eyes. He felt suddenly weary, especially of this interrogation. Like the old days in Berlin. But without authority. Without having examined the evidence himself, without having seen the bodies. Except for Julie Neuberg's.

'Not especially,' Pardoe replied nervously. 'Look, I'm a single man. I've never married. But I'm not homosexual. I like women. I never married because . . . because I never seemed to be in one place for very long. I was engaged for a short time when I was seconded by the Navy to Cambridge . . . But it didn't work out.'

'Why did it not work out?'

'It just didn't. She wanted me to give up the Navy, get a job as a civilian physicist. I didn't want to. She didn't want to become a navy wife, simple as that.'

'And Julie Neuberg?'

'What about Julie Neuberg?'

If he was innocent, he wouldn't know about her death, Lohmann told himself. He'd left Washington the morning her body had been discovered. Of course, if he was guilty he

131

would claim he knew nothing about it.

'You knew her?' he pressed on.

'Yes, I know her. Why . . . why the past tense? She isn't . . . ?'

'The same as the others. She was found the morning you left for New Orleans.'

'God!' A hiss of breath.

'Where did you meet her?'

'A reception. At the French Embassy. She was with her uncle, Senator Neuberg. And bored stiff. I danced with her. She seemed to find me amusing . . .'

'You saw her again?'

'Twice. Took her to the theatre. And another time to dinner.'

'Were you ever in her apartment in Georgetown?'

'Once. After the dinner date. She asked me up for a drink. I had a drink and left. That was all.'

'When was this?'

'About three weeks ago. I asked her out again, phoned her up but she made excuses. I got the impression she was seeing somebody else.'

Lohmann suddenly wished he could see Pardoe's face. He used to pride himself on being able to tell whether or not someone was lying. But now, in the darkness, he couldn't be sure. Except for one thing. Beside him, Pardoe was trembling. The shock of hearing about Julie Neuberg's death? Or something else? Fear, of what he had done?

Lohmann took a deep breath. 'So you didn't kill these women?'

He waited for the instant denial. It didn't come.

'I don't know,' Pardoe said.

The reply surprised Lohmann. He was expecting denial. Instead he got uncertainty. Frightened, nervous uncertainty.

'Tell me about it.' he said.

Pardoe now sat very still. They were passing through Baton Rouge. Not that they could see much of the town. Street lamps, illuminated signs, misted by the rain on the car window.

'You're some kind of policeman?' Pardoe said.

'I was.'

'But you're not British.'

'I have a British passport now,' Lohmann replied. And decided to tell Pardoe of his origins. Trust, he'd found, was infectious. Talk about yourself, you encourage the other to talk about himself. It often worked.

'I was a policeman in Berlin.'

'German!'

'But not a National Socialist. In 1934, I fell into disfavour, shall we say, with some powerful people. Hitler for one. Rheinhardt Heydrich for another. I got my daughter out – my wife is dead – and I left Germany in a hurry. Ended up in London. A very early refugee. Two years later I was involved in a matter involving the government. At that time, I met Winston Churchill. He brought me into this affair.'

'Why you?'

'I had police experience of serial murder. That is what we call this, serial murder. Also being a German, it was thought I might be more useful if my former countrymen tried to . . . to abort your mission. Which they are obviously trying to do.'

'Yes. Yes, they are, aren't they?'

Yet another silence as they drove out of Baton Rouge, catching a glimpse of the Mississippi, dark water reflecting the lights of the town. 'You said you didn't know whether or not you had killed these women,' Lohmann said. 'Tell me about that.'

'Is it possible, Lomond? To kill without knowing?'

The man was moving in the passenger seat now; restless, disturbed, perhaps again frightened.

'It is possible. A fugue. That is what it might be called. A period when you have no memory of what has happened. Perhaps the fugue is induced *because* of what has happened.'

'You mean, because the . . . the man has killed?'

133

Lohmann nodded. 'The guilt is too strong. The memory has to be driven away. But then I am not a psychologist.'

Pardoe suddenly seemed to change tack. 'There was another woman. The first, I suppose. If it was me.'

He reached in his pocket and produced a battered packet of Lucky Strike cigarettes. He proffered one to Lohmann who refused it. He lit his own with a brass lighter, hands shaking. In the flame Lohmann could see his face. Shining with sweat.

'It was in Singapore. Just before I came to London. A Chinese girl. I suppose she was a prostitute. Anyway I was lonely in Singapore. Fed up with the usual navy and government crowd. And I had memories of the girl at Cambridge. Anyway I . . . I took up with the Chinese girl. I'm not ashamed of that. Why should I be? She was very attractive. And caring, in her own way. Then, not long before I was posted back to London, she was found dead. Oh, I wasn't involved. I wasn't around. At least I don't think so. Anyway, nobody knew about us. I read about it in the newspapers. Dead. Murdered. Mutilated.'

He took a deep breath. In the glow from the dashboard he looked ill.

'That . . . beautiful body. Cut wide open. I had nightmares about that for a long time. As if I had been there. As if I'd seen it. Blood all over the room . . . everything . . .'

Lohmann kept his eyes firmly on the road.

'Can you be sure you weren't?' he said quietly.

'That's just it,' Pardoe said in a hoarse, rasping tone. 'Can I be sure? Can I? I don't know.'

He was trembling again. Lohmann could feel the seat shaking.

'What were you doing the night she was killed?' Lohmann asked, still calm and quiet. Let him talk, that was the old method, don't make demands; simply steer the conversation in the direction you wanted it to go.

'I'm not sure. I was drinking in the earlier part of the evening. With a friend, and American. Jimmy Straight . . .'

'He was in Singapore?' Lohmann trying to keep the surprise from his voice.

'I met him in Singapore. We got very drunk. Loaded. That's what he called it, loaded. I liked him. He was a change from the stuffed shirts. I think he's homosexual but he never showed that side of himself to me. And God knows, that night he had a chance. I was so drunk he put me to bed. I do remember that. Then I passed out. So you see, I couldn't have killed her, could I?' He stubbed out his cigarette viciously in the ashtray on the dashboard. 'I couldn't have killed Sue Linn. I couldn't. I wasn't in love with her but . . . but I was fond of her. And she would have done anything for me. There was no reason to kill her.'

'People don't always need reasons.'

'Then, if I did kill her . . . without reason . . . I'd be insane. I don't think I'm insane, Lomond. Do you think I am?'

Lohmann took a moment to reply. What was insanity? The old joke about the people who think they're Napoleon? The bewildered old man who doesn't know who he is? The fantasist who can't tell the real world from the world that exists only in his mind? The psychotic who seems as normal as the next man, but slaughters children every time there is a full moon?

In life it was not easy to differentiate.

'I've no reason to think so,' Lohmann finally replied. The lie came easily – it was a half truth, he had no reason to think Pardoe was sane, either.

'Tell me, have you any idea what time the girl in Singapore was killed?' he went on.

'The papers said, sometime in the early morning. Four, five o'clock, I think.'

'And what time did Straight put you to bed? Can you remember?'

'How could I remember that? Probably around midnight.'

'So it is possible you could have gone out later and killed the girl?'

'I told you, I was drunk. And . . . and surely I would have known . . .' Pardoe's voice tailed off. He was arguing the unarguable. There was no certainty as to what he could or could not have done.

There were lights ahead. A small town. The first sight that came into the beam of the headlights was a filling station, Shell Oil covering the world. A hamlet north of Baton Rouge, on the banks of the Mississippi. A battered wooden sign said, 'Welcome to —ville. Pop. 1054. Elevation 10 feet.' The name of the place seemed to have peeled away.

The lights on Main Street, —ville were minimal. Sagging street lamps barely illuminated one- and two-storey clapboard houses, white paint peeling from the wood. A drugstore, the only shop open, presented a grubby window on the world. A crumpled Confederate flag decorated a corner of the window. The place was lit up and, faintly, as they passed, they caught the sound of a popular standard. Glenn Miller. 'Little Brown Jug.' A block further on was an inn, also lit up, but dimly. A crooked sign said simply, 'Tavern'. Soundless. They were silent drinkers in —ville.

Lohmann was driving slowly, window down, looking for some kind of hotel or boarding house.

He found it a moment later. Hardly the Waldorf Astoria; it was clapboard, two storeys of it with a raised patio, and a blatant, yet modest sign, 'Commercial Hotel.' Lohmann pulled the Chevrolet into the kerb beside yet another small sign, 'Hotel parking only'. He turned to Pardoe who had been silent, staring ahead into the darkness, still back in Singapore searching his mind for a memory that was not there.

'We need sleep. Tomorrow we'll head for the nearest airport.'

Pardoe was beyond arguing. He nodded and stepped from the car, Lohmann locked both front doors and they climbed the few steps to the patio.

The foyer was like the foyer of a thousand such establishments in America before the motel began to dominate. It was also the lounge. Ageing armchairs, the leather cracked and in some places open to reveal horsehair stuffing, stood beside equally ageing small tables. There were even two spittoons at strategic points. Two elderly men, one in overalls, the other in shirt and denim slacks, sprawled half-asleep on two chairs. At the rear of the room, to the side of a staircase leading up to darkness, was the reception desk. Behind it a small man with a bald head, in waistcoat, striped shirt and polka-dotted bow tie was studying a newspaper on the desk and sipping from a bottle of Doctor Pepper's. As they entered he looked up wearily.

'Do sumptin' fur yuh?'

The two elderly men opened their eyes and surveyed the new arrivals bleakly.

'Have you two single rooms?' Lohmann asked of the small man.

'We got twelve rooms. All empty. Each of 'em kin be used as single or double. How long you want 'em fur?'

'One night.'

'Pity. Could do you a good deal on three days. Better deal on a week.'

'Just one night.'

The clerk half turned, reached out a thin arm and lifted two keys from a line of twelve, hanging from hooks. He placed the keys in front of Lohmann.

'Jest sign the register. Payment in advance. Five dollars a room. Be ten dollars. We don't do food but Charlie's Diner's next door, open 'til midnight, get a good deal there, recommend the blue-plate special. Got to be good – Charlie's ma brother-in-law. You people Yankees?' All this without drawing breath. Another minute and they'd hear the history of the town, maybe the history of the whole south.

'We are from Europe,' said Lohmann, signing the register as Muller and Smith. Pardoe watched him in silence.

'Europe, eh?' said the clerk. 'Got a brother went to Europe once. Didn't like it.'

137

'Many people don't, just now.' Lohmann lifted the keys. 'First two rooms, top of the stairs. Want a drink, I can get you a bottle of bourbon. Another five dollars. Want some company, we got two nice ladies willing t' oblige. Cost you 'nother five dollars each.'

'Thank you, no,' Lohmann said, a quick glance at Pardoe.

'Everything in this town costs five dollars,' said Pardoe, mildly amused, oblivious to the German's glance. He seemed to have put from his mind the conversation with Lohmann during the journey.

'Sure enough. This is a five-dollar town. Can you take your own cases up?'

They did so, Lohmann examining both rooms. They were identical. Each had a large uneven bed, a wardrobe, a chair, a wash basin (Lohmann's hot tap did not work), and a daguerreotype of Huey Long side by side with an equestrian sketch of General Robert E. Lee leading a cavalry charge.

They ate at Charlie's. The blue-plate special was roast turkey and corn grits, Louisiana style, which turned out to be much the same style as roast turkey anywhere else. They finished up with apple pie and coffee.

'Been quite a day,' Pardoe said. 'I could sleep for a week.'

'Do it,' Lohmann replied. 'But for eight hours only. Tomorrow we drive to the nearest airport. I'll see you at eight in the morning.'

Lohmann, alone in his room, undressed and stretched out under one sheet. In darkness. Except for a street light below his window, which cast light around the corner of the curtains and patterned the ceiling. He didn't sleep for some time, as if he was too tired to sleep – which he was.

He stared at the ceiling and the light patterns stared back at him. Could always find a face in a pattern if you looked hard enough. He looked and part of the pattern was a slim Robert E. Lee in plumed hat.

His mind slipped back into the past. To Berlin and his wife. Then there was another woman. Lucy. Lucy, remembered

138

with affection. What would she be like today, five years on? If she was still alive. She'd been one of Madame Kitty's girls. A whore. A cliché, the whore with a heart of gold. Not that it had mattered. What had he been in those days? One of society's sewer cleaners. City ratcatcher. After all, what else was the function of a policeman but to clean the city sewers of rats. The vermin of society had been his business and his quarry. He wished now Lucy had left Berlin with him. He'd made the offer. Maybe it hadn't been much of an offer: give up whoring and live on the edge of nothing in Paris and London. She'd been a practical girl – make enough money at Kitty's establishment, then marry a farmer who didn't know her past. Or open a café somewhere and become her own boss; never having to rely on men. Or ratcatchers. Trouble was, the rats had taken over the country.

And taken over Lucy. Would they allow her to get out of her profession? He doubted it. She'd be heavier now, she was the type, in that kind of business. With thick hips and tired eyes. If she was still alive.

Don't think any more on Lucy. It meant pain and longing. There had only been one other woman since then. In London. Rue Scott-ffolliot. There was regret there too. There could have been something more, but he had let it go. The practical Herr Lohmann. Worlds apart from Rue Scott-ffolliot. Better that it finished. She was married now to someone from her own world. No place in his.

Think of his daughter then, growing up in America, New York. He would see her soon. When this business was over. The one part of his own world that was left.

There was nothing else.

He finally fell asleep.

Dreaming: *Some kind of western movie, with a saloon that looked like the foyer of this hotel. No old men but swaggering cowboys straight from John Ford movies. Tim McCoy, Hoot Gibson, Buck Jones . . . all the movie cowboys were there. And the bad man in the black hat facing up to Lohmann. Daring him to draw his six-gun. Which turned into a Mauser. As if again he was going to have to kill somebody. Like von Glauber back in '34 in Berlin.*

Someone shouting, 'You can't shoot von Glauber. He's a Nazi party member.'

Nonetheless he'd shot von Glauber. That was reality. Another multiple murderer he'd been forced to shoot. To save a kid's life. Now he would be forced to kill again, the bad man who was challenging him to draw.

'Gotta do sumptin'.' The clerk's voice. 'Cost yuh five dollars a shot . . .'

'Okay! Drop them guns. I'm the sheriff . . . Sure enough, I'm the sheriff . . . just open up . . .'

'Open up! I'm the sheriff . . . !'

A banging on wood. Lohmann struggled to consciousness.

'Open up!' Someone was banging on the bedroom door.

'Won't do you no good, playin' doggo. Sheriff Ricky Cox. You in there, Mister Muller. Open up. You're under arrest!'

TWELVE

The offices of the sheriff of —ville, in —ville County, in the State of Louisiana. Although the outer office was simple, typical of many sheriff's offices - a counter for greeting visitors and complainants, and three desks for the three deputy sheriffs - the inner office was different. The walls had been lined with stained dark wood panels, there was a large desk and two deep armchairs. A bookshelf took up one wall and was filled with what looked like volumes on the law,

140

although a closer inspection would have revealed that they were a job lot of obscure tomes purchased for effect. A number of framed photographs on the other walls showed the sheriff shaking hands with Huey Long, with an aged William Jennings Bryan and a gentleman in white robe and pointed mask described below as the Grand Dragon of the KKK. Another photograph showed the sheriff being embraced by the late Will Rogers. It looked like the office of a high-priced city lawyer.

Behind the desk, lolling rather than sitting, was Sheriff Richard Cox. He was in his sixties, a big man in all directions. Yet his face was thin, with an assumed look of melancholy. His uniform was clean and fresh, if stretched taut by the large body underneath.

In front of the sheriff, in the two chairs, sat Lohmann and Pardoe. They showed every sign of having dressed hastily, Lohmann's tie askew, the top button of his shirt open. Pardoe, being accustomed to dressing quickly, was immaculate but, like Lohmann, unshaven.

Sheriff Cox was speaking, an amiable smile on his face.

'See because you came quietly and because you don't seem to be native born Americans . . . may indeed be visitin' foreigners . . . I got you in here, all friendly and comfortable. Anybody else, you'd be back in one of my cells.'

'We are citizens of the United Kingdom,' Pardoe asserted with some irritation. Lohmann was silent, biding his time.

'Now what kingdom would that be, mister?' said Cox bleakly.

'Great Britain!' Pardoe could not hide his exasperation. This was not good, Lohmann thought.

'That right, mister?' Cox gave what might have passed for a smile. 'Britishers, eh! Still foreigners to me. Now I don't got nothin' against foreigners. Although I'll tell you, they ain't popular in this county. Folk just don't like them pokin' round here. Always think, they do, foreigners should stick to them foreign places they come from.'

Lohmann decided to join the conversation. He spoke quietly and with almost over-elaborate politeness.

'I most certainly agree with you, sir. And indeed, having been touring some of your beautiful country on vacation, we are in fact returning to New York to proceed home. You will appreciate that there is a war at home and it is our duty to return to assist in the defence of our country.'

Cox assumed an expression that might have been construed as of benevolent understanding. ' 'Preciate your feelin's, sir. Be glad to speed you on your way but for one li'l ole matter.' He picked up a paper on his desk. 'You don't happen to have come from New Orleans?'

'We passed through.'

'Surprised you didn't stay longer. Mighty beautiful city. Even with all them niggers and foreigners. You did stop in time to hire yo'self a car there.'

'We'd been travelling by Greyhound buses but decided we'd get back north quicker if we hired a car,' Lohmann said easily. If the lie was good it was always easy.

'Look, why are we being kept here?' Pardoe cut in, irritation overflowing, causing Cox to frown.

'Because I consider it necessary, sir,' came the reply.

'In what way?' Lohmann, preserving the polite niceties.

'Before we get to that, you registered in the hotel here as Muller and Smith. Am I right?'

'You are.'

'You got passports with you?'

'I have my passport,' Lohmann replied with a shrug, and almost reluctantly passed over his British passport in the name of Lomond.

'And Mister Smith here?'

'The name is Pardoe,' said the Englishman, passing over his diplomatic passport.

Cox studied the two passports. 'Kin I ask why you registered as Smith and Muller? That's a kind of felony in this part of the world.'

Pardoe looked at Lohmann. The German took a deep breath.

'Captain Pardoe is on a diplomatic mission. It is a confidential matter and I felt that we should not reveal our real identities.'

Cox rubbed a chin, dark with stubble.

'And you, Mister . . .' he glanced at the passport. '. . . Lomond . . . ?'

'I am Captain Pardoe's assistant.'

'Okay, okay, so supposin' I accept all that. What's this mission all about?'

Lohmann now left it to Pardoe to respond.

'I am afraid, Sheriff Cox, I am unable to reveal that. It is a diplomatic matter which I can't go into.'

'Sounds to me as if you're confessin' to be spies. Agents of a foreign power, mebbe.'

'I assure you we are not acting against the interests of the United Stares. If you wish confirmation of my . . . of our identity, the British Embassy in Washington will provide it. Also the fact that we can claim diplomatic immunity. And if you wish assurances that we are not acting against the interests of your country, J. Edgar Hoover would give you such assurances.'

Cox leaned back in his seat and surveyed his polished brown shoes. 'That's a very pretty speech, Mister Pardoe. But first I wanna tell you I am the law in this county and not J. Edgar Hoover or any of his panty-waist G-men types.'

Cox suddenly shot forward in his seat, thrusting his jaw out, all amiability vanished. 'Me, mister! Richard J. Cox. And, as far as Richard J. Cox is concerned, that there diplomatic immunity don't mean nothin' when a serious crime is involved.'

'What serious crime?' Lohmann said. With a feeling within him that he already might know the answer to his question.

'Murder of a prominent New Orleans citizen.' Again, Cox glanced at the papers on the desk in front of him. 'Perfessor

Duplessis by name. This perfessor was found dead in some shack he owned out on the bayou.'

'And what has this to do with us?' said Pardoe, to Lohmann's surprise.

'Boatman. A Cajun, name of Joseph Boniface, took two men out to this perfessor's shack. Got their names. Pardoe and Lomond.'

'That's not possible. He didn't . . .' Pardoe said excitedly, but Lomond cut him off.

'Captain Pardoe and I deny the charges. I believe we are permitted to make a telephone call?'

The sheriff twisted in his chair, stomach threatening to burst the buttons of his shirt. 'Kinda pity our telephones are out of order . . . some fault on the line. Maybe they'll be okay by tomorrow.'

Lohmann leant forward. 'Sheriff Cox, I have to emphasise again that Captain Pardoe and I are entitled to diplomatic immunity. Even if there was some evidence of our involvement in the death of this professor, that immunity is irrevocable. You have to let us proceed.'

The sheriff's face contorted into what passed for a grin. 'Look, Mister Lohmann, I only got your word for it about this diplomatic immunity.'

'You have our passports!'

'Very fancy, but they don't mean a thing to me.'

'You could telephone the British Embassy.'

'I ain't gonna spend the county's money on expensive telephone calls,' Cox insisted. And then added as an afterthought, 'That would be, if the telephones was workin'.'

'You could be in trouble,' Lohmann said quietly.

'Lomond, I never been in trouble. Not the whole of my life. See, my daddy owned this town. And when he died, he left it to me and my two brothers. Now I'm the sheriff, my younger brother is the county judge and my youngest brother, he's county prosecutor. Also, not that it matters but that young deputy standing at the door behind you, that's my nephew by

144

marriage. Judson. In charge of the jail. And the two boys outside are second cousins. We are the law around here. What we say, goes. And no Washington Embassy or the FBI has any jurisdiction in county affairs. So you see, you're my prisoners until I decide what to do with you.'

'And when will that be?'

The sheriff toyed with an ornate paper knife.

'I reckon you stay here until the New Orleans Police Department send one of their people up here to . . . to dispose of you. Just mebbe they'll listen to this diplomatic immunity stuff. Me, I'm concerned you might be wanted men. Otherwise why are you heeled?'

In the hotel room, he had removed the Mauser from Lohmann's suitcase. Now he produced it from a drawer and placed it on the table.

'You carrying that without a permit.'

'I have a permit in Washington,' Lohmann said. Knowing he was lying. He'd never applied for a gun permit. But he didn't think Cox would even bother to check. Even if the telephone was working. 'As a foreign national attached to the embassy, I am permitted –'

Cox cut in on him with every evidence of being weary of the conversation. 'You don't have no permit from me, mister. But I won't bother booking you on that. Not while we're waiting for the New Orleans boys. So, until they get here you'll be the guests of Judson back there in the jail. You jest take 'em down, Jud, boy.'

'You've informed the New Orleans police?'

'First thing this morning before I picked you up, I was on the phone to them.' Cox said. 'Jest before the phones went out, that was. They'll be on their way. Meanwhile you want some breakfast, you can have the standard jail breakfast . . . that's coffee and a roll, or you wanna pay for it yourself, you jest give Judson the dough he'll get you bacon, eggs sunny-side up, pancakes, anythin' you like from Charlie's.'

Cox stood, signifying the interview was over.

145

Pardoe said: 'But, look here . . .'

'I done all my lookin', Mister Pardoe. You talk now to the city boys from New Orleans. Lock 'em, Judson.'

Judson, the nephew by marriage and deputy sheriff, took them to the lock-ups at the back of the building.

It was like every jail Lohmann had seen in every Hollywood movie. Realism, he told himself, was everything in these movies. There were no cells as such but areas barred off from other areas. Cages for people. Pardoe was locked in one cage, Lohmann in the next. Each area was separated only by bars. There was no bed, but a bench ran along one wall. Above the bench, high in each cage, was a small window, barely large enough for a small dog to get through, without glass but with thick bars. A primitive form of ventilation, Lohmann decided. Beyond the window was a fragment of grey sky.

'You be wantin' breakfast?' Judson asked, yawning.

'Bacon, eggs and coffee,' Lohmann said, 'For both of us.'

'Two dollars each plus a dollar for the service. Five dollars, that'll be.'

'Everything here still costs five dollars.' Lohmann handed over a five dollar bill. 'Do you pay the county executioner five dollars a time?'

'Right 'nuff,' said Judson laconically. 'That's Sheriff Cox's cousin from Baton Rouge.'

A groan came from the cage opposite. A bundle of begrimed clothing lay on the bench, breathing almost imperceptibly between groans.

'Pay no heed to him,' Judson said. 'Town drunk. One in every town. He's jest sleepin' it off.'

'Another relative, I presume.'

Judson frowned, thinking about it. But he made no further comment and went out. Lohmann looked across at Pardoe and leaned against the bars separating them.

'I have an uncomfortable feeling,' Lohmann said. 'In there you were going to say something about the Cajun boatman?'

Pardoe nodded. Worried. 'The sheriff was lying. About the

146

boatman. I never told him my name. Or the fellow who impersonated you. How could the New Orleans police be looking for Pardoe and Lohmann?'

'I thought it was something like that. Better though you say nothing to Cox. Perhaps it is something we keep up our sleeve.'

'But we're supposed to be held here, waiting for the police. If they don't come, what happens?'

'We wait and see. It could be interesting.'

They waited. A half hour later, Judson returned with a tray on which were two breakfasts. Both were cold. He shoved the two trays under the bars of each cage.

'For another five dollars could we have had them hot,' Lohmann said acidly.

Judson blinked.

'Any sign of the New Orleans police?' Lohmann went on.

'Guess they'll be here when they're here.' The deputy scratched his stomach and loosened his gunbelt. He went out again.

The bundle in the other cell groaned and sat up. A begrimed face with large eyes tinged with red, peered at them.

'I got company,' the face said.

'Good morning,' Pardoe said politely.

'Ain't that much good. God, I'm thirsty.'

'Would you like some coffee?' Lohmann estimated if he stretched out and the begrimed face stretched out, he could hand over the mug of coffee. Which tasted pretty foul anyway.

'You wouldn't have any corn liquor? No, don't reckon you would. Be obleeged fur the coffee.'

Lohmann held the mug out and a dirt-streaked hand grasped it.

'Thanks, mister. Name's Hod. Hod Gramercy.'

'Hod Gramercy.' Lohmann echoed the name.

'Pretty fancy name for a drunk, eh?' Hod Gramercy said, grinning and showing a row of uneven brown teeth.

'At least it's not Cox,' Pardoe said.

'Would be on the other side of the bars if it was. Still, I prefer Gramercy. Cajun name. Origin, French. See, I may be a drunk but I ain't an uneducated one. You got in Cox's bad books?'

'I think we have.'

'Bastard. Tin-pot dictator. Thinks he's Mussolini around here. You heard of Mussolini?'

'We have heard of him.'

'Only Cox's worse. Me, I reckon a night on corn whisky'll get me a year on the county prison farm. Gives 'em cheap labour. Chain gang stuff. You best be ready for that.'

'I think he has other plans for us,' Lohmann said.

'Unless he's after money. He after your money?'

'More than that, I believe.'

'Christ, you in bad luck. There's only your money or the prison farm, or one other thing.'

'And that is . . . ?'

'You don't want to know.'

'I would like to know, Mister Gramercy. My name, incidentally is Lohmann. And this is Mister Pardoe.'

Gramercy rubbed a hand across his forehead. An area of pink and comparatively clean skin appeared above his eyes.

'Mister Lohmann, Mister Pardoe, that there Sheriff Cox don't like wasting county money. You pay him, or you go to the prison farm, or else he got a big grudge against you. That happened before. The fellers it happened to ain't been seen since. 'Cept for one who was hauled out of the Mississippi down near Baton Rouge. Cox said he must have fallen in the river. Been in for five days, floated up all filled with gas and putrefaction. An' he was the one was found. Others, they jest disappeared in the swamp country.'

Pardoe looked nervously at Lohmann. Who looked away. Thinking.

'Otherwise they jest disappeared in the swamp country.' After whoever was coming from New Orleans arrived. And whoever

148

it was, Lohmann felt sure it wasn't the New Orleans Police Department.

Gramercy went on: 'Now I reckon you two ain't in a situation where you could pay him off. Else you would've. An' I don't think he'll be lookin' at you as prison farm fodder.'

Lohmann looked curiously at the begrimed face and red-rimmed eyes. 'How do you know all this?'

Gramercy grinned, exhibiting the brown teeth yet again. 'I ain't never as drunk as they think I am. Afore you came in. I was sitting upstairs, looking like I was in the world of corn whisky. Good at lookin' like I'm asleep, I am. I heard the phone call from N'Orleans that set Mister Big-Belly Sheriff Cox after you. Then I heard the deputies talkin'. So I figger you boys is more important than jest a couple of trout he might catch for a little extra in the treasury.'

'Who made the phone call to Cox?'

'Didn't hear that. But I guess the guy was phonin' around everybody. Hit lucky with Cox.'

'Could it have been the New Orleans Police Department?'

'Heck, no! Cox was much too polite to be talkin' to the New Orleans bulls. This is his kingdom, remember. He don't give an alligator's spit for any other law. Also, they might jest get on to what he's up to around here. He wouldn't take too kindly to that.'

'What's he saying?' Pardoe said evenly. 'What does it mean for us?'

'It means, if we can't get out of here, then your mission will come to a rather abrupt end,' Lohmann replied.

'They'd kill us?' Pardoe look across to Gramercy's cell.

'They'd enjoy doin' it, mister. You might recognise 'em. They're that kind of jest plain folks.'

THIRTEEN

They were left alone until well into the afternoon. Pardoe insisted on pacing his cage nervously and for the first hour talked incessantly about the need to be back in Washington. Lohmann, following Hod Gramercy's example, stretched out on the bench in his cage, closed his ears to Pardoe's lamenting and his eyes to the greyness of the one wall, the spiders' webs and the cockroaches which made tentative appearances from under the benches. He dwelt on the ironies of his life reviewing them, parading them in his mind like an inspecting general. Until five years before he had been responsible for putting people behind bars. In Germany in 1934, the cells were probably less salubrious than the one he now occupied. But then he believed those he had placed in cells had been, at the least, deserving of their incarceration. Murderers, thieves, swindlers, Lohmann had been convinced of his own rectitude in imprisoning these people. He was still so.

Dwelling on the ironies of his life Lohmann realised he had come to the greatest democratic nation in the world, the self-dubbed home of the free and the brave, only to find, at least in one small town, the rule of the dictator held sway here too as in Germany. Gramercy had described Sheriff Cox as a small-town Mussolini. Closer to Hitler, Lohmann told himself. A thief and a swindler, from all Gramercy had said. And a murderer. With his own minute empire, in which his word was law. How could such a state exist within the great democracy?

It was nearly three o'clock when the outer door to the cage area opened and Cox came in followed by a fat, balding man with a round red face, a pitted sun balanced on a thick neck. He had small myopic eyes and Lohmann estimated he was in his early forties. He was followed by a silent Judson.

'These are your fugitives, Mister Colescott,' Cox said indicating Lohmann and Pardoe with a expensive wave of his hand.

'Fit the description all right,' the man called Colescott replied, peering at the two prisoners. His accent, Lohmann noted, lacked the southern flavour of Cox and his compatriots.

'Mister Colescott is ... eh ... from the New Orleans P.D.,' Cox said speaking to Lohmann.

'That is so?' Lohmann said. 'He will of course have his identification?'

Cox flushed. 'I'm his goddam identification! Mister Colescott is an old friend.'

'I have heard of him,' Lohmann smiled coldly. 'From a small black man called Billy Bones, also called Amboise. William Amboise. It was a brief acquaintance. Terminated too quickly. A pity.'

Cox looked baffled. But Colescott turned even redder, if that was possible. He suddenly noticed Hod Gramercy sitting in his cage, eyes half shut, taking in everything.

'Who the hell's that?'

'Eh? Oh, that's Gramercy. Town drunk. He don't know nothin' about nothin'.'

'Get him out of here!'

Cox acted with alacrity. He nodded to Judson who at once went over and unlocked Gramercy's cell. Wearily Hod rose and shuffled forward.

'Lettin' you off this time, bum,' Cox said. 'Should be thankin' Mister Colescott for that.'

Hod shuffled past Colescott. 'Obliged to yuh, sir,' he said, gave Lohmann a sympathetic knowing look and allowed Judson to hustle him out.

'Now I'll just have a word with these two,' Colescott said. 'Stay around, Cox. After all, they are your prisoners.'

The sheriff nodded obsequiously. Lohmann thought, the dictator has met the *great* dictator. What was it the English writer said? Fleas have little fleas and on the little fleas are even smaller ones. Something like that. Cox was one of Colescott's little fleas. And Colescott would not hesitate to scratch Cox out of existence if it suited him. Just as he would not hesitate to remove Lohmann and Pardoe, if he thought he could get away with it, – which he probably could.

Colescott faced Lohmann and ignored Pardoe. As if assuming Lohmann was the man in charge. 'The sheriff here tells me you claim diplomatic immunity?'

'We do. Also we are entitled to a telephone call which so far we have been denied.'

Colescott gave a small smile. His eyes became even smaller, almost vanishing into the surrounding flesh.

'Sheriff Cox is in charge here. Wouldn't want to interfere in matters relating to his jurisdiction.'

'He'll be in trouble,' Pardoe spoke for the first time to the new arrival. 'Once the Embassy finds out where we are.'

'Of course, first they'd have to find out, Mister – sorry, *Captain* – Pardoe. They'd have no reason to know you're here, would they? You'd have to get out of here to be able to inform them.'

'Oh, we'll inform them, sir,' Pardoe insisted. 'Indeed we will.'

'*If* you get out of here. And, if you don't, who's going to know you ever been here? Sheriff Cox, you got no record of these two vagrants, have you?'

Cox grinned. 'Never even heard of them.'

'You see, Captain? You left New Orleans, you could have gone anywhere. Of course, if we charge you with the killing of that good old man, Professor Duplessis, then they'd have to know.'

'We didn't kill Duplessis!'

152

'You would say that. And I guess, even if you were charged, you'd plead that there diplomatic immunity and get off without losing even a hair. Don't like that, Captain Pardoe. Don't like it at all. Do you like it, Cox?'

'Don't like it one little bit,' Cox echoed.

'Y'see, gents, we don't like folks coming into our country, murdering people and getting away with it. We're old fashioned. We believe in justice. As in the Bible, an eye for an eye . . .'

Lohmann glanced at Pardoe, who replied with a bleak look. 'In this case, two eyes for an eye. Yes?'

'You got it. See, we got our own law around here, when the regular law don't work.'

'And who administers that?' Lohmann asked.

'Oh, you'll see, mister, you'll see. Tonight. Meanwhile, we're not inhuman. A little later we'll order the blue-plate special for you from the local eating house. At our expense.'

With a wide grin, he turned on his heel and went to the outer door. Cox followed, the pet dog in the steps of his master. At the door, Colescott stopped and swung around to face them again.

'I won't say I'll see you later . . .'

'You keep yourself away from the heat, Mister Colescott?' said Lohmann.

Colescott tapped his nose with his index finger. 'What I don't know, I can't talk about.' He paused, thoughtful. 'One thing might help, mind. Get you a stay of execution, you might say. I heard from the sheriff you was on some kind of mission here in the U.S. of A. Now if you was to give me some details of that mission, Captain Pardoe, we might just think twice. See, I got friends up north who might just be interested in that mission of yours.'

Pardoe looked at him without speaking. The Captain has courage, Lohmann told himself. And he would need it. They would both need it.

'Well anyway, you just think about it,' Colescott said. 'You

153

got a few hours. Mind you, the longer you take, the more difficult it'll be to keep the local boys from getting their pound of flesh. So you better think fast.'

Colescott went out followed by the sheriff. They were alone. At least, Lohmann thought, Hod Gramercy had been released, this time he would escape the prison farm. Lohmann missed the grubby little man. He represented some kind of honest humanity in this obscure little town.

Pardoe leant against the wall of his cage disconsolately. 'We're in big trouble,' he said.

'It would seem so. The men in the black hats have us.' Lohmann thought of Reiner and his fascination with movies. The man in black hats . . . the bad guys.

'What do we do?'

Lohmann shrugged. 'Think. Await opportunity, if there is an opportunity. Anyway we relax. Conserve energy. Also, pray a little, if you believe in the efficacy of prayer.'

Lohmann again stretched out on the bench, staring at the smooth, whitewashed ceiling. Pardoe followed suit. Lohmann was inwardly cursing himself. He should have prepared for the possibility of interception by the other side. He should have contacted Greenock, informed him of what had happened in New Orleans and the route they proposed to take to get back to Washington. It was an elementary rule: never attempt anything without *Unterstützung*. What the Americans would call back-up. Now they were on their own and could easily end up simply disappearing into the swampland. Their bodies would never be found. He wondered vaguely if Pardoe had any family, anyone who would miss him. The man was unmarried but his parents could be alive. Or he might have brothers or sisters. And, if the killings continued, the investigation would have to start all over again. Without Ernst Lohmann.

And there was himself. Only one person would miss him. Anna, daughter of ex-Inspector Ernst Lohmann, formerly of the Berlin Criminal Police. Perhaps she would not miss him too much. Four years apart, a long enough time for a child to forget. Time enough to lose the picture in the mind. Even love did not ensure that memory would last. His own recollection was of a fourteen-year-old child on the brink of womanhood. Today she would be nineteen and he was always afraid, when they did meet, they would meet as strangers. It was possible he might not even recognise her. Perhaps it was best that way. If he was to die, for a time Anna would miss the memory of her father, but it would be easier to mourn a memory than a person.

Yet he would so much liked to have seen her again. He would like to have seen her grow up even more.

Who else would mourn? Reiner, a little, as a friend. Lucy, in Germany, if she was still alive. If she ever learnt of his death. But only as a nostalgic memory. They had already lost each other, four years ago. And there would be Rue Scott-ffolliot, back in England. But then Rue was married, taken up with a husband and a young family. There'd be only a small sadness there. What more could he expect?

The feeling of self-disgust came over him. Self-pity followed by self-disgust. What did it matter that few would mourn him? Even if he were mourned by regiments he wouldn't be around to appreciate it. What the hell was he doing, sinking into a pit of self-absorption, draping his mind in black for himself? Where the hell was the Inspector Lohmann, known for his cool pragmatism, his resourcefulness, his dogged determination? Too many years as a refugee, too many years of living easily, his profession abandoned?

Now it was time to tell himself he was again a working policeman. He was in an alien environment, working virtually on his own. And whatever back-up he had, he'd ignored. That didn't mean he had to give up. He had to be ready for the opportunity that would present itself. He had to consider what action his opponents proposed to take and what methods they determined to carry out.

He forced himself to sit up.

He stared across at Pardoe. The Captain was asleep. Good. If he was able to sleep while under the threat of death, he could be relied upon when the time came to act. Which had to be soon.

Time passed. Beyond the cell window the grey sky had turned to black. A deep velvet black.

'Hey! You in there!' The whisper came from outside. From below the window. 'Kin you hear me, in there?' The hoarse voice of Hod Gramercy. Hoarse but sober.

'I can hear you,' Lohmann whispered back.

'You okay, so far?'

'So far.'

A pause. Then, 'You're in bad trouble.'

'We know it.'

'They got the white linen out.'

What the hell did that mean? Lohmann stood on the bench. The top of his head was in line with the foot of the small window.

'Don't like to see all that white cloth,' Gramercy went on. 'Bastards going to have a midnight picnic. With you two on the menu. Anythin' I can do?'

'You couldn't get hold of the keys and get us out of here?'

'No way. Mighty sorry, but only Cox and Judson have the keys. Cox is eatin' with that feller from New Orleans and Judson's probably sittin' playin' pinochle with the other deputies. Mind you, the others'll be going off to dress up pretty soon. Still, nothin' I kin do there. Anythin' else? Want me to phone friends?'

'They are in Washington.'

Lohmann heard Gramercy stifling a cough. 'Not much help there, either. Even if they sent anybody from New Orleans, you'd be cold meat floatin' deep down in the swamp before they got here. Be no trace anywheres. They make sure. They even tore the page from the hotel register. They know all the tricks.'

It was true. Even if Gramercy could contact Washington and they could call on help from New Orleans it would be too late.

Another idea. Lohmann thought longingly of his Mauser lying on Cox's desk. 'Can you get hold of a gun? Pistol or revolver.'

'I got an old long barrel Smith and Wesson. Use it fur shootin' tin cans off the fence. When I' m drunk. Used to be ma daddy's.'

'Ammunition?'

' 'Bout twelve rounds, at the foot of a drawer. Wait a minute: what you thinkin'?'

'Would it get through the bars of the cell window?'

A pause. Gramercy was working it out. 'Reckon so. You plannin' to shoot anybody?'

'Not unless I have to.'

'You got to remember, you get away but I got to keep on livin' around here.'

'I will remember that, Mister Gramercy. But you will remember they are planning to kill us. I tell you I would only fire your gun, if they try to kill us.'

Another pause while Gramercy considered this.

'Yeah. Okay.' Another paroxysm of suppressed coughing. 'What you goin' to do with it, if you ain't gonna shoot anybody?'

'I think maybe frighten Judson.'

The third pause. Then a cackle of laughter. 'I like it, I like it. You wait. Be back.'

Lohmann waited. Thinking he should awaken Pardoe. Then decided it was too soon. When and if Gramercy brought the weapon would be time enough.

Fifteen minutes went by. Would Gramercy come? Had anyone heard them whispering? Lohmann found himself pacing the cage now as Pardoe had been doing. Then there was a clattering sound against the bars of the cell window, followed by a muffled oath from outside.

157

'Is that you, Gramercy?' Lohmann whispered.

'I missed the window,' came the reply. 'Wait! I'll git somethin' to stand on.'

There followed a scuffling sound and then two dull thuds. A hand appeared at the foot of the window and a small package wrapped in greasy paper fell through the window and landed at Lohmann's feet.

'That's the slugs,' Gramercy said. 'I got to be careful. I'm standin' on a wooden packing case. I fall, I gonna make a helluva noise.'

Then the hand appeared again, with a larger package. This time the package had to be manipulated through the bars. Finally it was manoeuvred through and Lohmann caught it. This time it was wrapped in oily rags. Lohmann peeled the rags away to reveal the long-barrelled Smith and Wesson .38.

'I have it. Thank you.'

Lohmann checked the sights. They seemed to be perfectly aligned. A pity he couldn't test the gun. Never mind, he had a lethal weapon in his hands. And they had a chance to get out of this place. If they were lucky.

'Mister?' Gramercy again.

'Yes?'

'You git out of there, you come back around here. I left somethin' for both of you.'

'What is that?'

'Some nice white linen. There's a lot of it around already tonight. You get into it, you can mingle with the rest of them.'

'I . . . I do not understand.'

'You will. Just get around back, you hear? You'll soon understand. When you do, don't try and git back to your car. They'll go there minute they know you're out. Head across Main Street and down to the river.'

'Why the river?'

' 'Bout a half mile upstream, Sheriff Cox's got hisself a nice little power boat. You can drive a power boat?'

Lohmann looked across at the still recumbent Pardoe. 'I

158

have a naval captain here. It should be possible.'

'The key's on the dashboard. Cox jest leaves it there. Reckons nobody would have the brass neck to steal his boat. If they did, they'd end up with the fishes. You got all that?'

'I understand.'

'An' by the way, iffen they catches you, you ain't never heard of ole Hod Gramercy. *Comprenez*?'

'Yes, of course. And thank you, Mister Gramercy.'

'Thank me when you're back in Washington DC.'

Another thumping sound from outside. Followed by footsteps squelching in mud. Hod Gramercy was gone. Having done his good deed for the day.

Lohmann unwrapped the bullets and fed them into the Smith and Wesson. There were six left when the weapon was loaded. Now it was time to waken Pardoe.

Lohmann called to him. 'Wake up! *Raus*! Time to move out.'

Pardoe sat up, blinking. 'What's happening?'

'We're getting out of here.'

Pardoe stared at the gun in Lohmann's hand. 'Where did you get that?'

'Our friend, Mister Gramercy.'

Quickly, Lohmann moved to the bars and called out. 'Judson! Mister Judson, come quickly.'

Two seconds later he called again. The outer door opened and Judson entered, hatless, chewing something which was more likely to be gum than tobacco.

'What you makin' all that fuckin' noise about?'

'Over here!'

The deputy ambled across to Lohmann's cage. 'Okay, okay. So what is it?'

'This!' Lohmann brought the Smith and Wesson from behind him, pointed it at Judson's chest.

'What the hell . . . ! Where'd you get that?'

'Not important. What I can hit, that is important. If I fire, it would be a most painful wound.'

159

'D . . . don't. Look, this ain't my doin', you bein' where you are. Nothing to do with me. I'm only obeying orders.' He repeated this last sentence, the great twentieth-century alibi, as it was to become.

'You have new orders,' said Lohmann, adopting the tones he had heard so often back in Germany; the authority of the gun and the whip, the arrogance of the black uniform and the Death's Head insignia. 'You will unlock the two cells – now!'

'Be . . . be worth more than my job . . .'

'Be worth your life to do it. Otherwise . . .' Lohmann shrugged. '. . . so messy.'

Judson, hands trembling, produced the keys from a ring on his belt and unlocked the cages. 'You won't get no distance, mister,' he said. 'There's hundreds out there'll be lookin' out for you.'

Lohmann came out of his cage and relieved the deputy of the keys.

'How does it come to be there are hundreds?'

'Came into town for the festivities . . . that's what Cox says. Give 'em liquor, sweat and executions and you keep 'em happy. What Coxie says.'

Lohmann unlocked Pardoe's cage. The captain stepped out as Lohmann pushed Judson in. 'Anybody else in the office?'

'They just gone. All getting dressed up for the . . . the . . . you know . . .'

'Tell them we're sorry we let them down.'

The two fugitives were now at the door.

'You just going t' leave me in here?' Judson asked.

'That is the idea.'

'Couldn't let me have the funnies off my desk? Get hellish bored in here on my own,' he pleaded.

'We are in a hurry, one noise, one shout from you, we come back and shoot you. In the stomach.'

They went out through the deserted office and onto the street. It was pitch dark except for a distant street lamp and a watery moon struggling through banks of cloud. Hugging the

160

wall, they made their way to the back of the building. What Hod Gramercy had left them was lying on the old packing case under the window of Lohmann's cell.

There were two sets, pure white, almost pristine. Long sheets and two hoods, side by side, ready for use.

Lohmann shivered and looked across at Pardoe.

'Now we know what we really have to be afraid of,' said Lohmann, lifting up the robes of a member of the Ku Klux Klan.

FOURTEEN

He should have known, Lohmann told himself. This was Klan country. And somebody was using the Klan to get rid of them. But not this time.

'Put on the robes.' he told Pardoe. 'And pull the hood down. Come on. I think you'll find we are able to mingle with our fellow Klansmen.'

He slipped the Smith and Wesson into his trouser band as they donned the robes. On the breast was the insignia of the particular branch of the Klan, the Louisiana chapter or whatever they called themselves. They were congregating tonight to execute two white men they had doubtless been told had murdered one of their fellow citizens. If all Lohmann had heard about the Klan was true, they would accept, without question, the executions. Indeed, from what he'd heard, the Klan didn't need a reason. These people enjoyed dispensing their own brand of so-called justice. They enjoyed killing people.

Side by side, they marched onto Main Street. And found themselves among other similarly clad figures. They moved singly or gathered in groups, one large group congregating outside the hotel. Some had their hoods down, making no secret of their identities. Others concerned to conceal their faces, had their hoods up, much to Lohmann's relief; otherwise, he and Pardoe would have stood out.

'Walk easily,' he whispered to Pardoe. 'We must appear to be talking to each other.'

They crossed Main Street, two old friends, discussing the events to come. Fellow Klansmen nodded to them, possibly imagining they recognised two comrades. They reached the group at the hotel and Lohmann felt a hand on his back.

'Going t'be an inneresting night,' said the voice of a tall, thin figure. A kind of Gary Cooper in white robes. 'We'll show 'em, eh?'

'We'll show 'em.' Lohmann repeated, praying his accent would not be apparent. He was lucky. The thin man laughed and moved on.

As they came to the hotel, two figures appeared on the patio. Both were in Klan robes, more ornate than the rank and file in the street. Cloth of gold and silver thread, Lohmann told himself. The first of the new arrivals, hood off, was Sheriff Cox. A cheer went up. The sheriff raised his hand to acknowledge and, at the same time, quieten the acolytes.

'Boys!' he said, clearing his throat, a dry rasping sound. 'Fellow Klansmen! You all know why we're gathered here t'night. To make sure justice is gotten for the death of one of our own by these two furriners! An', because of the importance of this action, we're mighty honoured to have with us, from the North, no less than the Imperial Wizard of the Invisible Empire himself, in person.'

A sound of wonder followed by an even greater cheer went up, as the portly figure was acknowledged. Colescott! Lohmann recognised the man by his shape. Not merely a Grand Dragon but the Imperial Wizard himself. Elected by all the Klans in America? Or self-appointed? But certainly the grand panjandrum himself. Lohmann noted that Colescott, despite the power of his position, kept his hood over his face. If there was ever retribution for the proposed night's work, the Imperial Wizard was going to make sure he wasn't identified as having been present.

Colescott stepped forward.

'It's a mighty great honour to visit the beautiful state of Louisiana in the heart of the southland of our great nation. Indeed, in the very county from which the Klan arose. As our ancestors pledged so we are pledged to keep America white, to keep the niggers in their place, and to brook no interference from Yids, Catlickers and foreigners. So, when foreigners not only come into our country but murder our distinguished brothers with impunity, we look for justice. And when we know the country is so perverted as to ignore that justice, we administer it ourselves . . . with the rope!'

This was greeted by an even louder cheer. Lohmann felt himself shiver. Be grateful, *dank Gott*, he and Pardoe were not still in the cages waiting to be lynched for the murder of Duplessis, a killing in which Lohmann was sure Colescott himself had been involved. And, another thought, Duplessis had surely been a fellow countryman of these Klan members, but from his background he had also almost certainly been a Catholic; himself an enemy of the Klan.

'So, Klansmen,' Colescott went on. 'White riders of the dark night, upholders of the purity of our nation . . . despite that Jew, Roosevelt, in the White House, let's show them foreigners Klan justice!'

With a gesture reminiscent of Adolf Hitler, hand in the air, Colescott acknowledged the cheering and strode down from the patio, through the mob. As he passed, hands slapped him on the back and more cheers arose. He was followed by Cox and the other Klansmen, as he led off the short march to the sheriff's office. Lohmann and Pardoe found themselves being swept along with the crowds.

163

Pardoe gripped Lohmann's arm.

'What do we do . . . ?' he whispered.

'Go with them. For now.'

Outside the office, the mob gathered impatiently as Colescott and Cox went inside. Murmurs of anticipation ran through the Klansmen.

'Now we'll show these murderin' furriners!' the hooded figure next to Lohmann said eagerly.

Lohmann nodded in response with assumed enthusiasm.

The murmurs became an almost animal sound as Cox, hood down, soon appeared at the door, his face contorted with rage. Behind him was a dishevelled Judson and the large figure of Colescott, face still concealed by his hood.

'They got loose!' Cox shouted.

A roar of anger came from the mob.

'They can't hiv got far,' Cox went on. 'So we got a hunt on. You're good hunters. Go get 'em, boys.'

He knew how to handle a crowd, Lohmann thought. The anger changed at once to an excited anticipation. A manhunt! The Klansman's idea of a good time.

'Connors, you and some of the others get on up towards the highway. Ferguson, you take the woods.' Cox, his rage dying, was beginning to enjoy himself. 'Some of us'll go towards the river. The rest of you spread out through the town. They may be skulking around the hotel. And take guns. One of them's armed.'

The crowd dispersed noisily. Lohmann gripped Pardoe by the arm.

'The river,' he whispered.

A group of twenty or so headed across Main Street and into the wooded area behind the houses. Lohmann and Pardoe, joining them, found themselves stumbling through bracken and gorse and into darkness. Ironic, Lohmann told himself; the first time in his career he was part of a manhunt where the quarry was himself. After some moments, Lohmann smelt the river, a damp odour of rotting vegetation, and felt the air cool.

164

'Upstream,' he muttered. 'We move upstream.'

They fell behind the Klansmen who were moving forward with considerable noise as they beat at bushes and peered into the undergrowth. Some were carrying hand torches, others had bound splinters of wood and twigs together and turned them into hand-held torches, Lohmann and Pardoe moved away from the lights, at first blundering into the darkness. But a feeble moon coming out from behind the clouds gave them some light, and in a few minutes they found themselves at the bank of the river. They moved on upstream of the main body of Klansmen. The broad dark expense of the Mississippi was at their side, the water moving sluggishly southwards to the sea.

After a time, they stopped, both of them breathless. Pardoe leant against a twisted tree.

'Where are we going?' he gasped.

'Gramercy told me Cox has a power boat somewhere upstream. Can you drive a power boat?'

'Yes. But we'll need keys.'

'On the boat, according to Gramercy. You can navigate the river?'

'Shouldn't be too difficult. It should be a flat bottomed craft.'

They went on. Stumbling and tripping. Moving as fast as they could away from the town and the searching Klansmen, sometimes, when the undergrowth became too thick, wading in the shallows at the water's edge. Later, climbing back onto the bank, they sank knee-deep into mud.

'Just hope there are no crocodiles here,' Lohmann said, his lungs heaving as he gasped for breath.

'No crocodiles in these parts,' Pardoe replied. 'Maybe the odd alligator. Certainly snakes.'

Lohmann swore nervously in German.

Pardoe said: 'There must be an easier way to get to this boat.'

'Probably a path somewhere. But we are safer this way.'

165

Fifteen minutes later, the moon cleared a cloudbank and they saw, in front of them, the outline of a wooden jetty.

'I think we are there,' said Lohmann.

They struggled across a bank of mud towards it.

Then the beam of a torch shot across the mud, momentarily blinding them.

'Well, well, now why would two good Klansmen be searchin' this far upriver?'

Pardoe stopped, ankle-deep in mud. 'Christ!' he said.

The outline behind the torch was familiar.

'Would they jest be too eager, or do they know somethin'?' said Sheriff Cox. 'Now don't you be movin', boys. I got this scatter gun in my hand, and I wouldn't want you messed up before we gits to the hangin'. Jest come forward very slow, like.'

The torch was moved to the side and they could make out dimly the features of the figure on the jetty. The Sheriff had discarded his robes and was in uniform, broad-brimmed hat on the back of his head.

'And both of you dressed in Klan robes. Now that was clever. Who'd ha' thought it. 'Ceptin' me. Boys ain't goin' to like you two in Klan robes. A kinda desecration, you could say.' He moved, balancing himself, legs apart, to better hold gun and torch. The jetty, a ramshackle affair, creaked and swayed under his weight. 'Now you be just comin' forward very slowly. Any sudden movement and I press this trigger. Sprays a lot of pellets. Couldn't miss. Pretty painful when you get them in the face. And they'd take in both of you.'

Lohmann let Pardoe move first, watching him step forward in the mud towards the jetty. The moon was full out now, and they could see the Sheriff clearly, his face shining with sweat, his mouth twisted into a mirthless grin.

'Don't know what made me think of my little old boat here, but lucky I did, ain't it? Pity you took the hard way to git here. I jest drove along the nice little track, all dry and comfortable.

166

But you did pretty well. Boat's here, waiting fur you. Another pity you didn't make it sooner. Might have got clean away.'

Pardoe reached the side of the jetty.

'You climb aboard at the far end, mister,' said Cox, gesticulating with the rifle towards the river and the end of the jetty. He switched off the torch and put it in his belt. The gun barrel was swinging between the two men.

'Don't get any ideas. This is a double-barrel gun. One for each of you. Mind you, I'd hate to do it. Spoil the hangings the boys are lookin' forward to.'

Lohmann thought, he talks too much. There was some advantage there. A man talking wasn't paying attention to the possibility of having to fire his weapon.

Pardoe climbed from the mud onto the end of the jetty. Again it shook and creaked, the wood aged and rotting. He hauled himself upright and, raised his hands in the air.

'That's it,' Cox said. 'Hands high and you get a little while longer to live. Man does a lot of things he don't like to keep livin' a half hour longer. Seen it often.'

Lohmann reached the edge of the jetty. He was off the mud now, treading the shallows of the Mississippi. He reached out to raise himself onto the planking with his left hand. His right hand under the Klansmen's robes, searching. As he appeared to be trying to drag himself up onto the planking, he put all his weight on the wood.

Again the jetty shuddered and rocked.

Cox swayed, trying to maintain his stance on the planking. 'Easy now,' he said.

Under the now wet and mud-streaked robe, Lohmann felt the cold butt of the Smith and Wesson on the palm of his right hand. He pulled it from his trouser belt.

'Watch it!' said Cox, as Lohmann exerted more pressure on the planking. Again the Sheriff swayed and the shot gun in his hand wavered.

Lohmann brought the Smith and Wesson up to the edge of

the jetty, praying it would be invisible to Cox. He levelled it at the middle bulk of the Sheriff's figure.

And remembered Gramercy. '. . . You plannin' to shoot anybody? . . . Remember, you get away but I got to keep on livin' around here.'

He lowered the gun and pressed the trigger.

The sheriff collapsed onto one knee even before Lohmann heard the roar of the revolver. Then Cox screamed the scream of a child. And, as if in slow motion, he seemed to fold up and fall, face forward, onto the wooden planking.

A moaning, weeping sound came from the shivering mass.

Pardoe's hand came down and pulled Lohmann up onto the jetty. The two men stood on the wooden planking, face inches apart. Lohmann could see the sweat and grime on the Englishman's cheeks and forehead. Pardoe's eyes were shining and he seemed to lick his lips with a kind of vicarious excitement.

'You didn't kill him.' Was there regret in the man's voice?

'I didn't aim to kill him,' Lohmann replied. 'I aimed for his kneecap.'

'The boat's here,' said Pardoe. It lay on the other side of the jetty, a new craft, clean lines gleaming in the moonlight.

'Check the key's there,' Lohmann said, 'and make sure there is enough petrol. Then wait.'

'What are you going to do?'

Lohmann nodded towards Cox. 'If we leave him there, he'll bleed to death. I put on a tourniquet, that will keep him alive. Then I take him to his car and leave him there. He should survive. He can use his police radio.'

'Why?' said Pardoe, and jumped into the boat.

'Because I do not wish an unnecessary killing on my hands.'

Cox was still moaning and shuddering in pain. Small eyes, twisted in agony, gazed up at the man who had been his quarry.

'Bastard!' he managed to gasp.

'Perhaps, both of us,' Lohmann replied, and knelt by the wounded man. His shot had been accurate and effective. The knee cap was smashed. Blood oozed from splintered bone.

'I can do nothing to stop the pain,' Lohmann informed him. 'But I can stop the blood. That way you will probably live. Which may be more than you deserve.'

He took off the muddied Klan robe and, tearing strips from it, tightly bound the sheriff's leg above the knee. Throughout, Cox whimpered pitifully.

Through gritted teeth, Cox said: 'They'll . . . get you. They'll get you . . . wherever you are.'

'And who are they?'

'Colescott knows. He'll make sure.' A spasm of pain forced Cox into silence. His eyes rolled back and he went limp. Lifting the now unconscious figure, not without some difficulty, Lohmann carried Cox back along the pier. He was a considerable weight and Lohmann was thankful when, some twenty yards along a narrow path, he came upon a wide track and the parked police car. He eased the wounded man into the driving seat and closed the door, breathing heavily.

Back at the jetty, Pardoe was waiting in the boat.

'The petrol tank is full.'

'Good. We get started then.'

'Where do we go?'

'North. Natchez, I think is the nearest sizeable town. If there is no airport there, we hire a car and drive to the nearest one.'

'They took our money in that jail.'

'So we phone the Embassy. Collect, that is what they call it, isn't it? They will arrange the flight and car hire. Now move the boat, if you are in a hurry to get back to Washington, the sheriff's friends may yet arrive.'

Washington

FIFTEEN

A slight snowfall during the night had turned Washington into a glistening white wedding cake. As the snow had recommenced falling around dawn, the streets had retained the white mantle, not yet turned by the traffic into a brown mire of mud and slush. The cold bit deep into Lohmann's bones after the mild humidity of Louisiana. He had wrapped himself in a large woollen pullover under his trench coat; a thick scarf, newly purchased that morning in a shop in the hotel's mall, embraced his neck as he and Pardoe drove from the Mayflower Hotel to the British Embassy.

They had arrived back in the city, dishevelled and ill-clad, the day before; and managed to sleep in their respective rooms for sixteen hours. Lohmann had felt a sense of relief at the return to Washington. There was a feeling of security in being back in the capital after the alien territory that was Louisiana. It was a return to civilisation for which he was grateful. He had nonetheless slept fitfully, aware that his task should be to keep a close eye on the naval officer and afraid that Pardoe might awake before him and go out into the city. He need not have worried. Pardoe was exhausted, dark shadows under his eyes giving him a strange haunted look.

On the plane to Washington, Pardoe had been at first silent, morose, depressive. Then, not long before they landed, he had broken his silence.

'I should thank you.' Said almost reluctantly.

Lohmann had shrugged without replying.

173

'You saved my life. Those people, the Klan, they would have lynched us.'

'The man, Colescott, was working for . . . someone else.'

'They want to stop my mission. They don't know for sure what it is. But they want to stop it.'

Lohmann nodded . . . 'You could say so.'

'You see how . . . how important that makes it.'

'I have been so informed,' he said with Germanic precision.

'The other thing. These killings. They aren't important.'

'To the victims, they are important.'

'Yes, but . . . after the mission is complete, you must find out who killed these women.'

Lohmann shifted awkwardly in his seat. He felt mildly airsick. He tried to put the nausea from his mind, Pardoe wanted to talk, he must be allowed to do so.

'I intend to. But if it is you who killed them . . . ?' A question left open.

Pardoe's face contorted as if the thought was agonising. As well it might be. He rubbed his hand across his face as if to erase the thought.

'Surely I should have a memory of . . . of these things?'

'Not necessarily. As I have said.' Lohmann was being very precise. As always.

Pardoe shuddered. He gripped the detective's arm. 'If . . . if you find I have killed these women, I want you to promise me . . . Lomond, I want you to promise me . . . you'll . . . you'll shoot me.'

Lohmann thought, he doesn't know that was already the order from London. And even if he couldn't prove his guilt, Pardoe was under a death sentence. The only thing that could save the man was if Lohmann could find the real murderer. If there was a real murderer.

Now as they drove to the Embassy, Lohmann behind the wheel, Pardoe began to recover from his depression. He became elated, almost manic. He exhibited a ghoulish sense of humour even about the possibility of being executed by his

174

companion. As if it might relieve his conscience.

'At least I'd have a clear conscience. I mean, what I don't know, I can't be blamed for. I shall be blameless.'

Lohmann kept his eye on the road, saying nothing.

'I can move forward now,' Pardoe kept talking. 'Despite Duplessis being killed, I think the mission can be completed. I have to phone New York. Perhaps we'll have to fly there. You'll be coming with me, of course?'

'Of course.'

'A few days. All I need. Oh, I phoned the Embassy from the hotel. We have to go to a reception tonight.'

Momentarily Lohmann took his eyes from the road, surprised. It was the first time it had been mentioned.

'Is this quite the time to get involved in social events?'

'You'll enjoy it, Washington society,' Pardoe went on with an intensity of enthusiasm that seemed excessive. 'I told them you had to come with me. That's right, isn't it? It's one of these parties thrown by some Washington hostess – top people from the government and the army. And most of the embassies . . . even includes the attachés. It'll be very lavish.'

'Should you not be concentrating on your mission?'

'That's the point. I will be. There will be people there who can help. I could cut a few corners if I can get to the right ones. And one in particular . . .'

Lohmann was conscious of the man's excitement. At cutting corners with his mission? Or was it something else? A heated intensity at being, once again, back in the Washington social scene. Julie Neuberg had played a part in that scene. Mary Lou Hancock had been on the darker fringes of it.

'Is it not about time you told me more of this mission?' Lohmann asked, as he steered the car over the white mantle of snow and onto Pennsylvania Avenue.

There was a moment of silence. Pardoe kept his eyes on the road ahead. When he finally spoke again, his elation was muted. 'You should know. God, if I can't trust you, Lomond,

175

who can I trust? But it's always been on a "need to know" basis . . .'

They were passing the modest edifice of Blair House. Pardoe stared at the building through the gently falling snow.

'I . . . I can tell you this,' he said. 'There are two men who've recently arrived in America. They're in New York just now. They're foreign nationals . . . not American citizens . . . not British. But I have to arrange that they meet and talk with the President. The meeting must be secret . . . and not appear to be sponsored by our government. Roosevelt must always be seen to be impartial in this war, and we are belligerents.'

Lohmann was curious. 'Are there not ways of simply applying to the White House?'

'It mustn't be done openly. Too many leaks in this city. Too many German sympathisers in the country. The Lindberghs and Father Coughlins. And . . . and even those people who may not be pro-German but are isolationist. Powerful people like Hearst and Colonel McCormick.'

Lohmann was beginning to realise he knew little of the American scene. He looked puzzled.

Pardoe caught the look. 'Powerful people. Own half the newspapers in the country. America Firsters, they call themselves. So you see, it all has to be done in secret. But there's one man I must speak to who'll be at this party tonight. Alexander Sachs. He's an economist, with top connections in the government. We believe he's sympathetic . . .'

Pardoe suddenly stopped as if he had already said too much. After a moment he spoke tersely. 'That's all I can tell you just now.'

They drove in silence again. After a time Lohmann said: 'I have no dinner jacket.'

Pardoe smiled. 'We're working on something that could change the entire course of the war, – and you're worried about having no dinner jacket. I think the Embassy can provide one. It wouldn't do for you to turn up at one of the Madge Van Essling's parties improperly dressed.'

'Van Essling?'

'Our hostess. Some of the wealthier women in this city make a career of throwing parties for the politicians. The attraction of power, I suppose. Madge is one of the wealthiest.'

'I have been at one of Madame Van Essling's parties,' said Lohmann. 'In London, three years ago.'

Pardoe raised an eyebrow. 'You never stop surprising me, Lomond. You must have had an extensive social life in London.'

'I was involved in another case of murder at the time,' Lohmann replied. 'It also concerned people in government.'

'And no doubt you apprehended the murderer?'

'He was killed,' Lohmann said.

It was as if the cold had suddenly invaded the interior of the car. Pardoe shivered visibly, his face suddenly assuming an ashen hue.

An hour later, alone in his tiny office at the Embassy, Lohmann waited. On his arrival the day before, he had left a message at the hotel. He was now waiting for the arrival of Reiner. He sat at his desk, sipping a hot cup of coffee and listening to the air-conditioning humming on the wall above him. At least it brought a warmth to the room. He wished there was a window. Without a view of the outside world he had a growing feeling of claustrophobia. As if he was in a cell waiting for something to happen – for Pardoe's next move? He knew the naval officer was in his office along the corridor, making phone calls concerning the mission, always concerning the mission. Although he had only Pardoe's word for that. What could happen?

When he had entered the Embassy this morning, he had at once been subjected to being measured for, as the Americans called it, a tuxedo. He had felt vaguely humiliated at the

177

operation. Carried out by a small man who had been hurriedly summoned and was most apologetic that there was no time to tailor a suit and he would have to hire one. Of course the little man assured him it would be a perfect fit. As if it was important to the embassy of a country at war. While others were engaged in the business of war as it affected them in America, he, Lohmann, was being measured for a tuxedo. And then left abandoned in a cell drinking coffee. Surely there were more important things in the world he could be doing?

He stared down at his desk, at an unmarked blotter, and a telephone.

The telephone rang.

'Lomond here.'

'A Mister Reiner to see you.'

At last. He could perhaps now get to work.

Reiner came in with every appearance of breathlessness. He was wearing a heavy dark overcoat and a wide-brimmed black hat. Both were speckled with snow. His face was flushed. He was excited, obviously he too was eager to be working.

'Glad to see you back, chief. How was New Orleans?'

'Warm. In many unexpected ways. Tell me what you have found out.'

Reiner took off his coat and hat, placed them carefully on the back of the chair and, producing a small notebook from his inside pocket, sat facing Lohmann.

'Straight. James Henry the Third. Son of James Henry Straight the Second. A millionaire. Money originally made from non-alcoholic drinks and chewing gum. But now with interests in oil and steel. That is the father. The son went to Harvard Law School where he just scraped a law degree . . . There was some sort of scandal but it was hushed up. Cost the father a large monetary donation to the college.'

'What kind of scandal?'

'James the Third has some perverse interests. One of his

old class-mates at Harvard said he was the kind who might be found in bed with man, woman or dog. And equally at home with all three.'

'Yet he's an FBI agent? Hoover has a reputation for puritanism.'

'Hoover can make exceptions when it suits him. Straight's father apparently helped Hoover when he had money problems a few years ago. In return Hoover made Straight a kind of agent. It was honorary only at first. When Straight started moving around the world at his father's expense Hoover began to use him. You see, the FBI has no mandate to operate abroad, but Hoover likes to know what's going on everywhere. Especially with regard to US embassy and diplomatic people. Straight started to furnish him with regular reports from abroad. Any diplomat who seemed too liberal was duly reported to Hoover by young Straight. All went into Hoover's files. They say he has massive files on every political and diplomatic figure in America. And abroad.'

'Reminds me of someone.'

'Himmler? Yes, I thought that. Anyway, you know Straight was in Singapore at the same time as your friend, Captain Pardoe? And a girl was murdered.'

'Pardoe told me about it.'

Reiner's eyes widened. 'Maybe Pardoe's cleverer than you think. Tell all and sound as if you have nothing to hide.'

'Or is he being honest?'

Reiner grinned. 'Trouble with you and I, chief, is we're not used to honest men. Anyway, Straight and Pardoe became good friends in Singapore. Which is surprising. No sign of any homosexual inclinations from Pardoe?'

'I haven't seen any.'

'So they were an unlikely pair to become friends. Pardoe seems very conventional, very normal – except that he might just like to eviscerate young ladies. Anyway, I talked to a US consular service man who was in Singapore and it seems

Straight and Pardoe and a few other British and Americans got together out there. They were a pretty wild crowd. Booze, girls, boys, a little drug-taking, anything went.'

'It doesn't sound like Pardoe.'

'I thought that myself. As I said, Pardoe seemed a typical, ordinary British naval type. It seemed, more than anything else, as if Jimmy Straight cultivated him rather than the other way round. Not that Pardoe minded. He was a kind of lonely type out there at first. And he has no private income of his own, but Straight would impress Croesus himself the way he throws money around.'

'And yet,' Lohmann broke in, 'he seems genuinely to be concerned about Pardoe's well-being. As a friend would.'

Reiner grinned. 'Unrequited love? Would love to make a pass at Pardoe but doesn't dare in case he's rejected?' The grin widened. 'Or maybe they're just good friends. Have you ever thought, chief, our old occupation gives us such a low opinion of humanity?'

'I've thought it.'

'On the other hand, I suppose it's possible Straight is our man,' Reiner suggested. 'With all the . . . the kinks he had, it wouldn't be difficult to think of him getting bored with his own specialised habits and taking up murdering women as a new hobby.'

A silence, both considering the thought.

'After all, Straight was in London when the woman was killed there,' the ex-sergeant added. 'And back in Washington when Mary Lou Hancock was killed.'

'Anything about her to tell me?'

'Not a lot that's new. The girl from the sticks, as the Americans would say. Real name Marie Pulaski. Had quite an extensive clientele. Of which Pardoe could have been one. His name appears in her address book . . .'

'Yet he denies knowing her.'

'I can't find anybody who actually saw them together. But

that would apply to half the names in her book. A lot of her clients would make a point of not being seen with her.'

'Did Straight know her?'

'Oh, yes. He was in the address book, and she was seen on his arm in various night clubs. Straight didn't seem to mind being seen with her. Even if she was a hooker.'

Lohmann looked puzzled. 'A hooker?'

'Slang for a whore. But if Straight was our killer, he didn't mind being seen around with his victims beforehand. Which could be one strike for him being innocent.'

'Not a very strong one. If these killings are done in a frenzy of insanity, then the killer might not be aware he is going to do them until the event.'

Reiner scratched his chin. 'I think I understand that. Probably come out clearer in German . . . no, no, it's all right. Anyway, Miss Hancock had a list of men in her diary as long as your arm. If it wasn't for the other murders we'd have half the males in Washington under suspicion.'

'Let's pass on to the Neuberg girl.'

'Not a lot you don't know there. Pardoe met her at some diplomatic junket. Took her out – only a couple of times as far as I know. And of course she knew Straight. Well, they were both on the scene here. Incidentally her uncle has offfered a $50,000 reward for the apprehension of her killer. But she had been out with a lot of guys. Although – and this is interesting – there's a rumour among her neighbours and one or two friends that she had found a regular boyfriend. Told people she was really in love, seemed sure it would come to something.'

'It did,' Lohmann sighed. 'Her death.'

'She was talking about love and marriage, and the whole thing. Very romantic, very broody. She wasn't pregnant, was she?'

'I hadn't heard. I will check up on that.'

'Anyway, nobody has an idea who the man was.'

'If he was innocent, surely he would have turned up. He

hasn't. So it could be one of our friends,' Lohmann said.

'It could hardly be Jimmy Straight. I mean, this big romantic figure . . .'

'Stranger things have happened. Anything else?'

'Nothing else. I'm trying to find the boyfriend.'

Lohmann leaned back in his chair, drumming his fingers on the desk. 'I've more work for you . . .'

Reiner made a face. 'Trouble with this job is, it's all legwork and no action or excitement. All right, tell me.'

'A man called Colescott.'

'Where do I find this one?'

'Exactly where at this moment, I don't know. He was in Louisiana, although I think he's from the north. He is also the Imperial Wizard of the Ku Klux Klan.'

Reiner's grin reappeared. 'That makes it easy. High profile. I think I've even heard of him in the papers. You want all I can get on him?'

'Please.'

A knock on the door.

Lohmann frowned. He knew Pardoe was busy, Greenock was out at a US Navy reception. And he had his dress suit now. Who else could want him?

'Come!' he called out.

Charlie Markham came in. 'Oh, I'm sorry. I thought you'd be alone.'

'It's all right.' He made the introductions. 'Mister Reiner was an associate of mine in the old days. He is now a United States citizen.

'Mister Markham is in charge of security in the embassy, Reiner. He no doubt wonders who you are. You satisfied, Markham?'

'Not why I came to see you, actually.'

Markham studied the carpet briefly and then looked up, enjoying himself in an introverted manner.

'We've had the Louisiana State Police on. Regarding the death of two men. One a Professor Duplessis, the other a

182

negro found dead in a cemetery. Also an unpaid hotel bill and
a sheriff of some village who has been shot in the knee. What
the hell were you two doing in Louisiana . . . conducting a
two-man crime wave?'

SIXTEEN

Lohmann said: 'You can take care of it, Markham.'

Markham smiled sardonically. 'I'm glad you have so much
confidence in me. You'd better tell me about it.'

'It is true, all these things happened. But apart from not
paying the hotel bill, neither Captain Pardoe or I were
responsible.' Lohmann was deliberately adopting as casual a
manner as possible. 'I believe Pardoe is sending a cheque to
the hotel today.'

'To hell with the hotel bill. What about all the rest?'

'To do with a man called Colescott and a sheriff called Cox.
Of course they will admit nothing. Neither will we. But *we* are
being honest. They are not. And, we have diplomatic
immunity, have we not?'

Markham ran his hand through thinning hair. 'For God's
sake . . . they could still ask for your removal from the
country.'

'I would try a complete denial. They would have trouble
proving anything. And they won't want anyone to dig too
deeply.'

Markham looked from Lohman to Reiner and back to
Lohmann. 'What are you two up to?'

'You'd have to ask Pardoe. And I don't think he'll tell you.

It is all on a "need to know" basis.'

'Don't you think I need to know?'

'No.'

The two men stared at each other for a long moment. Markham finally looked away. 'Captain bloody Pardoe. Everywhere he goes, he brings problems.'

Lohmann continued to stare at him. But a puzzled expression had come into his face. 'What do you mean, everywhere he goes?'

'I've come across him before.'

'Where?'

'I was attached to the Governor's office . . .'

'In Singapore?'

'How did you know?'

'A guess. Tell me about Pardoe in Singapore.'

'He was attached to the Flag Officer, Pacific Fleet out there. I was with intelligence. He . . . he made some ill-advised friendships.'

'What does that mean?'

Markham sat on the edge of the desk. There was nowhere else for him to sit. He looked at Reiner.

'Should he be here?' he asked Lohmann.

'Sergeant – er, Mister – Reiner is completely trustworthy,' Lohmann replied, suddenly aware of his own pomposity. 'Tell me more about Pardoe.'

'There was nothing like this New Orleans business. It was simply that, as a naval officer with considerable responsibilities, he was tangled up with a pretty wild set. Heavy drinking, gambling, women. Maybe other kinds of sexual activities.'

'You could have had him recalled.'

'Eventually he would have been. But London did it for us. Admiralty wanted him back. So he went. I think the naval staff were glad to see him go. He was becoming a security risk.'

Lohmann rubbed his chin. 'Since I've known him, he has

184

preserved the security of his mission only too well.'

Markham contemplated his own right hand. 'It wasn't that we could accuse him of anything. But you have to understand how Singapore is. Place is crawling with possible agents. Chiang Kai-shek's Chinese, Communist Chinese, Japanese, Germans posing as Dutchmen, Americans posing . . . as Americans . . .'

Reiner said: 'I thought the British considered America a friendly nation.'

'Oh, we do,' Markham replied wryly. 'But they still have agents spying on us. Want to know what we're up to. Whether British policy doesn't clash with American policy. You should know, Lomond. You're in intelligence.'

'I'm comparatively new. Police work was more my forte.'

'Interesting. I knew there was something about you,' Markham said. 'Thought I knew most of MI6's people. Still, for your information, in the intelligence world, nobody quite trusts anybody else. Even those supposed to be friendly. The friendlys are only amiable when it suits them.'

'A selfish world.'

'Indeed. We are all preoccupied with ourselves. Never trust your best friend. It's a good rule.'

'I can imagine,' said Lohmann. 'So you ran across Captain Pardoe in Singapore. But all you really have against him is his association with a hard drinking crowd.'

'Of foreigners. Alien corn. Almost certainly out to milk him of information.'

'What kind of information?'

'He had knowledge of our Pacific Fleet. He knew about defence fortifications in Singapore. Stuff the Japanese, for example, would find extremely valuable. Oh, yes, we frowned upon his associations.'

'You have evidence that he gave away naval secrets?'

Markham shook his head. 'No, no. No evidence. Just the company he kept.'

'People like James Henry Straight?'

Markham raised his eyebrows. 'You've been doing your homework. Yes, Straight was one example. He is an operative for a Federal Agency.'

'The FBI. An internal agency, surely?'

'You have to understand, Lomond, our American friends are children in the world of espionage. They have, at this time, a rather embryonic intelligence service. So they have to make use of what is to hand. Like James Straight. Who is himself possibly not the most reliable of agents. He has his own special . . . proclivities.'

'Yes, I know about that,' said Lohmann, with a glance which might have been acknowledgement at Reiner. 'Well, thank you, Mister Markham for all your information. I'll keep it in the front of my mind. Meanwhile, Captain Pardoe is on a specific assignment. Which he seems to be handling with discretion, and which must not be hindered. You will not hinder him. You will handle this New Orleans business in the manner I have suggested . . .'

'You're giving me orders, Lomond?'

'If you choose to take it that way. However, your people in London will back me up, if you care to check with them.'

Markham lifted himself from the desk. 'I'll check. And handle New Orleans. But it will be a lot of trouble. If anything like that is liable to happen again, let me know in advance. I like an easy life.'

'One thing more, Markham . . .' Lohmann said.

'Yes?' Wearily, from the door.

'These activities of Pardoe's in Singapore. Were any of them of a criminal nature?'

Markham looked suitably surprised. 'Criminal? Good God, no. Wouldn't have expected that. Booze, yes. A loose tongue maybe. But nothing criminal. He was, *is* a senior naval officer. That's why I believe you about New Orleans.'

Markham went, closing the door behind him. Lohmann turned to Reiner.

'I know,' said Reiner. 'Your Mister Markham was in

186

Singapore. Probably when the girl was murdered out there. You'll want me to check on where he was when the others were murdered?'

'Can you do that?'

'My boss Solomon has a store in Singapore. I have connections.'

'Good. Do it,' said Lohmann. 'He's an interesting man, Markham. Wise yet naive.'

'Naive?'

'He believes in the purity and innocence of British naval officers in criminal matters. Or affects to do so. He obviously has never met the likes of Rheinhardt Heydrich. He too started off as a naval officer.'

There was a pause.

'Very well, Reiner, you know what to do.'

Reiner nodded. 'And you?'

'I shall be in Washington as long as Pardoe is here. Tonight, I go to one of the city's big social events. You see, Paul, the man in charge gets all the . . . what's the word . . .?'

'Perquisites.'

'Yes, exactly.'

When Reiner departed, Lohmann sat back and lit a cigarette. Not that he liked American cigarettes, with their peculiar toasted flavour. But they were all he had to hand. An unopened packet in the desk drawer. He inhaled, brooding. It seemed, since he had arrived in America he had spent most of his time protecting Pardoe. Apart from the visit to the scene of Julie Neuberg's murder, there had been no investigation of the allegations that Pardoe might have killed the three women. It wasn't the way he had worked in the old days. But then he had had the force and backing of a complete criminal investigation department behind him. Here, he only had Reiner to do the legwork.

He reached forward and lifted the telephone. 'Get me the Federal Bureau of Investigation.'

He was duly connected, and asked for Whitney Collins. He

waited for a long two minutes. Finally Collins came on the line.

'What can I do for you, Mister Lomond?'

'It is regarding the murders of these two women. I was wondering if I could see the police and medical reports on them?'

A pause. 'These cases are being investigated by the FBI since they took place in the Federal District of Washington. The police are not involved except peripherally.'

'Then may I see the FBI files?'

'FBI files are not available to members of the public. Or to foreign nationals.'

Lohmann sighed. It was what he should have expected. 'I would remind you, Mister Collins, that since the case concerns one of our nationals and I have been sent here to investigate him myself, our interests coincide.'

Another pause. Lohmann imagined he could hear a muffled voice in the background. Then Collins again. 'I appreciate all you say, but no files could be released without the express permission of the Director.'

'Very well. Will you please connect me with Mister Hoover's office?'

'It happens I am speaking from there. I'll see whether he can speak to you. He's a very busy man . . .'

'Aren't we all, Mister Collins?'

The phone seemed to become muffled. A hand over the receiver. Another minute passed.

'Herr Lohmann! This is Edgar Hoover, Herr Lohmann. Y'know, I just can't get over a German working for the English as an investigator. Just can't get over it.'

'It doesn't worry the British, Mister Hoover.'

'Maybe their investigating organisations aren't as particular as ours. Collins here tells me you'd like to see the reports on the two killings.'

'My job is to investigate from our side.'

'So it is, so it is. Y'know, Agent Collins would like to have a word with your Captain Pardoe . . .'

'It can be arranged, I'm sure.'

Another silence. Hoover considering. 'This afternoon?'

'Why doesn't Mister Collins come along to the Embassy?'

Hoover gave a sound like a snort. 'On *your* territory?'

'For a start.'

'All right, Lomond. Or Lohmann . . .'

'Can we stick to Lomond?'

'Lomond. Agent Collins will come to your Embassy at three o'clock. He will bring you the files on the two killings. He will hand them over provided he can see Captain Pardoe.'

'Thank you, Mister Hoover.'

'Oh, by the way Lohmann . . . Lomond. We've been getting some strange stories from our New Orleans office. They're running around down there like headless chickens. Couple of killings took place. You know anything about what went on down there?'

'A little. Enough to assure you we were not responsible.'

'We might talk about that.'

'I think your people in New Orleans might be better talking to a man called Colescott. And a sheriff called Cox – he has a bad knee.'

Unexpectedly, at the other end of the line, Hoover started to laugh. It was harsh, grating sound.

'Good, good! I'll bear that in mind, Mister Lomond. Doubtless we'll meet again.'

'Possibly. Thank you for your co-operation, Mister Hoover. Goodbye.'

'*Auf Wiedersehen*, Mister Lomond!'

Lohmann replaced the receiver and at once lifted it up again. 'Connect me with Captain Pardoe.'

A moment later, Pardoe came on the line.

'Lomond here. This afternoon an FBI agent, a Mister Whitney Collins, will come and ask you some questions.'

'This afternoon! I don't know, Lomond. I have a great deal of work, and this party tonight . . .'

189

Was there, in Pardoe's voice, a trace of panic? Or was he imagining it?

'See him, Pardoe. It is necessary.'

'But . . . but what do I tell him?'

'The truth, Pardoe, try the truth. As you remember it. If he asks anything about New Orleans, also the truth. You will do that?'

'Yes, all right.' Reluctantly, for a man who professed his innocence. Or at least his uncertainty.

At three o'clock, two large files were handed in to Lohmann's office. Every document was photostat. And there was no way of telling whether there were any documents withheld. Still, Lohmann told himself he could not complain. The files *seemed* complete.

He started to read.

The scene-of-crime reports were already familiar to him. Pardoe's name appeared in both women's address books. All right, that he already knew. There was also the British naval officer's brass button. Something he would have to ask Pardoe about. Collins would certainly do so. Anyway there were many British seamen and naval officers in and out of the United States at this time. Also, the button had not been wrenched from the killer by the victim; it had merely been lying in the room. Dropped off a jacket accidentally, or deliberately placed there? A thought worth considering.

He turned to the medical reports. Compiled by the little man, Sanders, with the pince-nez.

Death by shock, caused by evisceration, loss of blood, severance of various vital organs as listed. A catalogue of horrors. The same for both women. And as the woman in London had died. With both American women, sexual intercourse had taken place before the assault. Semen and blood in the genitalia. And the incision ran from just above the genitalia upwards to the throat. Like gutting a fish,

Lohmann thought. It would take a powerful hand and a sharp blade to do it.

The blade had no serrations and had to be abnormally sharp, and two inches long at least. The report ruled out old fashioned razors, and most knives. As Lohmann had suggested at the scene of the Neuberg murder, the weapon would seem to have been a scalpel with a fairly long blade. A two-inch blade. Not usual for a scalpel but not impossible.

Sanders' report indicated mild bruising on the torso and on the arms. The bruises on the arms were commensurate with both women having been held down, pinned by the arms during intercourse. And afterwards, when they had been killed.

Both murders had taken place late in the evening. Time enough for the victim and the killer to drink, dine, and have sexual intercourse, and be followed almost at once by murder.

Recipe for a psychopath's evening out.

Lohmann read through the reports and then read through them again. Stamping the image on his mind. Asking himself, could the man he had known closely for two days have committed these crimes? Not that two days was much time. But under the tension they had endured in New Orleans and —ville, men learned quickly about each other. Still, he could not answer that question.

Later, as he drove Pardoe back to the Mayflower Hotel to change for the Van Essling party, he asked him about Collins' questioning.

'I told him I knew Julie Neuberg,' Pardoe replied, shifting nervously on his seat. 'I told him I didn't know the other woman . . . what was her name?'

'Mary Lou Hancock.'

'Don't know how my name got into her address book. I did what you told me to do, Lomond. I told the truth.'

'And he believed you?'

'I don't know. You'll have to ask him. Persistent, he was.

191

To the point of deafness. Kept having to repeat my answers. Like a parrot. Over and over.'

'And the button? The British naval officer's button found in the Neuberg apartment?'

Pardoe stared out of the car window. It was starting to snow again. The snow was yellow under the street lights.

'Not mine. I have two uniforms and my dress uniform. And no buttons missing. Anyway it wouldn't be hard to get hold of a button like that. The Embassy has a supply. There are souvenir shops here and in New York where all sorts of insignia can be bought. Even Nazi Party buttons and medals.'

'And British navy buttons?'

'Yes.'

'Convenient.'

'Anybody could have picked one up and left it in the girl's apartment.'

'Or, if they'd lost one, easily found another one to sew on?'

Pardoe glared out at the falling snow, his lips tightly shut, a straight line terminating the conversation. Lomond turned his mind to the evening ahead . . . uneasily.

SEVENTEEN

They used Lohmann's car, Pardoe in white mess jacket under his greatcoat sitting silently in the passenger seat. Nervous, Lohmann thought. Lohmann himself was in the tuxedo provided by the Embassy. Still feeling uneasy. He was long unused to social events. Especially such exotic ones as he suspected this would be.

The house was at the far end of Massachusetts Avenue.

To call it a mere house was an understatement. It was a mansion, a pseudo-Grecian edifice, the frontage pillared and imposing. It stood in its own grounds, back some distance from the road, windows ablaze; like a stone Christmas cake decorated by the myriad lights in the windows. The shadows of skeletal willow trees fell on the lawn, winter thin sentinels bare of greenery. A plush red carpet covered the steps under the pillars. Attendants in plum coloured uniforms matching the carpet scurried around outside as they relieved the arriving guests of car keys and cars, which were then parked God knew where, ready to be brought back at a moment's notice. The efficiency of wealth. It all seemed to say, this could be yours too, if your descendants hung on for two hundred years and exploited the country with one ruthless object, the acquisition of the riches on display this night.

Inside the main door of the house a rake-thin senior footman, and attendant staff, relieved the guests of their coats and hats. Beyond the footman, a major-domo, the butler, obese and pompous, announced the names of the guests, like a bell tolling the arrivals. And in some cases, where necessary, he added a modicum of information on those with lesser known names who needed further identification.

'Senator and Mrs Robert La Follette.'

'Mister Bernard Baruch.'

'Captain Robert Pardoe, Naval Attaché, British Embassy, and Mister Ernest Lomond, British Embassy staff.'

'Countess di Frasso and Mister Gary Cooper.'

The hostess, a youth of seventeen at her side, greeted her guests. Madge Van Essling had not changed a great deal since Lohmann had been a guest at the dinner party she had thrown in London some three years before. With the years her hair had turned even more blonde, her face smoother, her body larger, her make-up thicker. She would admit to thirty-nine while rapidly approaching fifty. She was dressed in a Paris gown certainly designed for a woman of thirty-nine. The youth, dressed in a new tailored tuxedo, was her son Eric, newly graduated from an exclusive high school, his face still marked by the eruptions of adolescence.

Those of her guests with whom she had a close acquaintance she greeted with a small, bird-like cry and an embrace. To those who were strangers, or passing acquaintances, she avoided shaking hands, leaving that to her son, and merely greeted them with an expansive, if set, smile. She had however a keen ear for the major-domo, picking up at once the names of the arrivals so that she could welcome Pardoe with a low voiced, 'So nice to see you Captain Pardoe. And welcome, Mister Lomond.'

Her eye caught Lohmann's and, for a moment, dwelt there. There was a spark of puzzled recognition which died as soon as it flared. The name Lomond was close enough to Lohmann, with which he had been introduced in London. But then he had been a German citizen, and was now a representative of the British Embassy. She was at once distracted by the couple behind them. She turned to embrace with a delighted cry the Countess di Frasso and the tall, gangling figure of her movie-star escort.

Lohmann and Pardoe went into the hall, Lohmann thinking how the movie-buff, Reiner, would have enthused over the famous actor behind them. And there was more Reiner would have enthused over. The hall was like every movie set for a wealthy family mansion ever shown on the screen. It might have been the actual hall of the house in *My Man Godfrey*. The wide staircase came down from above in a majestic sweep. The decor around it was art nouveau and perhaps already dating fast. The hall itself was crowded. Guests greeted strangers like old friends, acquaintances embraced acquaintances like lovers. Among the men, handshakes were forcibly firmer than usual, an assertion of power and masculinity. Among the women the embraces were more ardent as if to emphasise a concern which might or might not be genuine but must be seen by others. But more striking than the people were the clothes. The latest creations from Paris were next to the newest models from Fifth Avenue. Around necks and wrists were the flashes and sparks of light from necklaces and bracelets which knew only Tiffanys and its like as their origins.

The men might have paled into insignificance but for their uniforms; dress uniforms, medals to be worn. The US Army, Army Air Corps, Marine Corps and Navy predominated. From young lieutenants – almost certainly the scions of influential families – to the highest ranks in the country. And there were the uniforms of other nations. There were officers of the French Army and Navy, Belgians and Dutch, a number of Italians, and at least one Chinese officer from a small diplomatic entourage. And closer to home there were officers of the Canadian Army, and in almost comic opera uniforms, the military and naval representatives of several Central and South American republics.

There were, Lohmann noticed, no representatives of Germany, Japan or Russia. Despite United States neutrality, Madge Van Essling was an Anglophile and had chosen to ignore the German Embassy. Nor would she have any truck with the Japanese, not since the rape of Shanghai. And, as far as the Soviet Union was concerned, the thought of entertaining a Bolshevik in her home would have been anathema to Madge, she had been proud to include among her friends the late dowager Empress of Russia.

To the left of the hall, with its crowded array of guests, was a large room, the ballroom. On a dais at the end of the room an orchestra of black faces were playing 'They Can't Take That Away From Me'. Lohmann glimpsed couples shuffling around the floor, appearing vaguely bored at the procedure. To the right of the hall was another large room, even more crowded, in which there was a long bar on one side and buffet on the other.

Lohmann was surprised at how many of the faces were familiar to him; at least two other movie stars apart from Gary

Cooper. And a great number of prominent politicians.

'Sam Rayburn,' Pardoe pointed out the squarish, grizzled figure of the Texan. 'The young fellow he's talking to, he's a congressman from Texas. Lyndon something or other . . .'

Pardoe, however, was not merely pointing out celebrities. He was searching for someone. Finally his eyes settled on a tall, thin man with grey hair standing alone near the bar.

'That's the man I have to see. Alexander Sachs. I'm going to have to leave you.'

'But you will not leave without me.' This was not a question, but a statement.

Pardoe looked sideways at him. 'You worry too much.'

'I have cause.'

'I have to see this man.'

'Who . . . what is he?'

'An economist. New Deal type. With access to people in high places.'

Lohmann nodded. 'I will wait here.'

'It's a party,' Pardoe said. 'Relax. I'm not going anywhere. For God's sake, circulate.'

Pardoe left him. Alone in a crowd. He stood for some minutes. Feeling awkward.

'Hello,' said the low female voice from behind him.

He swivelled around to face blonde hair, shining under the lights of the chandelier above. The hair flowed downwards to moulded bare shoulders in almost perfect symmetry. The gown below was simple but stylish, black velvet cut low. The face, made up to appear *sans* make-up, was high cheek-boned, a face of startling and unusual beauty. Also, it was familiar to Lohmann.

'Hello!' he replied hesitantly, trying to think where had he met her, if he had indeed met her. And how could he have possibly forgotten? He searched back in his mind. London or Paris or even Berlin? No, not Berlin, nor Paris. And surely if he had met this creature in London, he would have remembered . . .

196

She seemed to read his mind. 'Captain Greenock's office,' she said with a smile. 'His secretary. Sweater, skirt, sensible shoes and only a double ring of pearls – cultured actually, but rather nice. Working clothes for an embassy girl.'

The blonde behind the desk only days ago. Then he had barely noticed her. How could that have been? Barely spoken to her. He remembered now a fleeting smile before being shown in to meet the naval attaché.

'You remember me now, Mister Lomond?' The question with a wider smile, but then, his reaction entitled her to smile.

'Of course I do.' He collected himself quickly and well or so he told himself. 'Miss . . . Miss . . .?'

'You never were told my name. Caroline . . . Caroline Norwood. Known as Caro.' The voice was pleasant; accent English, tinged with American.

'Miss Norwood.' Acknowledging her like an echo. Had he always been so awkward in front of women, he asked himself. Probably so, since his wife had died. It had taken him time to know and relax with Rue Scott-ffolliot back in England.

'Mister Lomond,' she said. 'Ernest. You see, I know your name. Documents pass across my desk.'

He thought, that's all you will know.

'Are you surprised I'm here?' she asked. 'Oh, we Embassy girls are never forgotten. Invited everywhere. We make up numbers at dinner parties, we look ornamental on occasions like this, we even meet future husbands here, if we're so inclined. And some are. Very powerful men are all around us, Mister Lomond. Power is a great aphrodisiac. As is money, and there's plenty of that around too; all with American nationality thrown in.'

'That's why you're here, Miss Norwood?'

She shook her head. 'Might be. But it's not. I have American nationality. And British nationality.'

He looked puzzled, and she saw he looked puzzled.

'My mother was American, my father was British. I was born in America – Bayonne, New Jersey. So, I have dual

197

nationality. Being British allows me a responsible job at the Embassy. And if I did want to stay on in the States, I wouldn't have to marry to do it.'

'You did give two other reasons for being here.' It was Lohmann's turn to smile.

'Actually I don't find money an aphrodisiac,' Caro Norwood went on. 'I have more than enough of it. For a secretary. Oh, all legal. I was an heiress. And, as for power, no, no aphrodisiac for me. Powerful men are too full of themselves. Interesting to study from a distance, but boring close up. No, if you wanted to know what interested me, even excited me, then I should say it was . . . mystery!'

'Mystery?'

'Like you and Captain Pardoe. Don't misunderstand me. I don't know or care what you two are doing here. But . . . but mysterious, it is. That I find exciting.'

'You'd be disappointed, Miss Norwood.'

'Caro. Call me Caro. Quicker and easier. Yes, I suppose I would probably be disappointed. But not my business . . . will never know . . . won't ask . . . in wartime, heaven forbid. But I can enjoy imagining. You know I once went out with a French diplomat – very small *fromage* but nice and I imagined he was an agent of French intelligence. We had a great time. As good friends, only. Although he did propose and I even considered it. But in the end I said no. It was just as well. He turned out to be some kind of accountant over here to check on his embassy's expenditure. What an escape! I could have ended up married to an accountant, the dullest thing in the world. Would you get me a drink? A highball.'

Lohmann blinked.

'It's a cocktail,' she said. 'Just ask at the bar.'

He did so, ordering a whisky for himself. Pardoe was at the side of the bar talking to the man called Sachs.

'He's written it,' Lohmann overheard Sachs say, in low and barely perceptible tones.

'Then why doesn't he send it?' Pardoe, asking the question.

'He, of all people knows what it might mean.'

Pardoe was about to reply when he caught Lohmann's eye. He nodded and taking Sachs by the arm, moved away towards a curtained window, an isolated spot in the crush of the room. Taking the drinks, Lohmann returned to Caroline Norwood. She was chatting to a young man who moved off as he arrived.

'My apologies,' said Lohmann. 'Was I interrupting?'

'No, no. An old acquaintance. He's something in the State Department.' She took her highball from him. 'May I show you around? Some of the sights of Washington are here.'

They moved into the ballroom. The lights were dimmed and the orchestra was playing a blues.

'Always the problem,' she said. 'When you want to see the sights, they dim the lights. Would you like to dance?'

'Are you not taking my lines from me?'

She laughed. 'I always do. My other problem. Every time I'm attracted to a man, I steal his lines and he resents it.'

'I don't resent it,' said Lohmann. 'I am just not a good dancer. But, if you wish to take the chance . . .'

He found she was easy to dance with, and it relaxed him, so that he was able to move with ease. When the orchestra ended the number, they walked from the dance floor, into the hall. And through the hall. They sat in a corner across from the buffet.

'Are you married, Mister Lomond?' she asked.

'Please don't call me Mister.'

'Ernest.'

'I hate Ernest. Lomond. Just Lomond.'

'Lomond, Okay, Lomond. Married?'

'I was. She is dead.'

'I'm sorry.'

'No. It is a long time ago.'

Why, he thought, do the conventions sound so stilted?

'That's Charles Lindbergh,' she said 'Over there. The tall thin man leaning against the pillar.'

199

He stared across at the lank figure of the aviator. The great American hero. Friend of the great and the good. And the bad.

'He disappointed me a time ago,' Lohmann replied. 'He is too friendly with the wrong people. Like Hermann Goering. And Hitler.'

'This country is neutral, Lomond.'

'It is difficult to be neutral with these people. I know them.'

Caro Norwood turned and stared up at him. 'You have a British Passport. I know that. I've seen it. But you don't sound British.

'I always thought my English was very good.'

'Oh it is, it is. But not quite . . . right. Not perfect.'

Lohmann shrugged. 'I am naturalised. I came to England as a refugee.'

'And you work for the Foreign office?' She had an expression of amused suspicion on her face. 'I didn't know foreigners could get into the diplomatic service. Even naturalised foreigners.'

'Sometimes they bring in those with specialized talents.'

'And you have specialized talents?'

'It could be said.'

Again the smile. 'I'm intrigued. I told you I like a mystery. I suppose I shouldn't ask you anything else. Official secrets and all that.'

'Something like all that.'

A pause between the two of them. Only the hubbub of the room.

She spoke first. 'I don't suppose you would tell me where you originally came from?'

'You "don't suppose" correctly.' His eyes were roving around the room.

'Spain? No, you're not Spanish. Nor are you Russian. Although you could have been a White Russian. But no. Not with that accent, however slight it is. That really only leaves –'

'I might be Lativan, Albanian, Estonian.' Still searching

200

the room with his eyes. Where Pardoe had been talking to the man Sachs, there was only Sachs, now, alone.

'But you're not. I think you're . . .'

'Can you see Captain Pardoe anywhere?' An urgency had crept into his voice. The man Pardoe had been talking to was standing alone at the bar, a mournful expression on his face. As if to say, such is the life of economists at social occasions.

Caro's eyes now searched the room. 'He's probably dancing. He'll turn up.'

'I have to find him.' Lohmann was on his feet.

'Come now, Lomond, you're not his keeper.'

He said nothing. She stood up beside him and stared into his face.

'Yes, you are,' she said. 'That's what you're here for. You're his . . . what? Keeper? Bodyguard? Something like that.'

'Good evening, Mister Lomond.'

James Henry Straight the Third, in front of them, the small figure immaculate in dinner jacket, blond hair slicked back, nothing out of place. With a strong aroma of aftershave.

'I see you have found a charming companion,' Straight went on, looking at Caroline Norwood. In the remark was a note of challenge, a competitor looking at a rival? 'Do introduce me.'

'Miss Norwood. Mister Straight.'

Straight gave a minute formal bow. 'I'm glad somebody is looking after him. Washington society is such a jungle. We should really run battle training schools to prepare the novice.'

'I think Mister Lomond will do very well,' Caro replied.

'Under your tuition, dear lady. Had he not found you, I would have been delighted to undertake the task myself. Oh, by the way Mister Hoover sends his regards.'

Lohmann was still searching the room. 'Very nice of him,' he said automatically.

'Oh, no,' said Straight. 'Hoover is never . . . nice. Also I gather he was very curious about your expedition to New Orleans. And not entirely happy.'

'Then he might arrest the criminals. I did pass on a few names.'

'And they all appear to be good Americans.'

'Excuse me,' Lohmann said, more to Caro Norwood than to Straight. 'Be back in a moment.'

He crossed to the bar and to the solitary figure of Alexander Sachs.

'Mister Sachs?'

Sachs seemed momentarily grateful for the company. 'Alexander Sachs. You are . . . ?'

A slight accent, Lohmann thought, probably Russian. Under the American. He'd been in this country a long time.

'I'm a colleague of Captain Pardoe's.'

'Captain Pardoe? I'm afraid you have the advantage of me. I do not know a Captain Pardoe.' The face was impassive. He was good. Admirable self-control.

'The British naval officer you were speaking to,' Lohmann explained.

'Was I? 'Sachs replied. 'So many people here. I don't recall a British naval officer.'

Lohmann felt cold. The man lying.

'A few minutes ago. You were talking to him. Over there, by the window.'

'You're mistaken. Someone else, sir, surely. I'm sorry. You'll excuse me. I see an old friend . . .' He moved off, to greet a tall young man, a thatch of hair hanging over a broad forehead.

Lohmann recrossed the room, easing his way through the throng. Still feeling cold. Back to Straight and Caroline Norwood.

'Lomond, Miss Norwood was telling me you're looking for Bobby Pardoe,' Straight said. 'But I just saw him outside in the hall.'

'In the hall?' Lohmann said, relief flooding through him. It was however a momentary sensation, as Straight went on.

'He was just leaving. Seemed quite preoccupied. Not that I thought anything of it, knowing you would not be far behind.'

The chill again. 'He was leaving?' Alarm bells rang in his head.

Lohmann turned to Caroline Norwood. 'You'll have to excuse me.'

She returned his look as he started to move away. 'I think I'll come with you,' she said. 'I may be able to help.'

As they moved away, Straight stared after them. 'Have fun, both of you!'

In the hall, Lohmann looked wildly around. 'He came in my car. How would he go?'

Caroline hurried up to the fat butler. 'The British naval officer. Captain Pardoe. He just left?'

'The British officer. Yes, miss. Some twenty minutes ago.'

'How?'

'We called him a taxi, miss. At his own request. He looked rather agitated. Taken unwell, I thought.'

Lohmann was at her side. Tight lipped. 'Damn!' he said under his breath.

It was her turn to stare at him. 'It's important?'

'It may be. Where the devil has he gone?'

'His hotel?'

'I only hope so.'

'You're very concerned. As his keeper?'

'Yes.'

'Then we'll find out where he has gone. And go after him.'

EIGHTEEN

Caroline Norwood was as good as her word. She asked the butler to find out where the cab had been ordered from and the name of the driver. They waited, Lohmann feeling suddenly weary. The woman, this embassy secretary, was exhibiting an efficiency which he found oddly lacking in himself. In Berlin, he would have been on to the cab driver, Reiner would have found him and brought him at once to police headquarters. Now it was left to a secretary not just to ask the questions, but to think of them in the first place.

The butler returned five minutes later to inform her that the driver had been contacted. He was returning from another fare and would be as quick as he could in reaching the Van Essling home.

As quick as he could was another twenty minutes. He was a small dark man with a distinctly un-Washington accent. He greeted them with a scowl.

'So what's it all about? Dere's other cabs waiting here. Why call me back? Was on my way home.'

Lohmann took over, recovering something of his former confidence. 'You took a British naval officer as a fare some three quarters of an hour ago?'

'Did I? Maybe. Maybe not. Take a lot o'guys a lot of places. Don't have to look at 'em. What's it to ya?'

'I want to know where you took him.'

The man bridled. 'The passenger got his rights. Where the guy goes is his business.'

Caroline was standing at Lohmann's side. It was starting to rain now, turning the thin layer of snow underfoot to slush. She ignored it.

'We really do have to find out where he has gone.' she insisted, affecting a wistful urgency.

It had no effect on the driver. He was a New Yorker, born in Brooklyn, enjoying showing off his native intransigence to these denizens of the good life in Washington. Who did they think they were? The guy all dressed up in fancy pants; the broad, like some high grade whore. But he was determined to show them he was not without honour in this modern Babylon.

'Look, lady, cab drivers is like dese professional guys, doctors, lawyers. The customer is entitled to his privacy,' said with head erect, and an assumption of prideful disdain.

Again Caroline made the next move. She opened her velvet evening bag and extracted a ten dollar bill. The driver looked at it, conflicting emotions on his face. But the conflict was minimal and the stronger emotion dominated, he took the bill.

'Picked the guy up from here about an hour ago. Dressed like some kind of commissionaire widout too much braid? And a Limey accent?'

'That is the man,' said Lohmann.' Where did you take him?'

But the driver ignored Lohmann. He beckoned Caroline towards him and, leaning from the cab window, whispered in her ear. After all, it was her ten dollars. She straightened up and stared down at him.

'You took him there?' she said.

'Where he wanted to go, lady.'

'Will you take us?' Lohmann cut in. 'Wait for us and bring us back?'

'Listen, buddy, I can take you dere. But I ain't waiting around dat neighbourhood. Dey take the sidewalks in at night dere in case somebody steals them. I wait for you, the cab goes, bit by bit. I open my mouth, dese guys down dere give

205

me a second mouth under my chin wid a shiv.'

'It's no use asking him.' Caroline said. 'You've got your car. I know how to get there.'

Lohmann turned to beckon a page, fumbled in his pocket, produced his car keys and handed them over to the page under the beady eyes of the cab driver.

'So yuh call me back here and den use your own lousy auto. Dat ain't nice.'

This time Lohmann reached in his pocket and handed the man a further ten dollars. This seemed to satisfy him. He nodded towards Caroline.

'You gonna take the broad down to dat place?'

Lohmann, looking out for the arrival of his own car, ignored the question. He did not know how to answer it. Caroline Norwood knew the address and presumably the route. It was necessary that he take her with him. Also she was willing.

'You don't know dis town, buddy. Wouldn't take King Kong down dere dis time night. Not widout a company of US marines.' The cab shot off down the drive.

'What did he mean?'

'He's the nervous type.'

'There's reason I should not take you there?'

'There's a reason you should. You don't know the way and I do.'

Lohmann nodded but without certainty. He wished he'd brought Reiner with him.

Two minutes later, his car arrived. 'If I drive, it might be quicker,' Caroline suggested.

He handed her the keys. They drove onto Massachusetts Avenue. 'This place we are going to, why did the taxi driver think I should not take you there?' Lohmann asked. 'Where are we going?'

She drove the heavy car without effort.

'Into Washington's ghetto,' she said.

'There is a Jewish ghetto?'

Caroline laughed. 'Not Jewish. The black area, negro district.'

'Ah, yes.'

'It's a very poor district. And dangerous. If you're white.'

They drove in silence now, Lohmann preoccupied by his own thoughts. What had prompted Pardoe to leave without telling his watcher? Why the negro district? Something to do with his mission? Highly unlikely. Something to do with another part of his being, the part that held questions to which only he knew the answers? The part that concerned his name in Antoinette Valois' address book back in England, a dead prostitute in Singapore, another in Washington, and the dead girl in Georgetown? Four violent deaths haunting one man. Not coincidence. Impossible that it was coincidence. Back in Berlin, before Hitler turned a beautiful city into a nightmare, Pardoe would have been in his own small nightmare by this time, in detention, being interrogated . . .

. . . except that the man was on some mission of importance to the pursuance of the war.

The car turned into a long narrow street of dark and decaying tenements. Half the street lights were broken, those that survived cast a feeble light over damp sidewalks strewn with the refuse of a society in seemingly permanent despair. A broken-down car sagged on its bare metallic wheels against the kerbside, windows long since smashed, bodywork long since dented and twisted, like a mutilated body abandoned, unburied.

Caroline drew up some distance past the wreck, at the dark entry to one of the tenements. Five storeys towered above ground level. There was no one in sight. As if the street had been drained of humanity, was waiting for something to happen.

'This is the number,' she said. 'Twenty-seven. Where the cab dropped Pardoe.'

Lohmann looked out of the car window. 'Not like the rest of Washington,' he said.

'This *is* the rest of Washington. More people live like this than like that.'

He nodded sourly, still checking the building. 'It seems deserted. You will wait for me?'

'It only seems deserted, Lomond. The people are here. You wouldn't expect them to stand out in the rain and the sleet? In the summer, this would be a hive. I think I should come with you.'

'I'll be perfectly all right.'

'It's not you I'm thinking about. It's not only old cars they strip around here.'

Lohmann opened the car door and stepped onto the wet surface of the road. Out of the corner of his eye he thought he saw a movement from an alley on the other side of the road, then decided he was mistaken. He patted his coat, feeling the comforting shape of Hod Gramercy's Smith and Wesson in the band of his trousers. It was large and uncomfortable but he was grateful he'd thought to bring it with him.

'The police are not in evidence,' he said.

'The police know better. When they come down here, they come in cars and in force.'

She joined him on the sidewalk. At the same time her eyes roved the street. There was still no one in sight.

'They're there,' she said, as if in answer to an unasked question. 'They're there, and they want to know why we're here.'

'Then let us find Pardoe and get away from this place.' He was nervous now. This empty street and its dark tenements induced nervousness. He eased the Smith and Wesson out of the waist band and into a damp palm. Still keeping it under his coat. The entry to the building gaped in front of them. A black hole in a black universe.

They went in.

The walls gave the entry an unhealthy damp odour. The blackness gave way to a pale sliver of light filtering through the transom above one of the two doors at the end.

'Which door?' said Lohmann. 'Did the cab driver tell you?'

'We go by guess and by God,' Caroline replied.

They moved forward. From the door with an illuminated transom they could hear voices. Harsh grating American, a Negro couple, voices raised in argument . . .

'God damn you, mudderfucking bitch, you always putting yo' nose in my business.'

'Doan know nothin' bout yo business. I's too busy wid my own business. Which be waitin' for you to hand over my dough.'

'Ain't no dough . . .'

'What you do wid it? I knows what you do. Gave it to dat fat cow, always sashyin' round you. Gave our money away to a whore.'

'If I did, it be cos I don't get nothin' from you . . .'

Lohmann peered at Caroline. 'Not that one, I think,' he observed in a half whisper.

'That one?' said Caroline, nodding to the other door.

'Could be so. But no lights. We better try upstairs.'

The stairs were rickety. Wood embedded on wood. *Honky go home!* was sprayed on one wall amidst scattered scrawls and other laboriously etched graffiti now just visible, as their eyes became used to the gloom.

They climbed the stairs which protested at their doing so with creaks and groans. On the first landing they were faced with three doors. Lohmann, with a slight shrug, moved as if to knock on the nearest. His companion grabbed his arm.

'No!' she said. 'Not yet. Best go to the top floor, see if there's any sign of which one he might have gone into. Best do it that way. Might find him without antagonising the others.'

They climbed to the next landing. Three doors and little light filtering through to the hallway. From behind one door the sound of a man singing off key.

'Bess, you is ma woman now. . .'

They climbed slowly, in silence. On the top landing two doors were firmly shut, the transoms in darkness.

The third door was half open.

Beyond the door, darkness. Caroline glanced at Lohmann and strode forward. But before she reached the door he pulled her back.

'You do not walk into the dark without care.' He drew the Smith and Wesson from his coat. He moved towards the open door and reached in to where there should be a light switch. He groped for some seconds before finding and depressing it. A bright light flooded the landing, dazzling them. Lohmann took a step backwards a moment before his eyes adjusted to the light.

The door opened directly into the brightly lit room. Now Lohmann stepped inside, Caroline behind him. He'd expected a run-down, seedy apartment living-room. Instead he was standing in a bright, garish room, striped wallpaper, deep soft armchairs covered in gaudy floral pattern, a print of a nude in an explicit pose on the wall in front of him. A cheap, flashy drinks cabinet was open, bottles on display. Another print on the wall to his right, a semi-nude briefly clad in leather.

'Looks like a whore's front room,' Caroline said. 'Not that I've ever been in one.'

'You have now,' Lohmann replied. 'That is exactly what it is.'

To his left was a door, ajar, leading to a shower room and a tiny kitchen. The shower room was not in the original design but built in from a section of the living room. Money had been spent renovating this apartment, however tasteless it might be. He doubted if any of the other apartments in the building were like this.

Another door to his right was shut. The bedroom, presumably. Lohmann walked towards it.

'Maybe this is the wrong apartment,' Caroline said, 'Not the kind of place Captain Pardoe would want to come to.'

'In which case we will have some explaining to do. But somehow I think this is the place.'

He opened the door. The room was in darkness.

But he knew at once he was not alone.

He didn't hear the breathing at once. It was simply a sense that someone was in the room. And there was an odour too, a sweet, sickly, musty aroma; and more, an under-smell, even more unpleasant. It was then he heard the breathing. Almost sobbing, coarse and deep, someone trying to control the breathing without much success.

Lohmann felt for the light switch and pressed it down.

Pardoe sat in a corner on a low stool in front of a cheap dressing table, his back reflected in the mirror behind him. And something else reflected there too, behind the image of Pardoe. First things first, Lohmann told himself. Concentrate on Pardoe.

He was still wearing his heavy coat, dress uniform underneath. His cap was on his lap in front of him. His face was drawn and tense.

He looked up. 'Sorry Lomond,' he said hoarsely. 'Didn't mean to desert you. But . . . but I got this message. To come here. And I couldn't find you in that crowd. So I just came on . . . here . . .'

His face cracked, seams appearing, mouth contorting. He looked across the room to the large bed.

Lohmann followed his eyes. Knowing what he was going to see. With a feeling of *déjà vu*.

I have been here before. Not only in Georgetown in the Neuberg girl's apartment. But before that, in Germany. Has anyone ever worked out the amount of times people are slain in bedrooms. How often had he, Ernst Lohmann been here. Senior officer in charge of criminal investigation, viewing the scene of the homicide. In reality enough times, in dreams over and over again.

She'd been a big woman, five foot ten or eleven, in her late twenties. She wasn't black but a deep chocolate brown. She was on her back, stark naked on a gaily coloured patchwork counterpane, a cover of many colours. But if the colours were many, they were marred by an uneven spread of rusty brown around the body. And also on the body. Large breasts spilled over her sides, nipples prominent. Between the breasts was the cut, a valley of dried brown blood and ravaged tissue, reaching down across the belly towards the pubic hair above the *mons Veneris*. The incision was clean and even, the outer skin cut but not torn. Above the torso, the face had an expression of surprise on it, dead eyes open staring at the ceiling, a questioning expression in them.

She had, to Lohmann's professional eye, been dead for some hours.

NINETEEN

Behind him, Lohmann heard a sharp intake of breath. Caroline Norwood was standing in the doorway staring past him at the body on the bed. On her face was a look, not so much of horror as of fascinated curiosity. It was an odd reaction, he thought. Yet he was glad she hadn't screamed. Too often he'd heard the scream of a woman at the scene of a crime. It always vaguely unnerved him at a time when he needed all his concentration.

'She's dead,' Caroline said, an entirely unnecessary statement of the obvious.

'If she's not dead, she would be making medical history,' he replied, with unusual callousness. While he had trained himself years before to be completely impersonal as regards the victims of violent crime, he could not resist a tone of acidity in his voice. She was too self-assured. Too unemotional. It unnerved him almost as much as if she had

212

screamed. He wished devoutly she was somewhere else.

Her head swivelled around to Pardoe, sitting head in hands. 'And . . . and he killed her?' A statement of fact tinged with awe. No horror, no disgust.

A cool lady.

Lohmann said: 'I don't think so. She's been dead for some time.'

Now she turned to face him. 'How can you know that?'

'The blood has long since dried.' He turned to Pardoe. 'This message you received – how and from whom?'

Pardoe looked up again, eyes dark and strained. 'Telephone call.'

'Somebody who knew you'd be at the Van Essling party?'

'Anybody could find that out. Simply telephone the Embassy. They knew where I was.'

'So who was the caller?'

'Said he was a man I know. Or rather I know of. Said to meet him at this address.'

'And you came like the sacrificial lamb . . . To one of the poorer districts in the city?'

Pardoe tried to straighten his shoulders and sit up. Without much success. He seemed merely to squirm in the chair. It was an attempt at mild indignation.

'I . . . I've never been in here before. How could I know what it would be like?'

'By looking when you arrived in your taxi.'

'The man might have been . . . in hiding.'

'What was his name?'

Pardoe hesitated. 'A man called Szilard. At least he said he was Szilard.'

'An American?'

'Hungarian originally. He worked in Germany for a time, but after Hitler came to power he became a refugee.'

'He told you he was a refugee?'

'It was known. Szilard is quite well known.'

Lohmann took a deep breath, looking around the room.

Nothing much to see. Nothing out of the ordinary. Except the body. And the blood. The dressing table was untidy, the disarray of an untidy woman. Pots of cream, make-up, powder and a box of tissues.

'So this man, Szilard, phoned and asked you to meet him here?'

'Yes. At least . . .' Pardoe hesitated, looking uncertain.

'At least what?' Lohmann pressed on.

'You see . . . I've never actually met Mister Szilard. I've heard of him and . . . and he is important to . . .'

'To what?'

'The reason I'm in America. I've written him, spoken to him on the telephone twice. Oh, I don't know . . . it's just . . .' He hesitated again, shaking his head. A puzzle?

'Again, what, Captain Pardoe? Is this Szilard friendly to you?'

'Oh yes. He's part of it all. Perhaps it all started with him.'

'Part of what?'

Pardoe shrugged without replying.

'Yet there is something else worrying you?' Lohmann went on.

'You never give up, do you, Lomond?'

'I hope not. There is more, yes?'

'Maybe. Probably. You see it sounded . . . yes, it sounded like Szilard but . . . but now I'm not so sure. It could . . . just might have been someone imitating him.'

'Why do you say that?'

Pardoe looked up, suddenly angry. 'Well, for God's sake, he's not here, is he? He tells me to come here and he'll be waiting. But he isn't. There's only . . . that!' With a nod towards the body on the bed.

'So you think you were deliberately lured here?'

'What else?'

'Do you know the . . . the victim?'

'Never seen her before in my life.'

Lohmann contemplated the body. A well-built young

woman. A waste of a life, whoever and whatever she was. He remembered so many such sights in his past. Dead bodies, young and old, the deaths, every one, an exercise in futility. Why? To satisfy another's perverse passion? Or for other reasons, as yet unknown.

'You'll not turn up in her address book, then,' Lohmann said acidly.

'I told you . . .!'

'All right, all right.' Lohmann walked around the bed, eyes on the floor. Then he knelt and looked under the bed. After a moment he straightened up.

'What are you looking for? Someone hiding?' Caroline asked with a touch of acid humour.

'The weapon. Knife, scalpel, whatever.' He gently lifted the counterpane and looked under. Then he turned away.

'Nothing. You didn't see a weapon when you came in, Pardoe?'

'No.'

'So, whoever did it took the weapon with him. Which means he could use it again.'

She returned the smile. Too easily, he thought, with a corpse in front of her.

'What do we do?' Caroline asked, a kind of excitement returning to her face. 'Phone the police?'

'You would wish to increase Captain Pardoe's predicament? Implicate him in another murder? Create a diplomatic incident?'

'Of course not.'

'Then we should go from here. As fast as we can. If the car is still in one piece. Pardoe, come.'

The car was still in one piece. The street still appeared to be empty. Yet instinctively Lohmann braced himself, fingered the Smith and Wesson. They crossed the sidewalk to the car, Lohmann leading the way.

A figure appeared in front of the car.

'T'ink you gonna go off jest like that, honky?'

The voice came from behind them. Lohmann spun around on his heel, adrenalin suddenly flowing. *I have been here before*. The inevitability was monotonous. *Why do I allow myself. . . ?* Somewhere there was a quiet life translating Goethe, Rilke, so many others, a quiet, non-violent life.

The voice, made flesh, was a tall black youth. Over six feet and muscular. Shoulders that could carry oxen, not that he would ever have seen an ox. The large body was dressed in dungarees over a polo-necked sweater and crumpled, stained trousers.

'Why should we not go?' Lohmann replied, glancing briefly at the youth's eyes. He wasn't going to hold that gaze; that would have been accepting a kind of challenge. If he tried it and looked away first, it would be considered a weakness. And it would only anger the black youth to force him to look away. Instead Lohmann coolly looked around. There were eight of them now. The man between them and the car, the big black youth, and three others on each side. An intimidating circle. All were large and black, all were young, about nineteen or so.

So often before, he thought again. Not black, but equally aggressive. Berlin in the twenties. The street gangs robbing to live, and not just to live. They always began to enjoy it; the violence, the excitement, the risks. They'd been drawn into the master race, violence given legality. In the SS, in the SA, in the army. But not here in Washington DC.

The big youth was taking his time to reply. Grinning and enjoying it.

Finally he replied. 'You in our territory, man. Don't know what you is doin' here, but it gotta cost you.'

Lohmann reached in his pocket and took out a ten dollar bill.

The youth grinned. 'Kinda cheapskate, that. What do you say, boys?'

Murmurs of agreement from his seven followers.

'You tell him, Billy.' From the one in front of the car.

'See, mister,' said the youth called Billy. 'Mean t'say, jest look at yous. Fancy tuxedo, fancy uniform and fancy lady. Ten dollars, that's a kind of insult. Might get away with it with white boys, but not with us.'

'What do you suggest, then?' said Lohmann.

'All the money you got might jest get you outta here.'

'Now, look here . . .' Pardoe began.

'Shut up, mister fancy uniform, or we mebbe cut you. I'm talkin' to the man.' A nod towards Lohmann.

'And if we did give you all the money we have . . . ' Lohmann asked.

'We might jest let you go. We might not. Or the lady there, she might jest want to stay and entertain us. Then we'd let her come home to you boys in the morning. But if you don't give us all that dough in your wallets, jest come to the same thing anyway. Only you might get cut up. Might even end up dead.'

He's an articulate young bastard, Lohmann told himself. He glanced at Caroline, and for the first time that night her face was ashen. She was tense, trying to stop herself from trembling. He couldn't blame her for that. These eight youths didn't often see dressed up, prosperous-looking whites in their territory in the small hours. Their appearance on a cold night was some kind of delinquents' bonus.

Lohmann cleared his throat. 'I will tell you what I'm going to do, Billy. It is Billy? Yes, it is. I will tell you now.'

'The black youth's grin widened. 'Cain't wait to hear.'

Lohmann took the Smith and Wesson from under his coat. The grin became slightly more set but stayed in place. 'Well, well, honky's got a big cannon. My, oh, my! See the big cannon, boys. Not that it do him much good. Mebbe get one, two shots off at the most, mebbe hit one of us, so what's a small hole, and then we got the three of you.'

Lohmann, feeling less like grinning than ever before, nevertheless forced himself to smile, matching the youth. As if the body upstairs in the tenement wasn't enough. . .

'You're right,' he said. 'I'd get one, maybe two of you. And

217

then you'd have us. But consider this, my friend. I wouldn't try and shoot anyone else. Only you. I'm a good shot. The first will be a belly shot. Have you ever been shot in the belly?'

The smile disappeared from the youth's face. Lohmann didn't wait for an answer but went on. 'Of course it probably won't kill you. Certainly not at once. But the pain is terrible. And it lasts. Afterwards you walk doubled up for a long time. And you never forget the pain. With luck I'll get a second shot, lower down. It will take off your testicles and probably the other thing. You'll be useless to the ladies for the rest of your life.'

The black face was tense. The youth laughed but it was a forced, nervous laugh. 'You t'ink you can shoot that good?'

'I know I can. Medals and a cup to prove it. Oh, your boys will get us, but you won't. You'll be hurting very badly. Most people with a belly wound will tell you they'd rather have been shot dead.'

He levelled the gun at the youth's midriff. Except for the splash of water dripping from a tenement roof into a rain barrel, there was no sound. Lohmann could feel the eight pairs of eyes fixed on them. Waiting for word from their leader. Two knife blades glinted in the dark. One youth was staring openly at Caroline Norwood, a look of anticipation on his face.

Then the big youth seemed to relax. He spread his hands out, palms upwards. 'Hey man, you ain't US citizens, is you?'

'No, we're not.'

'Could tell. Could tell from the fancy accents. Where you from?'

Pardoe answered. 'We're British citizens.'

'Limeys, eh? Well then, we ain't unfriendly to foreigners. We just don't want honkys wandering around our territory. Supposin' I jest allow you folks to get into your car an' drive 'way. You sure won't come back here.'

'We wouldn't,' said Lohmann.

'Okay, then. Freddy, let them pass.'

The youth in front of the car hesitated. One of the others swore.

'Fuck it, Billy, that ain't no fun!'

'Freddy! Move! And Joey, you just button your lip.'

Grudgingly Freddy moved away. The others relaxed, except for the one called Joey, a natural dissident.

'You jest let 'em walk away?'

'They is visitors, Joey. So I let them walk away. You wanna make something of it?'

Joey's dissent stopped at wanting to make 'something of it'. Lohmann indicated that they get into the car. Caroline took the driver's seat, Lohmann at her side and Pardoe climbed into the back.

'Move, before they change their minds,' said Lohmann quietly.

Later that night, they were in Pardoe's room at the Mayflower, joined by Reiner, whom Lohmann had wakened from his bed. Pardoe was sitting, as he had been in the bedroom of the dead woman's apartment, eyes bleak, staring into the middle distance. Somewhere else.

Caroline Norwood had ordered coffee from room service and sat in a corner, cup held in both hands. Shivering still from delayed shock. At the body or at the threat the black youths had presented, Lohmann could not decide, but thought it was probably the youths. She had been too cool in the presence of the body. When she had finished her coffee, she asked Reiner to call her a cab to take her home. Lohmann did not object.

When he came back to the room. Reiner poured more coffee for the three of them. Lohmann turned to the dazed Pardoe.

'I want you to listen to me, Captain. I am going to outline my problems to you. You may then be able to help. Or otherwise. But you will know the problems.' He launched into a recital of events and Pardoe's involvement. 'A

219

prostitute killed in Singapore. Another in London. A third in Washington. Then Senator Neuberg's daughter.'

'Wait a minute,' said Reiner. 'The pattern is broken here, she was not a prostitute.'

'True, Reiner,' said Lohmann. 'But not entirely broken. Miss Neuberg had many male friends. And a number of affairs. Our murderer does not perhaps differentiate between the amateur and the professional. Again also in this case, while Captain Pardoe left for New Orleans the morning after the killing, he is uncertain how he spent the night.'

'In bed, here. I think,' Pardoe said, running his hands through his hair.

'Through all this we know you are subject to fugues, Captain. Brief blackouts. Temporary lapses of memory. So, we have little definite evidence against you – even the button from a British naval uniform on the Neuberg girl's apartment is circumstantial. You agree?'

'I suppose so.'

'However, the circumstantial evidence is strong. You were in place, shall we say, when all these women were killed. And they were all killed by the same method.'

'But . . . why . . . why would I kill them?' Pardoe burst out plaintively.

'That we don't know. If you did commit these crimes, perhaps only a psychiatrist could tell us. But – there was one other person in these places at the same time as the women were killed. James Henry Straight the Third.'

'You don't think Jimmy would . . . ?'

'We have no evidence, Pardoe. It is simply that he was in the cities when the crimes occurred. A very slim chance, but we keep it in mind.'

'There may have been someone else too,' Reiner said quietly.

Lohmann swung around in his chair to face his old assistant. 'Who?'

'Told you I had connections in the FBI back home. My

connection has connections. The British agent at the Embassy, Charles Markham, he too was in Singapore when the whore was murdered.'

'He told me so.' said Lohmann.

'But did he tell you he was back in London when the killing occurred there?'

'No.'

'And he could just have been in Washington when the other two were done. But I have to check on that.'

'Do so.' Lohmann turned back to Pardoe. 'So we come to tonight. The black girl is dead in her apartment and you are called there. Why? To frame you? Perhaps. But the girl had been dead for some hours. So it appears you are clear of this crime. So far. It is a point in your favour.'

'I'm glad something is,' said Pardoe. 'Could I have some more coffee?'

Reiner poured him a tepid coffee. 'You want me to order another pot?'

Pardoe shook his head. 'This'll do. Go on, Mister Lomond. It's fascinating to see oneself as a possible mass murderer.'

'That is the serial murder case,' Lohmann sat back and accepted a cigarette from Reiner. 'Now we come to what may well have no connection with these killings. That is, your mission in America. That has already resulted in two other killings, which you had nothing to do with – Professor Duplessis and the man in the cemetery in New Orleans. It is just possible you killed Duplessis but I doubt it. So . . .' Lohmann inhaled deeply from the cigarette '. . . we come to the mission itself. It is time, Pardoe, I knew more about it.'

Pardoe swallowed a mouthful of coffee, avoiding looking at Lohmann. 'I told you, it was on a "need to know" basis.'

'No longer good enough, Pardoe. Someone tried to frame you tonight. In New Orleans, Duplessis died. I want to know why.'

Pardoe clattered his coffee cup onto his saucer. 'All right, all right! I'll tell you some of it. I just have to think where to start.'

'Start with Duplessis.'

'Yes, well . . . he was an old friend of Franklin Roosevelt. I have to get certain people to the President to . . . to convey certain information to him.'

'Why not use the British Ambassador?'

'I told you before. The United Kingdom, as a belligerent, must not be seen to be involved. We were planning to use Duplessis to get to the President.'

'We? Who is we?'

'Szilard and . . . and others.'

Szilard and who else, Lohmann asked himself. But decided to let it pass for the time being. 'The Germans know of this mission?'

'No! No, there is no reason to think they do.'

'Yes they probably killed Duplessis. And are trying to stop you. They must know.'

'They can't.'

'But they could know about you. And want to know why you are here.'

'How could they?'

'Your friend Straight is very curious to know why you are here.'

Pardoe looked up, irritated. 'He's an FBI man. He's not on the German side. They've even been arresting German agents in America.'

'Perhaps with some reluctance?' Lohmann suggested. 'Hoover is a very careful man. I do not think he's keen to antagonise the isolationist and pro-German elements in America.'

'Waiting to see which way the cookie crumbles,' Reiner added with a smile. Lohmann glared at him; the phrase was foreign to him. He turned back to Pardoe.

'Your mission . . . the next step?'

'I have another way of getting Szilard to Roosevelt. I

222

have to go to my second source.'

'That is . . . ?'

Pardoe hesitated again. 'Look, Lomond, I don't want to find my second source dead on my arrival.'

'You know I shall accompany you.'

'Yes, of course.' Pardoe glanced across at Reiner. 'You will know the man when we get there. Day after tomorrow.'

'Very well. But you go nowhere without me. Understood?'

'All right. Nowhere without you. Now I would like to get some sleep.'

Lohmann rose and Reiner did likewise. 'I'll see you tomorrow, Captain.'

In the deserted corridor, Reiner said, 'I've been working for you, chief.'

'Tell me.'

'The man you wanted me to check up on. Colescott.'

'Go on.'

'James A. Colescott. Formerly a veterinarian. From Terre Haute, Indiana. Been in the Ku Klux Klan for 14 years. Became Imperial Wizard, the Klan's top man, last June. Worked for a time in the Indiana political machine. Says he's against hangings and floggings.'

'He didn't seem so when I met him,' observed Lohmann.

'Well, he's a broad-minded man in a narrow kind of way,' Reiner replied. 'He is rumoured to have had connections with the Amerika-Deutscher Volksbund a few years ago. Was friendly with Fritz Julius Kuhn, their leader. But Kuhn went to prison for embezzlement early this year and Colescott then became very close to his successor, William Kunze. Also I heard Colescott went down to New Orleans a few days ago.'

'Duplessis, you mean?'

'It all shows that Colescott, through Kunze, may well have connections with the German Embassy and German intelligence.'

'That would be logical,' said Lohmann. 'I should like to meet Kunze.'

223

'I thought you might, chief. It just so happens there's a public meeting of the Bund in Washington tomorrow. You would like to go?'

'It might be awkward if Colescott was there.'

'He's still in New Orleans.'

'Then I'll certainly go. Under the name on my other passport. Muller.'

'And I'm sure Kunze would like to meet Herr Bruno Muller, a new visitor from Germany. Tomorrow?'

'Tomorrow. Good night, Reiner. And good work.'

'You never said that back in Germany.'

'Perhaps you didn't do any good work in those days!'

Lohmann let himself into his room. And, even before he could put the light on, became aware he was not alone.

TWENTY

The damp sweat of fear rose on the back of Lohmann's neck. He reached for the Smith and Wesson and moved sideways out of the doorway, aware he had been a perfect target, silhouetted against the light from the corridor.

'No need for panic, my dear Lomond,' said the familiar voice. 'And please put the gun away. So dangerous, these guns . . . and so phallic.'

Lohmann switched on the light. James Henry Straight the Third was lounging in an armchair at the foot of the bed, still elegant in his immaculate tuxedo.

'What are you doing here?' Lohmann said, quietly angry.

'Came to see you, old man.'

224

'How did you get in?'

'The FBI runs courses in picking locks. Doors are easy. One course I made sure I took. Told myself it would certainly come in useful. Especially for getting into hotel bedrooms. Thought I'd just wait here for you in comfort. You see, I just wanted a word.'

'You always wait in a dark room?'

'The light was too bright. Hurts these old, alcoholic peepers of mine.'

'What do you want?'

'Among other things, to assure myself you arrived home safely from your little trip to beautiful downtown Washington. Incidentally, I thought you handled the coloured boys rather well. Would have been such a pity if you'd shot the big one. Especially the second shot you threatened. He was such a beautiful specimen. Oh, the waste if you had shot him.'

'You were there?'

Straight produced a gold cirgarette case, offered it to Lohmann. 'American that side, Turkish the other. That's what they always say in these dreadful E. Phillips Oppenheim novels about spies. Do have one.'

'No thank you.'

Straight selected a cigarette for himself, lit it with a matching gold lighter and slipped the case back into his pocket.

'Of course I was there. But, knowing the district, I kept a low profile. I've been there often. What do they say . . . looking for a bit of rough? But one has to be rather careful.'

'How did you know we were there?'

'I followed you from the Van Esslings' of course. Curiosity. And being an agent of Mister Hoover, even if only part-time, it could be said to be my job. I saw the dead woman, too. After you'd gone. It appears Captain Pardoe has been at it again.'

'If you saw her, you'd know that was not so. The woman had been dead for hours. Pardoe couldn't have . . .'

'Of course he could. Have you asked him what he was doing this afternoon?' Lohmann suddenly felt sick. 'While you were in your office this afternoon, Captain Pardoe went out. You see, we have a man keeps an eye on the British Embassy – for the Embassy's protection, of course. And Mister Hoover does like to know what everybody's up to. Oh yes, Pardoe went out while you were presumably in your office.'

'You know where he went?'

'He's a very clever man, Pardoe. Our man tried to follow him but he lost him. In the Smithsonian Museum. From there Pardoe could quite easily have gone to the tenement to visit the negro lady.'

'You don't know that he did.'

Straight drew on his cigarette. It was one of the Turkish variety, with a heavy acrid odour.

'No, I don't. But I don't know that he didn't. All I'm saying, Mister Lomond, is that he had the time and the opportunity.'

'Why would he go back there this evening?'

'Who knows? Perhaps he left something there he had to go back for. As he could have done at the Neuberg killing. Left a button there, didn't he?'

'Or one was planted.'

'Of course, that is a possibility. But don't you think it has become too coincidental. Every time we have one of these killings, Pardoe is around. Singapore, London, Washington?'

'Other people are around too.'

Straight raised one eyebrow. 'Really? Who?'

'James Henry Straight the Third, for one.'

Straight sat up. 'My dear Lomond . . .'

There was phlegm at the back of Lohmann's throat. He wondered whether he had said too much. Still, he pressed on. 'Singapore, London, Washington. You were there.'

Straight rose to his feet. 'You surely don't think . . .'

'Like Pardoe, you're a possibility.'

With an expression of distress on his face, Straight stubbed

226

out his cigarette on an ashtray at his side. 'It's hardly my . . . thing. My bag, as they say. Carving up ladies? Really, Lomond. Couldn't this be that Germanic imagination of yours?'

'You too were around. Fact.'

'Yes, but . . .'

'Where were you, yesterday afternoon?'

'I . . . I was . . . I was at the movies.'

'Alone?'

'Yes. Alone. I was just . . . just passing time until the Van Essling party.'

'Were you? Or were you in downtown Washington? You have admitted you knew the area. Probably better than Pardoe. Oh, yes, you could have been there.'

Straight's thin frame was shivering now. And the shivering was distinctly visible. 'I told you, I was at the movies.'

'Which cinema? What did you see?'

'The . . . the Circle, yes that was the one. I think. On Pennsylvania Avenue. I saw . . . oh, what was it . . . ? I should be expected to know the title . . . yes, I remember . . . it was a revival. Of *G-Men*. James Cagney, Barton MacLane. Big man . . . marvellously ugly. Barton MacLane . . .' His voice tapered off. He was staring down at the carpet.

'Did anybody see you?'

'Lomond, or Lohmann, or whatever your name is – I'm not a suspect in these killings . . .'

'Maybe not to the FBI, but you are to me. Did anybody see you?'

'How should I know?'

A long silence. From somewhere out in the city there came the faint sound of a police siren. Straight lit another cigarette. His hand trembled as he lit it. Lohmann thought, first time he'd seen the man discomfited. It gave him some degree of satisfaction.

'I should be going now,' Straight said. 'It's late and . . . and it's been a long day.'

Lohmann acknowledged the statement. 'We'll talk again.'

Straight looked up quickly. 'Remember, I'm the one who has always tried to help Bob Pardoe. In Singapore, here in Washington. Me! Helping. Remember that.'

'It's a good tactical move, Straight.'

Straight went slowly, almost reluctantly, to the door. He stopped, hand on the doorknob.

'I . . . I informed the FBI of that black woman's murder. They'll be there tonight. I didn't mention you or Pardoe or that woman of yours being there.'

'Good of you.'

'It would have made everything so complicated.'

'Did you tell them why you were there?'

He stood erect now, some of his confidence back. He gave a small sad affectation of a smile. 'Oh, I didn't tell them it was me. I made an anonymous telephone call. Rather naughty of me. But I couldn't think what else to do. You see, I was protecting you and Pardoe.'

'And yourself.'

Straight shrugged and went out, shutting the door behind him.

Phlegm returned to Lohmann's throat, nausea to his body. He felt exhausted, a feeling of desolation taking over. Despite the horror of finding the black woman's body, there had been a sense of relief at noting she had been dead for some time. That fact alone seemed to exonerate Pardoe; and might well provide the first break in the line of circumstantial evidence that pointed to him. But now Straight's story had brought back all the previous suspicions. Where had Pardoe been that afternoon? Another question to be answered. Or was Straight simply redirecting suspicion away from himself?

Questions without answers. He should be used to that. But this case was different. His task was to protect his chief suspect, at least for the time being. And afterwards? Afterwards there was to be no diplomatic incident. If Pardoe was guilty or if he appeared to be guilty he was to be removed. It was little consolation to Lohmann that he himself had refused to be the executioner. He would still be the one to point the finger. And there had already been enough killing.

Crossing the room, he opened his suitcase and produced an unopened bottle of Scotch he had bought in Canada. In the bathroom he found a glass and poured himself three fingers. He went back into the bedroom and sat on the edge of the bed, contemplating the glass.

Remembering. He had first come out of Germany, to Paris, 1934. After his daughter had departed for America, Ex-Inspector Lohmann was alone in the city of light, his only acquaintances other refugees fleeing from Nazi persecution. Sad eyed Jews, many once prosperous, now living on the edge of nothing, haunting cheap cafés. Those were the days of mourning. Dead fathers and sons, lost friends and relatives. Dead careers. Talent wasting away in the gutters of all the cities surrounding Germany. Lohmann himself had turned to the solace of the bottle. And even in London had found, at first, only the same consolation.

Sitting in the drinking club in Soho, the Gog and Magog, day after day. Work became a few translations from German to English for a hack publisher in order to pay for the drink. Slowly he had pulled himself out of an alchoholic haze, become involved in a private investigation that had revealed Nazi infiltration into British politics. It had been the beginning of a new life.

Now he was back at something approximating to the work he knew. Yet everything was different. Nothing simple. No firm definitions. Now, everything was uncertain, no one to be trusted. No defining of guilt or innocence.

He had first met Robert Pardoe in New Orleans, and began to like the man's tenacity, his determination to carry out his mission, began to believe too, that if Pardoe was a murderer, the man himself was unaware of it. There was medical jargon to define his condition. Fugue. Paranoid schizophrenia. The Jekyll and Hyde syndrome? Or he was innocent and were

229

there other more sinister, forces at work?

Lohmann stared at the untouched whisky glass. He had no official standing here. No official standing anywhere. Only the word of a politician back in London. It would be so easy to forget it all, get drunk and stay drunk, even fly to New York, see Anna . . . God, how he wanted to see his daughter. *Wait until after the job was done*, that was what they'd said. Why wait? Why not get out of the whole murderous business? Was it his war, fighting against his own people?

But they weren't his people. Not the Hitlers and Himmlers and Heydrichs. Remember Heydrich. The charming, perfectly mannered ex-naval officer, now an SS General, and multiple killer, Himmler's executioner.

He lay back on the bed, remembering, Kristallnacht, the broken windows of small shops. Remembering the old bookseller who had once sold him law books when he had been a young policeman; he hadn't even realised the old man was a Jew until he'd met him in the dark of night, hiding on a rubbish dump, trying to survive. And the others who had happened to be his friends and happened also to be Jews, the ones who simply disappeared and were never seen again . . .

He fell asleep, the whisky untouched. He was back again on the banks of the Wannsee on a perfect summer's day, picnicking with his wife and small daughter. Knowing the linden trees were in bloom in the city. And none of the rest had ever happened. It was a kindly dream.

Another day. More snow. Starting to fall in the early morning, it had gone on falling until every tree in the city looked like a Christmas tree and the dome of the Capitol was again an enormous iced cake.

Lohmann was in Pardoe's office.

'We leave tomorrow morning,' Pardoe said. 'It's not a long drive. And once I see the man I'm going to see, the end of the job is in sight.'

230

'If "they" don't get to your man first.' Lohmann said quietly.

Pardoe looked up. 'Nobody knows. Except Alexander Sachs, and I can trust him.'

Lohmann indicated his assent. Taking his time. Waiting to achieve the greatest effect. Before asking the question.

'You dining with me tonight?' Pardoe said.

'No. I have to go out for a time with Reiner. You'll stay in the hotel?'

'Where else?' A pause. 'Look, Lomond, I won't go out. You'll have to trust me.'

Lohmann nodded. 'Bill Greenock's asked you to dine with him. At the hotel.' It was something he'd arranged that morning with the naval attaché. Greenock would be with Pardoe while he and Reiner were out.

'Good!' Pardoe replied. 'I'd like that. Naval reminiscences. Probably bore you. Who served on what ship and when. Verbally stick out our tongue at our superiors. Good for the soul. If not for prospects of promotion.'

He was off guard now, Lohmann reckoned. Time to ask the question. As casually as possible.

'Where were you yesterday afternoon, Pardoe?'

He thought at first Pardoe hadn't heard him. The Captain was flicking through papers on his desk. Then he looked up, a mildly puzzled expression on his face.

'Yesterday afternoon? I was here. Until I went back to the hotel with you.'

'Yes. You are sure?'

A deepening frown on Pardoe's face. 'Why do you ask?'

'You went out.' It was a statement, not a question.

Pardoe's frown deepened. 'Did I? Oh, wait – I may have gone for a stroll. To get some air. This American central heating, it can become oppressive when you're not used to it.'

'So you went out. For how long?'

'I'm not sure. I remember strolling down Massachusetts Avenue. And then . . .' He stopped abruptly. As if he was lost.

231

Trying to recollect something not quite right.

'You went to the Smithsonian?'

'Did I? Yes, I'd always wanted to go there. It was something to do.'

'It's a long walk.'

'I . . . I took a cab. Yes, I did . . .'

'And said nothing to me?'

'It didn't seem important.'

'When did you get back here?'

The man's eyes moved over his desk. Looking for something. Some kind of reassurance. 'I don't know. I remember being here afterwards. Sitting here . . . and then thinking, time I collected you. We went back to the hotel to change for the Van Esslings'.'

'You didn't take a taxi from the Smithsonian? Go somewhere else?'

Now Pardoe looked up from the desk. 'Where . . . where would I have gone . . . ?'

'Downtown. To the black girl's apartment.'

A long silence. Pardoe still staring up at the German. His face at first expressing only mild puzzlement. Then the face broke up, creased into an agonised expression. He appeared to be still questioning, but added to it was naked fear. He finally broke the silence.

'For God's sake, Lomond . . . you're thinking . . . ?'

'That you are not absolved from last night's killing.'

'You're thinking I killed the black girl. And, if I killed her, I killed all the others. That's it. All over again. You believe that?'

'I believe that it is again a possibility.'

'Lomond, would I . . . could I kill like that? Do that to a human being?'

'Somebody did. Why not you?'

'God, no! No, no, no! I swear to you . . . the first time I was in that room was last night.'

'Perhaps. Or perhaps you simply had no memory of being

232

there before. It does not mean you were not there.'

'That thing . . . what do you call it? A fugue. Loss of memory. As if I was some kind of Jekyll and Hyde.'

'You put it correctly.'

Pardoe leant back, limp in his chair. It was an attitude of hopelessness compounded with frustration.

'I don't know,' he said through clenched teeth. 'I don't know.'

'Why *did* you go to that apartment last night? To find something you'd left behind? Another button from your uniform?'

'No! No, I told you, I received that message, thought it was from Szilard . . .'

'And he phoned the Embassy and was told you were at the Van Esslings'?'

'Yes, I suppose so. Otherwise how could he know I was there?'

'It can be checked. All calls to the Embassy are registered.'

Lohmann reached forward and lifted the phone on Pardoe's desk. 'Exchange? Can you tell me, was there a call for Captain Pardoe here last night?'

He waited. Looking at the figure behind the desk. Pardoe was breathing heavily. After a moment Lohmann spoke again. 'Thank you. Did the caller leave a name? Ah, yes. Again, thank you.'

He replaced the receiver. Pardoe looked up, hopefully.

'Well?'

'There was a phone call. From someone called Szilard.'

Relief took over. Pardoe sat back. 'There! It proves something.'

'It proves someone phoned and called himself Szilard,' Lohmann said dryly. He leaned forward. 'Pardoe, you could have phoned yourself. Called yourself Szilard. Asked for yourself .'

'That's crazy.'

'Or rather clever.'

233

'But, if I am subject to these . . . these fugues . . . ?'

'Or if you simply like to kill women, and know it? Then it would inevitably be part of the planning of the killing. To cover yourself.'

'And I planned the others too, I suppose?'

'If you did, there was no need to. A prostitute dies in Singapore. Nothing to connect you with her, except your own knowledge of the woman. The same in London. Except that she kept an address book. And in Washington . . .'

'I never knew that woman!'

'Again your name turns up. And Julie Neuberg . . .'

'I admit I took her out a couple of times. Would I have done that if I intended to kill her?' Pardoe moaned.

'You had to. You may have been seen out with her. You see, it could be a fugue.' Lohmann hesitated, for maximum effect. 'Or it could be an irresistible impulse.'

Pardoe was trembling now. Fearful of himself.

Lohmann added. 'Or of course, someone could be framing you.'

'You sound as if you don't believe that any more.'

'I don't know, Pardoe, I just don't know, not yet. But I will know – in the end. You'll stay with Greenock tonight.'

Pardoe nodded, exhaustedly. Lohmann moved to the office door.

'I phoned Szilard,' Pardoe said. Lohmann stopped in mid stride. 'This morning. Asked him if he had phoned me last night. Sounded quite stupid. *Did you phone me last night? Did I speak to you?*'

'And . . . ?'

'He didn't. He is waiting to hear from me. When I have word for him.'

Lohmann said: 'Let it be soon. Just now, the casualty rate is becoming too high.'

On the way back to his office he met Caroline Norwood in the corridor.

'I was coming to see you,' she said. 'How is Captain Pardoe?'

'Frightened, I think.'

She was dressed in her working clothes, sweater, skirt and sensible shoes. This time no pearls. She looked tired.

'I had a nightmare last night. About that poor woman,' she said ruefully.

'I am not surprised,' he replied, but he was surprised, after her coolness earlier. But then, he thought, perhaps a delayed reaction.

'Lomond, come and have dinner with me tonight,' she went on. 'At my apartment. I . . . I don't want to be on my own. And . . . and I'd like you to come.'

'I have some work to do.'

'Couldn't you postpone it?'

He thought quickly. How long would he be with Reiner? The Bund meeting could not last all evening. Unless something developed and there was small chance of that.

'It is not possible,' he said reluctantly. 'But I could perhaps come later. After ten o'clock. If you still want me to?'

She gave a sigh of relief. 'Yes, I'd like that. I could make you a late supper.'

'You're sure?'

She gave a nervous laugh. 'I really would like some company . . .'

'Yes, well, I shall certainly come.'

He nodded and was about to move away. But she reached out and touched his arm. The smile had gone from her face. She said: 'You see, after last night, Lomond, after last night, I . . . I'm afraid.'

He looked into her eyes. Deep, dark brown. Reflecting something. Or was it the image at the back of his own mind, reflected in her eyes? Of the dead girl sprawled across the bed? No, not just one girl . . . five dead girls sprawled across the world . . . ?

TWENTY-ONE

They took a taxi. Reiner said 'How are you going to handle this, chief?'

'I was on to London this afternoon,' Lohmann said. 'Coded wires exchanged. Asked them a few questions.'

'Late homework, eh? You got answers?'

Lohmann nodded. 'William Kunze, according to MI6. An interesting portrait. American born. Philadelphia. Took over as leader of the Bund earlier this year from Fritz Kuhn when he was arrested on embezzlement charges. Kunze had already been recruited by Abwehr II as agent at large in the USA.'

'Abwehr II?'

'In charge of sabotage, insurrections and assassinations. They have become very departmentalised since our day, Reiner. Kunze also works closely with a man called Anastase Vonsiatsky, known as the 'Millionaire'. This man married a rich American woman, Marian Ream. Vonsiatsky is the head of a Ukrainian paramilitary group and founder of something called the International Russian Fascist Party. They apparently hide their pro-Nazi work under the guise of anti-Soviet activities.'

'This Vonsiatsky is important?'

'Weapons,' Lohmann said quietly. 'A small arsenal on his estate in Connecticut. Any of them want armour, they can call on Vonsiatsky. So London tells me. That man you pointed out to me in the bar at the hotel, that first night . . . do you remember, you said he was Mafia?'

'He looked like Mafia.'

'I asked about him in the hotel later. He was a Ukrainian. Refugee from Russia. Fortunately I don't think he was watching me. He was there to report on Pardoe.'

'But wouldn't they know Pardoe was in New Orleans?'

'They would take no chances. In case they had been misinformed. He would be told to wait there. They already had a man waiting in the hotel in New Orleans.'

'Such Prussian efficiency!' said Reiner, looking around the hall. The audience were beginning to take their seats. The noise of wood on wooden floor was loud harsh and grating.

'So what does it mean?' he said.

'Somebody had to supply the alternate Lohmann in New Orleans,' Lohmann replied. 'To kill Duplessis and try and kill Pardoe. If he couldn't be discredited. As a guess, I'd say the people who organised that were probably Ukrainians. Vonsiatsky's people. With local help, like Billy Bones, who died because of it. Of course when Pardoe and I got out of the city, they were able to call on Colescott and his Klan people. Pity I can't prove it. But it feels right.'

Reiner gave a small smile. 'It's getting like the old days in Berlin. You get hunches . . .'

'Only in Berlin I could prove them.'

'So what next?'

'After the meeting, I introduce myself to Kunze. And you leave it to me.'

'When do I ever do anything else?'

The hall was an unimposing building in downtown Washington. But large. It had been some kind of drill hall used in the past by a local unit of the National Guard. But not recently. And not on this night.

A notice at the entrance proclaimed, in small letters:

"German-American Bund"

Below this, in larger letters:

"HEAR WILLIAM KUNZE!
DEFEND AMERICA AGAINST THE JEWISH-
BOLSHEVIK

CONSPIRACY!

Every red blooded, white skinned American welcome.''

A bustling crowd had gathered at the entrance when Lohmann and Reiner arrived. At each side of the double doors were large men in white jackets and brown shirts. They also sported armbands with small swastikas over the word Steward. They were carefully scrutinising everybody who entered.

In front of the door a rotund figure, red-faced, small eyes inset in fleshy features, was attempting to light a cigar. He looked up at Lohmann and Reiner and nodded affably.

'Evening, boys. You goin' in to the meetin'?'

'That is the intention,' Reiner replied.

'My first time,' said the fat man. His accent, Reiner judged, was mid-Western. 'You been to any of these shindigs before, son?'

Although the man could not have been much older than Reiner, the ex-police sergeant accepted the patronising appellation of 'son' with amusement.

'I have,' Reiner said. 'But not my friend.'

The fat man, however, showed no interest in replies to his questions. He was concerned only with his own thoughts. 'I'm from Oklahoma,' he said. 'Greatest li'l state in the Union. Own a lot of property out there. Yeah, I do pretty well . . .'

'Nice for you.' Reiner, still amused.

'Land. That's the thing. Land. Picked it up for peanuts durin' the depression. Enterprise, that was. The good ol' American way. Bet you're wonderin' what I'm doin' here, eh?'

'Yes, indeed,' Reiner forced himself to reply, trying to lead Lohmann around the ample figure towards the entrance.

' 'Course, I ain't no Kraut,' the fat man went on. 'Though they do say my great-grandpappy came from Hamburg.' A melon-slice-like grin was carved out of the plump face. 'Would make him some kinda hamburger, eh?'

238

'You'll please excuse us,' Lohmann said. But to no avail. Circumventing the man's bulk was almost impossible.

'Mind you,' the Oklahoman went on, 'jest mebbe this Hitler guy's got the right ideas. Yes sir, Kraut or no Kraut, he's mebbe got the right idea 'bout them goddam Reds. And the Yids. *They* get in everywhere. They tell me they started this war in Europe. Them and the English in cahoots. You know, when I was lending money to them dirt farmers, and when they couldn't pay up, I was bein' forced to foreclose on their land, and damn Jewish Commie agitators were comin' from the city and bad-mouthin' me all over Oklahoma City. Can you imagine that?'

'Unbelievable,' Reiner said dully.

'I mean, I don't blame the farmers but I was good enough to loan 'em dough. Not my fault they couldn't pay up. Not my fault interest rates were high. Man's gotta live. Always pay my own debts, sure enough. Jest had to take up the land. That was the deal. That's the American way, ain't it?'

'Nothing for nothing and damn little for a dollar,' Reiner said quietly.

'True enough,' the fat man replied, and then momentarily looked uncertain. Before pressing on, 'I kinda like the way them Bunders say things. I mean, you leave it to Roosevelt an' we'd all be fighting the Englanders' war for 'em. Did it the last time. They never learn. An' kin I help it if there was oil found on that land of mine. Them dirt farmers wouldn't have known what to do with all that oil. An' I sure do. S'why I'm in Washington, doin' business with the big guys. Yeah. Playin' with the big boys now. So it benefits the country too, don't it?'

The man's mind moved in narrowly decreasing circles, Lohmann thought. Like so many of his fellow citizens in the old days in Germany.

'Very interesting, sir, but we have to go in. You will please let us past.' Lohmann said.

'Sure, sure, you go right on, friend. Me, I'm jest waitin' for a buddy who's going to take me in. Old Bund member, told me about the whole thing, mebbe you know him. Conrad Hoffmann? Con was good enough to send me all the paper 'bout the Bund, not that I'm a readin' man but I guess he would be knowing I would agree with most of it. Helluva a nice guy, ol' Con, you surely know him?'

'I'm afraid not.'

'Nice, nice guy. Real folks. Knows what side his bread's buttered on . . .'

'Very important,' said Reiner. 'Otherwise you get a hand covered in greasy butter. Good to have spoken to you . . .'

They finally managed to push past.

One of the brown-shirted stewards stepped in front of them. 'You members?'

'I am considering joining the Bund,' said Reiner. 'I have been at meetings in Cincinnati.'

'So have some fuckin' Reds,' the steward replied. 'We gotta be careful.'

Reiner produced his social security card. 'You can see my name is Reiner . . . I was born in Berlin.'

The steward still looked doubtful. Lohmann showed him his German passport, manufactured in London. And date stamped on his entry to the USA a week before. Also done in London.

'I have recently arrived in America. From Berlin. I am also a member of the German National Socialist Party. I am here on business on behalf of the Third Reich. Also I wish to meet my comrades and fellow countrymen living in America.'

The steward was impressed by the passport with the eagle and swastika emblazoned on the cover.

'Of course, Herr Muller. Very glad to see you. Please go in.'

The interior of the hall was half full but filling rapidly. Several hundred people at least.

'One of their smaller more intimate gatherings,' Reiner explained icily.

Large men in lounge suits rubbed shoulders with men in

240

denims and check jackets. Words of greeting were exchanged, some in English with a variety of American accents, some in German, the German usually in louder tones as if they were showing off their knowledge of the language of their fore-fathers.

'*Wie geht es. . . ?*'

'*. . . Guten abend. . .*'

'*. . . Ach, Willi, mein alter freund. . .*'

Lohmann surveyed the hall. Stewards around the walls, large men like the two at the entrance. More like bouncers in some dubious night-club or bar. No, like *Sturmtruppen*! A sight once familiar to him, an image from the past. The SA. Same faces, same expressions, same physiques. Under more posters advertising the Bund.

"HEAR WILLIAM KUNZE TELL THE TRUTH! HEAR ABOUT THE JEW ROOSEVELT'S CONSPIRACY TO TAKE OVER AMERICA FOR THE REDS!"

But it was only when Lohmann turned to face the platform at the end of the hall that he experienced the true *frisson*; ghosts from the past; shadows in the back of the mind; memories of Berlin. Behind the speaker's lectern, on the back wall of the hall was draped an enormous swastika banner. Hanging next to the Stars and Stripes.

He shuddered.

Reiner said: 'You all right?'

'Something walked over my grave.'

'I know,' Reiner shrugged. 'Gave me a sick feeling the first time I saw it in Cincinnati.

They took their seats in the back row. The hall was now full and loud with echoing conversation. Several hundred people talking at once, it is like waves crashing on rocks. But, the sound died as a tall figure strolled onto the platform.

'August Klapprott,' Reiner whispered. 'I recognise him.

Came to Cincinnati. Deputy Führer of the Bund.'

The man called Klapprott banged the lectern with a small gavel. 'Fellow Americans!' he shouted. 'It is good to see you tonight, here in the heart of our beloved America. And to know that, by your very presence, you are strengthening the bonds between America and the Fatherland!'

It was, Lohmann had to admit, well orchestrated. At the mention of the word Fatherland, a hidden loud speaker blared out 'Deutschland Uber Alles', followed immediately by 'My Country 'tis of Thee'. The assembled company stood for both anthems.

Then, the music dying, Klapprott went on, 'Now I wish to introduce our leader, Gerhardt Wilhelm Kunze.'

Wild cheering broke out and, as the figure of Kunze strode on to the platform, the audience rose to its feet. 'Sieg Heils' rang out, a thunderous acclamation. The meeting suddenly ceased to be an American gathering and became, unashamedly, a Nazi rally.

Kunze stood, basking in the approbation of his people, turning ever so slightly to the left and then to the right, acknowledging his reception from all parts of the hall. Away from the platform he would have been an insignificant figure, completely nondescript. But then, Lohmann told himself, Adolf Hitler had been such a figure. Lohmann had not only seen Hitler at the enormous rallies of the Party in Germany but he had also met him. And had seen the dangerously insignificant appearance of the man. Dangerous because of that very insignificance; with the icy detemination to assert himself, to ensure by any method that everything went as he, and only he, wanted and demanded; the lust for absolute power.

The cheers and the heils died down as Kunze raised a hand. Again the gesture was reminiscent of Hitler. Everything was a studied impersonation. And this mob would accept it, already had accepted it. If they couldn't have the original, they were delirious to settle for the duplicate.

242

Kunze started his peroration. And again Lohmann could see he had studied Hitler; the deliberate gestures, the throwing back of the head, the pauses, they were all modelled on the Führer – as was the speech. Indeed, but for being in English, it might well have been a Hitler oration. Lohmann did not bother to follow it. He simply noted the emphasis on certain words and phrases . . . the word *Jew* spat out at intervals with appropriate assumption of contempt and disgust. Phrases like *Jewish Bolshevik conspiracy* underlined and thrown to the assembly as if throwing meat to starving animals. Roosevelt was referred to as the *Jewish President* in the pay of the *Jews of Wall Street*. A reference to the good German-Americans was received with rapturous applause. The speech ended with a wild hymn of rhetorical praise to National Socialism and the multitudinous benefits it would bring to America.

When he had finished, Kunze took a step backwards and waited again to receive the demanded and expected ovation. Which inevitably he got. It lasted some minutes, although Lohmann noticed it was kept going with the active encouragement of the stewards around the hall who led the cheers, glared at those who faltered or were not enthusiastic enough.

The trestle tables at the side of the hall were uncovered and the crowd was permitted to rise, mingle, seek coffee and sandwiches. While they were doing this, the stewards went into the midst of them, accosting those who were not wearing the small button hole swastika and Stars and Stripes badge that denoted active membership of the Bund. Those who were not wearing the badges were ushered towards yet another trestle table, a recruiting corner where they were over-actively encouraged to join and pay at once their membership and entrance dues. Lohmann had to admit to himself that it was well organised. He had been to similar Fascist rallies in London, where Sir Oswald Mosley had spoken. There, the stewards had also to be physically active but in a more violent manner. In London there had been outbreaks of violence as dissenters had tried to make themselves heard. They had been beaten up. Or else, on occasion, there were sufficient of them in a group to beat up the stewards. Blood had flowed and heads had been broken. But here, there was not dissension, only acquiescence. The stewards had done their work well. They had excluded dissenters.

'You guys ain't members?' It was Lohmann and Reiner's turn to be approached by a steward, a large man with a scarred forehead, and deep-sunken eyes almost swallowed up by fleshy cheeks.

Lohmann stiffened, back like a ramrod. The Prussian stance, he had once called it. His face became a mask of arrogance. He had seen it often enough in Berlin to affect it with conviction. Reiner, inwardly amused, was silent.

'I am,' said Lohmann, 'a member of the National Socialist Party of the Third Reich. Enrolled in Prussia in 1926.'

The steward was nonplussed, and with not the brightest of minds behind the sunken eyes, he managed to appreciate that he was face-to-face with what he could just about comprehend was a real Nazi Party member. But, he was under instructions to recruit, with force if necessary, for the German-American Bund. Did being a German National Socialist allow this stranger who affected also a broad German accent, exemption? He was uncertain.

Across the hall under the platform, William Kunze had descended from his elevated position, condescending to mingle with his admirers. He was flanked by his deputy, August Klapprott and another figure, a smaller, darker man. The steward in front of Lohmann looked over the head of the crowd as if seeking guidance from his leader. But Kunze was too far away to help.

Lohmann decided to break the deadlock and put the man's fears to rest.

'I am here to see Gerhardt Wilhelm Kunze. On behalf of

244

certain authorities in Berlin,' he announced with assumed pomposity.

Of course it worked. The steward backed away apologetically. 'Yeah, yeah, sure. I'll tell him . . . tell Mister Kunze.' The uncertain American had taken over from the Bundist steward. Faced with obvious authority he crumbled into abject humility.

'How do you think you can get away with this?' said Reiner in a nervous undertone.

'Conviction, Reiner. Believing in yourself, being utterly assured. That way you can get away with anything.'

Lohmann stared over the heads of the crowd to where the steward was talking animatedly to Kunze and pointing in their direction. Kunze said something, the man nodded and started to make his way back through the crowd towards them.

'I feel like a man who can't swim,' said Reiner. 'And about to go over Niagara Falls in a cardboard box.'

'You can only drown once.'

'Once is enough.'

The steward reached them, 'Kunze will see you. Back room. You follow me.'

They were shown into a bare, dusty, high-ceilinged room with one trestle table, some boxes underneath the table, three or four upright chairs, one broken, and no other items of furniture.

'Wait here!' said the steward and went out, shutting the door behind him.

They were alone. Reiner watched Lohmann look around the room, the way Lohmann always did it; getting to know the geography of the place wherever it was. Looking for exits and entrances. Ways of escape. Old habits die hard, he thought. And thank God for it. There were windows but high up on the wall, unreachable, no way out there. There was another door at the far end of the room. Reiner gently tried it.

'Locked,' he said, returning to Lohmann's side. 'As Mister

Hardy says to Mister Laurel, "Here's another nice mess you got me into." '

'I only hope this does link with the Pardoe business. Otherwise, what are we doing here?'

'It should. Through Colescott. Friend of Kunze. Why would the Ku Klux Klan be interested unless instructed by someone connected with Berlin? Kunze is the only apparent connection.'

They waited. The silence held. Minutes passed.

The door from the main hall opened and Kunze came in. He was flanked by two large stewards. Behind him was the small dark man.

'Guten abend, mein herren!'

Lohmann straightened up. The Prussian stance again. *'Guten abend, Herr Kunze.'*

'You wish to see me?'

The two stewards moved to either side of the doorway, silent sentinels. Waiting for any action that might be required.

'I have come from Berlin,' Lohmann said. 'My name, on this occasion, is Bruno Muller.'

'And on the other occasions, Herr Muller?'

Lohmann forced himself to smile. As sardonically as possible. 'I'm sorry but that is none of your affair.'

Kunze returned the smile affably. 'So. What is your business?'

'Among other matters, to see you. I am from Abwehr II.'

Reiner felt his knees trembling. Stage fright. Asking himself, what could happen here? They were in Washington DC. The capital of the greatest country in the world, the bastion of democracy, land of the free and the brave. And, he thought, with more murders per capita than any other country in the world. The trouble with America was, it was too big. People could simply disappear and never be seen again. If these people so desired. Could happen to them.

'You have identification?' Kunze asked. Still affable.

Lohmann laughed now, with heavy sarcasm. 'Oh, certainly. I should carry a card with my name and number on it, stating I am with German intelligence? Do you carry such a card, Kunze? You too are Abwehr II. You are perhaps crazy enough to do so? I am not.'

He reached into his jacket and produced his passport.

'I have my passport. You will see my recent entry date. Bruno Muller on the front. Businessman. Here to arrange the purchase of non-belligerent material for the Third Reich. To be exact, cottons, linens and other cloth. That is my reason for being here, as far as the American government knows.'

Kunze flicked the passport open, glanced at it, returned it.

'So you are a German citizen. That is all it tells me.' The smile in place.

'But I tell you much more, Kunze,' Lohmann replied coldly. 'I tell you you are an agent of Abwehr II. Is that common knowledge?'

Kunze glanced around at the two stewards. A nervousness in his manner now. 'Leave us,' he told them. The stewards went out. The small dark man stayed.

'You'll have to tell me a great deal more, my dear fellow,' Kunze went on. 'Otherwise I might not believe you. And if I don't believe you I shall have to act like the villain in the Dick Tracy strip. That would be a pity.' He took a deep breath, glancing at his companion. The small dark man drew out a large Luger pistol. 'You see,' Kunze said. 'I have to apologise, but I am prepared for all eventualities. If you cannot tell me more, such a pity. Then I'm afraid you will tell no one anything ever again. I'm sorry – that does sound so melo-dramatic, doesn't it?'

'No, no, your sense of security is admirable,' Lohmann said.

Suddenly Kunze seemed to relax again. 'However, before we come to what might be unpleasant, let's have a drink. Anastase, would you be good enough . . . ?'

The dark man whose name was Anastase handed the pistol

247

to Kunze and went over to the table. He reached down and produced a tray from the floor under the table. On the tray were glasses and a bottle.

'Schnapps,' said Kunze. 'The real thing. Imported from Germany. You see how lucky we are. A good German drink. After all it is in the great American tradition. If we cannot give them a hearty breakfast, Anastase, at least the condemned men are entitled to a last drink.'

TWENTY-TWO

The drink was warm at the back of Lohmann's throat. Yet the old familiar taste brought back again so many memories. He drained the glass and looked at Gerhardt Wilhelm Kunze. American born, what did he really know of Germany? He was a plastic imitation of Hitler, a poseur with an unoriginal pose. And the small dark man with him, holding the gun. Anastase. Vonsiatsky? Almost certainly the 'Millionaire', the Ukrainian who married money, the paymaster of the Bund. With a pistol in his hand.

Lohmann suddenly laughed aloud, in character as Bruno Muller. His two antagonists looked up at him in amazement. Reiner kept quiet, sipping his schnapps. Leaving it to Lohmann.

They're playing games, Lohmann told himself, bad actors giving ham performances. Even though they were pro-Nazi, they couldn't help but create their roles from Hollywood movies. He laughed again.

'You find it funny, Muller?' said Kunze, discomfited and

unable to conceal his irritation. A man faced with a gun and the threat of its use should not be laughing. The man who held the gun held the power. And this stranger was seemingly unable to acknowledge that fact.

'I find it amusing, Mister Kunze,' Lohmann replied. 'You threaten to kill me? You, by yourself, not using hired people, never having actually killed before. And here in America too. Oh, I've no doubt it could be done, and my body disposed of. You might get someone to do it. But you yourself won't do it . . .'

'You believe that?' This from Anastase Vonsiatsky. Curious.

'Because, Mister Vonsiatsky . . . you are Vonsiatsky? Yes, of course you are. Because, neither of you has any such orders from Berlin, and without orders you will be too afraid . . . of making a mistake . . . of actually killing anyone. It's such a messy business and I'm sure when you had to do it in the past, others did it for you. Also of course, you cannot do anything without orders from Colonel Lahousen in Berlin. He *is* your chief at Abwehr II. You have to be either under direct orders from him . . . or his man in America. That is the man above you. Lahousen or his man will not be pleased if I am executed.'

Vonsiatsky, white faced, looked at Kunze. 'He . . . he knows of Lahousen.'

Lohmann felt easier. He'd known Lahousen in the old days, knew now, from MI6, that Lahousen was in charge of Abwehr II. 'Of course I know Lahousen!' he barked. 'I am here at his orders.'

Kunze said nervously: 'Why come to us? Why not go to the control here?'

'I would hardly go to a man whose efficiency is in question!' Lohmann slammed his fists together in a gesture of impatience. 'I am here to check on whether the job is being done properly. Since the results so far have not been satisfactory.'

Reiner could only stare at his chief with ill-concealed admiration. That was okay, he told himself. He would be expected to admire an envoy from Berlin. And his genuine admiration was for Lohmann's unerring ability to improvise in a tight situation. Not that it should have surprised him. He'd seen it often enough in the past. But not in quite this situation. He was browbeating these two with the unabashed arrogance and bravado of the part he was playing.

Lohmann went on: 'So you knew that Captain Pardoe was going to see the old man, Duplessis. You had your people kill Duplessis. You did this before you knew why Pardoe wished to see Duplessis . . .'

'Our people tried to find out. They reported that Duplessis claimed he had no idea why Pardoe wanted to see him. Eventually it was decided to kill Duplessis as the only way to frustrate Pardoe.'

'*Falsch*!' Lohmann barked. 'We had to know the purpose of his mission. We do not know that, do we?'

'We are still working to that end,' Kunze replied uneasily. 'And we could easily kill Pardoe. It would have been done by Colescott if he had not had the other man with him.'

'There is no need to kill Pardoe. Except as a last resort. You know this. You are aware of our intention to discredit him, to disgrace the man?' Lohmann was striding up and down now, assuming an intolerant impatience. Again he slammed his fists together.

'We only know something of it. But we are not involved in that part of the operation . . .' Kunze spluttered.

'Ach! You should be aware of the entire plan . . .' Lohmann petulant now. Pacing up to Kunze and staring him in the face with something approaching contempt. 'I shall speak to your control on this matter. You should have been kept in the complete picture.'

Kunze took this as a kind of approbation. A smug smile spread across his face. 'I agree. How can one carry out orders when one is kept in ignorance of the full picture?'

Lohmann swung around on his heel and brought his face close to Kunze. Thinking, the man had bad breath. But then shouldn't one's enemies always prove so unpleasant?

'We are displeased with the whole operation in New Orleans!' he barked yet again. 'You were given permission to use this man Colescott?'

'No, but he is sympathetic . . .!'

'He is a member of the Ku Klux Klan! The Führer does not approve of such clandestine organisations. They can be dangerous and subversive to the aims of the Reich. And you use them to eliminate Duplessis!'

Lohmann turned again and strode up to Vonsiatsky. 'You have weapons and people of your own, yet you assign such tasks to others. Are you afraid of the necessary elimination of enemies? And yet you can stand here and threaten me with a pistol!'

He reached out, grasped the barrel of the Luger and prised it unconcernedly from the Ukrainian's hand.

'You will have no need of this, Herr Vonsiatsky. You wouldn't kill me, in case I am what I say I am. Also, if I am not what I say I am, you will still not kill me. It is not an easy thing to do. So very messy . . .*unangenehm*. . . you'd leave other people to carry out this task. Too afraid to be involved.'

He weighed the Luger in his hand.

'We will go now to speak to your control.' He turned to Reiner. '*Kommen*!' He strode to the door, pocketing the Luger as he went. Reiner followed, white faced. At the door, Lohmann turned and spoke once again to Kunze.

'You would be better off confining your activities to propaganda work, Herr Kunze. It needs a strong stomach to function as a party assassin. Good evening.'

He went out into the hall followed by Reiner. The stewards were cleaning up and a few Bundsmen were still congregated in groups volubly discussing the meeting. Lohmann walked through them, looking neither to the left nor the right.

★

251

A short time later they were in a bar. Reiner swallowed a large brandy.

'I'm not used to this. Maybe I was once. But not any more. You can handle these things.'

'It's been a long time for me also,' Lohmann grinned. 'I suppose it's like riding a bicycle – you never forget.'

'But how did you know they wouldn't fire?'

'I didn't. Not for certain. But Kunze has too much to lose. Head of the Bund; he would call himself Führer. Too much to lose to be involved personally in a killing – his predecessor went to prison for embezzlement. Kunze wouldn't take that chance. Also, they believed I might well be from Germany, they wouldn't dare kill an emissary of the Reich, not without checking with their control. Oh, if necessary, they would have found someone to do the job, given time. They thought the Luger would intimidate us. The last thing they would expect is that we turn and walk out on them. Like yourself, Reiner, they believe in all the myths fostered by the American cinema. People don't ignore guns when pointed at them. The trouble is, unless you are in a panic, it's not easy to kill someone.'

Reiner drained his glass. 'Thank God you were right. But was it worth it?'

'Ah, yes. We know for certain that there is a German agent on station here who is organising action against Pardoe's mission. Perhaps later we can use them to catch this agent. Also, while they know Pardoe is on a mission, they do not yet know the purpose of it. So, they are working in the dark.'

'Like us,' Reiner said glumly. 'Your Captain Pardoe is not exactly forthcoming about the nature of his job, and we're on his side.'

'He's been cleverer than we give him credit for. He's done something rare in the intelligence world. He's kept a secret. It's a rare ability.'

'So what now?'

'You go back to the hotel. Tomorrow I go with Pardoe.

Wherever. Perhaps then I'll know what it's all about. Meanwhile, keep an eye on Kunze and Vonsiatsky. But I think they will now keep a low profile. If they believe I am from Berlin, they will leave me to deal with their controlling agent. And, if they do not believe, they will be too frightened to act. Might force the man into the open.'

'Where we want him.'

'Meanwhile,' Lohmann looked at his watch, 'I have a supper engagement.'

The apartment was off 2nd Street, in a high block. It was small but tastefully furnished. A living-cum dining-room, bedroom, bathroom and a kitchenette. The dining table was at a large window which looked out over the lights of the city and the illuminated dome of the Capitol. Candles glowed and the rest of the lighting in the room was suitably subdued. Lohmann was impressed and showed it.

'You're surprised, Lomond?' Caroline Norwood said.

'Most pleasantly.'

'It's not all furnished on the salary of an Embassy secretary. I was left a great deal of money when my father died. He was in oil. And rubber. Made a fortune out of contraceptives. The self-made man endeavouring to stop people making any more of his type.'

'Unusual,' Lohmann said.

'Very. When he died I ran the company for a couple of years. Went all over the world. In the end, didn't like it, sold out, came back to this job. Poor daddy, he was always embarrassed by the uses of all that rubber. I mean, he didn't mind being in trade . . . after all, Neville Chamberlain was in trade. And I was grateful for the money he left me. Enough to keep a regiment of wolves from the door. I've told you all about me. What's your story?'

'What an impressive view.'

She let it go. 'Yes, isn't it? Sit down. Relax.'

'Thank you.' He sat at the table awkwardly.

'Supper is nearly ready. Since I didn't know when you'd arrive, I got a couple of steaks. But next time I will have a full dinner prepared.'

'Oh, I am to be asked again?'

'Probably.' She smiled and disappeared into the kitchen-ette. Calling as she went. 'Help yourself to a drink – on the sideboard – Whisky: Scotch and rye – and gin. We're having wine with the supper.'

He rose and poured himself a small Scotch.

'May I get you something?' he called.

'Gin and tonic. I won't be long.'

He sat again at the table, contemplating the city lights, wondering about why he was here, about what was expected of him? If anything. There was something about Caroline Norwood that reminded him of Rue Scott-ffolliot. She came from the same class. Though, if there was such a thing as class, Lohmann hated to acknowledge it. He told himself he was above such distinctions. His only criterion among people was their honesty or otherwise. Caroline at least worked for a living. Unlike Rue who made a career out of indulging in her own personal pleasures. There was something else about Caroline, a cold practicality, she would never do anything without calculation. Like asking Lohmann to supper? Why?

She came out of the kitchenette. 'Won't be long,' she said, lifting the gin and tonic he had poured for her.

'No hurry.' He was beginning to relax. And she was the first woman he had been able to relax with since Rue.

'You're looking pale,' Caroline said.

'It is always so.'

'Too much excitement, too many late nights.'

'Only recently, and that will pass.'

'Your work is nearly finished?'

'Hopefully.'

'To do with Pardoe and that dead woman last night?'

Lohmann shrugged. 'There is a connection.'

'She's something to do with the reason he's here? . . . No, I shouldn't have asked that. Forget it.' She put down her glass and went back into the kitchen.

'How do you like your steak?'

'Eh . . . undercooked.'

'One rare steak coming up.' A few minutes later they were at the table eating. Lohmann had slung his jacket over the back of his chair, as if he was at home, pleased to be lulled into the sense of ease after the events of earlier in the evening. He found he was hungry – too much tension, too much dashing around snatching whatever was handy to eat. The steak was enormous and appetising, garnished with mushrooms and sauté potatoes. Caroline picked at her food, one elbow balanced on the table.

'You see,' she said, 'not just a pretty face but a good cook. The way to a man's heart and all that . . .'

He looked across the table at her face in candlelight. She was looking down at her plate, eating in the American fashion with only a fork, avoiding his eyes.

'That is your purpose, then?' he said, smiling.

'You're an interesting man,' she replied, eyes still down. As if embarrassed. 'Why not?'

'Why? In this city, surrounded by all these wealthy and handsome young Americans?'

'They are so synthetic. And their interests are so narrow – their own politics, and money. And trying all the time to get you into bed.'

'You think I would not do that?'

'I think, Lomond, you would wait until you were asked.' Now she looked at him, eyes showing amusement.

'It certainly makes it easier.'

'Anyway, let's leave it until you come for a proper dinner, then we can see what develops when you come back from your trip with Captain Pardoe.'

It was an open invitation. And not just to dinner.

'I shall look forward to that,' he replied.

'You're going off tomorrow morning?'

255

'As far as I know, it is entirely up to Pardoe, only he knows where we are going. All I know is we are going north. We should not be away for more than two or three days.'

'Then the first evening you are free, you will come for dinner.'

He was bemused. He felt she was making the running and he was trailing behind, not with reluctance, but with a degree of curiosity. Why him? He was, in his own eyes, a battered late-forties remnant of too much living. A lined face and a scarred body. Was that attractive to women? Or at least to this woman? He wasn't conceited, and had, in London, resigned himself to a lonely, almost monastic existence. And now Caroline Norwood was setting a pace that vaguely unnerved him.

Dinner finished with a glass of brandy and it was time for him to go. She came to the door of the apartment.

'You're flying north?'

'It is, Pardoe tells me, not as far as New Orleans. I shall drive him. It will be easier that way.'

She put a hand on his arm. 'Be careful.'

'I am used to driving on icy roads. And the snow is not yet too thick.'

'I wasn't thinking of the weather. It's . . . it's the other side . . . whoever they are.'

'Perhaps, if I was a better investigator, like the ones in detective stories, I would be able to say, "Ah yes, but I know who they are." Unfortunately I don't.'

'You will be careful?'

'Of course. I have a dinner engagement when I return. I wouldn't wish to miss that.'

She leaned forward, put her hand behind his neck and brought his head down to her lips. She kissed him, a long open-mouthed kiss, tongue probing to meet his.

'When you get back, Lomond . . .' she said. Leaving the sentence unfinished.

*

256

Back at the hotel, he went straight to bed. He booked a call for seven o'clock and then lay in the darkness, thinking. About Caroline at first, then about Pardoe. If Pardoe was right, the mission would soon be over; but the murder investigation would go on. And he was not looking forward to that.

He slept. Dreaming. Of the girl in Singapore, the woman in Shepherd Market, and the others in Washington. All of them merging into one. A black, white, Chinese, English, American girl. All one, lying on a bed, dead, mutilated, a multiplication of corpses. There must be no more, his own voice as he stared down at a body, *no more*.

There were three men standing around the body.

Pardoe, Straight and Markham.

One of three.

Which one?

Or was there someone else?

Shuffle the three cards and deal. Like the men who stand in a lane behind Leicester Square playing 'Find the Lady.' Only this time it wasn't the Queen they were asking him to find; another card altogether. The Ace of Spades, the death card? Or the Hanged Man in the tarot pack?

Asking himself then, how do you tell which one is the killer? How do you know which one is a maniac killing women in some ghastly aberration of the sex act? The act of love becoming the ritual of death. Mass murderers were always so ordinary.

I run towards death. . .

A line of poetry. He couldn't remember the rest of it.

In his head, a bell was ringing. Groping in the darkness, he switched on the bed light and, forcing his eyes open, he picked up his watch. They'd got it wrong. It was only six.

He lifted the telephone on the table by the side of the bed.

'Look . . . asked for a call at seven . . .' his voice hoarse with sleep.

'Lomond!'

'Wha' is it?'

'Jimmy Straight here.'

'What do you want?'

'I thought I should phone you.'

'So?'

'We picked up a small-time pimp tonight. Wanted under the Mann Act – that's transporting women across the state lines for immoral purposes. I sometimes wonder what other reason there is for anything . . .'

Lohmann squirmed under the bedclothes. 'You're going to tell me what this has to do with me?'

'Just that. The pimp is a three-time loser. He goes to prison for life this time. Also he has a boyfriend. So perverse, these people. He was only too willing to give us information regarding his boyfriend, if we were kind to him. Information received taken into account when he's charged. Anyway Mister Hoover decided we should listen to him . . .'

'This is a long story, Straight.'

'You are so impatient. Our pimp's boyfriend has been approached to do a little job of work. He reckoned the job's political, but not our politics. Yours, old man, between you people and the little man with the Charlie Chaplin moustache.'

'What's the job?'

'That, our pimp didn't know. But his friend is an Italian-American called Boom-Boom Marchetti. A freelancer but he does a lot of work for the Mob.'

'The Mob?'

'Gangsters, old man, gangsters. Blows safes for them. Hence the nickname Boom-Boom.'

'Has the British Embassy safes that need to be blown?'

Straight's high pitched laugh echoed down the phone. 'Who knows? It's not just safes he blows, but people too. An expert with jelly, TNT and all that. Of course it may have nothing to do with you, but on the other hand . . . you and Bobby Pardoe are targets for somebody. Just thought I'd tell you.'

Lohmann was silent for a moment. 'Thank you, Mister Straight. I'll bear it in mind.'

'Do that. Oh, by the way, don't mention I phoned you to Mister Hoover. I don't think he'd like it. I think he has the idea that it would be a good thing if you and the others all blew yourselves up. Save us all-American boys such a lot of bother. But I felt I had to let you know. After all, Bobby Pardoe's an old friend. And I wouldn't care to have to identify you both after you'd been scraped off some filthy pavement.'

TWENTY-THREE

An hour later, in Pardoe's bedroom.

'You want a coffee?' the Captain asked. He was sitting at a small table finishing his breakfast. Washed, shaved, dressed in a dark civilian suit.

Lohmann went to the window. 'I've had my breakfast.'

He looked down at Massachusetts Avenue. The traffic was beginning to pile up. Faintly he could hear the sound of indignant automobile horns protesting against the morning's delay. 'Isn't it time you told me where we are going?' he asked.

'Princeton, New Jersey,' Pardoe replied.

Lohmann had heard of Princeton. A university town. Why there? He decided not to press Pardoe at this time. There were other things to be concerned about. He looked around the room thinking of Boom-Boom Marchetti. The bed was already made. Almost as if it hadn't been slept in. Pardoe noticed his look.

'The chambermaid just made it,' he said. 'She'll tell you, if you ask her. Don't worry. I spent the evening in the restaurant downstairs with Bill Greenock. And later, in the bar. Then came to bed. No fugues, no trips downtown. Bill will tell you. He came up for a nightcap. Almost put me to bed.' And, as if turning any possible accusation around, Pardoe added, 'Where were you?'

'Talking to the people who arranged for Duplessis to be killed,' Lohmann replied quietly.

Pardoe's head came up. 'Good God! You know who . . .'

'*Arranged* it. Not did it.'

'Can't you have them arrested?'

'No evidence. A link with Colescott, that's all. Thin. But it's useful. Know the enemy. If not all of them. Yet.'

Lohmann's eyes settled on a briefcase lying against the foot of the bed.

'Yours?' he asked.

'Of course. It's coming with us.'

'May I open it?'

'Why?'

Lohmann smiled. 'To examine it's contents.'

'It won't mean anything to you. What is this?'

'I had word this morning. About a man called Boom-Boom Marchetti. A demolition expert who specialises in people.'

Pardoe rose. 'You're joking.'

'I'm not joking.'

Pardoe opened the briefcase. It contained a folder filled with typewritten papers.

Lohmann shrugged. 'We have to be careful.'

'Yes. All right.'

Pardoe donned a heavy overcoat and a dark soft hat. Lohmann wore his trench coat over a pullover, and a scarf around his neck. Pardoe stared at him.

'It's cold out there. You be all right?'

'Yes. Shall we go?'

Pardoe headed towards the elevator but Lohmann steered

260

him past it to the staircase. 'We'll walk down.'

'We're eight floors up!'

'It's good exercise. Also, if anyone is waiting for us, they will expect us to take the elevator.'

'God! This isn't going to be New Orleans all over again?'

'I hope not. We may not be so lucky this time.'

They descended to ground level, coming out at the side of the foyer of the hotel. Lohmann looked around. The foyer was busy. Tourists and residents. The after-breakfast crowd milling around the reception desk, the news stand, the front entrance. Lohmann was scanning faces. One face familiar but only from the newpapers; an eminent southern senator, with flowing white locks, a string tie and a loud voice, who resided at the hotel. No other faces he knew. They turned to the stairwell that led down to the underground car-park, it had a low roof, and concrete pillars between the rows of cars. Cadillacs, Pontiacs, Chevrolets, Fords. There were two Rolls-Royces, one new, one vintage and in a corner, a vintage Cord, in pristine condition gleaming under the bulkhead light fittings. Lohmann felt the hair at the back of his neck bristle. This was the ideal place for an ambush. Any amount of assailants could be concealed behind the pillars and the cars. He stopped Pardoe at the door, gripping his arm.

'Where's the car?' They were to use a Pontiac supplied to Pardoe by the Embassy.

'The attendant parked it when I got back from the Embassy last night. It'll be jammed in at the back somewhere.'

Lohmann nodded. And found himself looking at a youth in smart overalls approaching them.

'Do sumpthin' fur yuh, mister?'

The overalls had the insignia of the hotel above the breast pocket. The youth, an acne-scarred version of a young James Cagney, was chewing gum and twitching his shoulders in accepted Cagney fashion.

'Where is Mister Pardoe's car?' Lohmann asked.

The youth looked past him at Pardoe. 'Oh, yeah, Mister

Pardoe. You're the Pontiac. Never forget a face or the car that goes wit' it. Parked that one way back since yuh wasn't usin' it last night. Keys on the hook on my board. I'll git 'em. Got to move a couple of others to git yours out.'

He turned on his heels and walked across to a small kiosk near the entrance. He reappeared a few moments later, three sets of car keys dangling from his fingers.

'Won't be long,' he called across to them, and disappeared into the jungle of cars.

Pardoe lit a cigarette, stamping his feet on the concrete.

'You are nervous?' Lohmann asked.

'Cold. Maybe a little nervous. Be glad when we're on the way.'

'I also.' Lohmann reached into his coat and under his jacket. The waist band of his trousers was weighed down. 'Take this,' he said, bringing forth the Smith and Wesson. 'You can use a pistol?'

Pardoe nodded, took the weapon from him, and held it in the palm of his hand, contemplating the shining metal. 'This the one you got from Gramercy?'

'Yes.'

The pistol disappeared under Pardoe's coat. 'But what about you? Shouldn't you . . .'

'I have a Luger in my belt. A present from a Ukrainian gentleman last night.'

Behind them a car engine roared. The youth was moving a Cadillac, all silver trimmings and shine. He parked it to one side and went back to a large Ford saloon. They watched as he moved this second vehicle in front of the Cadillac. He had now cleared a lane for the dark Pontiac to move out. Lohmann took a step towards the lane, followed by Pardoe. But the youth was ahead of them.

'I'll get it out for yuh. Don't want you scraping any of my other customers.'

As the youth unlocked the Pontiac and climbed in, Lohmann stopped, waiting . . .

. . . and, suddenly felt a chill run through his body, a horrific knowledge of what he would have done to stop them if he had been the opposition . . .

'Wait!' he called out. 'Don't start the engine.'

He was too late. The youth had switched on the ignition and the engine spluttered to life. For a second Lohmann felt relief flood through him. He'd been wrong.

. . . the flash came first. A dazzling, blinding ball of yellow light bursting outwards in instant expansion and turning almost at once into scarlet flame. Then the sound hit their eardrums, sudden almost unbearable pressure, deafening them. At almost the same time the force of the explosion struck their bodies, sending them staggering back against the concrete wall.

Inside the fireball, the Pontiac disintegrated. The roof split and part of it rose into the air and bashed against the ceiling. Other fragments of metal and glass flew through the air smashing windows and the sides of adjacent cars. Lohmann and Pardoe had instinctively thrown their arms up to protect their eyes. Lohmann could feel pinpricks across his face as tiny fragments of glass whipped against them despite their distance from the explosion.

When Lohmann lowered his arms he glanced at Pardoe. There were tiny flecks of blood on the man's forehead.

'You . . . you all right?'

'Christ!'

They were peering through smoke at the smouldering wreck of what had once been the Pontiac. At first they could see little of the attendant but, as the smoke seemed to clear, they were able to make out something in the driving seat. It looked like a bundle of rags. Lohmann moved towards the wreck. Fragmented windscreens were all around, and glass and metal covered the concrete floor like hard snow.

The driver's door of the Pontiac was nowhere to be seen. Lohmann looked straight into the front seat. The youth, he reckoned, mercifully had been killed instantly. Surprisingly

263

his face was untouched, but below his waist there was nothing but a mass of blood.

Lohmann half turned. 'Boom-Boom Marchetti.'

Within twenty minutes the car-park was full of police officers and firemen. Charlie Markham appeared from the embassy, looking vaguely surprised to see Lohmann and Pardoe.

'What kept you?' Lohmann said sardonically.

Markham glared back at him. 'I got a phone call at the office. This has to do with you?'

'Embassy car. Given to Pardoe last night.'

Markham surveyed the wreck now surrounded by police officers. 'Someone's going to have a lot of paperwork to do to write that one off.'

'Someone is going to have to write off their son too,' Lohmann replied grimly.

A large, untidy figure in a crumpled suit lumbered up to them. He was instantly recognisable.

'Morning, Chief Thompson,' Markham said with a slightly excessive degree of deference.

The chief of Washington PD's detectives ignored Markham. He gazed steadily towards Lohmann and Pardoe.

'You two some kind of double act?'

Pardoe flushed. But Lohmann looked straight at the chief of detectives. He could sympathise with a man trying to do a job in which higher authority would always frustrate him. 'You'll have to look elsewhere for this one,' Lohmann replied.

'That so? And would you have any idea where I might look?'

'I've a name for you,' Lohmann went on. 'Marchetti. Known as Boom-Boom.'

Thompson's eyes became slits. 'You've learned your way around this city pretty quickly.'

'Information received,' Lohmann said.

'Who was the victim?'

Markham stepped forward. 'The garage attendant. Young fellow. Nobody important.'

Thompson spoke to him without looking at him. 'He was a US citizen. That's important enough.'

'Yes, of course, but . . .'

'I know Marchetti. He doesn't go in for garage attendants. He only blows away important guys for big money. Mob guys, guys that get in the way of the mob. Maybe sometimes politicos somebody got annoyed with. Sure he'd blow anybody if the price was right. Who'd want to take out a garage kid. The car was taken from the British Embassy pool for you, Lomond?'

'Not for Lomond,' said Pardoe. 'It was in my name.'

'You're Pardoe, aren't you? Your name keeps croppin' up in funny places. Well, I guess we take you all in and we talk. We talk until I make some sense outta this. Unless you're gonna plead diplomatic immunity. Which ain't gonna look nice.'

The voice came from behind Thompson. Sharp and clear. 'Not this day, Thompson.'

The chief of detectives spun round to face Whitney Collins. And behind him, small, pale and wearing a small, pale smile, James Henry Straight the Third.

'The FBI,' spat Thompson. 'I shoulda known. What interest can the FBI have in the death of a garage attendant?'

'You said it yourself, Chief. He was a citizen.'

'Murder is my territory,' Thompson insisted.

'We're not interested in the kid. We just want you to let Mister Lomond and Captain Pardoe go about their business.'

'But they were the target,' Thompson protested.

'All right. They were the target. But not the perpetrators. And hasn't Lomond given you a likely name?'

'Marchetti?'

'Dear old Boom-Boom,' said Straight from behind Collins, in a wistful voice.

'Almost certainly,' Collins went on. 'Did the job, I reckon, late last night.'

'Okay, okay!' Thompson barked. 'So I'll pick him up.'

'Normally I'd encourage you. But it's pretty futile now. Boom-Boom Marchetti has gone to a higher court, for which relief we must be grateful.' Collins scratched his nose meditatively. 'We went to see him early this morning. We saw him, but he didn't see us. He was very dead. Somebody used him on this job and then trashed him. Your case is closed already, Chief.'

Thompson scowled, not at Collins but at Lohmann, and walked abruptly off to survey the wreck.

Collins nodded to Lohmann. 'I don't think they need you any more around here. Were you going somewhere?'

'Yes. We'll go now.'

Lohmann took Pardoe by the arm and steered him towards the garage exit. As he did so, Straight sidled up.

'Glad you're all right, Bobby,' he said to Pardoe.

'Thanks, Jimmy. We're both fine.'

'Happy to have been of help, Mister Lomond.'

'I'm glad to have received your help, Mister Straight.'

Straight gave a nervous nod and hurried over to rejoin Whitney Collins. Markham followed Lohmann and Pardoe to the garage entrance.

'You'll be wanting another car from the Embassy?'

Pardoe agreed. 'Yes, we'd better . . .'

'No!' Lohmann's tone was decisive. 'No car this time. We'd be vulnerable on the road. No, we can get the train to New York. From there we can reach . . . reach our destination quite easily.'

Markham looked dubious. 'You'd be leaving yourself wide open on a train. Look, Lohmann, somebody's after the two of you, that's clear enough. And whoever it is is a meticulous bastard. They cut Marchetti's throat to keep him from talking to the police . . .'

'They're certainly getting desperate. At first they were

266

content to smear Captain Pardoe. Because they wanted to find out why he was here. Now they're getting nervous. They'd be just as happy to see him dead.'

'I see that now,' said the security man. 'Look, I can come with you . . . get one or two more men for additional protection . . .'

Lohmann looked at Pardoe. The naval man shook his head. 'Thank you for the offer, Mister Markham, but once we get to New Jersey too large a presence might become obvious to too many people. I'm sorry but I think we'll be taking the train on our own, as Lomond says.'

Markham smiled. 'That's how you want it, I won't argue. Anything I can do for you?'

'A taxi to Union Station,' said Lohmann.

Markham went out into the street.

'Are we doing the right thing?' Pardoe asked.

'I hope so,' Lohmann replied without looking at him. 'Yes, I hope so. But you have the Smith and Wesson and I have the Luger. If everything works out the way I think it will, we'll need them.'

'But isn't that why we're taking the train? Because it'll be safer?'

'That's the point, Captain Pardoe. Whichever way we go, we have trouble now.'

Maryland–New Jersey

TWENTY-FOUR

The train, like a dark worm, writhed its way across the snow-covered fields of Maryland. They had a Pullman compartment to themselves, arranged by payment of a ten dollar bill to the cheerful black porter who accepted the bill with genuine reluctance.

'Nobody much travellin' today,' the porter said. 'You didn't need to give me no ten dollars. Train only half full. Or half empty if you is a pessimist. Guess the snow's keepin' people at home. Makes it easy for me. You folks be wantin' lunch? I kin get you seats in the dining car.'

'We will take lunch. Meanwhile can we lock this door from the inside?'

'What the lock's there for,' the porter replied, leaving them to the luxury of the Pullman. They took off their coats and sat in the comfort of the ageing seats.

It was typical American overnight compartment though the journey would be entirely by day. Small, cell-like, without windows to the corridor but a large window with a panoramic view of the passing snow-covered fields; above their heads the cupboard-like arrangements that could come down to provide the sleeping facilities; a small toilet-cum-washroom off one side of the compartment.

Pardoe, grey and strained, looked around with a shiver. His shoulders seemed to fold in on each other, his chest a hollow concavity between them. 'I keep thinking of that young garage attendant.'

'You were not responsible.'

'Perhaps. Perhaps not. But this whole mission . . . the people who've died violently because of it. First Duplessis, then the man in the cemetery in New Orleans, now the boy in the garage . . .'

'War casualties.'

'It's not even their war. I feel responsible.'

'You weren't. Not for *their* deaths.'

Outside the carriage window the white fields flashed by, a glaring blur that could barely be looked upon. The train gathered speed. Pardoe was staring intently at Lohmann.

'The women. For God's sake, surely I would know . . .' Pleading, but in a quiet undertone which somehow underlined his desperation. 'All your talk about fugues . . . you really believe that?'

'I told you. It has been known.'

'If it's true, that means I'm . . . I'm insane.'

'It is a kind of insanity, yes.'

'But . . . but in a court, would it be considered insanity?'

'I cannot answer that.'

Pardoe took a deep breath, stared out of the window. But the intensity of the snowy glare caused him to look quickly away.

They sat in silence. Finally Lohmann spoke. 'Isn't it time I knew more about our reasons for going to Princeton?' he said.

Pardoe's expression remained bleak, reluctant to come out of his personal terror. Another pause. When he spoke, it was quietly, slowly.

'We were too late to reach Duplessis. He would have been able to get to the President. You see, he was a close personal friend of Roosevelt's. Now we're going to see someone else. He has enough of a reputation to reach Roosevelt.'

'A physicist?' Pardoe looked vaguely puzzled. 'It's the common factor,' Lohmann explained. 'Duplessis was a professor of physics, you have a degree in physics – must be fairly rare in a naval officer – which is why you were chosen for this mission. So we are going to see another physicist. I believe there is one particular theoretical physicist at Princeton.'

'I wonder if it matters,' Pardoe mused.

Lohmann said: 'It matters if it is to do with the war.'

'Oh yes, it's to do with the war.' Pardoe gave a long sigh. 'Thank God this business will soon be over. No more murders.'

'We must hope so.'

A sudden urgency came into Pardoe's voice. 'You . . . you said we weren't followed from the hotel. You said that.'

'It may be they had no need to.'

Pardoe's eyes widened. He looked nervously towards the locked door. 'You think they could still try and stop us?'

'We have to be prepared for all possibilities.'

Lohmann leaned back in his seat and closed his eyes. Fifteen minutes went by, Lohmann at the edge of sleep. As always, waiting. He thought, they must be halfway towards the first stop. City of Baltimore, where Edgar Allan Poe had lived; all he knew about the place. But then the mind always filled with useless information, that surfaced at the edge of sleep . . .

The knock at the compartment door brought him back to consciousness. He reached under his jacket, feeling the cold comfortable metal of the Luger. It was a sharp urgent knock, a demand for attention. Surely not the knock of the negro porter. He glanced across at Pardoe; wide awake, eyes round, staring back at him. Questioning . . .

Lohmann took the Luger from under his jacket and held it in his lap. Motioning Pardoe to do the same. Pardoe brought out the Smith and Wesson with a kind of fearful reluctance.

The knock on the door was repeated.

'Yes?' Lohmann said, affecting the weariness he had just shaken off.

'Porter, sah!' The reply was muted. A dim affectation of a Southern accent. Not quite right.

'Wha' do you want?'

'Need a word, sah.' An inadequate answer.

He wondered how many there would be. At least three, he presumed, making sure they outnumbered their quarry. He looked towards the washroom. Too small, too obvious to conceal himself. Had to be some other way.

Pardoe, aware that something was wrong, aware that the voice beyond the door wasn't the porter they had already talked to, was staring at Lohmann, waiting for a lead. Why shouldn't he? Lohmann was the bodyguard. His was the decision.

Lohmann looked towards the window. God, not the window. He'd seen that too often in the movies. Reiner could have listed them. The hero clinging to the side of the moving train, did he have to do that? Did the window even open?

He rose, lowered it to a blast of ice cold air, and the roar of the train. He looked out and down. There was a kind of ledge, barely a foothold. Easy in the cinema, maybe possible in reality if there was something above which he could hold onto. He looked upwards. There it was, a line, a ridge of metal above the window. There was also the wind pressure created by the train moving at some sixty miles an hour. Enough, without a firm hold, to blow him from the side of the train, smash him back against the carriage and then throw him off onto the line running alongside, to be broken on metal and stone chips. One slip into oblivion, If he was going to do it, he couldn't afford to think too long about it. And if he was going to, how far along was it to the carriage door? Or to another window that might be open? Which would be unlikely in icicle weather.

He looked back into the compartment. Pardoe was staring at him in amazement.

'You don't expect us to go out there?' Pardoe said, his voice almost lost in the blast of air.

Lohmann shook his head, and pointed to himself. He held up three fingers and shouted, 'Three minutes and then let

274

them in.' His voice would be masked from the men beyond the door.

'You're leaving me . . . ?' Astonishment and fear.

Lohmann closed the window to cut off the sound.

'I go around,' he said quietly, aware that he was suddenly breathless. And he had only contemplated the other side of the window. 'Hold them off. Tell them you're washing. Just give me time . . .'

Pardoe nodded uncertainly. Another knock.

Lohmann leant against the door and called out a reply. 'You'll have to wait. I am in the washroom.'

No response seemed to indicate an acknowledgement. He crossed back to the window, took his jacket off, and replaced the Luger firmly in his waistband. Then he took a deep breath and lowered the window again. And again an icy blast of freezing air hit him in the face. He put one leg over the edge of the window, foot searching below for support. Finding the ledge he brought his other leg over and balanced himself, gripping the edge of the open window.

The air tore at his body, a weight of solid ice pressing against him. Not possible, he thought, not possible. His fingers would be torn from their grip on the open window, and he could not reach up to the ridge above it. But, even with it closed, he could grip a ridge of metal at the foot of the window. Now, if he could reach over to the next window . . . He looked up and saw Pardoe, pale-faced, staring down at him.

He moved one hand down, supporting himself by the newly discovered ridge below the glass. And staring up at Pardoe, he shouted, 'Shut the window!'

Reluctantly, and with infinite care, Pardoe pulled the window up. And Lohmann was alone, hanging from the side of the carriage.

He thought: *'Christ, I'm nearly fifty years of age, out of condition and I'm hanging from the outside of an express train from my fingernails like some hero of one of those silent serials except that it isn't silent there's a hell of a noise beating against my eardrums and the wind force is battering against me I can't move and I have to move and whether I do or I don't this is the nearest thing to suicide will I ever see Anna again? that's a question have to move now away from this window and I feel as if I'm paralysed only can't allow myself to be paralysed. . .'*

He took the fingers of his left hand from the ridge and strained towards the window of the next compartment. It was like moving one arm against a solid force. Which it was. A force of nature plus the thrust of the moving train. Sixty miles an hour against a wind that must double the miles per hour pressing against him. He strained to the left.

Touching the ridge under the next window.

His fingers scrabbled against the ridge. The metal was iced up, his fingers were freezing cold and scrabbling to gain a grip . . .

And did so, after what seemed like ages. He edged himself along the side of the train. The right hand now! Take it off the ridge and move it under the next window.

He made it. Arms aching, back stiff and cold and agonised.

Three more to the carriage steps and entrance. Easing along the second window. *'Thank God it wasn't a British train doubt if it could be done apologies to Robert Donat in the 'Thirty-Nine Steps' or did he just jump off a moving train? now that would be easy just let go and die quickly anyway a British train wouldn't have the observation area between carriages, and what the hell did it matter anyway except that if he fell off the train Pardoe would be killed or something the bloody mission would probably fail and did that mean Germany would win the war? he doubted it but then who was he?'*

The same straining and edging and pain and cold.

He made it. Two more to go.

'Pardoe might be dead by now and all this would be pointless, Anyway, isn't this where in all the best movies a train comes along on the next rail and gives everybody a thrill . . . would he fall off or not? but bless somebody or other no train not yet

*anyway maybe if he fell off he'd land in a snow bank and suffer
only minor injuries like breaking both legs or he would land on his
head and fracture his skull stop thinking and move before you
freeze to death.'*

Another window. And stabbing pains in the arms now.

*'Maybe all this was good exercise everybody should crawl
along the outside of a moving train for at least fifteen minutes
every day I was a teenage nine-stone weakling until I crawled
along the side of a train God bless you Charles Atlas stop thinking
and move to the next window before you stick to the side of the
train frozen in ice.'*

Another window. He edged again towards it.

One foot slipped into the rushing slipstream. He pulled it
back, gulping air.

*'Close that was both feet and he would have been gone stop
thinking stop thinking.'*

And moved on, slowly, slowly, with infinite care. The last
window. Half reaching, half sliding along. Not far now.

Feet slithering below him.

*'I can't fall off I'm on the good side one of the men on the white
horses stop thinking every time you think you stay immobile like a
fly stuck to the metal move and don't think.'*

The last window . . . and where it ended so did the finger
grip. He would have to swing himself forward and hope his
feet would land on the step between the carriages and let him
grab the handrail.

He reached out and propelled himself forward. Against the
gale which seemed to be lessening. For a fraction of a second
his feet were in nothingness; then his hands were firmly
gripping the handrail. Sweating in spite of the icy cold,
panting for breath, he pulled himself into the step. The train
was slowing down. He climbed onto the solid metal floor
between the carriages and looked back over his shoulder. The
fields had gone and in their place were buildings, sheds,
factories, and a mesh of other rail lines opening up and
twisting across soggy ground. The snow was patchy now and

turning to mud and slush. They were on the outskirts of Baltimore.

He opened the carriage door and went into the corridor, easing the Luger from his waistband. When he reached the compartment the door was shut. With Pardoe and whoever was pursuing them inside. Lohmann leant back against the corridor window and, Luger in his right hand, kicked out at the door. There was a sharp crack of splintering wood as it flew open. Lohmann propelled himelf into the compartment.

Pardoe was sitting in the corner against the window. A large man with a pistol in hand was facing him, the weapon pointing at Pardoe's chest. Another large man with close-cropped hair was standing leaning against the window. And, as Lohmann burst in, a familiar figure, small and dark came out the washroom.

'You were looking for someone, Vonsiatsky?' Lohmann said, pointing the Luger at the Ukrainian's head.

Vonsiatsky gaped at him.

'Muller!'

Lohmann slipped into his role of last night. 'Congratulations. I didn't think you would apprehend Captain Pardoe. You've been working hard since last night. But now I will take over.'

Vonsiatsky stiffened. 'We have our orders. To take Pardoe and Lomond.'

'You seem to have mislaid Lomond.'

'He came on the train with Pardoe. He has left the compartment. He will return.' Vonsiatsky hesitated. And then went on. 'Unless he already had returned. Our . . . our control informed us last night he had no knowledge of anyone from Germany called Muller. And he also believed that Lomond was himself of German origin.'

'You're very quick, Herr Vonsiatsky. Now you'll please tell your associate at the window to throw his gun on the floor.'

The Ukrainian gave a small, amused shrug. 'Why should I? His gun is pointed at Pardoe, yours at us. A kind of stalemate.

You might be equally advised to throw your gun on the floor.'

Another ridiculous situation, Lohmann told himself. Life so like the stuff of bad melodrama. Them and us. And guns in between. Like the old days.

'*I have been here before*,' Lohmann thought. '*Has to be resolved*.'

He swivelled the Luger around and fired one shot. It struck the man facing Pardoe on the wrist. The man screamed, his weapon clattered to the floor.

'One has to be very fast in such stalemate situations,' Lohmann said, the Luger again pointing at Vonsiatsky. 'If you continue to argue, the next bullet will go through your forehead. The entry hole will be small but the exit will take away the back of your head. Don't make me do that, Vonsiatsky, I am not of a bloodthirsty nature.'

The Ukrainian was ashen faced. Behind him, the wounded man was moaning, clutching his wrist trying to stop the blood. The third intruder had flattened himself against the wall, staring down at him.

Lohmann said, 'Captain Pardoe, will you please pick up that weapon and relieve the other gentleman of the one he undoubtedly is carrying. And then search Herr Vonsiatsky here.'

Vonsiatsky studied him for a long moment. 'You are Lomond?'

'Too late to deny it now.'

The small dark man was silent. A moment later Pardoe had three guns in his hand.

'The window, I think,' said Lohmann. Pardoe threw them out.

'I seem to be taking guns from you all the time,' Lohmann said to the Ukrainian. 'I'm grateful, but how many can one man carry at one time?'

'You will still be stopped,' Vonsiatsky said.

'But not by you.'

The train was still slowing down, moving at not more than

fifteen miles an hour. Outside the window the backs of tenements.

'We should be in Baltimore station very soon. It's time for you to disembark. At this speed, the worst that can happen is probably a broken leg. To the window . . .'

'You can't . . .'

'Either jump or I fire again. The choice is yours. Make it now.'

The wounded man jumped first, then his companion. Lohmann glimpsed the two figures land on the muddy track and roll over. As the train moved slowly on, he could see one of them struggle to his feet. Vonsiatsky was last. He opened his mouth to protest, thought better of it, and jumped.

Lohmann pulled the window up at once, and turned to Pardoe. 'You all right?'

Pardoe nodded as if in a mild state of shock.

'Sit back, Pardoe, and relax.' He looked at himself in the mirror on the back of the washroom door, saw a dishevelled figure, face, hands, and clothes smeared with soot, hair awry. 'While I have a wash. I must look not too disreputable when we get to Princeton.'

TWENTY-FIVE

Another figure with hair awry. He seemed an old man although in fact he was only sixty. But the wild hair was grey to white, as was the moustache. The eyes were deep sunken, sad and yet with a sparkle which lent a suggestion of humour

280

to the seamed face. And despite his lack of inches, he dominated the room.

'Already I have written to President Roosevelt but not with any great urgency,' he said with an accent Lohmann identified as Viennese. 'The good Mister Sachs wants me to write again, as does Szilard. And now you.'

Standing back to the window he was facing Pardoe who was in front of the untidy desk. Behind them Lohmann was ensconced in a deep leather armchair. The room was comfortable but as untidy as was the desk which was covered in papers. From the window there was a view of grey ivy-clad walls and green grass flecked with snow – the campus of Princeton's Institute of Advanced Studies.

Lohmann ached, the muscles in his legs and arms were reacting to the punishment he had inflicted on them. But for the pain, the train journey might have been a recent nightmare which he would gladly and easily have forgotten. He could only hope Vonsiatsky and his associates were experiencing as much pain from their fall from the train. Nevertheless, he was alert, and fascinated by the small figure of the old man in the knitted pullover and baggy, crumpled trousers.

'I can give you some idea of the urgency of the matter,' said Pardoe, opening his brief case and extracting a file of papers. 'I would urge you to read these documents.'

Professor Albert Einstein shrugged, waving his hands in the air, palms upwards. 'Papers, papers, I am reading papers all day. You tell me the gist of them. That will be enough. But they are prepared by your British government?'

'Collated by them,' Pardoe replied. 'They are written by people you know, or know of. Fellow scientists. Very few of them British.'

'Don't mistake me, Captain. I have sympathy with your government in this war. But the Americans are very . . . very nervous about involvement in the conflict, as you will know.

And my own position as a refugee is delicate. After all I am only a private citizen.'

'Hardly that, sir . . .'

'You think I am special. Not so. However, please . . . these documents, tell me about them.'

'First of all, Dr Szilard, while working at Columbia University, has become increasingly concerned about information coming out of Germany regarding the possibility of Germany gaining control of the uranium deposits in the Belgian Congo. Although Belgium is neutral, the Wehrmacht could so easily invade Belgium as they did in the last war. The world's greatest deposits of uranium could become theirs.'

'I have heard of this. Szilard visited me.'

'You may know then that Szilard has further information relating to the work of Otto Hahn and others . . .'

'You are telling me nothing new, Captain Pardoe.' Einstein was exhibiting a degree of impatience, albeit amiably.

'We also know that Germany has been conducting experiments with heavy water.'

'Now that is of interest.'

'And Dr Goebbels has released hints about a new bomb which the Nazis are reputed to be developing.'

The old man's bushy eyebrows rose. 'They have said this?'

'They have let it be known. We are perhaps fortunate that they have caused so many of their best scientists to seek refuge in this country. Apart from yourself and Szilard, there's Teller, and Hans Bethe, Von Neumann, Ulman . . .'

Albert Einstein turned back to the window to contemplate the campus. 'I have expressed doubts as to the possibility of such a weapon being created. As has your own Sir Henry Tizard. These new phenomena concerning the fission of uranium or even plutonium to create a bomb are only theoretical.'

'Perhaps at present, sir. But it is conceivable, Szilard believes it possible. And the result – an extremely powerful bomb, which could very well destroy an entire town.'

Lohmann was leaning forward now, aching muscles forgotten, fascinated by the discussion.

Einstein was silent for a moment. Then he spoke. 'Such a bomb may never be possible. Indeed I hope it is not possible. Physicists should not deal with the making of bombs!'

'I agree with you, sir. But do you think the German government would hesitate?'

Einstein looked over at Lohmann. 'You are from Germany, sir?'

'Like yourself I am a refugee.' Lohmann replied, shifting awkwardly in his seat. 'I also had the . . . *die privilegiert zweifelhaft. . .*' A glance at Pardoe, '. . . the dubious privilege of meeting Hitler himself.'

The professor gave a small, ironic smile. 'A difficult gentleman, I believe?'

'As you say, Herr Professor. And a man who, given the possibility of owning such a bomb, would not hesitate to authorise its use.'

'So,' said Einstein, 'this the Americans should have before Hitler. This is what you are saying?'

'This is what I would say.'

'Things move so fast,' Einstein said. 'So many experiments for the benefit of mankind. Yet so many unpleasant side effects. Ach, bombs, this is not the purpose of our work.'

'You see the necessity, Professor?' Pardoe said.

'Can the British do nothing?'

'We have the ability but hardly the resources. Our supplies of Uranium 235 are minuscule. Here in America, there are some small deposits. And Canada has considerable resources. Between ourselves and the United States it may be possible to deny Germany the Congo deposits. But there is no certainty of that. Yet certainly the resources of the United States could and should be utilised.'

'And the abilities of so many talented refugees,' Einstein added. 'If they are willing.'

'These are the very people who believe it essential,' Pardoe responded.

Again the old man contemplated the view from the window. 'If such a bomb is possible . . . the results would be horrific.'

'Especially in the hands of Adolf Hitler,' Lohmann added. It was all so new to him, yet the concept frightened him.

Einstein nodded. 'I have already written another letter to Roosevelt. But I have not yet sent it. I will incorporate what you say in this letter and I will send it to President Roosevelt. In fact I will give you a copy today to take with you. Szilard has already written me. I will enclose a copy of his letter.'

'You will involve yourself, sir?' Pardoe asked.

'I am a theoretical physicist, Captain. Any papers of mine will be available, but others will have to do the practical work. Szilard, Hahn, Teller, Fermi . . . and so many others, this would be their kind of work. I will advise the Americans to turn to Szilard. You will excuse me while I have amendments made to the letter I have already written. Please relax, gentlemen. You will take some tea.'

The last was an instruction not a suggestion. Einstein went to the door of the room.

'It is ironic,' he said. 'We work, as the popular journals would say, for the benefit of mankind. We explore the universe in theory and practice. I have always believed that was our function. Now I find myself recommending the making of a bomb. I do not like it. It makes me feel uncomfortable. But I suppose it has to be done.'

He went out.

Pardoe turned to Lohmann. 'Now you know.'

'This bomb . . . is possible?'

'Some doubt it. There are even those who think that if such a bomb went off, it might trigger off an infinite chain reaction.'

'What does that mean?'

Pardoe stroked his chin. 'The destruction of the world.

284

Atom splitting atom, splitting atom, *ad infinitum* the earth explodes. It's a thought. But fortunately unlikely.'

'You are sure?'

'Nothing is certain in this area. Einstein, as you've heard, isn't at all sure such an atom bomb can be made. Sir Henry Tizard thinks the same and Churchill's friend Lindemann is sure it's impossible.'

'I think I hope they are right.'

'Myself, I think it can be done,' Pardoe said quietly. 'Makes other . . . other deaths seem trivial.'

A plump housekeeper brought in a tray with tea and a plate of biscuits.

Twenty minutes later Einstein rejoined them. He handed an envelope to Pardoe. 'Your copy of the letter. The other copy will go direct to Washington. I suggest you take that at once to Alexander Sachs.'

He sat facing them and allowed Pardoe to pour him a cup of tea. As he drank it, his face became infinitely sad.

'I can only pray, that this bomb is an impossibility. And if it is made, that it will never be used against Germany . . . against any country.'

They drove back to Washington that evening. The journey was uneventful, and Pardoe appeared to sleep for most of the trip. Lohmann could not stop himself thinking of the meeting with Einstein. And of the bomb. What had Pardoe called it? The atom bomb. A destructive force many times greater than any normal explosive. He echoed Einstein's thought that it never be used.

It was after midnight when they arrived back at the Mayflower Hotel.

'I'll telephone Sachs at once,' Pardoe said when he reached his room. 'And when Roosevelt receives this letter my work is finished here. We'll have done everything we can.' His hands and his forehead were damp with perspiration. 'But then, I suppose your work goes on?'

'But not for long,' Lohmann replied.

Once in his own room, Lohmann phoned Reiner. The former sergeant appeared a few minutes later, dressing gown over his pyjamas.

'Pardoe's mission is almost over,' Lohmann told him without going into the details of the visit to Princeton.

'So where does that leave us?' Reiner asked.

'Still searching for our serial killer.'

'Pardoe?'

Lohmann took off his jacket and sat on the end of the bed. 'It's still possible. Either these killings were carried out to discredit Pardoe or . . . he is our man. A psychopathic personality. He may genuinely have no knowledge of his actions at the time he kills. Or he may be a very good actor.'

'You've no leads to anyone else?'

Lohmann looked up. 'Oh yes, I have leads. But whether to a killer or . . . to something else, I'm not sure. Also, there is one other thing.'

Reiner smiled, 'You're going to tell me?'

'At the completion of his work here, if Pardoe is not proved to be innocent, the British government wants him . . . eliminated, rather than arrested by the Americans.'

'They could plead diplomatic immunity on his behalf.'

'In a multiple murder case? The Germans would enjoy that. No, the British would simply eliminate him. Excuse it as an action necessary in time of war.'

Reiner abstractly produced a packet of Camels from his dressing gown and lit a cigarette. 'No trial? No further investigation?'

'Unless I can prove his innocence.'

'Which you cannot.'

'If he is innocent, I need time,' Lohmann leaned forward, extracted a cigarette from the packet in Reiner's pocket and waited for his former assistant to offer him a light. Reiner did so quickly.

'Sorry, chief – getting mean in my old age. If Pardoe's to be killed, who does it?'

'They haven't given me that information.'

'Which means you have to work fast.'

Lohmann rose from the bed, inhaled the cigarette and paced the room irritably. 'Serial murder is not something that can be solved quickly. And certainly there is much evidence against Pardoe. Although all of it is circumstantial.'

'What else can it be? Short of catching him in the act. Short of catching anybody in the act. Pardoe would appear to have the opportunity every time. He can be linked to the victims. He admits to knowing most of them . . .'

'Except for Mary Lou Hancock. And the coloured girl.'

'Yet his name was in the Hancock girl's diary. And we found him in the black girl's place.'

'Some hours after the murder,' Lohmann interjected.

'He could have been there in the afternoon. We know that.'

'*Could*,' Lohmann insisted. 'We have no proof.'

Reiner raised his eyebrows. 'Sounds as if you don't believe he is the killer.'

Lohmann continued to pace the room. 'I have been with him in circumstances of some jeopardy for both of us. Perhaps I have saved his life. Perhaps he has saved mine. Now I have to either prove his innocence, or expedite his death. It is not easy to . . . how can one say it . . . ?'

'Go into reverse gear?'

The telephone rang. Lohmann crossed to the bedside phone and lifted it.

'Lomond here.'

'I have spoken to Sachs.' Pardoe was at the other end of the line. 'And he's been on to the White House. He has made an appointment for tomorrow morning.'

'That is good,' Lohmann replied, feeling it was exactly the opposite. If the interview at the White House was successful, then the mission was over. And the British government would want action on the murders. Time was running out.

287

Pardoe went on, 'Sachs insists we accompany him. I have told him, as a serving British officer, it is not wise. But it seems Roosevelt wants to meet us. You'll be ready to leave with me at ten o'clock in the morning.'

'I'll be ready.'

He replaced the receiver. Time was running out for Captain Pardoe.

Washington

TWENTY-SIX

It was a bright, cold morning. A weak sun shone over the city, and most of the previous day's snow had disappeared. The Potomac flowed high under the Arlington Memorial Bridge, its waters dark and sluggish. Pigeons on the steps of the Capitol pouted and puffed out their feathers to keep themselves warm. The Washington Monument, that 550 foot obelisk dedicated to the founder of the Republic, reflected the rays of the yellow sun off its polished marble surface.

Lohmann breakfasted in his room, at the window overlooking the city. He had taken some care in dressing. His one suit had been sent down early to be cleaned and pressed. It wasn't every day, he told himself, he had an appointment with the President of the United States. He had of course seen newsreels of Roosevelt and, through the man's pronouncements, admired the image created and the work done. Not that the New Deal was over. Slowly it had dragged the USA from the depths of depression. In so many ways Roosevelt had brought the country out of the slough of poverty into which so many had fallen. Lohmann was curious to know whether he would admire in the flesh this man who had achieved so much.

He determined, when the meeting at the White House was over, to return at once to the Embassy and contact London by telegraph. He would request more time from the Admiralty on the murder case. He had developed an increasing admiration for Pardoe's single-mindedness in pursuing his task despite the attempts on his life and the fear that was visible within him regarding the murders.

A knock on the bedroom door. It was James Henry Straight the Third. Looking paler than usual. And, as always, impeccably dressed.

'Good morning.' The hands fluttering.

'I am sorry but I haven't much time . . .'

A smile from Straight. 'I know. You have an important appointment.'

Lohmann showed his surprise. 'May I ask how the hell you know that?'

'Mister Hoover has connections in the White House. They keep him informed.'

'Does the President know this?'

'Probably not. But then it is Mister Hoover's duty to know all that is happening at the White House. In order to protect the President. So Mister Hoover says.'

Lohmann rose from his breakfast table . 'Perhaps, before I go, you might tell me quickly what you want?'

'To warn you. Within the next day or so, Hoover plans to get a warrant for Captain Pardoe's arrest.'

'On what charge?'

'He believes there is enough evidence to detain Pardoe on suspicion of murder. In fact there will be enough evidence to charge him."

Lohmann felt suddenly angry. 'Charging him would surely be a local police matter.'

'Washington is a Federal District. Hoover can exert jurisdiction. Or simply hand over any evidence to the police.'

'All the evidence is circumstantial. You know that.'

'I know it, you know it, even Chief Thompson knows it. But Hoover seems to believe that within the next day or two he will have additional evidence.'

'Why have you come to tell me this?'

The small man shrugged. There was a sadness in his expression. 'I . . . I like Bobby Pardoe. I've told you that before. Of course you think I'm just an ageing queen on the make for a navy man who . . . who has no real interest in me beyond friendship. And . . . and you're right. But I don't want to see this happen. I want you to get him out of the country. As soon after your White House appointment as possible. Before Hoover produces his evidence.'

'It won't save him,' Lohmann said evenly. 'If British Intelligence believes he killed those women, they will issue orders to . . . get rid of him. Eliminate him. Without the scandal of a trial.'

Straight stared at Lohmann, a look of horror spreading over his face. 'You're not his guard. You're his executioner!'

'No. I was sent to watch him. If possible, stop these murders.'

'You've hardly been successful.'

Lohmann blinked. It was a partial truth. Had he stayed with Pardoe, the black woman might have lived. The others he could not have prevented. But at least he had ensured Pardoe's mission had been carried out. He glanced at his watch.

'I have to leave. You've no idea what this new evidence is that Hoover expects to get?'

'He plays things close to his chest.'

At the door of the room, Lohmann hesitated, hand on the door knob. 'Do you believe Pardoe killed these women?'

Straight shuffled his feet awkwardly on the carpet. 'I don't know. Sure it's possible. But it could have been someone else.'

'*You* were around in Singapore, London and Washington.'

Straight giggled. 'Not my bag, old man, killing women. I . . . get the old rocks off in other ways.'

'So you say.'

'But I could be lying, that's what you're telling me? I'm not. I like Bobby Pardoe, but not enough to take his sins upon myself. Anyway, there were others around.'

'I know. But you seem so anxious to help him. As if his arrest might be on your conscience.'

He left Straight helping himself to the last of the breakfast toast.

Pardoe was waiting in the hotel foyer, briefcase in hand. With Reiner in attendance.

'We have to pick up Sachs in ten minutes. I have a car waiting,' Pardoe said. He was dressed in a civilian suit. Careful not to be seen as a British officer entering the White House.

'I'll join you in a minute,' Lohmann said, taking Reiner aside. Pardoe looked puzzled but went out to the waiting car.

'Chief?' said Reiner.

'When we come back from this appointment, I shall drop Pardoe here. I want you to stay with him. Outside his room will be good enough. But you have to make sure he doesn't leave. I'll inform him.'

'You think he might go . . . hunting . . . again?'

'I think he has to be watched. Once his work is over, he may have strange ideas about relaxing.'

'In other words, you think he killed these women?'

'Do it, Reiner! It'll be over soon and then you can get back to Cincinnati.'

The car was a long, shining black Cadillac, supplied by the White House. Lohmann decided the driver, in smart grey flannel suit with a bulge under the left arm, was one of the elite Secret Service men who protected the President. With a brief 'Good morning, sir' to Lohmann, the man showed him into the back seat beside Pardoe.

A few moments later they picked up Alexander Sachs from a small house in a quiet street on the edge of Georgetown. He too was carrying a briefcase. They drove to the White House.

The Cadillac went in by a side entrance. They were greeted by a black manservant with a pleasing smile. He ushered them into the building, through a high ceilinged hallway and up a staircase, the walls of which were lined with portraits of previous occupants of the building. As they climbed the manservant commented on the portraits.

'That's President Grant . . . they say he had a mighty strong likin' for corn whisky. Now President Fillmore, we just doan't know much 'bout him. Or him there, that's President Chester Arthur. And that's President McKinley, they assassinated him. Before my time, that was. An' that's Mistah Coolidge, he was here when I first came. Very quiet gentleman.'

The figure behind the Oval Office desk, with the large, leonine head and familiar pince-nez, was instantly recognisable.

'Come away in, gentleman,' said Franklin Roosevelt with an expansive wave of a large hand. 'How are you, Alexander? The other gentlemen'll forgive me if I don't rise. The steel braces are acting up today.'

Sachs went over to the desk and shook hands with the seated President. Pardoe followed.

'Mister . . . no, Captain Pardoe, isn't it? And this will be Mister Lomond.'

He shook hands with them both, the wide smile in place ready to embrace the world. 'Sit down, sit down. I've ordered coffee but if any of you would like anything stronger, say the word. We have branch water here that enhances anything.'

They settled in comfortable chairs facing the President. Another black servant brought in a tray of coffee and served them in silence.

'Well now, I believe you have a letter for me from Professor Einstein, Captain Pardoe? A copy of that letter has already arrived.'

Pardoe reached for his briefcase.

'Oh, don't worry, Captain. I've already read the letter. I'm already *au fait* with the contents. Not that I am particularly knowledgeable in this branch of science.'

Alexander Sachs opened his briefcase and produced a large volume. 'I brought this along, Mister President. There's a

295

paper in here, Aston on "Forty Years of Atomic Theory". I thought it might be of use to you.'

'Thank you, Alex. Leave it with me. Of course what you want is to see that the Nazis don't blow us up.'

'That would be so.'

'You will get no argument from me there. You agree with Alex, Captain Pardoe?'

'I do, sir.'

Roosevelt leaned across his desk and pressed the button on an intercom machine. A female voice came through the machine.

'Mister President?'

'Missy, will you ask General Watson to come in. And bring Lyman Briggs with him.' Roosevelt switched the machine off and leaned back, head up in a pose familiar to newsreel viewers. 'So you truly believe this bomb could be made, Captain Pardoe?'

'Yes, sir.'

'I have discussed this with various of my people this morning. And indeed when I received the earlier letters from Einstein. Colonel Adamson believes research on this bomb would be a waste of time. Take at least two years to develop . . . if it were possible. And then he tells me it wouldn't win any war. Adamson believes wars are won by the morale of the soldier in the field and not by fancy new weapons. His words, gentlemen.'

'If such a bomb is possible then there would be no morale,' Lohmann said quietly. 'And possibly no soldiers.'

Roosevelt looked at him through the pince-nez and then suddenly threw back his head and laughed. 'A point, Mister Lomond, a point.' He swivelled around in his chair. 'You know, these physicist friends of yours, Captain Pardoe, Dr Szilard, Signor Fermi and the others, they have told me they need two thousand dollars to pursue their experiments. Oh, there's no problem there. If they'd asked for much more, my people might have been suspicious. But two thousand is so little. I . . . I have informed Adamson to authorise it.'

'That will be most helpful,' Pardoe said.

'I somehow think I'm not going to get a bomb for two thousand dollars,' the President went on. 'But any more and the Senate would have been on to me. That's one small problem. If we go ahead with this business, we're going to have to find money without informing the Senate. You see the problems I anticipate already.'

The door opened and two men entered. General Edwin M. Watson, known as Pa, the President's secretary, was a neat man of medium height with a tired face. His companion, Doctor Lyman J. Briggs, had the air of a civil service executive. He was indeed Director of the Bureau of Standards.

'Well, Pa, how have you been getting on?' Roosevelt said, head back again.

'A three-man committee, Mister President. Colonel Adamson representing the Army, Commander Hoover, the Navy. And Lyman here will be in charge.'

The pince-nez moved to focus on Briggs. 'Well, Lyman you know what we want of you.'

Briggs nodded calmly. 'We determine the possibilities of such a bomb being created. And determine the next step. I'm arranging a meeting with Szilard, Teller and Wigner.'

'Good, good! And the whole matter to be top secret. That includes Congress at this time.' The President then turned to Sachs and Pardoe. 'There you are, gentlemen, if this bomb of yours is possible, then we'll make it. And with good American technology, we'll make it before Herr Hitler does.'

'There is another problem, sir,' Briggs cut in. 'Doctor Szilard and his colleagues . . .'

'They are a problem?'

'While we can talk with them, and they can use their two thousand dollars on their research, they cannot be further involved in our work.'

The President took off his pince-nez and proceeded to

polish the lens with a handkerchief.

'These men have brought this whole concept to us, and you're telling me we can't use their expertise?'

'Mister President, they are aliens. Even if they wish American citizenship, it would take five years to grant it to them. Except by Act of Congress. Which we dare not ask for without revealing our reasons for such a move.'

'Yes, I see. Thank you, Lyman. They will have to be excluded after your one meeting. Very well. Proceed in that manner. Good morning, Pa, good morning, Lyman.'

The secretary and the civil servant were dismissed. When they were gone, Roosevelt turned to Pardoe.

'You see how we wrap ourselves in civil service red tape. I'm only sorry George Duplessis is dead. He would have cut through it all. But don't worry, gentlemen, I'm sure before this business is finished Szilard, Teller and the others will be deeply involved. I suspect we need them. Just as I suspect this is going to cost us much more than two thousand dollars. Thank you for coming, gentlemen. And, I need hardly say it, this meeting never happened.'

A smile flitted across the President's face. 'Of course, Captain Pardoe, you will inform Mister Churchill of the meeting that never was.'

Back in the hotel foyer, Pardoe was grim faced. 'That's it, Lomond,' he said. 'Mission complete. Now for the other problem.'

Lohmann nodded.

'Can we settle it back in London?'

'If the FBI will permit. Which I doubt.'

'It's strange. Up until the time we saw the President, I was a kind of asset to Great Britain. Now I am an unpleasant problem.' He stopped momentarily, bleakly staring into space. 'What do I do now?'

'You do exactly as I tell you. Go to your hotel room and wait there. Lock the door and don't go out.'

'I have to inform London of the meeting . . . I have to send a coded wire . . .'

'Write it out. I'll see it's coded and sent off from the Embassy. You'll do it in your room now. And then you wait.'

Lohmann left Pardoe's room half an hour later. Outside, he met Reiner.

'You stay here,' he informed his one-time sergeant. 'Make sure he doesn't leave the room, far less the hotel.'

'Where can I contact you?'

'The Embassy. But I will contact you. I have a feeling we are approaching a conclusion. Whether it will be the one we want, is another question . . .'

TWENTY-SEVEN

The cypher room was in the basement of the British Embassy. The senior cypher officer was alone when Lohmann gave him Pardoe's message to transmit.

'For the Admiralty. Top priority.'

'I'll code it up and get it off at once.'

'Any reply to the message I sent yesterday?'

The officer shook his head. 'Not yet. But then the Admiralty's got a lot of traffic going in and out. There's a German pocket battleship roaming around the South Atlantic. The *Graf Spee*.'

'So everybody has problems. The minute you get a reply . . .'

'I'll send it up to your office.'

In the corridor outside the cipher room Lohmann met

Caroline Norwood. She was carrying a bundle of papers.

'You're back,' she said, looking pleased and not bothering to hide her pleasure. 'In that case Captain Greenock wants to see you.'

'He's free now?'

She nodded.

'Good.'

'Lomond? The job you were on . . . it's finished?'

'Well . . . Captain Pardoe's work is completed,' he said, somewhat inconclusively.

'Fine. Celebration? You and I?'

'But I'm not sure *my* work is over.'

She smiled. 'Come on. You look like you need to relax. I promised you a dinner cooked by my own fair hands. Tonight? My place again.'

He hesitated and then made a decision. 'Why not?'

The smile broadened. 'Nine o'clock. Prompt. Everything I cook is meticulously timed. You come early, you put me off my cooking, you come late, it'll be ruined.'

'I shall be meticulous.'

'Good. Don't plan to leave early. Must dash.' She indicated the papers in her arms. 'For the cypher room.'

Captain Greenock was at his desk, charts spread out in front of him. He glanced up as Lohmann entered and then went back to studying his charts.

'Take a seat, old man. Big flap on at the Admiralty. There's a –'

'– German battleship in the Atlantic. I know.'

'Trouble is, we don't know where it is. Already sunk too many merchantmen for comfort. The whole Atlantic fleet's looking for it. They seem to think it might just head for a neutral deep water port. Wanted to see you – Pardoe's been on the phone. Tells me he's finished his job here.' The change of subject was effected without a breath.

Lohmann said, 'And mine may have just begun.'

Greenock looked up from his charts. 'You still haven't

300

proof he killed these women?'

'The evidence is purely circumstantial so far.'

'That means he may not be guilty.'

'No, Captain Greenock, it means he is probably guilty. How many people in this building know he is under suspicion?'

'You, me, Markham . . .'

'That's all?'

'As far as I know.'

'And your secretary.'

'Caroline? Not from me!'

'My fault,' said Lohmann. 'She accompanied me to the scene of the last killing. It was accidental,' he added quickly. 'We followed Pardoe from the Van Essling reception. He led us to another scene of crime.'

Greenock cast his charts aside and rose from his desk, taking in the implications. 'There was nothing about another killing in the newpapers.'

'I think that was J. Edgar Hoover's doing. And now I have heard he has additional evidence aginst Pardoe. But what, I don't know.'

'We can't ask for diplomatic immunity over multiple murder.' He walked to the window and stared morosely down at the Embassy gardens.

'You could, but it would not be popular,' Lohmann said.

'That is a masterpiece of understatement.'

'However, it will not come out,' 'Lohmann went on in low tones. 'If Pardoe is guilty, I think you will find there will be an accident . . .'

Greenock turned to look at him. Shock on his face; followed quickly by a questioning look.

Lohmann shook his head. 'I am merely the watcher, the detective. But I need more time, Captain. I have telegraphed London for that time. It may be that Pardoe is . . . what do the Americans call it? . . . in a frame. I want your support in this.'

'Yes, of course. Has London replied?'

'Not yet. But a message from you might help.'

'I'll get it off at once.'

'Thank you.' Lohmann rose now. 'One other thing. Has Markham reported anything on the leak from this Embassy?'

'Not yet. He can find no indication so far. Could any leak be simply "careless talk"?'

'Someone knew exactly where Pardoe was going when he went to New Orleans. They also knew I was following him. That was not careless talk. There is an enemy agent in this building. You have informed the Ambassador?'

'Markham told Lord Lothian of the possibility. The Ambassador authorised him to investigate and security was tightened up. I have to say Lothian doubted the whole story.'

'His Lordship is mistaken. But I think the agent has already revealed himself. Another reason I need time.'

'If you know something, Lomond, it is your duty to inform . . .'

'*When* I know something, Captain Greenock. Good day.'

He went back to his own office, sat behind his desk, placed several sheets of blank paper in front of him, and started to write. He set down in detail everything that had happened to him since he had arrived in Washington. It was an old exercise for him. Write everything in detail. Read and rewrite. Recall everything. He was still writing as darkness fell over the city.

It was past seven o'clock when a cipher officer came into his office. 'The reply to your London message. Knew you were anxious so I brought it up myself.'

'Thank you. Captain Greenock was sending a telegraph on the same subject . . .'

'He sent it. This reply covers both messages. I've decoded it for you.'

'Again, thank you.'

The officer left. Lomond stared at the decoded reply.

'Since Pardoe's mission completed, no further time

302

allowed. Decision at highest level. Arrangements are being made. Thornhill.'

Lohmann crumpled the paper in disgust. He lifted the telephone and dialled the Mayflower Hotel and was put through to Pardoe's room.

'Lomond. Is Reiner with you?'

'No. But I'm doing what you told me. Haven't been outside the room. In fact, I've been sleeping. Did you get my message off to London?'

'It has been received and acknowledged. Reiner will be outside in the corridor. Ask him to come to the phone, please.'

Another few moments, sounds in the background of a door being opened, half-heard voices. And then Reiner. 'Chief?'

'Our request for more time has been refused.'

'You mean, whether or not . . . .?' Reiner let the question tail off into silence.

'They have made up their minds. This means you are not only protecting Pardoe from himself, and the other side. You are also protecting him from British Intelligence. You will do that.'

'I understand.'

'We may have a few hours, we may not. Stay with Pardoe as before. You're armed?'

'Yes.'

'Good. Be prepared to use it.'

'Against . . .' he hesitated, aware of Pardoe's presence. '. . . our friends?'

'Against the British and the Germans. Try not to shoot anybody unless you have to. If you do, shoot to wound and claim the man was an intruder, a thief.'

Reiner sounded nervous now. 'Any authorisation?'

'No.'

'That's nice.' With heavy irony.

'We could perhaps hand Pardoe over to the FBI if we can be sure they are genuine. They may charge him with murder, but they should not harm him. In their custody might be the best place for him, I will investigate the possibility. I'll phone you on it. But don't leave him until I get there. Which may be late.'

Lohmann replaced the receiver and then, lifting it again, dialled the FBI building.

'I wish to be connected to Mister Straight.'

'Please hold on.'

The connection was made. 'Straight here.'

'Lomond. Is it safe to talk?'

'I'm alone.'

'Has your chief got his evidence yet?'

'Not so far as I know.'

Lomond took a deep breath. 'If Pardoe was in FBI custody, would he be safe? And could an arrest be made without publicity?'

'No to both questions. Hoover lives on publicity. And if a wanted man is killed, Hoover will ensure he is thought guilty. And shot while attempts were made to apprehend him. They can always use that one.'

'Could you arrest him? Or appear to. Put him in a safe place?'

'I know all the safest places in Washington.'

'Good. Do it. Before Hoover gets his evidence. Pardoe's at the Mayflower with my old assistant, Reiner. He will help you. You'll pick them up there?'

'Delighted. How long will this be for?'

'Until I can get him out of the country. If I can get him back to London alone, I may just be able to save his life.'

'So that London can try him for murder?'

'Better that than have him executed without trial. Once you have him in your safe house, you'll contact me?'

'Leave it to me.'

Lohmann replaced the receiver, lifted it again and was reconnected with Reiner.

'Pardoe must only be handed over to an FBI agent, James

Henry Straight. No one else. You can go with him and Pardoe. Straight will contact me later.'

'Understood.'

'Good.'

Lohmann replaced the receiver and sat back. His hands were trembling. He was determined to save at least one life, if possible. At least until he was sure that Pardoe was guilty. If otherwise, he could do little. Possibly in London he would be given a fair trial. Even that worried him. It was too much like the old days in Germany. They were able to dispense with the rule of law. Now, in wartime, the British were prepared to do the same. It went against everything in which he believed. A man, guilty or not, deserved his day in court.

Lohmann turned back to the papers in front of him. And read on.

At eight-thirty he rubbed red-rimmed eyes and folding up his notes, put them in desk drawer. He felt drained, exhausted, wanting only to go back to the hotel and sleep. But that was something he could not do. He was committed to going to Caroline Norwood's apartment. It was something he could not go back on, not now.

At two minutes before nine o'clock he arrived outside Caroline Norwood's apartment building. Impeccable timing, he told himself as he entered the building. The porter's desk was empty. The man was off duty. He went to the elevator and pressed the floor button. Nothing happened. The elevator was obviously out of order. He was forced to take to the stairs. Arriving finally at her floor, he swiftly walked the corridor to her door and rang the bell.

At first the only sound was his own breathing. He thought, I'm out of training. After all the exertions on the train the day before, he was feeling the effects. He waited, breathing heavily.

And waiting, heard the scream.

A shrill scream from behind a closed door. Her door. But clear, distinct and hollow with fear.

For seconds, it seemed, he stood staring at the polished wood in front of him.

And there was a second scream.

The next moments registered in his eyes as an under-cranked film, jerky and speeded up.

He took a pace backwards and kicked out at the centre of the door. A cracking of wood registered the door's protest, but still it remained closed.

Another pace backwards and another kick. His third kick matched the third scream. More wood splintered and the lock gave. The door hung open.

Lohmann forced it wide with his shoulder and went in, moving fast, the Luger in his hand.

The living-room was lit, but empty. The bedroom door was ajar. From beyond it came a low keening sound, another anticipation of fear. Lohmann went into the bedroom.

The only illumination was from the light on the bedside table. She was half lying, half sitting on the bed. Her dress was ripped open from the neck to the waist and one breast hung over the ripped brassiere. Below the neck was a thin scarlet line, from which blood was seeping down onto breast and brassiere. She was no longer screaming but moaning to herself. Her eyes were glazed with terror and she gave no indication she saw Lohmann.

Lohmann swung around, aware of someone else in the room. He saw the knife before he saw the man. It was lying on the carpet, the blade glinting in the light from the bedside lamp. The point of the blade was stained scarlet. The man standing over it was to the right of the door, a shadowy figure, hair wild, swaying forward, about to bend and pick up the knife.

Lohmann's reaction was automatic. He struck out at the man's head with the barrel of the Luger. The metal connected with the left cheek bone and the man went backwards and downwards. The back of his head hit the edge of the heavy wardrobe with a heavy thud. The man slid down the side of the wardrobe and was still.

Behind him, he heard Caroline Norwood's voice, hoarse and strained.

'Lohmann! . . . thank God . . . Lohmann.'

He turned. She was struggling up from the bed, her hands clutching the front of her torn dress, trying to cover her naked breast and the wound above it. Blood was oozing onto her hands. She started to talk, a flood of words.

'He . . . he rang the door bell. I . . . I thought it was you. And . . . and then . . . when I saw him . . . I invited him in. And then he had the knife in his hand and I ran in here . . . Oh, God, God, God . . . Lohmann, it was like the coloured girl . . and the others . . . he was going to . . .'

He went over to her and gripped her by the shoulder with one hand. He pulled aside the torn dress and stared at the wound. 'It's not deep. Go into the bathroom and wash it. Have you any antiseptic? And sticking plaster?'

She nodded.

'Good. Go in and wash the wound. I don't think it needs stitches, but we'll get the Embassy doctor.'

She did as she was told, disappearing into the bathroom, silent now. He lifted the bedside phone and dialled the Embassy number. All the while eyes on the figure lying against the wardrobe. Unconscious? Or dead? No, the blow and the head striking the wood wasn't enough to kill.

An urgent call for the doctor left with the Embassy switchboard, he replaced the receiver. The figure lying against the wardrobe stirred and moaned. Lohmann crossed to the door and, switching on the centre light, turned to face the semi-conscious figure. The man moaned again, hand going up to his bruised cheek. He opened his eyes.

Lohmann looked down into Robert Pardoe's face.

TWENTY-EIGHT

It seemed the final confirmation; the knife on the floor, the man lying against the wardrobe. And the terrified woman on the bed; the wound above her breast; the scream he had heard from behind the door. Everything resolved. The man caught in the act.

Pardoe opened his eyes and stared up at the figure bending over him.

'Lomond!' Dull, flat tones.

'Yes?' Matching his tone. No emotion. At the same time, replacing the Luger in his waistband. Knowing he wouldn't need it now.

'Why . . . why did . . .?'

'I hit you. To stop you.' He looked towards the bathroom. He could hear the sound of running water. 'Don't say anything. I have to get you out of here.'

'Yes, yes . . . out of here.'

Lohmann took the man by the shoulders. 'Pardoe, listen to me! You're a target now. For the FBI. For the Washington police. For British Intelligence. And for me. But I'm not your judge or your executioner. I want to get you out of here. Now, on your feet.'

Pardoe heaved himself up and stood awkward and unsteady. A livid bruise discoloured his cheek where the Luger had struck him. He swayed.

'The . . . the woman . . . did she . . . ?'

'She's all right. Wait there. Don't move.'

He went to the bathroom door. She was at the washhand basin, a strip of plaster in her hand.

'How are you?'

'It hurts. And . . . I feel so shaky.'

'Delayed shock. I'm going now.'

'No, for God's sake, don't leave . . .' She turned towards him, eyes again wide with fear.

'The doctor's on his way.'

'Lomond, he tried to kill me!'

'I know.'

'He . . . he is the one who killed the others . . .?'

He didn't reply to the question but said, 'I'm getting him out of here. That's my job. You'll be safe now.'

'Please. Don't go . . .'

He thought, she's well enough now. He'd arrived just in time. Yes, just in time. In time? She's fortunate? Or is she?

'I have to go,' he said. 'You'll be fine. Let the doctor in. I'll see you later.'

He retraced his steps across the room, took a handkerchief from his breast pocket and stooping, lifted the knife by the blade. He wrapped it in the handkerchief and went over to the dressing table. He stared down at bottles of lotion, powder, combs and brushes. And a small gold compact. He lifted the compact and placed it beside the knife in the handkerchief. He wrapped them up in the folds of the handkerchief and put it in his pocket. And addressed himself to Pardoe.

'You'll come with me now.'

'Yes . . . yes.'

In the street outside, Lohmann hailed a cab. He instructed the driver to take them to the Mayflower Hotel.

A sudden, sickening thought came into his mind. He faced Pardoe. 'What happened to Reiner?'

'He went out of the room. I didn't see him again.'

It wasn't like Reiner. Reiner did what he was told. Something else had happened. 'So he left you. And you went out. Despite my telling you not to.'

'Because you phoned again.'

'I phoned? I phoned only to speak to Reiner.'

Pardoe's voice trembled. 'No, after that, at about eight o'clock. You phoned, told me to come to her apartment. To Caroline Norwood's apartment. You . . . you told me, Lohmann. On the telephone . . .'

He was good, Lohmann thought. A considerable actor. Or he had convinced himself, believed it all. Or there was the other possibility . . .

Lohmann changed the subject. 'James Henry Straight, did he come to the hotel?'

'Jimmy? No. Not before I left. You did phone me, Lohmann. It . . . it was you . . . or it sounded like you.'

He stopped, hesitant momentarily, staring out at the lights of the city. Eyes lost, barely focused.

The foyer of the hotel was busy celebrating an old American custom. The Convention. A banner was draped above the reception desk 'WELCOME TO THE SHRINERS CONVENTION.' The area was filled with middle aged men; short, tall, fat, thin; loud in their greetings to each other, heads bedecked with small caps, jackets adorned with rosettes and other insignia. Lohmann and Pardoe moved through them and went directly to Lohmann's room.

'Sit down!' Lohmann said to Pardoe. 'Do you want a drink?'

'I could use a Scotch.'

Lohmann phoned room service and ordered two double whiskies. Nothing was said while they waited for the drinks. Pardoe washed his bruised face and afterwards sat, smoking a cigarette, hand trembling visibly. The drinks arrived carried by a flushed waiter.

'Sorry if I was a time, gents, but we're rushed off our feet downstairs.'

Lohmann tipped him; and he left at speed, the convention calling him. Lohmann handed Pardoe his drink and sat on the edge of the bed facing the naval officer.

'So, Captain Pardoe, it is as if we are back at the beginning. But now you have no mission to use as an excuse. And now also I have told you, you are in great danger, from a number of directions. It is time you told me the truth. Your truth.'

The hand still shook. 'I've told you the truth. All the time. It's just that I can't tell you what I don't remember.'

'Very well. Now tell me what you remember about tonight.'

'That's the strange thing. I remember it all. I told you, you phoned . . .'

'Not I.'

Pardoe inclined his head, suggestion of a shrug. 'It was someone who sounded like you, then.'

'Like the Szilard call? So we are dealing with an impressionist. Go on.'

'I took a taxi to her address. Miss Norwood's. Where you said you were. She answered the door. Invited me in. I asked for you. She said she was expecting you. Was she expecting you?'

'Yes.'

'So I was to wait . . . she gave me a drink. Everything normal, ordinary at first. And then . . .' He grimaced, rubbing his hand across his eyes. 'Let me get it right. She excused herself, went into the bedroom. Yes, she called me from the bedroom . . . that was it. Could I help her?'

'She asked you to help her? In what way?'

'I'm not quite sure. As if she'd dropped something . . . couldn't reach it . . . so . . . so I went in. She was . . . was lying on the bed. As you saw her. Dress torn, cut on her chest . . . and . . . and this is the crazy bit. She was smiling. Yes, she was smiling. It sounds insane, I know . . .'

'Never mind how it sounds. Tell me the rest.'

'She threw something towards me. Not hard, just tossed it to me. It fell on the floor. It was the knife, that knife you lifted. Blood on the tip. She must have cut herself with it. And then she started to scream. I think I just stood there. I didn't

311

expect the screaming. She . . . she screamed and screamed . . . and then you came in. And hit me. That's . . . all.'

Pardoe drained his whisky glass. 'Lomond, that is what I remember. Unless . . . unless I . . . I blacked out.'

Lohmann looked into his own glass. He was feeling slightly nauseated. Knowing now. For sure. There were no doubts. The proof was there. And it all added up. He stood up, moved to the door. 'You will please wait here. I shall lock you in. You will not open the door. You will not answer the telephone. You understand this?'

'I understand.'

Lohmann went to the door.

His hand was on the doorknob when Pardoe spoke again. 'Lomond. I'll do as you say. If I can. If . . . if nothing happens. No . . . no fugue.'

'There will be no fugue.' Lohmann said.

In the corridor, he made sure the door was locked. And walked to Pardoe's room. This door was also locked. He bent down and studied the lock. A simple one he could open in a few seconds. Trouble was, he didn't feel he had seconds to spare. He looked around. The corridor was empty. He took a step backwards and, for the second time that night, kicked out at the door lock. This one was easier than the other, one kick was enough, no snapping of wood. The door swung open with a click. He went in.

The body was on the floor in front of the bed. Lying face downwards. The back of the head was covered in blood, fragments of bone and whitish matter. An exit wound, the size of a fist. The man had been shot from the front and had twisted around as he fell.

Nausea again, phlegm at the back of his throat. He crossed the room and knelt down beside the body. He moved the head around, and stared into the dead left eye of James Henry Straight the Third – and last.

Oddly, he felt a sadness. He had asked Straight to come to the hotel.

The man had been shot in the centre of the forehead by someone taller than him. Something like a .33 or .35 bullet. Let the FBI determine that. From the position of the exit wound, the bullet had blasted downwards through the brain and exited just above the neck. The body was still warm. Been shot within the last hour, hour and half. He looked around. No sign of a weapon. Pity. Because, if the timing was right, the Bureau would accuse Pardoe. Before he left to attempt to kill Caroline Norwood. That would be the story.

He stood erect. Thinking about Caroline. Somebody would ask, why her? Out of all the women in Washington, why her? And they would answer that Pardoe knew her at the Embassy. He'd simply targeted her. Oh, it was very neat. Jimmy Straight, because he knew too much, and then Caroline. And Straight was dead and Caroline was alive. Only because he, Lohmann had arrived at the scene on time. Exactly on time. *Nine o'clock. Promptly. Everything . . . meticulously timed.* Of course. Had to be. While Straight was killed. For being there? Or for coming at all?

The voice behind Lohmann said, 'Ach, Gott!'

He turned and faced Reiner at the door of the room, holding the back of his neck, looking groggy.

He was staring past him at the body.

'Pardoe?'

'James Straight. Pardoe is in my room. What happened? Where were you?'

'I was here. With Pardoe. Then somebody knocked on the door.'

'Pardoe just said that you'd gone out of the room.'

'He was in the toilet when the knock came. I opened the door. Very carefully.'

'So?'

Reiner opened his hands, palms upwards. He looked shamefaced. 'No one. Then I forget the old days. I stepped out. Nothing else. Blackness. An expert. The blunt instrument or the side of the hand to the neck. He must have been

313

waiting at the side of the door. I woke up in my room a few minutes ago. With this pain.'

'In your own room? How did you get there?'

'Room key is in my pocket. Whoever hit me must have carried me there. Probably didn't want unconscious bodies lying around the corridor for hotel staff to trip over.'

'Or for Pardoe to trip over when he left for the Norwood apartment.'

'He went there?'

'I'll tell you about it later. You didn't shoot Straight by any chance?'

A look of disgust spread over Renier's face. 'Ach! You tell me to expect this man Straight. Anyone else I can shoot but not him. But I didn't shoot the man who hit me, either. I didn't even see him.' He looked down at the body again. 'What do we do? Phone the police?'

'No. The last thing we do. Let someone else find him. But I want you to go to the police.' Lohmann reached into his pocket and producing the handkerchief containing the knife and compact he handed it to Reiner. 'Take this to Chief Thompson. Ask him to get the fingerprints from it. Tell him to check his records. Tell him I may have something for him – rather than for the FBI. He'll like that. When he has done what I ask, phone me either here or at the Embassy, and tell me the result. Understood?'

'Understood.'

Reiner disappeared into an elevator and Lohmann returned to his room. Pardoe was sitting on the edge of the bed, head in his hands. When Lohmann entered he looked up, his face grey and drawn.

'What now?' he asked of the detective.

'I was hoping to take you to a safe house. But that is not going to happen. Perhaps the Embassy will be the best place. You should be safe enough there. They wouldn't dare try and eliminate you in their own Embassy.'

Pardoe sat up erect now, ramrod straight. 'You say everyone is trying to . . . kill me. Why? And who . . . who are they?

314

The mission is complete. What point is there?'

'Captain Pardoe, you are an embarrassment. To a great many people. The British government for one. The FBI would also like to get their hands on you. And they would not be averse . . . to killing you while you try to escape. And I think our more recent adversaries would still be happy to see you discredited.'

His hand brushed nervously across his brow. 'What can we do?'

'I think we will wait. I think also we will have a visitor. It might prove illuminating. Also I am expecting Reiner to contact me. Yes, we will wait.'

They waited.

TWENTY-NINE

They waited for over half an hour. After some minutes Pardoe rose from the bed and paced the room. He expressed impatience; fear and uncertainty of what was ahead of him, puzzlement as to why they were waiting. Lohmann said little. He was waiting, but for what he would not say. He was used to waiting; in the past as a young policeman, later, in the Berlin days, as a senior officer. Patience was an old virtue but a necessary one. He could remember old Strauss-Kruger, his first chief . . . Inspector Gunther Strauss-Kruger, long dead and that before the rise of Adolf Hitler. In the twenties Strauss-Kruger had once arrested Hitler.

'*That evil, ugly , little man,*' as he had once called Hitler. '*Every idea in his head is sick. He has one virtue just now. He has *patience. With enough patience he might even come to power. Then he'll lose his patience and destroy himself...*' If Lohmann could only be sure Strauss-Kruger had been right. But then he had also preached patience to Lohmann. *After the investigation is complete, everything has been done, then the detective has to wait. If he has done his work properly, then the end will present itself. But one must have the patience to wait.*'

That word. Patience! *Geduld*! To be able to wait, knowing the end was in sight.

Thirty-seven minutes later there came the knock on the door. It was a tentative, uncertain knock, a knock that perhaps did not want to be answered.

Pardoe twisted around to face the door, tense as drawn wire. He opened his mouth but Lohmann motioned him to be silent. Waiting for the second knock. Keep the new arrival waiting, keep his nerves as tense as one's own, that was the method.

The second knock was only slightly louder than the first. Lohmann went to the door, turned and indicated that Pardoe should go into the bathroom. Frowning, Pardoe obeyed, shutting the door behind him. Only then did Lohmann open the door.

Charlie Markham was standing in the corridor. Hat and heavy raglan coat, hands in pockets, tall, dapper, Markham with his thin face and long upper lip. The would-be Tory squire but with a greater arrogance. A more familiar arrogance, to Lohmann. And always giving the impression of bow-string taut intensity. Lohmann told himself, sententiously, he should have noticed this before.

Markham stepped into the room, eyes searching.

'Where is he, Lomond?'

'You are looking for someone?'

'You know I'm looking for Pardoe. Caroline Norwood phoned me. She told me what happened. This time he's been caught in the act.'

'And you think he is here?'

'He left Caroline Norwood's apartment with you. And you haven't had time to get him into a safe house.'

Lohmann suddenly smiling. Which surprised himself. 'Who said anything about a safe house?'

Markham hesitated. For a fraction of a second. It was enough. Before he could open his mouth, Lohmann went on, 'The only person who knew I was looking for a safe house was James Henry Straight. And a short time ago somebody shot him.'

Markham blustered, 'I don't know anythng about that . . .'

'No surprise that Straight's been shot? Whoever shot him would show no surprise.' A pause and a deep breath. 'Did you shoot him, Markham?'

Lohmann could see the bubbles of perspiration breaking out on Markham's brow. The eyes moved from left to right and back again. Searching. No longer for Pardoe. For a way out?

'I didn't come here to talk about Straight . . .'

'The FBI will want to know who killed James Henry. They don't like their people being killed.'

'They'll believe Pardoe killed him!'

'But we know he didn't. So, to get away with that story you have to kill me as well.' Lohmann took another deep breath. 'And my assistant, Reiner. And Captain Greenock . . . oh yes, I've spoken to him on the phone . . .' The lie came easily. It was additional insurance. 'Have to be a regular "night of the long knives," Markham. Even the FBI won't be able to blame Pardoe for that trail of corpses. Because either you'll have killed him, or he'll be in custody.'

Markham made the half expected move. He drew out the .35 automatic from his coat pocket and levelled it at Lohmann. It was a bulky object with the distorting shape of a silencer over the barrel.

'You're very confident for a man at the wrong end of a gun, Lomond.'

'I've been there before.' So very true. So many times before

317

– had gone with the job in the old days. Also he thought how difficult it was to pull the trigger while staring into the eyes of the target. Unless one was trained to do so.

Markham, he knew, was trained to kill. His one chance, Lohmann reckoned, was to keep talking. Markham would be curious as to how much he knew. Had to keep that curiosity alive.

'Pity you killed Straight,' Lohmann said. 'Took out one of my three suspects. Pardoe, Straight, and yourself, Markham. You were all in Singapore when this thing started. And in London and Washington. Or did it start before Singapore? Serial murder usually starts with lesser attacks on women. Building to the actual killing. Then, after the first killing, it becomes easy. But I expect from the nature of the murders you started to kill early. There could be no substitute for what you did to those women. You'd find it . . . stimulating. Yes, that would be the word. Stimulating . . .'

'That was Pardoe!' He was suddenly loud. 'You know it was Pardoe. You caught him in the act tonight.'

'I was meant to, wasn't I? But it wasn't Pardoe. That was too neat. Too nicely timed. Too prepared for.'

'You . . . you saw him trying to kill her.'

'I saw what I was meant to see. The FBI were expecting new evidence yesterday. Who told them to expect it? You, Markham? Or your "control". You have to have a control . . .'

'I don't know what you're saying!'

'I was told to be at Caroline Norwood's apartment at nine o'clock exactly. Not just told – stressed that if I was there too soon or too late I would spoil the dinner. It was a flimsy excuse but it had to work. I had to arrive at exactly nine in order to rescue Caroline from another of Pardoe's murderous sallies. That was how it was supposed to look, wasn't it? That was the evidence the FBI were told to expect. It was to end the case. Discredit Pardoe, even if it was too late . . . even if his mission was complete? Even now if he was proved to be a murderer, Roosevelt might be persuaded to have second

318

thoughts about the mission . . .'

'Very ingenious, Lomond. If anyone would believe it . . .'

'They will. It isn't as if I've just discovered it was you, Markham. You confirmed it the other day, you know. After the car bomb went off, you were the only one I told we were going by train. And we weren't followed from the hotel. Yet three gentlemen turned up looking for us on the train. You had to have arranged that. Through your connections with the Bund, I presume? Earlier too, you were one of two people who knew I was going to New Orleans. The other was Captain Greenock. He hadn't been in Singapore or London when the women were murdered there. But you had. You and Straight and Pardoe.'

'I told you. It's Pardoe! It has to be Pardoe!'

'No. Tonight's little charade disproved that. I was meant to catch Pardoe in the act, shoot him – if you were lucky – case closed, no further investigation. Nobody would need to look further into the spy in the Embassy who worked for the Germans. . . or should I say two spies. You and Caroline Norwood? Incidentally, was she in Singapore when you killed the prostitute?'

Markham's face was ashen. The hand holding the revolver trembled. Lohmann thought, *God I have to be careful. Drive him too far and he'll fire the thing*.

'That's what she was,' Markham said. 'A Chinese prostitute . . . a whore . . . who'd miss her?' He looked up at Lohmann, a mildly excited look. 'I'd done it before you know. Once before . . . in Berlin . . . unsolved murder. Was attached to the Embassy in Berlin . . . one of your whores in the Unter den Linden . . . under the linden trees, Lomond. In your native land. Oh, I know who you are . . . or were. Lohmann, Berlin police. Until the Nazis took a dislike to you. I'm right, aren't I?'

Humour him, Lohmann told himself. *Keep him happy*.

'You're right, Markham. How did you know? The Abwehr?'

'Something like that, yes, something like that . . . but . . .

319

but it was your people who taught me . . . Military Intelligence . . . how to kill . . . they taught me that. They even suggested mutilation could be used. To disguise the real motive. Very clever, that. You eliminate an enemy of the state and make it look as if some maniac's been at work . . . so . . . so, I thought . . . get rid of the whores . . . make it look as if I was insane. That was how to do it . . . starting in Berlin .

It came to Lohmann then. The reason. The why of Markham. What makes him run. Who winds him up.

'They caught you in Berlin,' Lohmann said.

Markham scowled. 'Eh . . . ?'

'The Berlin police. They arrested you, a British intelligence man working under cover from out of the British Embassy. And he mutilates a whore. Only he gets caught.'

'I . . . I allowed them to catch me. You see, I admired the system. The Nazis . . . so efficient . . . I didn't mind them knowing. They were down on whores too . . .'

The phrase was familiar to Lohmann. *Down on whores.* Jack the Ripper was *down on whores.*

He said aloud, 'The Ripper case.'

'He had the right idea,' Markham said. 'And he was never found. You see, all taught to me by my own people.'

'And the Germans made it work for them. Yes, I see how it would work. The police hand you to the Gestapo. And the Gestapo agree to release you, if you work for them. They had another agent inside British Intelligence, and they had a killer who enjoyed his work. That's how it was, Markham.'

The man blinked. Tall figure, long legs now, like his hand, slightly but visibly trembling.

'They understood. They were trying to cleanse their country. I was only assisting. You see, I had sympathy for their cause. I agreed to work for them. And . . . and . . .' He giggled now, not high pitched but a stuttering sound from the back of his throat. 'And they didn't care if I killed a dirty whore or so.'

'Was it their idea in Singapore?'

'No, no, that was mine. Pardoe was . . . using this whore. Top class Chinese piece . . . pretending she wasn't what she was . . . and I thought, if I killed her and . . . and made Pardoe believe he'd killed her . . .'

'You'd have created another agent for Germany.'

'Why not? He was a career officer. He could be useful. Oh, he was drinking a lot in those days. We all were but, if he didn't get into trouble he was marked for higher things.'

'Future staff officer. Useful if he could work for the other side. And there was no war on then.'

Markham nodded. 'I was looking to the future. The trouble was . . . there was that little queen, James Henry Straight the Third. A comedian, that one. He was following us around. We thought he was just a rich tourist, with a not too healthy friendship with Pardoe. And Pardoe humoured him. Unbeknown to Straight, he was helping me, keeping Pardoe drinking.'

'So you could kill the Chinese girl and Pardoe would be so drunk he wouldn't know whether he'd done it or not?'

'I killed the Chinese tart one night after he'd left her. Then I got Pardoe and Straight so drunk they didn't know what they'd been doing. After that night, when he heard she'd been murdered, it wasn't hard to place the thought in his mind . . . *'What did you do after you left us, Bobby? . . . Where did you go? . . . Did you read about the Chinese whore got carved up . . .?'* Oh, yes, he got worried all right. Then he was posted back to London. It was easy in London. He didn't even know the Valois woman was a whore and I made sure she got to know him. Then I could kill her in the line of duty.'

'Pardoe never wondered about you?'

'I was never near him in London. I worked through the whore. And when I came to Washington and he saw me, I think he wanted to avoid me. Afraid I might mention Singapore.'

'But you couldn't turn him into a German agent?'

'Wasn't necessary any more. He had this mission. And the

321

Abwehr wanted to find out what it was all about. If they couldn't do that, then we had to discredit him. Try and make him crack . . . two more killings . . . the Hancock tart and the Senator's niece . . . that was a good move . . . a senator's niece . . . everybody got excited. Including the FBI. And then Pardoe went off to New Orleans. We didn't know why but we knew he had tried to contact this Professor Duplessis.'

'You didn't kill Duplessis. You were still in Washington.'

'The Bund handled that part of it. They had contacts in New Orleans.'

'The Ku Klux Klan?'

'What I like about your fellow countrymen, Lohmann, they utilise everything to hand – the Bund, the KKK – just as they utilised me . . .'

'With Caroline Norwood as your control in Washington?'

Markham smiled. Ravines appeared on the cheeks of the thin face. The tall figure was stooping now. Weary. 'You weren't meant to know that,' he said.

'Difficult not to, after tonight's *Märchenkomödie* . . . pantomime. Yes, a pantomime. All the precision about the time, and the knife . . . I sent it to be checked for fingerprints. Pardoe said she threw it to him, she hoped he would catch it, but he didn't, he was too shocked. I think we'll find the prints on the knife are Caroline Norwood's.'

Suddenly Markham straightened up. 'We talk too much, don't we, Lohmann? Keep me talking. The oldest technique. Now the talking's done. Where is Captain Pardoe?'

'You think I would keep him with me?'

Markham frowned. 'No, I . . . I think you'd have more sense . . . where is he?' He made a menacing movement with the gun.

'You're going to shoot me?'

'Tell me where he is.'

'Either way, you shoot me. You have to now.'

'I'll find him anyway. Without you as his keeper, he won't be hard to find.'

Lohmann caught his breath. His body tensed. He'd been shot before, a long time ago. In the side and in the shoulder. There'd been pain, but his memory of it had gone. Now he was relying on the man he was supposed to protect, to protect him. If Pardoe mistimed it . . .?

The bathroom door slammed open.

Markham, surprised, half turned.

Pardoe came out low, in a rugby tackle.

And Lohmann dived forward under the gun.

Pardoe got to Markham first. Head to one side, arms wrapped around the tall man's legs. Markham folded towards Lohmann who grabbed his body.

There was one muted gunshot.

Then the gun was slithering across the carpet.

Lohmann felt nothing. And prayed it hadn't hit Pardoe. He levered himself up with his left hand and hit Markham on the back of the neck with the open palm of his right hand. The old blow he'd learned a long time ago. Resistance stopped. Markham went limp. Lohmann rolled aside and onto his knees. Seeing the automatic on the carpet. His hand went out to it as did another hand. The other hand reached it first.

Pardoe stood erect, unhurt, the weapon in his hand. Behind him there was a bullet hole in the wall just above the skirting board. Pardoe threw the automatic to Lohmann.

'You seem to collect these,' he said.

Some minutes later. Markham was conscious again. He began talking immediately, sitting on the bed with Lohmann pointing the automatic at him, talking, and grinning.

'It doesn't matter,' he said. 'Whichever side of the gun I'm on. Nothing much matters now, you know, the way things are . . . you see that, don't you?'

'He can't stop it,' said Pardoe, who was at the window, looking on the dark city below.

'Once they start, they have so much they want to get rid of,' Lohmann responded. 'It's typical.'

Markham said: 'Typical? I'm not typical, not me. Of course you think I'm insane. It's always the way. Anything you don't want to understand is placed-in the box marked insanity.'

'That is so,' Lohmann agreed easily, feeling a deep sense of relief. He was still alive. That was enough reason for feeling so, he told himself.

'So what now? You think you have choices. Prison, asylum, institution, whatever you like. Doesn't matter. Won't happen. So where to?' Markham, still grinning, rambling on.

Lohmann met Pardoe's eyes. 'The Embassy. To inform London. And hand Markham over, to whoever.'

Lohmann and Pardoe donned their coats. And motioned Markham to his feet.

'I have your gun in my coat pocket,' Lohmann addressed Markham. 'You run, I shoot you. In the back or the back of the kneecap. Either is painful, the first may be fatal. We are going through the foyer to get a taxi to the Embassy.'

'I won't run,' Markham replied. 'There's no point. We're all dead men already. Walking dead. Soon we'll stop walking.'

They descended in an empty elevator. And came out into a packed foyer. The Shriners were still milling about, still greeting each other even more loudly. A great volume of drink had been consumed inspiring an air of great bonhomie. Pardoe pushed his way through the crowd with Markham following and Lohmann behind Markham, hand encircling the .35 in his coat pocket.

They were halfway across the foyer when the figure of what seemed to be a large, plump Shriner appeared in front of Pardoe.

'Evening, boys,' the Shriner said and, drawing something from inside his jacket, shot Pardoe twice in the chest. Markham, surprised, took a step forward. The plump man turned towards him and shot him in the forehead.

Later, Lohmann wondered about the killing of Markham. Was it a reflex action by an assassin who feared an attempt to stop him after he had completed his task? It had to seem to the man that Markham was a threat to him and to his escape.

Lohmann also acted without thought. He was still gripping the automatic in the pocket of his coat, the weapon he had taken from Markham. He didn't take time to draw the gun from his pocket, but brought it up inside his coat.

The man was turning, about to push his way back through the crowd towards the main doors of the hotel. The crowd however seemed to freeze momentarily at the sound of the shots, blocking a passage to the doors. A second later they would panic and rush, screaming and shouting, to the sides of the foyer. But not yet. The gunman turned back, seeking another way of escape. His eyes met Lohmann's just as the ex-detective fired from inside his pocket. The bullet travelled in an upward trajectory, entering the gunman's mouth and continuing to plough upwards through the brain.

The assassin's was the third body to go down in the hotel foyer. There was an expression of surprise on his face as he fell.

THIRTY

In those seconds Lohmann felt he had finally awakened in the centre of a nightmare. It was a long nightmare taking in the past days in New Orleans and Washington, the present, the here and now in the foyer of the Mayflower, and some part of the future. That, he could only anticipate. What followed confirmed that he was right. Only later, in New York, would he come out of it. Meanwhile he had to follow it through.

Ignoring the two other bodies, both of them so obviously dead, he stepped over them and knelt beside Pardoe. Pardoe's eyes flickered.

'What . . . what happened? Feel as if I'd been kicked by a mule . . .' His eyes narrowed, flickered again. 'Have I been shot? I think I have . . .'

'We will get help,' Lohmann said and looked around him into pandemonium. They were in the centre of the foyer, isolated, an undisciplined ring of Shriners and hotel staff around the walls of the hotel; the noise was ear-shattering.

Lohmann shouted then, above the noise, with a sudden rage. 'An ambulance! Gott! Will someone get an ambulance and a doctor!'

His cry created some activity at the reception desk. And a figure pushed its way through the Shriners and across a space towards the three bodies and the kneeling Lohmann.

'I'm a doctor.'

'This one,' Lohmann indicated Pardoe. 'The other two will be dead.'

The doctor knelt beside Pardoe, taking the pulse beat with his right hand, and with his left, gently moving aside coat and jacket, unbuttoned the shirt to reveal the wounds. Then, grimly, he looked at Lohmann and shook his head.

'Funny,' said Pardoe, oblivious to the doctor. 'Don't feel any pain. Did . . . did he miss? Just . . . just feel cold. Very cold.'

He visibly shivered, smiled apologetically at Lohmann and, closing his eyes, died.

The nightmare went on.

Lohmann stood up. He'd seen death often enough to take it without fear, but always with sadness. The horror this time was in the ambience, the very ordinariness of the hotel foyer. And in the speed with which death had overtaken three men. And, in Pardoe's case, he felt even more saddened and infinitely weary. As if all his efforts had failed when they were both close to waking.

326

He was vaguely aware of sitting down in one of the deep armchairs in the foyer. The doctor seemed to have taken charge, getting the hotel staff to ring off the area in which the bodies lay. Panic having died down, the Shriners approached with unconcealed curiosity. The arrival of two uniformed police officers forced them away again, although they still loitered at the fringes of the scene, talking in low, excited tones.

A thoughtful page boy handed Lohmann a glass containing a large brandy. As it swam into his vision, he took it with his left hand and drained it gratefully; he became aware then that his right hand still gripped the automatic he had taken from Markham. He also became aware that he had the Luger still in the waistband of his trousers. It was as if throughout the whole business, he had been collecting other people's guns. So many guns. Each one representing a death, perhaps? So many deaths now. A nightmarish thought in a nightmare series of events. He shouldn't be here. He should be in London. He considered London his home now. In London, at first, it had been Berlin he had considered home; the city he had missed. But now it was London. That was reality. Yet here he was in the middle of this other reality that seemed so unreal. Not simply a nightmare but the American nightmare.

'So it's you, Mister Lomond!' The voice was instantly familiar. He looked up and focused on the face of Chief of Detectives Thompson.

'Chief,' he acknowledge the detective's arrival.

'I can see tomorrow's papers on this one,' said Thompson. "Massacre at the Mayflower". Could even rank with the gunfight at the OK Corral. Guess we'd better have a quiet talk. They tell me you got a room here. Let's go.'

They took the elevator to Lohmann's floor. Passing the door of the room containing Straight's body.

'There's another one in there,' Lohmann said, feeling surreal.

'Another what?'

'Body. James Henry Straight. The Third.'

Thompson swore loudly and obscenely. And went in to view Straight's body. Lohmann waited in the corridor. After a few minutes, Thompson came out.

'Christ!' he said. 'You know he's FBI?'

'I know.'

'Rigor setting in. He's been dead a while. Your work?'

'No. Markham.'

'Yeah, you'd say that, wouldn't you? I guess we'll see soon enough. I phoned for the murder boys to come up here when they finished down below. You got quite a story to tell me.'

They went to Lohmann's room. Untidy. Can a room be dishevelled? There was the rumpled bed with the impression on it where Pardoe had rested; a coffee table on its side, knocked over in the scuffle with Markham, fragments of a broken ashtray.

Thompson faced him. A large face, with large round questioning eyes. 'I was wrong about the OK Corral. This is more like the world war. With Pardoe as the fuckin' Kaiser.'

'Not Pardoe. Markham is the one you want . . . wanted.'

'You keep sayin' it. Maybe you're the one I should be after. Downstairs they tell me this guy shot your two pals and then you shot him. That right?'

'I shot the man. He had a gun and he was using it. To escape he would have used it again. I had to shoot him. I don't know who he was or why he was shooting.'

'You sure you don't know who he is?'

'I have never seen him before.'

Thompson sighed heavily. 'You go shootin' complete strangers? Most times around here, when hoods shoot each other up, they know who they're shootin' at.'

'Perhaps you have identified him, Chief?'

'Didn't even know his face, and I know a lot of faces. Guy had no identification. No wallet, no drivin' licence. Nothin'. Not even name tabs on his clothes. Or maker's tabs. A few dollars in a back pocket.'

328

'Only a professional works like that.'

'I already figured that. So start talking, Mister Lomond.'

Heard this dialogue before, Lohmann thought, in a hundred Hollywood gangster movies. It wasn't real, words thought up by a script writer in a celluloid factory. Perhaps that is where the dialogue of a nightmare comes from?

Silently the bedroom door opened. No knock, no sound of the door handle being turned. Whitney Collins came in, followed by two other men. In Brooks Brothers grey flannel suits. And still wearing hats. Americans wore their hats all the time, he should have noticed that before, perhaps he had been doing so subsconsciously, as if the hats were part of their heads, non-detachable.

'Okay, Chief,' Whitney Collins said. 'We'll take over.'

Thompson moved his lips, swearing again, with feeling.

'Mister Hoover's waiting to see you, Lomond,' Collins went on. 'Chief Thompson will tidy up here. But no press statements, Thompson. Mister Hoover will handle that.'

'You know your guy, Straight,' Thompson said, with relish. 'He's in a room along the corridor. Stone cold.'

Collins showed no emotion. 'He was. We're taking him away now. Let's go Lomond.'

The bad dream continued in Hoover's office. It was after midnight. He could study the framed photographs on the walls of the office. J. Edgar Hoover with President Hoover (frowning), with President Roosevelt (grinning toothily), with Henry Ford (very old), with Charles Lindbergh (very young), with Jack Warner (of Warner Brothers). And with so many others, perhaps even with God . . . Behind the desk the heavy moon-face of the Director himself. Hovering at his shoulder, a tall thin man, introduced curtly as Clyde Tolson, associate of the Director. Lohmann was again sitting facing Hoover. He was aware of Whitney Collins looming behind him. Nothing was real – except that it was happening.

Hoover spoke: 'You may leave us, Collins.'

The agent looked surprised. He opened his mouth to say something, thought better of it, and left the room.

Hoover fastened his small eyes on Lohmann. 'I have a report here of all that has happened this evening at the Mayflower Hotel.'

Lohmann shrugged. 'And the events leading up to that?'

The Director's hand waved through air. 'I am aware of all that. With the death of Pardoe, we seem to have closed the case files on the serial killings of these women.'

'Not with the death of Pardoe,' Lohmann said. 'Pardoe didn't kill these women.'

Tolson coughed. Hoover frowned.

'We have evidence. A statement here from Caroline Norwood, a secretary at the British Embassy. Pardoe tried to stab her, in fact did cut her superficially. You arrived in time to stop him.'

'No. It was meant to look like that. Caroline Norwood cut herself.'

'I find that difficult to believe.'

'Do you, Mister Hoover? I don't think so. You knew all about it. You knew it was going to happen. That was the evidence you were expecting. Straight told me you were expecting evidence. You were expecting that evidence two days before it happened.'

The Director flushed angrily. 'Go on,' he said, tight lipped.

'Caroline Norwood cut herself and threw the knife to Pardoe. He was meant to catch it, but he didn't. Chief Thompson has it now, comparing fingerprints on it with prints on a powder compact of Miss Norwood's. I'm sure they will be one and the same.'

'And why would Miss Norwood do this?'

'To give you the final evidence that Pardoe was guilty. Which he wasn't. Also she wanted to protect Charles Markham.'

'Why should she want to do that? We know Markham was a British Intelligence agent seconded from MI6 to work as a

330

security officer in the British Embassy,' said Hoover.

'Because Markham was also a murderer. A psychopath. I believe Abwehr, the German intelligence bureau, found this out and turned him. He was working for them.'

Hoover grinned. It was a cold, mirthless grimace. 'I was told that you were once an efficient police officer, Lohmann. I didn't expect some fantastic story from the pen of Phillips Oppenheim.'

'You forget the cliché, Mister Hoover: Truth is stranger than fiction. Markham's own paranoia about killing women played into the hands of the Abwehr. His immediate job here was to turn Pardoe, or discredit him. Captain Pardoe could not be turned. Therefore Markham's control decided he was to be discredited. They were working on him in London and here, blaming him for the killings of these women, Markham's victims were to become Pardoe's. And Pardoe didn't even know for sure whether he was killing these women. He had a drink problem which Markham encouraged.'

'So why was he killed tonight? And why was Markham also killed?' The cold smile was still on Hoover's face. 'Who was this unknown assassin? Surely the Abwehr wouldn't want to kill Markham?'

Lohmann faltered. The one question mark in his mind. Who was the assassin? 'I . . . I don't know. Your people?'

Hoover shook his head. 'Not mine. We will leave that for the time being. This control of Markham's you talk about, can you identify him?'

Lohmann took a deep breath. 'Caroline Norwood,' he said.

'One of the British Embassy staff!' Hoover assumed a surprised look.

'There was a leakage of information. We knew that. A German agent or a traitor inside the Embassy . . .'

'Would that not have been Markham?'

Lohmann shook his head. 'Markham was one source. But I believe there had to be one already in place before Markham

331

and Pardoe and myself even arrived. It has to be Caroline Norwood. Before he was killed, Pardoe told me someone impersonated me and invited him to come to the Norwood apartment. Probably Markham. They cleared the way for Pardoe to be there before me. I was instructed to come at exactly nine o'clock – to arrive when Miss Norwood was staging her charade. She had to be working with Markham, was probably his control.'

'An assumption, Lohmann.'

'A reasonable one. She made the initial advances towards me. I think she was also in Singapore when a Chinese prostitute was murdered by Markham. That was the beginning of the framing of Pardoe.'

'You have proof she was in Singapore?'

'No. But it can be found, I'm sure. She told me she inherited a company from her father. Oil and rubber. Rubber spells Malaya. It brought it to mind.'

'All assumptions again, Lohmann.'

'I haven't the facilities to investigate and prove these assumptions. You have, Mister Hoover. You could do so.'

Hoover looked at the spotless white blotting paper on his desk in front of him. 'Not possible. The FBI are empowered only to work within the continental United States. Isn't that so, Clyde?'

'It is, Mister Hoover.'

'You don't stick to that,' Lohmann heard himself protest. 'James Straight worked for you abroad.'

The FBI director scowled. 'He travelled abroad on leave. Nothing to do with the Justice Department.'

'You say so?' Lohmann, with a touch of insolence.

Hoover slammed the flat of his hand on the desk. 'I say so!' The small eyes peered at Lohmann. 'And another thing. Miss Norwood will not be touched!'

Lohmann was now genuinely surprised. 'But if she's a German agent . . .'

'Then I've no doubt she will no longer be working in the

British Embassy. But we will not touch her unless it suits us.'

'But if she's part of a Nazi spy ring . . . working with the German-American Bund . . .? I thought you people arrested enemy agents?'

Hoover leaned back in his chair now, at once relaxed and easy again.

'We're not at war, Herr Lohmann. You are as much the agent of a foreign power in working for the British as Norwood might be working for the Germans . . . if that is what she is doing. You see, my only interest is the United States of America. I know President Roosevelt has sympathy with your British cause, but Roosevelt will not be President for ever. Sympathies can change. Especially as the Germans get stronger. I don't take sides, Lohmann. Not until I see which side will win. That is the side that will benefit the United States.'

'I don't think Roosevelt would agree with you.'

'But I will still be here when he has gone.'

It was Lohmann's turn to stare at the director of the FBI. He realised the man considered himself above presidential authority. At least until such authority was tested.

Hoover went on. 'I repeat, you will leave Caroline Norwood alone. We know she works for German Intelligence.'

The lights seemed to flicker in the room. Or was it his own eyes blinking? Lohmann couldn't be sure. He was exhausted, he knew.

Hoover said, 'You look surprised. How do you think we knew we would have evidence against Pardoe? Because Miss Norwood arranged the little farce with you catching Pardoe in the act. It was a good idea. Would have worked. Cleared up the murders. Embarrassed the British. Unfortunately, you saw through it. Pity.'

'You . . . you want to embarrass the British?'

Hoover thumped the desk again, this time with the fist. 'I already embarrassed the Germans when I arrested some of their spies early this year. It was the turn of the British. You are enemy agents in the USA as much as the Krauts. You want us in this war on the side of the British. I want us out of European wars. This time we don't pull your chestnuts out of the European conflagration. Not a second time.'

'You support the isolationists, Mister Hoover?'

'I support my own interests, which are the interests of this country. I hold one of the few non-elective offices of the USA. Me, Lohmann, I am continuity, not Roosevelt or whoever comes after him. Me!'

The paranoia was showing, Lohmann told himself. He forced himself to stand up, albeit unsteadily.

'I think it's time I left,' he said.

Hoover sat back yet again. 'You will be returning to London?'

'Yes.'

'Good. One thing. This mission of Pardoe's . . . ?'

Something Hoover didn't know. Lohmann was pleased at that.

'I should ask President Roosevelt. I believe he knows.'

'But you . . . do you know, Lohmann?'

The lie still came easily. 'I didn't have to know. I was merely his bodyguard . . . his watcher.'

Hoover smiled. A cold smile. 'And in the end you failed. Goodbye, Herr Lohmann.'

Two days later, the nightmare persisted. Lohmann had vacated his office in the Embassy, after making his farewells to Bill Greenock.

'Sorry it ended this way,' Greenock had said. 'But at least you cleared Pardoe.'

'I wonder whether it matters to him now.'

' 'Course it matters, 'Greenock had insisted. 'Pardoe was a naval officer. You cleared his name. That would have been important to him.'

They had shaken hands on it and Greenock handed over Lohmann's instructions. Back to Montreal and then await a seat on a plane to London. His degree of priority was lower than it had been on the journey from London, and he had permission to go via New York.

Packing in his room at the Mayflower, he was nervous about New York, about seeing Anna. After nearly four years. Would she recognise him? Reiner, who had come to say his goodbyes, was enthusiastic.

'*Kinder* do not forget, chief,' he insisted. 'She'll be as nervous as you, believe me.'

The trouble is, Reiner, I . . . I can't remember her face. After five years. I can't bring her face into mind. Me! Lohmann! The great detective . . . cannot remember his own daughter's face.'

Reiner laughed. 'Because you've thought of it too much. That's natural. One thing, though. You sent a schoolgirl to America. A fourteen-year-old child. In New York you meet a young woman.'

'I'll try to remember.'

Reiner glanced at his watch. 'Time I was going. Train to Cincinnati'll be off soon. Back to the security business. Still, been good working together again, chief.'

'It has, Reiner.'

'Well . . .' A nervous shrug of regret. '. . . next time, eh?'

'Next time. And my sincere regards to your wife.'

'Thanks. 'Bye, chief.'

And Reiner was gone. Lohmann finished packing his case. Wondered whether he would ever see him again. A good man, and one of the few he could trust. In this tortuous world there were so very few.

Behind him the bedroom door opened.

'Came to say goodbye, Lomond. Or should I call you Lohmann?'

He turned to face her. Caroline Norwood. Alone. In a smart tailored coat, hatless. Hair down to her shoulders. Washington chic had taken over. She was no longer the English secretary.

335

'Couldn't very well come to the Embassy,' she said. 'Not *persona grata* there any more.'

'I think you would be liable for arrest there, on British territory. On a charge of high treason.'

'We have something in common, Lohmann. I believe, on German territory, you too would be so liable.'

Lohmann shrugged. 'I will alway believe there is a difference. These people in Germany today, they do not represent the real Germany.'

With a small, twisted smile, she perched on the arm of a chair, 'It's one point of view. On the other hand my late father admired Hitler very much, thought he was the future of the Aryan race.'

'Forgetting there are other races? With equal demands on life and liberty.'

'And the pursuit of happiness. Oh, Lohmann, you believe all the words. I don't believe any of them. Theirs or the others.' I confess, I'm in it for the money. I was slightly inaccurate when I said my father had left me a fortune. He left me a bankrupt rubber company, some oil shares, and more than a nodding acquaintance with Hermann Goering and some of the others. Particularly Admiral Canaris – he offered me a lot of money. Especially when he knew I could get back to my old job in the diplomatic service . . . humble secretary sure enough, but hearing so many worthwhile fragments of information.'

'And you recruited Markham?'

'That was easy. As long as I kept him away from knives in my presence. We took advantage of his little weakness. And of Pardoe's. Markham's was killing ladies, Pardoe's slightly more innocuous: drink. But it enabled us to transfer the guilt to poor Captain Pardoe. Would have convinced him if it hadn't been for you.'

'It is good to know I was of some use. But you will have to be careful. Hoover knows all about you.'

'Of course he does. He was another source of revenue. He

didn't care about my work for Germany. As long as I worked for him as well.'

It had been there in front of him, Lohmann told himself. But the confirmation still surprised him.

'His interests became the same as the Germans',' she went on. 'Find out what Pardoe's mission was and, if possible, stop him. Oh yes, Hoover wanted that . . .'

'Why should he?'

'Why should he not, Lohmann. He doesn't want America involved in a European war. His whole philosophy is isolationist. Even more than that I would say Mister Hoover has more sympathy with Germany than with England. It was even his idea that I should make it appear Pardoe had attempted to kill me. Unfortunately, and the credit is yours, Lohmann, you didn't fall for it. Such a pity.'

'And . . . and Hoover's man then killed Pardoe and Markham?'

Caroline Norwood frowned. 'No. That was something else. I don't know who. Perhaps those amateurs in the Bund. Although they deny it. No, at the end, Hoover would rather have taken Pardoe alive. Been a blow to the British to have one of their envoys accused of being a double murderer. Ah well, it doesn't always go the way we want it to go.'

Lohmann donned his trench coat and picked up his suitcase. 'Anyway,' he said. 'I am about to leave. Unless you've come here to stop me?'

She rose from the arm of the chair. He was aware of her perfume, Chanel of course, aware of more than the perfume, the lines of her body under her coat, the curve of her cheekbone. A memory of Rue Scott-ffoliot again. Did the devil have more than the best tunes? Also the most attractive women?

'I'm sorry you have to rush back to Europe,' she said. 'I was hoping you might have had a few days' leave. You see, you really do interest me, Lohmann. It wasn't merely a tactical move on my part. I would have liked us to know each other better. But we were the victims of circumstance. Unless you stay on a day or two longer.'

He walked past her to the door. 'I wouldn't be able to sleep nights, Caroline. Someone in Germany might offer you a few dollars to kill me. And you wouldn't be able to resist the offer. Also I have an engagement with a lady in New York.'

He opened the door, hesitated, and faced her for the last time. 'I should be careful, Caroline Norwood. Mister Hoover may have to divest himself quite soon of any pro-Nazi feelings. And then I think you would find yourself . . . what is the word? . . . *entbehrlich* . . .?'

'Expendable?'

'Exactly. And then you too will be expended.'

New York–London

EPILOGUE

New York. Scott Fitzgerald called it Babylon on the Hudson. Big. Noisy. All the clichés applied. Streets like concrete canyons, people like scurrying ants. The New World in a hurry. The pursuit of happiness overtaken by the pursuit of the dollar. This was the place to which he had sent his daughter to start a new life. And he was filled with doubts at the thought now.

The doubts dissipated. In a brownstone house in a quiet street, in a quiet, old fashioned room his late wife's relatives brought his daughter to him.

At first, a silence. At the beginning like two strangers at their first meeting. Also as if neither was sure of the identity of the other.

Then she moved. Not as a child but as a young graceful woman running to him with arms outstretched. But with the word of a child.

'Papa!'

It was a long embrace and there were the inevitable tears. A brief silence and then a tidal wave of words. They talked and talked; question, answer, statement, explanation. And laughter.

They talked of how different it was here in New York from Berlin. Later they talked of Berlin under the National Socialists. She had been nearly seduced by National Socialism. But now he was pleased she could talk about her relief at being away from Germany.

341

They spent two days together. Walking, talking, eating, sightseeing. And she ended his nightmare.

Then his departure was imminent.

After the war . . . after the war . . . those were the promises that were made. She would come to London, he would come to New York, did it matter which? Always *after the war*. She asked if he had to return to London. And he found it a moral imperative; a journey he had to make.

Reluctantly he said his farewells, there were some tears, not too many, and then he drove to Montreal. He waited another two days before he found himself on a plane to London.

It was an office under the Admiralty building. Down deep. Stretching under Admiralty Arch to the Mall. He was in some kind of a briefing room, the walls covered in maps, facing an officer in Naval Intelligence, a stranger to him. And a familiar face; Thornhill greeting him with a half smile.

'You did a good job,' the naval officer said. He was a sharp featured man with tired eyes and a public school accent.

'The First Lord was pleased,' Thornhill added.

'Was he?' said Lohmann. 'I wasn't, I should have brought Pardoe back. He was innocent of those killings.'

'Your report has been noted,' said the naval officer.

'He shouldn't have died. He carried out his mission . . .'

'Thanks to you,' Thornhill said. 'We have a job for you. If you want it.'

'What kind of a job?'

'Nothing too active. You've done that bit. Monitoring German radio. You'd be attached to Military Intelligence. And have a reasonable income. Army captain's pay.'

'I will think about it.' Suddenly he wanted away from this office. He was warm, too warm, the air heavy around him. He wanted to be in his own room overlooking the British Museum, where he could see the trees surrounding it, even though they would be dark and skeletal at this time of the year.

342

He stood up. 'Yes, thank you. I will think about it.' Knowing he would take it. Nothing else for him to do. One small way of fighting National Socialism. But taking his time to accept. Do not show too much enthusiasm. That way you ended up in new nightmares. Also there was something else here. Something he had known but had not admitted to himself.

They talked a little more, Lohmann on his feet. The naval officer asking about Captain Greenock; about the feeling in America towards the war. About Roosevelt. They were impressed he had been at the meeting in the White House. Then Lohmann went to the door.

'Pity you had to kill our man, though,' the naval officer said bleakly. 'Yes, pity about Rand. Of course you weren't to know. John Rand, he was the man you killed in the Mayflower Hotel. The man who shot Markham and Pardoe. One of our agents. Licensed to kill. He was only to shoot Pardoe, but I suppose Markham was a bonus. As it turned out.'

'Pardoe was innocent of the murders.'

'Of course we know that now. But then he was the number one suspect. We couldn't afford to have him arrested for murder. So, his mission over, we took the necessary precautions.'

'And killed him.'

A touch of the nightmare returning. Even more now, Lohmann wanted away from this place. From the naval officer with the tired, cold eyes. With certainty he knew this man had ordered the killing of Pardoe. Doubtless following orders from above, but the direct order had come from this man.

He had been introduced by Thornhill on his arrival, he remembered the rank but the name eluded him.

'You are . . . Commander . . . ?'

'Fleming. Ian Fleming. Nice to have met you, Mister Lohmann. Or will we be calling you Lomond from now on?'

Outside, in Trafalgar Square, he breathed in the cold air of the winter morning gratefully. It would soon be Christmas. First wartime Christmas; no Christmas trees blazing with light; an austere Christmas, sandbags for decorations. And then sometime soon the war would really start.

Shivering, he pulled his coat around him and walked across the square. The nightmare was over. Until the next one. Oh yes, there would undoubtedly be another.